7/91

D0952248

Dawn

Books by V.C. Andrews

Flowers in the Attic
Petals on the Wind
If There Be Thorns
My Sweet Audrina
Seeds of Yesterday
Heaven
Dark Angel
Garden of Shadows
Fallen Hearts
Gates of Paradise
Web of Dreams
Dawn

Dawn

V.C. ANDREWS

POCKET BOOKS
New York London Toronto Sydney Tokyo Singapore

An *Original* Publication of POCKET BOOKS

POCKET BOOKS, a division of Simon & Schuster Inc.
1230 Avenue of the Americas, New York, NY 10020

Jacket illustration by Richard Newton

Printed in the U.S.A.

Quality Printing and Binding by:
Berryville Graphics
P.O. Box 272
Berryville, VA 22611 U.S.A.

Dear V.C. Andrews Reader:

Those of us who knew and loved Virginia Andrews know that the most important things in her life were her novels. Her proudest moment came when she held in her hand the first printed copy of **FLOWERS IN THE ATTIC.** Virginia was a unique and gifted storyteller who wrote feverishly each and every day. She was constantly developing ideas for new stories that would eventually become novels. Second only to the pride she took in her writing was the joy she took in reading the letters from readers who were so touched by her books.

Since her death many of you have written to us wondering whether there would continue to be new V.C. Andrews novels. When Virginia became seriously ill while writing the Casteel series, she began to work even harder hoping to finish as many stories as possible so that her fans could one day share them. Just before she died we promised ourselves that we would take all of these wonderful stories and make them available to her readers.

Beginning with the final books in the Casteel series we have been working closely with a carefully selected writer to organize and complete Virginia's stories and to expand upon them by creating additional novels inspired by her wonderful storytelling genius.

DAWN is the start of a new V.C. Andrews series. We believe it would have given her great joy to know that it will be entertaining so many of you. Other V.C. Andrews novels will be published in the coming years and we hope they continue to mean as much to you as ever.

Sincerely,
THE ANDREWS FAMILY

Dawn

Momma once told me that she and Daddy named me Dawn because I was born at the break of day. That was the first of a thousand lies Momma and Daddy would tell me and my brother Jimmy. Of course, we wouldn't know they were lies, not for a long time, not until the day they came to take us away.

1
ANOTHER NEW PLACE

The sound of dresser drawers being opened and closed woke me. I heard Momma and Daddy whispering in their room, and my heart began to thump fast and hard. I pressed my palm against my chest, took a deep breath, and turned to wake Jimmy, but he was already sitting up in our sofa bed. Bathed in the silvery moonlight that came pouring through our bare window, my sixteen-year-old brother's face looked chiseled from granite. He sat there so still, listening. I lay there listening with him, listening to the hateful wind whistle through the cracks and crannies of this small cottage Daddy had found for us in Granville, a small, rundown town just outside of Washington, D.C. We had been here barely four months.

"What is it, Jimmy? What's going on?" I asked, shivering partly from the cold and partly because deep inside I knew the answer.

Jimmy fell back against his pillow and then brought his hands behind his head. In a sulk, he stared up at the dark ceiling. The pace of Momma's and Daddy's movements became more frenzied.

"We were gonna get a puppy here," Jimmy mumbled. "And this spring Momma and I were gonna plant a garden and grow our own vegetables."

I could feel his frustration and anger like heat from an iron radiator.

"What happened?" I asked mournfully, for I, too, had high hopes.

"Daddy came home later than usual," he said, a prophetic note of doom in his voice. "He rushed in here, his eyes wild. You know, bright and wide like they get sometimes. He went right in there, and not long after, they started packing. Might as well get up and get dressed," Jimmy said, throwing the blanket off him and turning to sit up. "They'll be out here shortly tellin' us to do it anyway."

I groaned. Not again, and not again in the middle of the night.

Jimmy leaned over to turn on the lamp by our pull-out bed and started to put on his socks so he wouldn't have to step down on a cold floor. He was so depressed, he didn't even worry about getting dressed in front of me. I fell back and watched him unfold his pants so he could slip into them, moving with a quiet resignation that made everything around me seem more like a dream. How I wished it were.

I was fourteen years old, and for as long as I could remember, we had been packing and unpacking, going from one place to another. It always seemed that just when my brother, Jimmy, and I had finally settled into a new school and finally made some friends and I got to know my teachers, we had to leave. Maybe we really were no better than homeless gypsies like Jimmy always said, wanderers, poorer than the poorest, for even the poorest families had some place they could call home, some place they could return to when things went bad, a place where they had grandmas and grandpas or uncles and aunts to hug them and comfort them and make them feel good again. We would have settled even for cousins. At least, I would have.

I peeled back the blanket, and my nightgown fell away and exposed most of my bosom. I glanced at Jimmy and caught him gazing at me in the moonlight. He shifted his eyes away quickly. Embarrassment made my heart pitter-patter, and I pressed my palm against the bodice of my nightgown. I had never told any of my girlfriends at school that Jimmy and I shared even a room together, much less this dilapidated pull-out bed. I was too ashamed, and I knew how they would react, embarrassing both Jimmy and me even more.

I brought my feet down on the freezing-cold bare wood floor. My teeth chattering, I embraced myself and hurried across the small room to gather up a blouse and a sweater and a pair of jeans. Then I went into the bathroom to dress.

By the time I finished, Jimmy had his suitcase closed. It seemed we always left something else behind each time. There was only so much room in Daddy's old car anyway. I folded my nightgown and put it neatly into my own suitcase. The clasps were as hard as ever to close and Jimmy had to help.

Momma and Daddy's bedroom door opened and they came out, their suitcases in hand, too. We stood there facing them, holding our own.

"Why do we have to leave in the middle of the night again?" I asked, looking at Daddy and wondering if leaving would make him angry as it so often did.

"Best time to travel," Daddy mumbled. He glared at me with a quick order not to ask too many questions. Jimmy was right—Daddy had that wild look again, a look that seemed so unnatural, it sent shivers up and down my spine. I hated it when Daddy got that look. He was a handsome man with rugged features, a cap of sleek brown hair and dark coal eyes. When the day came that I fell in love and decided to marry, I hoped my husband would be just as handsome as Daddy. But I hated it when Daddy was displeased—when he got that wild look. It marred his handsome features and made him ugly—something I couldn't bear to see.

"Jimmy, take the suitcases down. Dawn, you help your momma pack up whatever she wants from the kitchen."

I glanced at Jimmy. He was only two years older than I was, but there was a wider gap in our looks. He was tall and lean and muscular like Daddy. I was small with what Momma called "China doll features." And I really didn't take after Momma, either, because she was as tall as Daddy. She told me she was gangly and awkward when she was my age and looked more like a boy until she was thirteen, when she suddenly blossomed.

We didn't have many pictures of family. Matter of fact, all I had was one picture of Momma when she was fifteen. I would sit for hours gazing into her young face, searching for signs of myself. She was smiling in the picture and standing under a weeping willow tree. She wore an ankle-length straight skirt and a fluffy blouse with frilly sleeves and a frilly collar. Her long, dark hair looked soft and fresh. Even in this old black and white photo, her eyes sparkled with hope and love. Daddy said he'd taken the picture with a small box camera he had bought for a quarter from a friend of his. He wasn't sure it would work, but at least this picture came out. If we'd ever had any other photos, they'd been either lost or left behind during our many moves.

However, I thought that even in this simple old photograph with its black and white fading into sepia and its edges fraying, Momma looked so pretty that it was easy to see why Daddy had lost his heart to her so quickly even though she was only fifteen at the time. She was barefoot in the picture, and I thought she looked fresh and innocent and as lovely as anything else nature had to offer.

Momma and Jimmy had the same shimmering black hair and dark eyes. They both had bronze complexions with beautiful white teeth that allowed them ivory smiles. Daddy had dark brown hair, but mine was blond. And I had freckles over the tops of my cheeks. No one else in my family had freckles.

"What about that rake and shovel we bought for the garden?" Jimmy asked, careful not to let even a twinkle of hope show in his eyes.

"We ain't got the room," Daddy snapped.

Poor Jimmy, I thought. Momma said he was born all crunched up as tightly as a fist, his eyes sewn shut. She said she gave birth to Jimmy on a farm in Maryland. They had just arrived there and gone knocking on the door, hoping to find some work, when her labor began.

They told me I had been born on the road, too. They had hoped to have me born in a hospital, but they were forced to leave one town and start out for another where Daddy had already secured new employment. They left late in the afternoon one day and traveled all that day and that night.

"We were between nowhere and no place, and all of a sudden you wanted to come into this world," Momma told me. "Your daddy pulled the truck over and said, 'Here we go again, Sally Jean.' I crawled onto the truck bed where we had an old mattress, and as the sun came up, you entered this world. I remember how the birds were singing.

"I was looking at a bird as you were coming into this world, Dawn. That's why you sing so pretty," Momma said. "Your grandmomma always said whatever a woman looked at just before, during, or right after giving birth, that's what characteristics the child would have. The worst thing was to have a mouse or a rat in the house when a woman was pregnant."

"What would happen, Momma?" I asked, filled with wonder.

"The child would be sneaky, cowardly."

I sat back amazed when she told me all this. Momma had inherited so much wisdom. It made me wonder and wonder about our family, a family we had never seen. I wanted to know so much more, but it was difficult to get Momma and Daddy to talk about their early lives. I suppose that was because so much of it was painful and hard.

We knew they were both brought up on small farms in Georgia, where their people eked out poor livings from small patches of land. They had both come from big families that lived in rundown farmhouses. There just wasn't any room in either household for a newly married, very young couple with a pregnant wife, so they began what would be our family's history of traveling, traveling that had not yet ended. We were on our way again.

Momma and I filled a carton with those kitchenwares she wanted to take along and then gave it to Daddy to load in the car. When she was finished, she put her arm around my shoulders, and we both took one last look at the humble little kitchen.

Jimmy was standing in the doorway, watching. His eyes turned from pools of sadness to coal-black pools of anger when Daddy came in to hurry us along. Jimmy blamed him for our gypsy life. I wondered sometimes if maybe he wasn't right. Often Daddy seemed different from other men—more fidgety, more nervous. I would never say it, but I hated it whenever he stopped off at a bar on his way home from work. He would usually come home in a sulk and stand by the windows watching as if he were expecting something terrible. None of us could talk to him when he was in one of those moods. He was like that now.

"Better get going," he said, standing in the doorway, his eyes turning even colder as they rested for a second on me.

For a moment I was stunned. Why had Daddy given me such a cold look? It was almost as if he blamed me for our having to leave.

As soon as the thought entered my mind, I chased it away. I was being silly! Daddy would never blame me for anything. He loved me. He was just mad because Momma and I were being so slow and dawdling, instead of hurrying out the door. As if reading my mind, Momma suddenly spoke.

"Right," she said quickly. Momma and I started for the door, for we had all learned from hard experience that Daddy was unpredictable when his voice turned so tight with anger. Neither one of us wanted to invoke his wrath. We turned back once and then closed the door behind us, just like we had closed dozens of doors before.

There were few stars out. I didn't like nights without stars. On those nights shadows seemed so much darker and longer to me. Tonight was one of those nights—cold, dark, all the windows in houses around us black. The wind carried a piece of paper through the street, and off in the distance a dog howled. Then I heard a siren. Somewhere in the night someone was in trouble, I thought, some poor person was being carried off to the hospital, or maybe the police were chasing a criminal.

"Let's move along," Daddy ordered and sped up as if they were chasing us.

Jimmy and I squeezed ourselves into the backseat with our cartons and suitcases.

"Where we going this time?" Jimmy demanded without disguising his displeasure.

"Richmond," Momma said.

"Richmond!" we both said. We had been everywhere in Virginia, it seemed, but Richmond.

"Yep. Your daddy's got a job in a garage there, and I'm sure I can land me a chambermaid job in one of the motels."

"Richmond," Jimmy muttered under his breath. Big cities still frightened both of us.

As we drove away from Granville and the darkness fell around us, our sleepiness returned. Jimmy and I closed our eyes and fell asleep against each other as we had done so many times before.

Daddy had been planning our new move for a little while because he had already found us a place to live. Daddy often did things quietly and then announced them to us.

Because the rents in the city were so much higher, we could afford only a one-bedroom apartment, so Jimmy and I still had to share a room. And the sofa bed! It was barely big enough for the two of us. I knew sometimes he awoke before me but didn't move because my arm was on him and he didn't want to wake me and embarrass me about it. And there were those times he touched me accidentally where he wasn't supposed to. The blood would rush to his face, and he would leap off the bed as if it had started to burn. He wouldn't say anything to acknowledge he had touched me, and I wouldn't mention it.

It was usually like that. Jimmy and I simply ignored things that would embarrass other teenage boys and girls forced to live in such close quarters, but I couldn't help sitting by and dreaming longingly for the same wonderful privacy most of my girlfriends enjoyed, especially when they described how they could close their doors and gossip on their own phones or write love notes without anyone in their families knowing a thing about it. I was even afraid to keep a diary because everyone would be looking over my shoulder.

This apartment differed little from most of our previous homes—the same small rooms, peeling wallpaper, and chipped paint. The same windows that didn't close well. Jimmy hated our apartment so much that he said he would rather sleep in the street.

But just when we thought things were as bad as they could be, they got worse.

Late one afternoon months after we had moved to Richmond, Momma came home from work much earlier than usual. I had been hoping she would bring something else for us to have for dinner. We were at the tail end of the week, Daddy's payday, and most of our money from the previous week was gone. We had been able to have one or two good meals during the week, but now we were eating leftovers. My stomach was rumbling just as much as Jimmy's was, but before either of us could complain, the door opened and we both turned, surprised to see Momma come in. She stopped, shook her head, and started to cry. Then she hurried across the room to her bedroom.

"Momma! What's wrong?" I called after her, but her only answer was to slam the door. Jimmy looked at me and I at him, both of us frightened. I went to her door and knocked softly. "Momma?" Jimmy came up beside me and waited. "Momma, can we come in?" I opened the door and looked inside.

She was facedown on the bed, her shoulders shaking. We entered slowly, Jimmy right beside me. I sat down on the bed and put my hand on her shoulder.

"Momma?"

Finally she stopped sobbing and turned to look up at us.

"Did you lose your job, Momma?" Jimmy asked quickly.

"No, it's not that, Jimmy." She sat up, grinding her small fists against her eyes to wipe the tears away. "Although I won't be havin' the job all that much longer."

"Then what is it, Momma? Tell us," I begged.

She sniffed and pushed back her hair and took each of our hands into hers.

"You're gonna have either a new brother or sister," she declared.

My pounding heart paused. Jimmy's eyes widened and his mouth dropped open.

"It's my fault. I just ignored and ignored the signs. I never thought I was pregnant, because I didn't have no more children after Dawn. I finally went to a doctor today and found out I was a little more n' four months pregnant. Suddenly I'm gonna have a child, and now I won't be able to work, too," she said and began to cry again.

"Oh, Momma, don't cry." The thought of another mouth to feed dropped a black shadow over my heart. How could we manage it? We didn't have enough as it was.

I looked to Jimmy to urge him to say something comforting, but he looked stunned and angry. He just stood there, staring.

"Does Daddy know yet, Momma?" he asked.

"No," she said. She took a deep breath. "I'm too old and tired to have another baby," she whispered and shook her head.

"You're mad at me, ain'tcha, Jimmy?" Momma asked him. He was so sullen, I wanted to kick him. Finally he shook his head.

"Naw, Momma, I ain't mad at you. It's not *your* fault." He swung his eyes at me, and I knew he was blaming Daddy.

"Then give me a hug. I need one right now."

Jimmy looked away and then leaned toward Momma. He gave her a quick hug, mumbled something about having to get something outside, and then hurried out.

"You just lay back and rest, Momma," I said. "I almost have the dinner all made anyway."

"Dinner. What do we have to eat? I was going to try to pick up something tonight, see if we could charge any more on our grocery bill, but with this pregnancy and all, I clean forgot about eating."

"We'll make do, Momma," I said. "Daddy gets paid today, so tomorrow we'll eat better."

"I'm sorry, Dawn," she said, her face wrinkling up in preparation for her sobs again. She shook her head. "Jimmy's so mad. I can see it in his eyes. He's got Ormand's temper."

"He's just surprised, Momma. I'll see about dinner," I repeated and went out and closed the door softly behind me, my fingers trembling on the knob.

A baby, a little brother or sister! Where would a baby sleep? How could Momma take care of a baby? If she couldn't work, we would have even less money. Didn't grown-ups plan these things? How could they let it happen?

I went outside to look for Jimmy and found him throwing a rubber ball against the wall in the alley. It was mid-April, so the chill was out of the air, even in the early evening. I could just make out some stars starting their entrance onto the sky. The neon lights above the doorway of Frankie's Bar and Grill at the corner had been turned on. Sometimes, on his way home on a hot day, Daddy would stop in there for a cold beer. When the door was opened and closed, the laughter and the music from the jukebox spilled out and then died quickly on the sidewalk, a sidewalk always dirtied with papers and candy wrappers and other refuse that the wind lifted out of overflowing garbage cans. I could hear two cats in heat threaten each other in an alleyway. A man was shouting curses up at another man, who leaned out a two-story window about a block south of us. The man in the window just laughed down at him.

I turned to Jimmy. He was as tight as a fist again, and he was heaving all his anger with each and every throw of the ball.

"Jimmy?"

He didn't answer me.

"Jimmy, you don't want to make Momma feel any worse than she already does, do you?" I asked him softly. He seized the ball in the air and turned on me.

"What's the use of pretending, Dawn? One thing we definitely don't need right now is another child in the house. Look at what we're eating for dinner tonight!"

I swallowed hard. His words were like cold rain falling on a warm campfire.

"We don't even have hand-me-downs to give to a new baby," he continued. "We're gonna have to buy baby clothes and diapers and a crib. And babies need all sorts of lotions and creams, don't they?"

"They do, but—"

"Well, why didn't Daddy think of that, huh? He's off whistlin' and jawin' with those friends of his who hang around the garage, just as if he's on top of the world, and now here's this," he said, gesturing toward our building.

Why hadn't Daddy thought of that? I wondered. I had heard of girls going all the way and becoming pregnant, but that was because they were just girls and didn't know better.

"It just happened, I guess," I said, fishing for Jimmy to give his opinion.

"It doesn't just happen, Dawn. A woman doesn't wake up one morning and find out she's pregnant."

"Don't the parents plan to have it?"

He looked at me and shook his head.

"Daddy probably came home drunk one night and . . ."

"And what?"

"Oh, Dawn . . . they made the baby, that's all."

"And didn't know they had?"

"Well, they don't always make a baby each time they . . ." He shook his head. "You'll have to ask Momma about it. I don't know all the details," he said quickly, but I knew he did.

"It's going to be hell to pay when Daddy gets home, Dawn," he said, shaking his head as we walked back inside. He spoke in a voice just above a whisper and gave me a fearful chill. My heart pounded in anticipation.

Most of the time when trouble came raining down over us, Daddy would decide we had to pack up and run, but we couldn't run from this. Because I always cooked dinner, I knew better than anyone that we didn't have anything to spare for a baby. Not a cent, not a crumb.

When Daddy arrived home from work that night, he looked a lot more tired than usual and his hands and arms were all greasy.

"I had to pull out a car transmission and rebuild it in one day," he explained, thinking the way he looked was why Jimmy and I were staring at him so strangely. "Somethin' wrong?"

"Ormand," Momma called. Daddy hurried into the bedroom. I busied myself with the dinner, but my heart started to pound so hard I could barely breathe. Jimmy went to the window that looked out on the north side of the street and stood staring as still as a statue. We heard Momma crying again. After a while it grew quiet and then Daddy emerged. Jimmy pivoted expectantly.

"Well, now, you two already know, I reckon." He shook his head and looked back at the closed door behind him.

"How we gonna manage?" Jimmy asked quickly.

"I don't know," Daddy said, his eyes darkening. His face began to take on that mad look, his lips curling in at the corners, some whiteness of his teeth flashing through. He ran his fingers through his hair and sucked in some breath.

Jimmy flopped down in a kitchen chair. "Other people plan kids," he muttered.

Daddy's face flared. I couldn't believe he had said it. He knew Daddy's temper, but I recalled what Momma said: Jimmy had the same temper. Sometimes they were like two bulls with a red flag between them.

"Don't get smart," Daddy said and headed for the door.

"Where're you going, Daddy?" I called.

"I need to think," he said. "Eat without me."

Jimmy and I listened to Daddy's feet pound the hallway floor, his steps announcing the anger and turmoil in his body.

"Eat without him, he says," Jimmy quipped. "Grits and black-eyed peas."

"He's going to Frankie's," I predicted. Jimmy nodded in agreement and sat back, staring glumly at his plate.

"Where's Ormand?" Momma asked, stepping out of her bedroom.

"He went off to think, Momma," Jimmy said. "He's probably just trying to come up with a plan and needs to be alone," he added, hoping to ease her burden.

"I don't like him going off like that," Momma complained. "It never comes to no good. You should go look for him, Jimmy."

"Go look for him? I don't think so, Momma. He don't like it when I do that. Let's just eat and wait for him to come back." Momma wasn't happy about it, but she sat down and I served the grits and black-eyed peas. I had added some salt and a little bit of bacon grease I had saved.

"I'm sorry I didn't try to get us something else," Mommy said, apologizing again. "But Dawn, honey, you did real fine with this. It tastes good. Don't it, Jimmy?"

He looked up from his bowl. I saw he hadn't been listening. Jimmy could get lost in his own thoughts for hours and hours if no one pestered him, especially when he was unhappy.

"Huh? Oh. Yeah, this is good."

After supper Momma sat up for a while listening to the radio and reading one of the used magazines she had brought back from the motel she worked in. The hours ticked by. Every time we heard a door slam or the sound of footsteps, we anticipated Daddy coming through the door, but it grew later and later and he didn't reappear.

Whenever I gazed at Momma, I saw that sadness draped her face like a wet flag, heavy and hard to shake off. Finally she stood up and announced she had to go to bed. She took a deep breath, holding her hands against her chest, and headed for her bedroom.

"I'm tired too," Jimmy said. He got up and went to the bathroom to get ready for bed. I started to pull out the sofa bed, but then stopped, thinking about Momma lying in her bed, worried and frightened. In a moment I made up my mind—I opened the door quietly and left to look for Daddy.

I hesitated outside the door of Frankie's Bar and Grill. I had never been in a bar. My hand trembled as I reached out for the doorknob, but before I could pull it, the door swung open and a pale-skinned woman with too much lipstick and rouge on her face stepped out. She had a cigarette dangling from the corner of her mouth. She paused when she saw me and smiled. I saw she had teeth missing toward the back of her mouth.

"Why, what you doing coming in here, honey? This ain't no place for someone as young as you."

"I'm looking for Ormand Longchamp," I replied.

"Never heard of him," she said. "You don't stay in there long, honey.

It ain't a place for kids," she added and walked past me, the stale odor of cigarettes and beer floating in her wake. I watched her for a moment and then entered Frankie's.

I had seen into it once in a while whenever someone opened the door, and I knew there was a long bar on the right with mirrors and shelves covered with liquor bottles. I saw the fans in the ceiling and the sawdust on the dirty brown wood slab floor. I had never seen the tables to the left.

A couple of men at the end of the bar turned my way when I stepped in. One smiled, the other just stared. The bartender, a short stout bald-headed man, was leaning against the wall. He had his arms folded across his chest.

"What do you want?" he asked, coming down the bar.

"I'm looking for Ormand Longchamp," I said. "I thought he might be in here." A glance down the bar didn't produce him.

"He joined the army," someone quipped.

"Shut up," the bartender snapped. Then he turned back to me. "He's over there," he said and gestured with his head toward the tables on the left. I looked and saw Daddy slumped over a table, but I was afraid to walk farther into the bar and grill. "You can wake him up and take him home," the bartender advised.

Some of the men at the bar spun around to watch me as if it were the evening's entertainment.

"Let her be," the bartender commanded.

I walked between the tables until I reached Daddy. He had his head on his arms. There were five empty bottles of beer on the table and another nearly emptied. A glass with just a little beer in it was in front of the bottle.

"Daddy," I said softly. He didn't budge. I looked back at the bar and saw that even the men who had continued to watch me had lost interest. "Daddy," I repeated a little louder. He stirred, but didn't lift his head. I poked him gently on the arm. "Daddy." He grunted and then slowly lifted his head.

"What?"

"Daddy, please come home now," I said. He wiped his eyes and gazed at me.

"What . . . What are you doing here, Dawn?" he asked quickly.

"Momma went to bed a while ago, but I know she's just lying there awake waiting for you, Daddy."

"You shouldn't come in a place like this," he said sharply, making me jump.

"I didn't want to come, Daddy, but—"

"All right, all right," he said. "I guess I can't do nothing right these days," he added, shaking his head.

"Just come home, Daddy. Everything will be all right."

"Yeah, yeah," he said. He gazed at his beer a moment and then pushed back from the table. "Let's get you outta here. You shouldn't be here," he repeated. He started to stand and then sat down hard.

He looked down at the bottles of beer again and then put his hand in his pocket and took out his billfold. He counted it quickly and shook his head.

"Lost track of what I spent," he said, more to himself than to me, but when he said it, it sent a cold chill down my back.

"How much did you spend, Daddy?"

"Too much," he moaned. "Afraid we won't be eating all that well this week, either," he concluded. He pushed himself away from the table again and stood up. "Come on," he said. Daddy didn't walk straight until we reached the door.

"Sleep tight!" one of the men at the bar called. Daddy didn't acknowledge him. He opened the door and we stepped out. I was never so happy to confront fresh air again. The musty smell of the bar had turned my stomach. Why would Daddy even want to walk in there, much less spend time there? I wondered. Daddy appreciated the fresh air, too, and took some deep breaths.

"I don't like you going in a place like that," he said, walking. He stopped suddenly and looked at me, shaking his head. "You're smarter and better than the rest of us, Dawn. You deserve better."

"I'm not better than anybody else, Daddy," I protested, but he had said all he was going to, and we continued to our apartment. When we opened the door, we found Jimmy already in the pull-out bed, the covers drawn so high, they nearly covered his face. He didn't turn our way. Daddy went right to his bedroom, and I crawled under the covers with Jimmy, who stirred.

"You went to Frankie's and got him?" he asked in a whisper.

"Yes."

"If I had been the one, he'd be furious," he said.

"No, he wouldn't, Jimmy, he'd . . ."

I stopped because we heard Momma moan. Then we heard what sounded like Daddy laughing. A moment later there was the distinct sound of the bedsprings. Jimmy and I knew what that meant. In our close quarters we had grown used to the sounds people often make whenever they make love. Of course, when we were younger, we didn't know what it meant, but when we learned, we pretended that we didn't hear it.

Jimmy drew the blanket up toward his ears again, but I was confused and a bit fascinated.

"Jimmy," I whispered.

"Go to sleep, Dawn," he pleaded.

"But, Jimmy, how can they—"

"Just go to sleep, will you?"

"I mean, Momma's pregnant. Can they still . . . ?" Jimmy didn't respond. "Isn't it dangerous?"

Jimmy turned toward me abruptly.

"Will you stop asking those kind of questions?"

"But I thought you might know. Boys usually know more than girls," I said.

"Well, I don't know," he replied. "Okay? So shut up." He turned his back to me again.

It quieted down in Momma and Daddy's room, but I couldn't stop wondering. I wished I had an older sister who wouldn't be embarrassed with my questions. I was too embarrassed to ask Momma about these things because I didn't want her to think Jimmy and I were eavesdropping.

My leg grazed Jimmy's, and he pulled away as if I had burned him. Then he slid over to his end of the bed until he was nearly off. I shifted as far over to mine as I could, too. Then I closed my eyes and tried to think of other things.

As I was falling asleep, I thought of that woman who had come to the bar door just as I was about to open it to enter. She was smiling down at me, her lips twisted and rubbery, her teeth yellow and the cigarette smoke twirling up and over her bloodshot eyes.

I was so glad I had managed to get Daddy home.

2
FERN

One afternoon during the first week of Momma's ninth month while I was preparing dinner and Jimmy was struggling over some homework on the kitchen table, we heard Momma scream. We rushed into the bedroom and found her clutching her stomach.

"What is it, Momma?" I asked, my heart pounding. "Momma!" Momma reached out and seized my hand.

"Call for an ambulance," she said through her clenched teeth. We didn't have a telephone in the apartment and had to use the pay phone on the corner. Jimmy shot out the door.

"Is this supposed to happen, Momma?" I asked her. She simply shook her head and moaned again, her fingernails pressing so hard and so sharply into my skin, they nearly caused me to bleed. She bit down on her lower lip. The pain came again and again. Her face turned a pale, sickly yellow.

"The hospital is sending an ambulance," Jimmy announced after charging back in.

"Did you call your daddy?" Momma asked Jimmy through her clenched teeth. The pain wouldn't let go.

"No," he replied. "I'll go do it, Momma."

"Tell him to go directly to the hospital," she ordered.

It seemed to take forever and ever for the ambulance to come. They put Momma on a stretcher and carried her out. I tried to squeeze her hand before they closed the door, but the attendant forced me back. Jimmy stood beside me, his hands on his hips, his shoulders heaving with his deep, excited breaths.

The sky was ominously dark and it had begun to rain a colder, harder rain than we had been having. There was even some lightning across the bruised, charcoal-gray clouds. The gloom dropped a chill over me, and I shuddered and embraced myself as the ambulance attendants got in and started away.

"Come on," Jimmy said. "We'll catch the bus on Main Street."

He grabbed my hand and we ran. When we got off the bus at the hospital, we went directly to the emergency room and found Daddy speaking with a tall doctor with dark brown hair and cold, stern green eyes. Just as we reached them, we heard the doctor say, "The baby's turned wrong and we need to operate on your wife. We can't wait much longer. Just follow me to sign some papers and we'll get right to it, sir."

Jimmy and I watched Daddy walk off with the doctor, and then we sat on a bench in the hall.

"It's stupid," Jimmy suddenly muttered, "stupid to have a baby now."

"Don't say that, Jimmy," I chided. His words made my own fears crash in upon me like waves.

"Well, I don't want a baby who threatens Momma's life, and I don't want a baby who'll make our lives more miserable," he snapped, but he didn't say anything more about it when Daddy returned. I don't know how long we had been sitting there waiting before the doctor finally appeared again, but Jimmy had fallen asleep against me. As soon as we set eyes on the doctor, we sat up. Jimmy's eyelids fluttered open, and he searched the doctor's expression as frantically as I did.

"Congratulations, Mr. Longchamp," the doctor said, "you've got a seven pound, fourteen ounce baby girl." He extended his hand and Daddy shook it.

"Well, I'll be darned. And my wife?"

"She's in the recovery room. She had a hard time, Mr. Longchamp. Her blood count was a little lower than we like, so she's going to need to be built up."

"Thank you, Doctor. Thank you," Daddy said, still pumping his hand. The doctor's lips moved into a smile that didn't reach his eyes.

After we went up to maternity, all three of us gazed down at the tiny pink face wrapped in a white blanket. Baby Longchamp had her fingers curled. They looked no bigger than the fingers on my first doll. She had a patch of black hair, the same color and richness as Jimmy's and Momma's hair and not a sign of a freckle. That was a disappointment.

It took Momma longer than we expected to get back on her feet after she came home. Her weakened condition made her susceptible to a bad cold and a deep bronchial cough, and she couldn't breast-feed like she had planned, so we had another expense—formula.

Despite the hardships Fern's arrival brought, I couldn't help but be fascinated with my little sister. I saw the way she discovered her own hands, studied her own fingers. Her dark eyes, Momma's eyes, brightened with each of her discoveries. Soon she was able to clutch my finger with her tiny fist and hold on to it. Whenever she did that, I saw her struggle to pull herself up. She groaned like an old lady and made me laugh.

Her patch of black hair grew longer and longer. I combed the strands down the back of her head and down the sides, measuring their length until they reached the top of her ears and the middle of her neck. Before long, she was stretching with firmness, pushing her legs out and holding them straight. Her voice grew louder and sharper, too, which meant when she wanted to be fed, everyone knew it.

With Momma not yet very strong, I had to get up in the middle of the night to feed Fern. Jimmy complained a lot, pulled the blanket over his head, and moaned, especially when I turned on the lights. He threatened to sleep in the bathtub.

Daddy was usually grouchy in the morning from his lack of sleep, and as the sleepless nights went on, his face took on a gray, unhealthy look. Early each morning he would sit slumped in his chair, shaking his head like a man who couldn't believe how many storms he had been in. When he was like this, I was afraid to talk to him. Everything he said was usually gloom and doom. Most of the time that meant he was thinking of moving again. What scared me to the deepest place in my heart was the fear that one day he might just move on without us. Even though sometimes he scared me, I loved my father and longed to see one of his rare smiles come my way.

"When your luck turns bad," he would say, "there's nothing to do but change it. A branch that don't bend breaks."

"Momma looks like she's getting thinner and thinner and not stronger and stronger, Daddy," I whispered when I served him a cup of coffee one early morning. "And she won't go to the doctor."

"I know." He shook his head.

I took a deep breath and made the suggestion I knew he wouldn't want to hear. "Maybe we should sell the pearls, Daddy."

Our family owned one thing of value, one thing that had never been used to mend our hard times. A string of pearls so creamy white they took my breath away the one time I'd been allowed to hold them.

Momma and Daddy considered them sacred. Jimmy wondered, as I did, why we clung to them so tenaciously. "The money it would bring in would give Momma a chance to really get well," I finished weakly. Daddy looked up at me quickly and shook his head.

"Your momma would rather die than sell those pearls. That's all we got that ties us, ties you, to family."

How confusing this was to me. Neither Momma nor Daddy wanted to return to their family farms in Georgia to visit our relatives, and yet the pearls, because they were all we had to remind Momma of her family, were treated like something religious. They were kept hidden in the bottom of a dresser drawer. I couldn't recall a time Momma had even worn them.

After Daddy left I was going to go back to sleep, but changed my mind, thinking that it would only make me feel more tired. So I started to get dressed. I thought Jimmy was fast asleep. He and I shared an old dresser Daddy had picked up at a lawn sale. It was on his side of the pull-out bed. I tiptoed over to it and slipped my nightgown off. Then I pulled out my drawer gently, searching for my underthings in the subdued light that spilled in from the bulb in the stove when the stove door was left down. I was standing there naked trying to decide what I should wear that would be warm enough for what looked to be another bitterly cold day, when I turned slightly and out of the corner of my eye caught Jimmy gazing up at me.

I know I should have covered up quickly, but he didn't see I had turned slightly and I couldn't help but be intrigued by the way he stared. His gaze moved up and down my body, drinking me in slowly. When he lifted his eyes higher, he saw me watching him. He turned quickly on his back and locked his eyes on the ceiling. I quickly drew my nightgown up against my body, took out what I wanted to wear, and scurried across the room to the bathroom to dress. We didn't talk about it, but I couldn't get the look in his eyes out of my mind.

In January Momma, who was still thin and weak, got a part-time job cleaning Mrs. Anderson's house every Friday. The Andersons owned a small grocery two blocks away. Occasionally Mrs. Anderson gave Momma a nice chicken or a small turkey. One Friday afternoon Daddy surprised Jimmy and me by coming home much earlier from work.

"Old man Stratton's selling the garage," he announced. "With those two bigger and more modern garages being built only blocks away, business has begun to drop off something terrible. People who are buying the garage don't want to run it as a garage. They want the property to develop housing."

Here we go again, I thought—Daddy loses a job and we have to move. When I told one of my friends, Patty Butler, about our many moves, she said she thought it might be fun to go from school to school.

"It's not fun," I told her. "You always feel like you've got ketchup on your face or a big mole on the tip of your nose when you first walk into a new classroom. All the kids turn around and stare and stare, watching my every move and listening to my voice. I had a teacher once who was so angry I had interrupted her class, she made me stand in front of the room until she was finished with her lesson, and all the time the students were goggling me. I didn't know where to shift my eyes. It was so embarrassing," I said, but I knew Patty couldn't understand just how hard it really was to enter a new school and confront new faces so often. She had lived in Richmond all her life. I couldn't even begin to imagine what that was like: to live in the same house and have your own room for as long as you could remember, to have relatives nearby to hold you and love you, to know your neighbors forever and ever and be so close to them, they were like family. I hugged my arms around myself and wished with all my heart that one day I might live like that. But I knew it could never happen. I'd always be a stranger.

Now Jimmy and I looked at each other and turned to Daddy, expecting him to tell us to start packing. But instead of looking sour, he suddenly smiled.

"Where's your ma?" he asked.

"She's not back from work yet, Daddy," I said.

"Well, today's the last day she's gonna work in other people's houses," he said. He looked around the apartment and nodded. "The last time," he repeated. I glanced quickly at Jimmy, who looked just as astonished as I was.

"Why?"

"What's happening?" Jimmy inquired.

"I got a new and much, much better job today," Daddy said.

"We're going to stay here, Daddy?" I asked.

"Yep and that ain't the best yet. You two are gonna go to one of the finest schools in the South, and it ain't gonna cost us nothing," he announced.

"Cost us?" Jimmy said, his face twisted with confusion. "Why should it cost us to go to school, Daddy? It's never cost us before, has it?"

"No, son, but that's because you and your sister been going to public schools, but now you're going to a private school."

"A private school!" I gasped. I wasn't sure, but I thought that meant very wealthy kids whose families had important names and whose fathers owned big estates with mansions and armies of servants and whose mothers were society women who had their pictures taken at charity balls. My heart began to pound. I was excited, but also quite frightened of the idea. When I looked at Jimmy, I saw his eyes had shadowed and grown deep and dark.

"Us? Go to a fancy private school in Richmond?" he asked.

"That's it, son. You're getting in tuition free."

"Well, why is that, Daddy?" I asked.

"I'm going to be a maintenance supervisor there and free tuition for my children comes with the job," he said proudly.

"What's the name of this school?" I asked, my heart still fluttering.

"Emerson Peabody," he replied.

"Emerson Peabody?" Jimmy twisted his mouth up as if he had bitten into a sour apple. "What kind of a name is that for a school? I ain't going to no school named Emerson Peabody," Jimmy said, shaking his head and backing up toward the couch. "One thing I don't need is to be around a bunch of rich, spoiled kids," he added and flopped down again and folded his arms across his chest.

"Now, you just hold on here, Jimmy boy. You'll go where I tell you to go to school. This here's an opportunity, something very expensive for free, too."

"I don't care," Jimmy said defiantly, his eyes shooting sparks.

"Oh, you don't? Well, you will." Daddy's own eyes shot sparks, and I could see he was maintaining his temper. "Whether you like it or not, you're both gonna get the best education around, and all for free," Daddy repeated.

Just then we heard the outside door opening and Momma start coming down the hallway. From the sound of her slow, ponderous footsteps, I knew she was exhausted. A sensation of cold fear seized my heart when I heard her pause and break out in one of her fits of coughing. I ran to the doorway and looked at her leaning against the wall.

"*Momma!*" I cried.

"I'm all right. I'm all right," Momma said, holding her hand up toward me. "I just lost my breath a moment," she explained.

"You sure you're all right, Sally Jean?" Daddy asked her, his face a face of solid worry.

"I'm all right; I'm all right. There wasn't much to do. Mrs. Anderson had a bunch of her elderly friends over is all. They didn't make no mess to speak of. So," she said, seeing the way we were standing and looking at her. "What are you all standing around here and looking like that for?"

"I got news, Sally Jean," Daddy said and smiled. Momma's eyes began to brighten.

"What sort of news?"

"A new job," he said and told her all of it. She sat down on a kitchen chair to catch her breath again, this time from the excitement.

"Oh, children," she exclaimed, "ain't this wonderful news? It's the best present we could get."

"Yes, Momma," I said, but Jimmy looked down.

"Why's Jimmy looking sour?" Momma asked.

"He doesn't want to go to Emerson Peabody," I said.

"We won't fit in there, Momma!" Jimmy cried. Suddenly I was so angry at Jimmy, I wanted to punch him or scream at him. Momma had been so happy she had looked like her old self for a moment, and here he was making her sad again. I guess he realized it because he took a deep breath and sighed. "But I guess it don't matter what school I go to."

"Don't go putting yourself down, Jimmy. You'll show them rich kids something yet."

That night I had a hard time falling asleep. I stared through the darkness until my eyes adjusted, and I could faintly see Jimmy's face, the usually proud, hard mouth and eyes grown soft now that they were hidden by the night.

"Don't worry about being with rich kids, Jimmy," I said, knowing he was awake beside me. "Just because they're rich doesn't mean they're better than us."

"I never said it did," he said. "But I know rich kids. They think it makes them better."

"Don't you think there'll be at least a few kids we can make friends with?" I asked, my fears finally exploding to the surface with his.

"Sure. All the students at Emerson Peabody are just dying to make friends with the Longchamp kids."

I knew Jimmy had to be very worried—normally, he would try to protect me from my own dark side.

Deep down I hoped Daddy wasn't reaching too hard and too far for us.

A little more than a week later Jimmy and I had to begin attendance at our new school. The night before, I had picked out the nicest dress I had: a cotton dress of turquoise blue with three-quarter sleeves. It was a little wrinkled, so I ironed it and tried to take out a stain I had never noticed in the collar.

"Why are you working so hard on what to wear?" Jimmy asked. "I'm just wearing my dungarees and white polo shirt like always."

"Oh, Jimmy," I pleaded. "Just tomorrow wear your nice pants and the dress shirt."

"I'm not putting on airs for anyone."

"It's not putting on airs to look nice the first day you go to a new school, Jimmy. Couldn't you do it this once? For Daddy? For me?" I added.

"It's just a waste," he said, but I knew he would do it.

As usual, I was so nervous about entering a new school and meeting new friends, I took forever to fall asleep and had a harder time than usual waking up early. Jimmy hated getting up early, and now he had to get up and get himself ready earlier than ever because the school was in another part of the city and we had to go with Daddy. It was still quite dark when I rose from my bed. Of course, Jimmy just moaned and put the pillow over his head when I poked him in the shoulder, but I flicked on the lights.

"Come on, Jimmy. Don't make it harder than it has to be," I urged. I was in and out of the bathroom and making the coffee before Daddy came out of his bedroom. He got ready next, and then the both of us nagged Jimmy until he got up looking more like a sleepwalker and made his way to the bathroom.

When we left for school, the city looked so peaceful. The sun had just come up and some of the rays were reflected off store windows. Soon we were in a much finer part of Richmond. The houses were bigger and the streets were cleaner. Daddy made a few more turns, and suddenly the city seemed to disappear entirely. We were driving down a country road with farmhouses and fields. And then, just as magical as anything, Emerson Peabody appeared before us.

It didn't look like a school. It wasn't built out of cold brick or cement painted an ugly orange or yellow. Instead, it was a tall white structure that reminded me more of one of the museums in Washington, D.C. It had vast acreage around it, with hedges lining the driveway and trees everywhere. I saw a small pond off to the right as well. But it was the building itself that was most impressive.

The front entrance resembled the entrance to a great mansion. There were long, wide steps that led up to the pillars and portico, above which were engraved the words EMERSON PEABODY. Right in front was a statue of a stern-looking gentleman who turned out to be Emerson Peabody himself. Although there was a parking lot in front, Daddy had to drive around to the rear of the building, where the employees parked.

When we turned around the corner, we saw the playing fields: football field, baseball field, tennis courts, and Olympic-size pool. Jimmy whistled through his teeth.

"Is this a school or a hotel?" he asked.

Daddy pulled into his parking spot and turned off the engine. Then he turned to us, his face somber.

"The principal's a lady," he said. "Her name's Mrs. Turnbell, and she meets and speaks to every new student who comes here. She's here early, too, so she's waiting in her office for both of you."

"What's she like, Daddy?" I asked.

"Well, she's got eyes as green as cucumbers that she glues on you when she talks to you. She ain't more n' five feet one, I'd say, but she's a tough one, as tough as raw bear meat. She's one of them blue bloods whose family goes back to the Revolutionary War. I gotta take you up there before I get to work," Daddy said.

We followed Daddy through a rear entrance that took us up a short stairway to the main corridor of the school. The halls were immaculate, not a line of graffiti on a wall. The sunlight came through a corner window making the floors shine.

"Spick and span, ain't it?" Daddy said. "That's my responsibility," he added proudly.

As we walked along, we gazed into the classrooms. They were much smaller than any we had seen, but the desks looked big and brand-new. In one of the rooms I saw a young woman with dark brown hair preparing something on the blackboard for her soon-to-arrive class. As we went by, she looked our way and smiled.

Daddy stopped in front of a door marked PRINCIPAL. He quickly brushed back the sides of his hair with the palms of his hands and opened the door. We stepped into a cozy outer office that had a small counter facing the door. There was a black leather settee to the right and a small wooden table in front of it with magazines piled neatly on top. I thought it looked more like a doctor's waiting room than a school principal's. A tall, thin woman with eyeglasses as thick as goggles appeared at the gate. Her dull light brown hair was cut just below her ears.

"Mr. Longchamp, Mrs. Turnbell has been waiting," she said.

Without a friendly sign in her face, the tall woman opened the gate and stepped back for us to walk through to the second door, Mrs. Turnbell's inner office. She knocked softly and then opened the door only enough to peer in.

"The Longchamp children are here, Mrs. Turnbell," she said. We heard a thin, high-pitched voice say, "Show them in."

The tall woman stepped back, and we entered right behind Daddy. Mrs. Turnbell, who wore a dark blue jacket and skirt with a white blouse, stood up behind her desk. She had silver hair wrapped in a tight bun at the back of her head, the strands pulled so tightly at the sides, that they pulled at the corners of her eyes, which were piercing green, just as Daddy said. She didn't wear any makeup, not even a touch of lipstick. She had a complexion even lighter than mine, with skin so thin, I could see the crisscrossing tiny blue veins in her temples.

"This here's my kids, Mrs. Turnbell," Daddy declared.

"I assumed that, Mr. Longchamp. You're late. You know the other children will be arriving shortly."

"Well, we got here as soon as we could, ma'am. I—"

"Never mind. Please be seated," she said to us and indicated the chairs in front of her desk. Daddy stood back, folding his arms across his chest. When I looked back at him, I saw a cold sharpness in his eyes. He was holding back his anger.

"Should I stay?" he asked.

"Of course, Mr. Longchamp. I like the parents to be present when I explain to students the philosophies of the Emerson Peabody School, so everyone understands. I was hoping your mother would be able to come as well," she said to us.

Jimmy glared back at her. I could feel the tension in his body.

"Our momma's not feeling that well yet, ma'am," I said. "And we have a baby sister she has to mind."

"Yes. Be that as it may," Mrs. Turnbell said and sat down herself. "I trust you will take back to her everything I tell you anyway. Now, then," she said, looking at some papers before her on her desk. Everything on it was neatly arranged. "Your name is Dawn?"

"Yes, ma'am."

"Dawn," she repeated and shook her head and looked up at Daddy. "That's the child's full Christian name?"

"Yes, ma'am."

"Very well, and you are James?"

"Jimmy," Jimmy corrected.

"We don't use nicknames here, James." She clasped her hands and leaned toward us, fixing her gaze on Jimmy. "Those sort of things might have been tolerated at the other institutions you attended, public institutions," she said, making the word *public* sound like a curse word, "but this is a special school. Our students come from the finest families in the South, sons and daughters of people with heritage and position. Names are respected; names are important, as important as anything else.

"I'll come right to the point. I know you children haven't had the same upbringing and advantages as the rest of my students have had, and I imagine it will take you two a little longer to fit in. However, I expect that very shortly you two will adjust and conduct yourselves like Emerson Peabody students are supposed to conduct themselves.

"You will address all your teachers as either sir or ma'am. You will come to school dressed neatly and be clean. Never challenge a command. I have a copy of our rules here, and I expect both of you to read and commit them all to memory."

She turned toward Jimmy.

"We don't tolerate bad language, fighting, or disrespect in any form or manner. We expect students to treat each other with respect, too. We frown on tardiness and loitering, and we will not stand for any sort of vandalism when it comes to our beautiful building.

"Very soon you will see how special Emerson Peabody is, and you will realize how lucky you are to be here. Which brings me to my final point: In a real sense, you two are guests. The rest of the student body pays a handsome fee to be able to attend Emerson Peabody. The board of trustees has made it possible for you two to attend because of your father. Therefore, you have an added responsibility to behave and be a credit to our school.

"Am I understood?"

"Yes, ma'am," I said quickly. Jimmy glared at her with defiance. I held my breath, hoping he wouldn't say anything nasty.

"James?"

"I understand," he said in a somber tone.

"Very well," she said and sat back. "Mr. Longchamp, you may resume your duties. You two will go out to Miss Jackson, who will provide you with your class schedules and assign a locker to each of you." She stood up abruptly, and Jimmy and I stood up, too. She stared at us a moment longer and then nodded. Daddy started out first.

"James," she called just as we reached the door. He and I turned back. "It would be nice if you shined your shoes. Remember, we are often judged by our appearance." Jimmy didn't reply. He walked out ahead of me.

"I'll try to get him to do it, ma'am," I said. She nodded and I closed the door behind me.

"I gotta get to work," Daddy said and then left the office quickly.

"Well," Jimmy said. "Welcome to Emerson Peabody. Still think it's going to be peaches and cream?"

I swallowed hard; my heart was pounding.

"I bet she's that way with every new student, Jimmy."

"Jimmy? Didn'tcha hear? It's James," he said with an affected accent. Then he shook his head.

"We're in for it now," he said.

3
ALWAYS A STRANGER

The first day at a new school was never easy, but Mrs. Turnbell had made it harder for us. I couldn't get the trembles out of my body as Jimmy and I left the principal's office with our schedules. In some schools the principal assigned a big brother and a big sister to help us get started and find our way around, but here at Emerson Peabody we were thrown out to sink or swim on our own.

We weren't halfway down the main corridor when doors began to open and students began to enter. They came in laughing and talking, acting like any other students we had seen, only how they were dressed!

All of the girls had on expensive-looking, beautiful winter coats made of the softest wool I had ever seen. Some of the coats even had fur trim on the collars. The boys all wore navy blue jackets and ties and khaki-colored slacks and the girls wore pretty dresses or skirts and blouses. Everyone's clothes looked new. They were all dressed as if this were their first day, too, only it wasn't. They were in their regular everyday school clothes!

Jimmy and I stopped in our tracks and stared, and when the students saw us, they stared, too, some very curious, some looking and then laughing to each other. They moved about in small clumps of friends. Most had been brought to the school in shiny clean buttercup-yellow buses, but we could see from gazing out the opening doors that some of the older students drove to school in their own fancy cars.

No one came over to introduce him or herself. When they approached us, they went to one side or the other, parting around us as if we were contagious. I tried smiling at this girl or that, but none really smiled back. Jimmy just glared. Soon we were at the center of a pool of laughter and noise.

I looked at the papers that told us the times for the class periods and realized we had to move along if we weren't going to be late the very first day. In fact, just as we got our lockers opened and hung up our coats, the bell rang to signal that everyone had to go to homeroom.

"Good luck, Jimmy," I said when I left him at the beginning of the corridor.

"I'll need it," he replied and sauntered off.

Homeroom at Emerson Peabody was the same as it was anywhere else. My homeroom teacher, Mr. Wengrow, was a short, stout, curly-haired man who held a yardstick in his hand like a whip and tapped it on his desk every time someone's voice went over a whisper or he had something to say. All of the students looked up at him attentively, their hands folded on their desks. When I entered, every head turned my way. It made me feel like I was a magnet and their heads and bodies were made of iron. Mr. Wengrow took my schedule sheet. He read it, pressed his lips together, and entered my name in his roll book. Then he tapped his yardstick.

"Boys and girls, I'd like to introduce you to a new student. Her name is Dawn Longchamp. Dawn, I'm Mr. Wengrow. Welcome to 10Y and to Emerson Peabody. You can take the next to last seat in the second row. And Michael Standard, make sure your feet aren't on the back of her chair," he warned.

The students looked at Michael, a small boy with dark brown hair and an impish grin. There was some tittering as he straightened in his seat. I thanked Mr. Wengrow and walked back to sit at my desk. Everyone's eyes were still on me. A girl wearing thick blue-framed glasses across from me offered me a smile of welcome. I smiled back. She had bright red hair tied in a ponytail, that hung listlessly down her back. I saw she had long thin pale arms and thin pale legs that were covered all over with pale red freckles. I thought about Momma telling me how awkward and gangly she was when she was my age.

I heard the public address system click on. Mr. Wengrow straightened into attention and glared around the room to be sure everyone was being attentive. Then Mrs. Turnbell came on and commanded everyone to rise for the Pledge of Allegiance, after which she made a series of announcements about the activities of the day. When she was finished and the public address system clicked off, we were permitted to sit down, but almost as soon as we did, the bell rang to begin the first-period class.

"Hi," the girl with the red ponytail said. "I'm Louise Williams."

When she stood next to me, I realized how tall she was. She had a long bony nose and thin lips, but her timid eyes held more warmth than anyone else's had yet at this school. "What do you have first?" she asked.

"Phys ed," I said.

"Mrs. Allen?"

I looked at my schedule card.

"Yes."

"Good. You're in my class. Let me see your schedule," she added, practically ripping it out of my hand. "Oh, you're in a lot of my classes. You'll have to tell me all about yourself, who your parents are and where you live. What a nice dress. It must be your favorite; you look like you're wearing it out. Where did you go to school before? Do you know anyone here yet?" She fired one question after another at me before we even reached the door. I just shook my head and smiled.

"Come on," Louise said, urging me along.

From the way the other girls ignored Louise as we passed through the corridor to our first class, I gathered that she wasn't very popular. It was always hard to break the ice in a new school, but usually there were cracks to find. Here, the ice around me seemed solid, except for Louise, who talked a streak from homeroom to our first class.

By the time we reached the gymnasium, I knew that she was very good in math and science and only fair in history and English. Her daddy was a lawyer in a family firm that went back just ages and ages, and she had two brothers and a sister who were still in grade school.

"Mrs. Allen's office is over there," Louise said, pointing. "She'll assign you a locker and give you a gym suit and a towel for your shower." With that, she hurried off to change.

Mrs. Allen was a tall woman about forty years old. "All the girls must take showers after class," she insisted as she handed me a towel. I nodded. "Come on," she said. She looked stern as we walked toward the locker room. The loud chatter eased up when we entered, and all the girls turned our way. It was a mixed class with girls from three different grades. Louise was already in her uniform.

"Girls, I would like you all to meet a new student, Dawn Longchamp. Let's see," Mrs. Allen said, "your locker is over there"—she pointed across the room—"next to Clara Sue Cutler."

I gazed at the blond girl with the chubby face and figure who was standing at the center of a small clique. None of them were in uniform yet. Mrs. Allen's eyes narrowed as she led me across the locker room.

"What's taking you girls so long?" she asked and then sniffed. "I smell smoke. Have you girls been smoking?" she demanded with her hands on her hips. They all looked at one another anxiously. Then I saw some smoke coming out of a locker.

"It's not a cigarette, Mrs. Allen," I said. "Look."

Mrs. Allen squinted and moved to the locker quickly.

"Clara Sue, open this locker immediately," she demanded.

The chubby girl sauntered over to it and worked the combination. When she opened it, Mrs. Allen made her stand back. There was a lit cigarette burning on the shelf.

"I don't know how that got in there," Clara Sue said, her eyes wide with what was obviously fake amazement.

"Oh, you don't, don't you?"

"I'm not smoking it. You can't say I'm smoking," Clara Sue protested haughtily.

Mrs. Allen lifted the burning cigarette out of the locker, holding it between her forefinger and thumb as though it were a cylinder of disease.

"Behold, girls," she said, "a cigarette that smokes itself."

There was some giggling. Clara Sue looked very uncomfortable.

"All right, everyone get dressed and quickly. Miss Cutler, you and I will have a talk about this later," she said, then pivoted and left the locker. The moment she was gone, Clara Sue came at me, her face red and bloated with anger.

"You stupid idiot!" she screamed. "Why did you tell her?"

"I thought it was a fire," I explained.

"Oh, brother. Who are you, Alice in Wonderland? Now you got me in trouble."

"I'm sorry, I . . . ."

I looked around. All the girls were glaring at me. "I didn't mean it. Honest. I thought I was helping you."

"Helping?" She shook her head. "You helped me into trouble, that's what you did."

Everyone nodded and the group broke up so everyone could finish dressing. I looked to Louise, but even she turned away. Afterward, the girls were very standoffish in the gym. Every chance she got, Clara Sue glared hatefully at me. I tried to explain again, but she wasn't interested.

When Mrs. Allen blew the whistle to end the period and send us to the showers, I tried to get Louise's attention.

"You got her in trouble," was all she would say.

Here I was only an hour or so in a new school and already I had made enemies when all I wanted to do was make some new friends. As soon as I saw Clara Sue, I apologized again, making it sound as sincere as I could.

"It's all right," Clara Sue suddenly said. "I shouldn't have blamed you. I just lost my temper. It was my own fault."

"Really, I wouldn't have pointed out the smoke if I'd thought you were smoking. I don't tattletale."

"I believe you. Girls," she said to those nearest, "we shouldn't blame Dawn. That's your name, right? Dawn?"

"Uh-huh."

"Do you have any brothers or sisters?"

"A brother," I said quickly.

"What's his name, Afternoon?" a tall beautiful girl with dark hair asked. Everyone laughed.

"We better get moving or we're going to be late for our next class," Clara Sue announced. It was easy to see that many of the girls looked up to her as a leader. I couldn't believe I'd had the bad luck to begin by getting her in trouble. Of all the girls to get in trouble, I thought, and breathed a sigh of relief, grateful for her forgiveness. I took off my gym uniform quickly and followed everyone to the showers. They were nice showers, clean stalls with flower-print shower curtains, and the water was warm, too.

"You better get a move on in there," I heard Mrs. Allen call.

I stepped out of the shower and wiped myself dry as quickly as I could. Then I wrapped the towel around my body and rushed to my locker. It was wide open. Had I forgotten to lock it? I wondered. I discovered the answer very quickly. Except for my shoes, all my clothes were gone.

"Where are my clothes?" I cried. I turned around. All the girls were looking my way and smiling. Clara Sue was standing by the sink, brushing her hair. "Please. This isn't funny. Those are my best clothes."

That made everyone laugh. I looked to Louise, but she turned away quickly, slammed her locker shut, and hurried out of the locker room. Soon everyone but me was leaving.

"Please!" I cried. "Who knows where my clothes are?"

"They're being washed," someone called back.

"Washed? What does that mean? Washed?"

I spun around, the towel still tucked in over my body. I was alone in the locker room. The bells were ringing. What was I going to do?

I started looking everywhere, under benches, in corners, but I found nothing until I went into the bathroom and checked the stalls.

"Oh, no!" I cried. They had thrown my clothes into the toilet. There was my pretty dress, my bra, and my panties. Even my socks, soaking with toilet paper floating around it all for good measure. And the water was discolored. Someone had urinated in there, too!

I fell back against the stall door and sobbed. What was I going to do?

"Who's left in here?" I heard Mrs. Allen ask.

"It's me," I bawled. She stepped into the bathroom.

"Well, what are you . . ."

I pointed down at the toilet, and she gazed into the stall.

"Oh, no . . . who did this?"

"I don't know, Mrs. Allen."

"I don't have any trouble guessing," she said sternly.

"What will I do?"

She thought a moment, shaking her head.

"Fish them out and we'll put them in the washer and dryer with the towels. In the meantime, you will have to wear your gym uniform."

"To classes?"

"There's nothing else you can do, Dawn. I'm sorry."

"But . . . everyone will laugh at me."

"It's up to you. You will miss a few classes by the time this is all washed and dried out. I'll go to see Mrs. Turnbell and explain what happened."

I nodded and lowered my head in defeat as I walked back to my locker to put on my gym uniform.

As the morning went on, I found most of my teachers to be kind and sympathetic once they heard what had happened, but the rest of the students thought it was very funny, and everywhere I looked I found them smiling and laughing at me. It was always hard to face new students whenever I went to a new school, but here, before I even got a chance to meet anyone and anyone got a chance to know me, I was the laughingstock.

When Jimmy saw me in the hallway and I told him what had happened, he was outraged.

"What did I tell you about this place?" he said loud enough for most of the students around us in the hallway to hear. "I'd just like to know who did it, that's all. I'd just like to get my hands on her."

"It's all right, Jimmy," I said, trying to calm him down. "I'll be all right. After the next class my clothes should be washed and dried." I didn't mention the fact that my dress would be wrinkled and need ironing. I didn't want him to get any angrier than he was.

The warning bell for the next class rang.

Jimmy scowled so hard at the students who were staring at us that most turned their heads away as they rushed to get to class.

"I'll be all right, Jimmy," I insisted again before starting toward my math class.

"I'd like to know who did it!" he called after me. "Just so I could ring her neck." He said it loud enough for everyone who was left in the hallway to hear.

As soon as I entered class, the teacher called me to his desk.

"You're Dawn Longchamp, I assume," he said.

"Yes, sir." I looked at the class, and of course, all the students were looking at me, smiles on their faces.

"Well, we'll introduce ourselves later. Mrs. Turnbell wants to see you immediately," he said.

"The Longchamp girl is here," Mrs. Turnbell's secretary announced as I entered the reception room. I heard Mrs. Turnbell say, "Send her in." The secretary stepped back and I entered.

Mrs. Turnbell's gaze was icy as she asked me to explain what had happened.

With my stomach jumping up and down and my voice shaking, I told her how I had come out of the shower and found my clothing in the toilet.

"Why would anyone do that to a new girl?" she asked. I didn't respond. I didn't want to get into any more trouble with the other girls, and I knew that was exactly what would happen if I mentioned the smoke.

But she knew already!

"You don't have to explain. Mrs. Allen told me how you turned in Clara Sue Cutler for smoking."

"I didn't turn her in. I saw smoke coming from this locker and—"

"Now, listen to me," Mrs. Turnbell ordered, leaning over her desk, her pale face going first pink, then red. "The other students at this school have been brought up in fine homes and have a head start on how to get along with other people. But that doesn't mean I will allow you and your brother to come in here and disrupt everything. Do you understand?"

"Yes, ma'am," I said hoarsely, tears choking me. Coldly Mrs. Turnbell eyed me and shook her head.

"Going around to class in a gym uniform," she muttered. "You march right out of here and go directly to the laundry and wait for your clothing to be washed and dried."

"Yes, ma'am."

"Go on. Get dressed and back to your classes as soon as possible," she commanded with a wave of her hand.

I hurried out, wiping the tears away as I ran through the hallway and down to the laundry. When I put on my dress again, it was so wrinkled it looked like I had been sitting on it. But there was nothing I could do.

I hurried up to make my English class. When I got there several students looked disappointed to see me in regular clothing again. Only Louise looked relieved. When our gazes met, she smiled and then looked away quickly. At least for now, my ordeal had ended.

After English class, Louise caught up with me at the doorway.

"I'm sorry they did that to you!" she cried. "I just want you to know I wasn't part of it."

"Thank you."

"I should have warned you right away about Clara Sue. For some reason most of the girls do what she tells them to."

"If she did this, it was a very mean thing to do. I told her I was sorry."

"Clara Sue always gets her way," Louise said. "Maybe she won't bother you anymore. Come on, I'll go with you to lunch."

"Thank you," I said. A few other students said hello to me and smiled, but for the most part Louise was the only raft for me to cling to in unfamiliar waters.

The cafeteria was fancier than any I'd ever seen. Here the seats and tables looked plush and comfortable. The walls were painted light blue, and the tiled floor was an off-white. The students picked up their trays and silverware at an area just before the serving counter and proceeded to the awaiting cashier.

I saw Clara Sue Cutler sitting with some of the other girls from our gym class. They all laughed when they set eyes on me.

"Let's sit over there," Louise said, indicating an empty table away from them.

"Just a minute," I said and marched up to Clara Sue's table. The girls all turned in surprise.

"Hi, Dawn," Clara Sue said, with a cat-who-has-eaten-the-canary look on her spiteful face. "Shouldn't you have ironed that?"

Everyone laughed.

"I don't know why you did this to me," I fired back in a hard voice as I eyed them all coldly. "But it was a terrible thing to do to someone, especially someone who has just entered your school."

"Who told you I did?" she demanded.

"No one told me. I know."

The girls stared. Clara Sue's big blue eyes narrowed to slits and then widened with an apparent softness.

"All right, Dawn," she said in a voice of amnesty. "I guess we broke you into Emerson Peabody. You're forgiven," she said with a queenly gesture. "In fact, you may sit here, if you like. You, too, Louise," she added.

"Thank you," I said. I was determined to mend fences and not disrupt Mrs. Turnbell's precious little school. Louise and I took the two empty seats.

"This is Linda Ann Brandise," Clara Sue said, indicating the taller girl with soft, dark brown hair and beautiful almond-shaped eyes. "And this is Margaret Ann Stanton, Diane Elaine Wilson, and Melissa Lee Norton."

I nodded at all of them and wondered if I was the only girl in the school without a formal middle name.

"Did you just move here?" Clara Sue asked. "You're not a sleep-over, I know."

"Sleep-over?"

"Students who stay in the dorms," Louise explained.

"Oh. No, I live in Richmond. Do you sleep over, Louise?"

"No, but Linda and Clara Sue do. I'm going to get my lunch," Louise declared and then pulled herself up. "Coming, Dawn?"

"I just need to get a container of milk," I said, putting my lunch bag on the table.

"What's that?" Louise asked.

"My lunch. I have a peanut butter and jelly sandwich." I opened my purse and found my milk money.

"You made your own lunch?" Clara Sue asked. "Why would you do that?"

"It saves money."

Louise stared at me, her watery, pale blue eyes blinking as she struggled to understand.

"Saves money? Why do you want to save money? Did your parents cut off your allowance?" Linda inquired.

"I don't have an allowance. Momma gives me money for milk, but other than that . . ."

"Money for milk?" Linda laughed and looked at Clara Sue. "What does your father do, anyway?"

"He works here. He's a maintenance supervisor."

"Maintenance?" Linda gasped. "You mean . . . he's a janitor?" Her eyes widened when I nodded.

"Uh-huh. Because he works here, my brother, Jimmy, and I get to go to Emerson Peabody."

The girls turned to each other and suddenly laughed.

"A janitor," Clara Sue said, as though she couldn't believe it. They laughed again. "I think we'll let Louise and Dawn have this table," she purred. Clara Sue lifted her tray and stood up. Linda and the others followed suit and started away.

"I didn't know your father was a janitor here," Louise said.

"You never gave me a chance to tell you. He's a supervisor because he's very good at fixing and maintaining all sorts of engines and motors," I said proudly.

"How nice." She looked around and then slipped her hands around her books and lifted them off the table. "Oh! I just remembered. I have to talk to Mary Jo Alcott. We have a science project to do together. I'll see you later," she said quickly and walked across the cafeteria to another table. The girls there didn't seem so happy to greet her, but she sat down anyway. She pointed at me and they all laughed.

They were snubbing me because they thought I was beneath them just because Daddy was the janitor. Jimmy was right, I thought. Rich kids were spoiled and horrible. I glared back at them defiantly, even though tears burned like fire under my eyelids. I rose and walked proudly to the lunch line to get some milk.

I looked around for Jimmy, hoping that he had been luckier than me and had made at least one friend by now, but I didn't see him anywhere. I returned to my table and began to unfold my bag when I heard someone say, "There any free seats here?"

I looked up at one of the handsomest boys I had ever seen. His hair was thick and flaxen blond like mine. It waved just enough to be perfect. His eyes were cerulean blue and they sparkled with laughter. His nose was straight and neither too long nor too narrow, nor too thick. He was just a little taller than Jimmy, but he had wider shoulders and stood straight and confidently. When I looked more closely at him, I saw that just like me, he had a tiny patch of freckles under each eye.

"They're all free," I said.

"Really? Can't imagine why," he said and sat down across from me. He extended his hand. "My name's Philip Cutler," he said.

"Cutler?" I pulled my hand back quickly.

"What's wrong?" His blue eyes sparkled wickedly. "Don't tell me some of those catty girls have warned you against me already?"

"No . . ." I turned and looked at the table of girls with Clara Sue at the center. They were all looking our way.

"I . . . your sister . . ."

"Oh, her. What'd she do?" His gaze darkened as he glanced back their way. I saw how it infuriated Clara Sue.

"She . . . blames me for getting her in trouble this morning in gym class. I . . . didn't you see me walking through the school in my gym uniform?"

"Oh, that was you? So you're the famous new girl—Dawn. I did hear about you, but I was so busy this morning, I didn't catch sight of you."

The way he smiled made me wonder if he was lying. Did Clara Sue put him up to this?

"You're probably the only one in the school who didn't," I said. "I was even called down to the principal's office and bawled out, even though it wasn't my fault."

"That doesn't surprise me. Mrs. Turnbell thinks she's a prison warden instead of a principal. That's why we call her Mrs. Turnkey."

"Turnkey?" I had to smile. It fit.

"And all this was my bratty sister's fault, huh?" He shook his head. "That figures, too."

"I've tried to make friends, apologize, but . . ." I glared at the girls. "They all turned on me when they found out what my father does."

"What's he do—rob banks?"

"He might as well for all they would care," I shot back. "Especially your sister."

"Forget her," Philip advised. "You can't let my sister get to you. She's a spoiled brat. She deserves whatever she gets. Where are you from?"

"Many places. Before Richmond, Granville, Virginia."

"Granville? I've never been there. Was it nice?"

"No," I said. He laughed, his teeth white and perfect. He looked at my bag and sandwich. "A bag lunch?"

"Yes," I said, anticipating his ridicule, too. But he surprised me.

"What do you have?"

"Peanut butter and jelly."

"Looks a lot thicker than the peanut butter sandwiches they give you here. Maybe I'll get you to bag me a lunch, too," he said. He looked serious about it for a moment, and then he laughed at my expression. "My sister is the biggest busybody here. She loves snooping in other people's business and then spreading rumors."

I studied him for a moment. Was he saying these things just to win my confidence or did he really mean it? I couldn't imagine Jimmy speaking so hatefully about me.

"What grade are you in?" I asked, trying to change the subject.

"Eleventh. I got my driver's license this year and my own car. How would you like to go for a ride with me after school?" he asked quickly.

"A ride?"

"Sure. I'll show you the sights," he added, winking.

"Thank you," I said. "But I can't."

"Why not? I'm a good driver," he pursued.

"I . . . have to meet my father after school."

"Well, maybe tomorrow, then. Hey," he said when I hesitated, searching for another excuse, "I'm perfectly harmless, no matter what you've heard."

"I haven't—" I broke off in confusion and felt my cheeks start to burn.

He laughed.

"You take everything so serious. Your parents gave you the right name. You're definitely as fresh as the birth of a new day," he said. I blushed even harder and looked down at my sandwich.

"So, do you stay in the dorms or live nearby?" he asked.

"I live on Ashland Street."

"Ashland? Don't know it. I'm not from Richmond, though. I'm from Virginia Beach."

"Oh, I've heard of it, but I've never been there. I heard it's very pretty there," I said and bit into my sandwich.

"It is. My family owns a hotel there: the Cutler's Cove Hotel, in Cutler's Cove, which is just a few miles south of Virginia Beach," he said sitting back proudly.

"You have a whole place named after your family?" I asked. No wonder Clara Sue was so swollen with her own importance, I thought.

"Yep. We've been there ever since the Indians gave it up. Or so my grandmother says."

"Your grandmother lives with you?" I asked enviously.

"She and my grandfather used to run the hotel. He died, but she still runs it with my parents. What does your father do, Dawn?"

"He works here," I said and thought, here I go again.

"Here? He's a teacher? And you let me say all those things about Mrs. Turnkey and—"

"No, no. He's a maintenance supervisor," I said quickly.

"Oh." Philip smiled and released a sigh of relief. "I'm glad of that," he said.

"You are?" I couldn't help sounding surprised.

"Yes. The two girls I know here whose fathers are teachers are the biggest snobs—Rebecca Clare Longstreet and Stephanie Kay Sumpter. Ignore them at all costs," he advised.

Just then I saw Jimmy come in. He was walking all by himself. He stopped in the doorway and gazed around. When he saw me, he flashed a look of surprise at the sight of Philip as well. Then he headed quickly to my table. He slapped his bag on top and flopped into a seat.

"Hi," Philip said. "How's it going?"

"Stinks," Jimmy said. "Just got bawled out for putting my feet on the rung of the seat ahead of me. I thought she would keep me there right through lunch."

"Gotta watch that around here. If Mrs. Turnbell comes by and sees a student doing something like that, she bawls out the teacher first, and that makes the teacher get even madder," Philip explained.

"This is Philip Cutler," said Dawn. "Philip, my brother, Jimmy."

"Hi," Philip said, extending his hand. Jimmy looked at it suspiciously a moment and then shook quickly.

"What do they think this place is, gold?" Jimmy said, getting back to his problem.

"Did you make any friends yet, Jimmy?" I asked hopefully.

He shook his head.

"I gotta get my milk." He got up quickly and went to the lunch line. The boys in front of him looked nervous when he approached.

"Jimmy's not overjoyed about being here, I gather," Philip said, looking his way.

"No, he's not. Maybe he's right," I added.

Philip smiled.

"You've got the clearest, prettiest eyes I've ever seen. The only one whose eyes come close is my mother."

I felt myself blush from my neck to my feet. I was absolutely beguiled by his flattering words, by the admiring look in his eyes. For a moment I couldn't speak. I had to shift my eyes away while I took another bite of my sandwich. I chewed quickly and swallowed, then turned back to him.

Some boys passing by said hello to him and then looked at me curiously. Finally two of his friends flopped down beside him.

"Aren't you going to introduce us to your famous new friend, Philip?" asked a tall thin boy with peach-colored hair and brown eyes. He had a crooked smile that brought the corner of his mouth up.

"Not if I can help it," Philip said.

"Aw, come on. Philip likes to keep everything to himself," the tall boy told me. "Very selfish guy."

"My name's Dawn," I said quickly.

"Dawn. You mean like 'it dawned on me'?" He and his companion laughed hard.

"I'm Brandon," the tall boy finally said. "And this idiot beside me is Marshall." The shorter boy beside him only nodded. His eyes were very close together and he had his dark brown hair cut very short. He wore a smirk, rather than a smile. I recalled Momma once telling me never to trust anyone whose eyes were too close together. She said their mommas, just before giving birth, must have been surprised by snakes.

Jimmy returned and Philip introduced him to the other boys, but he sat quietly eating his sandwich. Philip was the only one who would talk to him, but Jimmy obviously didn't care. I saw from the way he looked at Marshall from time to time that he didn't like him much, either.

The bell rang to end the lunch period.

"Going to gym class?" Brandon asked Philip. "Or do you have other plans?" he added, gazing at me and smiling. I knew what he meant, but I tried to look like I didn't understand.

"I'll meet you," Philip said.

"Don't be late," Marshall quipped, speaking out of the corner of his mouth. The two boys went off, laughing.

"Where are you heading, Dawn?" Philip asked.

"Music."

"Good. I'll walk along with you. It's on the way to my gym class," he said. We started away from the table. When I looked to the side, I saw how Clara Sue and her friends were staring at us and whispering. They looked so hateful. Why? I wondered. Why did they have to be this way?

"Where's your next class, Jimmy?" I asked.

"I gotta go the other way," he said and scurried off before I could say a word. He elbowed his way through the crowd of students heading out the doors to the corridors and disappeared quickly.

"Have you been going to this school all your life?" I asked. Philip nodded. As we went along, I noticed many girls and boys nod and say hello to Philip. He was obviously very popular.

"My sister and I even attended the kindergarten associated with it." He leaned toward me. "My parents and my grandmother make sizable contributions to the school," he added, but he didn't sound arrogant about it. It was just a statement of fact.

"Oh." Everyone around me seemed so sophisticated and so wealthy. Jimmy had been right. We were like fish out of water. My daddy only worked here, and what would I wear tomorrow? What would Jimmy wear? If we stood out like sore thumbs now, what would happen tomorrow?

"We both better get a move on before we're thrown to Mrs. Turnkey," he said and smiled. "Think about going for a ride with me tomorrow, okay?"

I nodded. When I looked back, I saw Clara Sue and her friends walking slowly behind us. Clara Sue looked very unhappy about the attention her brother was giving me. Maybe he was sincere. He was so handsome and I felt like doing something to annoy her.

"I'll think about it," I said loud enough for the girls to hear.

"Great." He squeezed my arm gently and walked off, turning once to smile back. I returned a smile, making sure Clara Sue could see, and then I entered the music suite just as the bell beginning the class rang.

My music teacher, Mr. Moore, was a rosy-faced man with dimples in his cheeks and hair as curly as Harpo Marx's. He had the sweetest disposition of any of my teachers I had met so far, and when he smiled, it was a smile full of warmth and sincerity. I saw that shy students shed their bashfulness when he coaxed them and willingly stood up to sing a few notes solo. He walked around the classroom with his tuning harmonica teaching us the scales, explaining notes, making music more interesting than even I imagined it could be. When he got to me, he paused and twitched his nose like a squirrel. His hazel brown eyes brightened.

"And now for a new voice," he said. "Dawn, can you sing Do re, mi, fa, so, la, ti, do? I'll give you a start," he began, bringing his harmonica to his lips, but I started before he had a chance to toot. His eyes widened and his bushy reddish-brown eyebrows lifted. "Well, now, a discovery. That's the best rendition of the scales cold I have heard in years," he said. "Wasn't that perfect, boys and girls?" he asked the class. When I looked around, I saw a sea of faces full of envy. Louise was especially jealous of the compliment Mr. Moore had given me. Her face was lime. "I think we might have found our solo singer for our next concert," Mr. Moore mused aloud, squeezing his round chin between his right forefinger and thumb as he looked at me and nodded. "Have you been in chorus before, Dawn?"

"Yes, sir."

"And do you play an instrument of any kind?" he inquired.

"I have been teaching myself the guitar."

"Teaching yourself?" He looked around the classroom. "Now, that's motivation, boys and girls. Well, we're going to have to see how far along you've come. If you're very good, you can put me out of a job," he said.

"I'm not very good, sir," I said.

He laughed, his cheeks trembling with his chuckles.

"There's something refreshing," he said, speaking to the rest of the class, "modesty. Ever wonder what that was, boys and girls?" He laughed at his own joke and went on with the day's lesson. When the bell ending the period rang, he asked me to remain a moment.

"Bring your guitar in with you tomorrow, Dawn. I'd like to hear you play," he said, his face serious and determined.

"I don't have a very good guitar, sir. It's second-hand and—"

"Now, now. Don't you be ashamed of it, and don't let any of the students here make you feel that way. I have an idea that it's a lot better than you think anyway. Besides, I can supply you with a very good guitar when the time comes."

"Thank you, sir," I said. He sat back in his seat and contemplated me a moment.

"I know the students are supposed to call their teachers sir and ma'am," he said. "But when we're working alone, could you manage to call me Mr. Moore?"

I smiled.

"I'll try."

"Good. I'm glad you're here, Dawn. Welcome to Emerson Peabody. Now you better hurry off to your next class."

"Thank you, Mr. Moore," I said and he smiled.

I started for my next class, but stopped when I saw Louise waiting for me.

"Hi," I said, seeing she wanted to be friends again. But that wasn't her first concern.

"I saw Philip Cutler sitting with you at lunch," she said, unable to hide the note of jealousy. "You'd better be careful. He's got a bad reputation with girls," she said, but her voice was still filled with envy.

"A bad reputation? He seems very nice. A lot different from his sister," I said pointedly. "What do they say that's so bad?"

"It's what he wants to do, even on a first date," she replied, her eyes big.

"What does he want to do?" I asked. She stepped back.

"What do you think?" She looked to the side to be sure no one could overhear. "He wants to go all the way."

"Did you go out with him?"

"No," she said, her eyes wide. "Never."

I shrugged.

"I don't think you should let people decide what you should and should not think about someone. You should decide for yourself. Besides, it's not fair to Philip," I added, his dazzling blue eyes still hovering in my thoughts.

Louise shook her head. "Don't say I didn't warn you," she advised.

"At least he didn't make me sit alone at lunch." My point, like an accurate arrow, hit the bull's eye.

"I'm sorry I left you . . . can we have lunch together tomorrow?" she asked.

"Probably," I said without sounding very definite about it. I was still feeling the scratches she and her catty friends had drawn across my heart. But that satisfied her enough to give me the benefit of another warning.

"If you think Clara Sue Cutler doesn't like you now, wait until she hears what Mr. Moore said."

"What do you mean?"

"She thinks she's going to sing the solo at the concert. She did last year," Louise said and punctured my balloon of happiness just as it was starting to inflate.

4
A KISS

At the end of the school day I met Jimmy in the lobby. He was very unhappy because his math teacher had said she thought he was so far behind, he might have to take the class over again.

"I warned you about missing all that school, Jimmy," I chastised softly.

"Who cares?" he replied, but I could see he was upset.

While we were talking, all the other students were hurrying out to catch buses or get into their cars. Those who slept in the dorms sauntered out slowly.

"All these rich kids got money to burn," Jimmy muttered, seeing some of them heading for their own cars. "Come on," he said, heading toward the stairway. "Let's see how long we've got to wait for Daddy."

I followed Jimmy down to the basement where Daddy's office was. There was a workroom right next to Daddy's office, which wasn't a big office, but he did have a nice wooden desk and two chairs in it. There were shelves on the walls and a large, hanging light in a dark blue metal shade draped at the end of a wire and chain just over the desk.

Jimmy sat down behind Daddy's desk and slumped back in the seat. I brought the other chair closer and opened my textbooks to begin doing some of my homework. Thoughts about the day whirled confusingly through my brain, and when I looked up, I caught Jimmy staring at me.

"Did you ever find out who did that to you?" he asked.

"No, Jimmy," I lied. "Let's just forget about it. It was all a misunderstanding." I didn't want him getting into trouble on account of me.

"Misunderstanding?" He shook his head. "They're all snobs here. The girls are stuck up and the boys are jerks. All they talk about are their cars and their clothes and their record collections. How come that guy named Philip was sitting with you in the cafeteria?" he asked.

"Philip? He came over and asked if any of the seats were free," I said, making it sound like nothing, when all along I had thought it wonderful. "When he found out they all were, he sat down."

"Funny, how he got so friendly so fast." Jimmy's eyes grew small as his mind worked overtime.

"He's just being nice." I myself had been unsure about trusting Clara Sue's brother, but for some reason I had to defend Philip to Jimmy. Philip was the only friendly soul at this school so far. I thought of his full lips curving into a lopsided smile and his blue eyes holding my own gaze hypnotically as he'd asked me to ride in his car. Just remembering made me shiver a little.

"Now that I think about it, I don't trust him," Jimmy suddenly concluded. He nodded, confirming his theory. "This all might be part of some joke because of what happened to you this morning. Maybe somebody made a bet with him that he couldn't get you to like him right away or something. What if he does something to embarrass you?"

"Oh, that can't be true, Jimmy. He's too nice to do anything like that!" I cried a little too desperately.

"If I'm right, you're going to be very sorry. If he hurts you," he added, "he'll have to deal with me."

I smiled to myself, thinking how good it was to have a brother who was so protective.

Just then Daddy appeared in the doorway. Unlike the end of his day's work at all of his other jobs, Daddy didn't look tired and dirty. His hands were as clean as they had been in the morning, and there were no smudges on his clothes.

I waited, holding my breath, expecting that by now he had found out about the gym class incident, but if he did know, he didn't say a word. And he didn't seem to notice how wrinkled my dress was.

"So?" he said. "How did your day go, kids?" He shot a very quick smile at me and stroked my hair for the most fleeting moment.

I glanced at Jimmy. We had decided we wouldn't tell Daddy what had happened to me, but all of a sudden I longed to bury my face in his chest and while safe in his arms cry a waterfall of tears. Even with the memories of Philip and music class to warm me, most of the day had been awful; now it was a blur of laughing faces swimming before my eyes. I knew I couldn't tell him, though—Daddy's temper was fiery and

unpredictable. What if he said something and got fired, or even worse—
what if Mrs. Turnbell convinced him everything was my fault?

"This place is just what I expected it to be: full of spoiled rich kids
and teachers who look down on you," Jimmy said.

"Nobody's looking down on me," Daddy replied gruffly.

Jimmy looked away and then glanced at me as if to say Daddy
wouldn't know if they did.

"Yeah, yeah. When can we get out of this place?" Jimmy demanded.

"We're leaving right now. I just want to enter some figures into my
record book here," he said, pulling a black and white notebook out of a
side desk drawer.

"You like this job, don't you, Daddy?" I asked as we were leaving. I
looked pointedly at Jimmy so he would understand how much this all
meant to our family.

"Sure do, baby. Well, let's get ourselves home to your momma and
see what her day was like."

When we arrived at our apartment, it was very quiet. At first I
thought Momma and little Fern were out, but when we peered into her
bedroom, we found them both curled up together asleep.

"Ain't that a picture?" Daddy whispered. "Let's just let them sleep,"
he said. "Jimmy, what'dya say me and you go get some ice cream for
dessert tonight? I feel like celebrating a little."

As soon as Daddy and Jimmy left, I took off my dress so Momma
wouldn't see how wrinkled it was, and I started to prepare dinner. Fern
woke up first and cried out for me. When I walked in to get her,
Momma opened her eyes.

"Oh, Dawn. Are you all back?" she asked and struggled to sit up.
Her face looked flushed and her eyes were glassy.

"Daddy and Jimmy went to get some ice cream. Momma, you're still
not feeling well."

"I'm fine, honey. Just a bit tired from a full day with Fern. She's a
good baby, but she's still a handful for anyone. How was your day at
school?"

"Did you go to the doctor?" I asked.

"I did something even better. I went out and bought the ingredients
for this tonic," she said and pointed to a bottle on the night table beside
her bed.

"What is this, Momma?" I turned the bottle of dark liquid around
and around in my hands. Then I opened it and smelled it. It stank.

"It's all sorts of herbs and such, my granny's formula. You'll see. I'll be better now in no time. Now let's not talk any more about me. Tell me about the school. How was it?" she asked, some excitement and brightness coming back into her eyes.

"It was okay," I said, swinging my eyes away so she couldn't see my lie. At least some of it was good, I thought. I put the bottle of herbal medicine down and took little Fern in my arms. Then I told Momma about Mr. Moore and some of the other teachers, but I didn't tell her about Clara Sue Cutler and the other girls, nor did I talk about Philip.

Before I was finished Momma closed her eyes and brought her hands to her chest. It looked like she was having trouble taking a deep breath.

"Momma, I'm staying home from school and watching Fern until this homemade medicine works or you go to the doctor!" I cried.

"Oh, no, honey. You can't start missin' days at a new school right off on account of me. If you stay home, I'll just be so upset, I'll get sicker and sicker."

"But, Momma . . ."

She smiled and took hold of my right hand while I held Fern in my left arm. As long as I held little Fern, she was content just sucking on her thumb and listening to me and Momma speak. Momma pulled me closer to her until she was able to reach out and stroke my hair.

"You look so pretty today, Dawn honey. Now, I don't want you worrying and denying yourself things on account of me. I can mend myself. I been in worse spots than this, honey, believe me. Your daddy got you and Jimmy into a fancy school where you're going to get advantages we never expected either of you would have. You just can't go on like you had to in the other places," she insisted.

"But, Momma . . ."

Suddenly her eyes grew dark and intense and her face was more serious than I'd ever seen it. She squeezed my hand so tight the bones in my fingers seemed to rub against each other, but the changes in her scared me so much I couldn't pull my hand away.

"You belong in this school, Dawn. You deserve this chance."

Momma's eyes glazed over a little, as though she wandered through an old memory. Her painful grip on my hand never loosened. "You should mix with the rich and the blue-blooded," she insisted. "There ain't one girl or boy at that school better than you, you hear?" she cried.

"But, Momma, the girls at this school wear clothes I'll never even get to try on and talk about places I'll never go. I'll never fit in with them. They seem to know so much."

"You deserve those same things, Dawn. Never forget it." With that her iron grip tightened even more, making me cry out a little. My whimper seemed to make her wake up, her eyes cleared, and she let my hand go.

"All right, Momma. I promise, but if you don't get better soon—"

"I'll go to a fancy doctor, just like I promised I would. That's a new promise," she proclaimed and raised her hand like a witness taking the stand in a courtroom. I shook my head. She saw I didn't believe her. "I will. I will," she repeated and lowered herself back to the pillow. "You better feed the baby before she starts letting you know you're late with her food. She can holler something awful when she's a mind to."

I hugged Fern to me and then took her out to feed her. Daddy and Jimmy returned and I whispered to Daddy that Momma was sicker than ever. A worried frown drew Daddy's dark brows together.

"I'll go talk to her," he said. Jimmy looked in, too, and then returned. He just stood by quietly and watched me feed Fern. Whenever Jimmy was worried and frightened about Momma, he would become as silent and as still as a statue.

"Momma's so pale and thin and weak, Jimmy," I said, "but she won't let me stay home from school to mind Fern."

"Then I'll stay home," he said through his clenched teeth.

"That would make her even angrier and you know it, Jimmy."

"Well, what are we going to do, then?"

"Let's see if Daddy gets her to go to a doctor," I said.

When he returned, he told us Momma had promised she would definitely go if the formula didn't work.

"Stubbornness runs in her family," Daddy explained. "One time her daddy slept on his shack roof just so he could get this woodpecker that was peckin' away at the shingles every mornin'. Took him two days, but he wouldn't come off that roof."

Daddy's stories had us all laughing again, but every once in a while I would look at Momma and then exchange a glance of worry with Jimmy. To me Momma looked like a wilting flower. I saw little things about her that filled my balloon of worry with more and more concern. I knew if it continued, I would burst into a panic.

The next day Philip Cutler surprised me at my locker right before the homeroom bell rang.

"Going to let me take you for a ride today?" he asked, whispering in my ear.

I had thought about it all night. It would be the first time I had ever gone for a ride with a boy.

"Where would we go?"

"I know a spot on this hill that overlooks the James River. You can see for miles and miles. It's beautiful. I've never taken anyone there," he added, "because I haven't met anyone I thought would appreciate it like I do. Up until now, that is."

I looked into his soft blue eyes. I wanted to go, but my heart felt funny, as if I were betraying someone. He saw the hesitation in my face.

"Sometimes you just sense things," he said. "I wouldn't ask any of these other girls because they're so spoiled they wouldn't be satisfied just looking at nature or scenery. They'd want me to take them to a fancy restaurant or something. Not that I don't want to take you to one," he added quickly. "It's just that I thought you might appreciate this the way I do."

I nodded slowly. What was I doing? I couldn't just go off with him without asking Daddy first, and I had to get back home to help Momma with Fern. And what if Jimmy was right and this was all some sort of secret prank engineered by Philip's sister and her friends?

"I've got to be home early enough to help Momma with dinner," I said.

"No problem. It's only a few minutes from here. Is it a date? I'll meet you in the lobby just after the bell rings."

"I don't know."

"We'd better start for class," he said, taking my books in his arms. "Come on, I'll walk you."

As the two of us walked side by side down the corridor, we turned a number of heads. His friends all smiled and said hello to me. At my homeroom doorway he handed me my books.

"So?" he asked.

"I don't know. I'll see," I said. He laughed and shook his head.

"I'm not asking you to marry me. Not yet anyway," he added. My heart fluttered and I felt as though Philip had been able to read my every thought. I hadn't been able to stop myself from making up stories —my own private fairy tale—before I fell asleep last night. I had imagined handsome Philip Cutler and me becoming the ideal couple, pledging undying love for each other, and becoming engaged. We would live in his hotel, and I would bring Momma and Daddy and Fern, and even Jimmy would come eventually because Philip would make him a manager or something. At the end of my fantasy Philip forced Clara Sue to be a chambermaid.

"I'll be after you all day," he promised and went off to his own class. His blue eyes seemed so sincere. This couldn't be a joke, I thought. Please, don't let it be a trick.

When I turned to enter homeroom, I saw the looks of surprise on the faces of some of the girls who had obviously seen me with Philip. Louise's eyes were as round as half-dollars and I could see that she couldn't wait to ask me questions.

"He wants me to go for a ride with him after school," I told her finally. "Do you think his sister put him up to it?" I asked, fishing for some clues.

"His sister? Hardly. She's mad at him for even talking to you."

"Then maybe I'll go," I murmured dreamily.

"Don't do it," she warned, but I could see the excitement in her own eyes.

Every time I passed from one class to the next, Philip was waving and asking, "Well?" Just after I sat down in my math class, he popped his head in the door and looked at me, raising his eyebrows, questioning. I could only laugh. He disappeared quickly when the teacher turned toward him.

The only sour incident occurred when I found Clara Sue waiting for me at the doorway to my next class. Linda was standing beside her.

"I heard that Mr. Moore is considering you for the solo at the concert," she said, her eyes small and watchful.

"So?" My heart was pounding.

"He's considering me, too."

"That's nice. Good luck," I said and started into the room, but she grabbed my shoulder and spun me around.

"Don't think you can come here and take over everything, you little charity case!" she cried.

"I'm not a charity case!"

Clara Sue inspected me from head to toe, releasing a disdainful sniff. "Stop deluding yourself, Dawn. You don't belong here. You're an outsider. You're not one of us. You never have been and you never will be. You're just poor white trash from the wrong side of the tracks. Everyone in school knows that."

"Yeah," Linda threw in. "You're nothing but poor white trash."

"Don't you dare say such things to me!" I protested angrily, fighting back the tears I could feel forming in the corners of my eyes.

"Why not?" Clara Sue asked. "They're true. Can't bear to hear the truth, Dawn? Well, it's about time you did. Who do you think you're fooling with your wide-eyed 'Miss Innocence' act?" she sneered. "If you think my brother is interested in *you,* you're nuts."

"Philip likes me. He does!" I declared.

Clara Sue raised an eyebrow. "I'll bet he does."

There was an undertone to her words . . . an undertone I didn't like. "What are you talking about?"

"My brother *loves* girls like you. He turns girls like you into mothers once a month."

Linda laughed loudly.

"Really?" I pushed my way to Clara Sue. "Well, I'll just tell Philip you said so." My words wiped away Clara Sue's smile, and for an instant she looked panicked. Without giving her a chance to retaliate, I left Clara Sue and her hateful words.

Philip did sit with me and Jimmy at lunch and spent a lot of time convincing Jimmy he should join the intramural basketball program. Jimmy was reluctant, but I could see that reluctance chipping away. I knew he liked basketball.

"So?" Philip asked me as we started for class. "Have you decided yet?"

I hesitated and then told him what had happened between Clara Sue and me in the morning. I didn't tell him exactly what she had said, however, just that she warned me against him.

"That little . . . *witch* is the only word that fits her. Wait until I get my hands on her."

"Don't, Philip. She'll just hate me more and try to make more trouble for me."

"Then come with me for a ride," he said quickly.

"That sounds like blackmail."

"Yeah," he said, smiling, "but it's nice blackmail."

I laughed. "Are you sure you can get me home early?"

"Absolutely." He raised his hand. "On my honor."

"All right," I said. "I'll ask my daddy."

"Great. You won't regret it," Philip assured me. I was so nervous about it, however, that I almost forgot to show Mr. Moore my guitar. I was really walking in a daze when I entered his classroom and took my seat.

"Is there really a guitar in there or is that just the case?" he asked when I didn't mention it.

"What? Oh, it's a guitar!" I exclaimed. He laughed and asked me to play. Afterward he said I had done very well for someone without any formal lessons.

The kind look in his eyes made me reveal my secret hope. "My dream is to learn how to play the piano and have one of my own some day."

"I'll tell you what," he said, sitting forward and bracing his elbows on his desk so he could rest his chin on his clenched hands. "I need another flute player. If you'll take up the flute for the school orchestra, I'll spend three afternoons a week after school teaching you the piano."

"You will?" I nearly jumped out of my desk.

"We'll start tomorrow. Is it a deal?" he said, extending his hand over the desk.

"Oh, yes," I said and reached out to shake. He laughed and told me I should meet him in the music rooms right after the last class of the day tomorrow.

I couldn't wait to run down and tell Daddy. When I told Jimmy, I was worried he would be upset that he would have to wait alone for Daddy in Daddy's office those afternoons. He surprised me with an announcement of his own.

"I've decided to join the intramural basketball program," he said. "One of the boys in my math class needs another guy on his team. And then I might join the cross-country team in the spring."

"That's wonderful, Jimmy. Maybe we can make friends here; maybe we just met the wrong people yesterday."

"I didn't say I was making friends," Jimmy replied quickly. "I just figured I could kill some time twice a week."

Daddy wasn't around, so I asked Jimmy to tell him I had gone for a ride and Philip would take me home.

"I wish you wouldn't get involved with that guy," Jimmy said.

"I'm not getting involved, Jimmy. I'm just going for a ride."

"Sure," Jimmy said and slumped down sadly in a chair. I ran back upstairs to meet Philip. He had a pretty red car with soft furry white sheepskin covers on the seats. He opened the door for me and stepped back.

"Madam," he said with a sweeping bow.

I got in and he closed the door. The car was even prettier inside. I ran my hand over the soft covers and looked at the black leather dashboard and gearshift.

"You have a beautiful car, Philip," I told him when he got behind the steering wheel.

"Thank you. It was a birthday gift from my grandmother."

"A birthday gift!" How rich his grandmother must be, I thought, to give him a car as a present. He shrugged, smiled coyly, and started the engine. Then he shifted into gear and we were off.

"How did you find this wonderful place, Philip?" I asked as we headed away from the school and in the opposite direction from where I lived.

"Oh, I was just cruising by myself one day and came upon it. I like to go for rides and look at the scenery and think," he said. He made a turn off a main street and headed quickly down a road without many houses on it. Then he turned again, and we began to climb up a hill. "It's not much farther," he said. We passed a few houses as we continued to climb, and then Philip turned down a rather deserted road that ran along a field and into a patch of trees. The road was only gravel and rock.

"You found this accidentally?"

"Uh-huh."

"And you haven't taken any other girl from Emerson Peabody up here?"

"Nope," he said, but I was beginning to have my doubts.

We drove through the small forest and came out on a clear field. There really wasn't any more road, but Philip continued over the grass until we came to the edge of the hill and could look out over the James River. Just as he promised, it was a spectacular view.

"Well?"

"Beautiful, Philip!" I exclaimed, drinking in the scene. "You were right."

"And you should see it at night with the stars out and the lights of the city. Think I can get you out at night?" he asked, with a crooked smile.

"I don't know," I answered quickly, but I harbored a hope. That would be more like a real date, my first real date. He edged closer to me, his arm over the top of the seat.

"You're a very pretty girl, Dawn. The moment I saw you, I said to myself, there's the prettiest girl I've seen at Emerson Peabody. I'm going to get to know her as fast as I can."

"Oh, lots of the girls at Emerson Peabody are prettier than me." I wasn't trying to be falsely modest. I had seen so many pretty girls with beautiful, expensive clothing. How could I compare to them? I wondered.

"They're not prettier to me," he said. "I'm glad you transferred to our school." His fingers grazed my shoulder. "Have you had many boyfriends?" I shook my head. "I don't believe that," he said.

"It's true. We haven't been able to stay in one place long enough," I added. He laughed.

"You say the funniest things."

"I'm not trying to be funny, Philip. It's true," I repeated, widening my eyes for emphasis.

"Sure," he said, moving his fingers to my hair and tracing a strand with his forefinger. "You have the tiniest nose," he said and leaned forward to kiss the tip of my nose. It took me by such surprise, I sat back.

"I couldn't help it," he said and leaned forward again, this time to kiss my cheek. I looked down as his left hand settled on my knee. It sent a tingle up my thigh. "Dawn," he whispered softly in my ear. "Dawn. I just love saying your name. You know what I did this morning? I got up with the sunrise, just so I could see the dawn."

"You didn't."

"Yes, I did," he said and brought his lips to mine. I had never kissed a boy on the lips before, although I had dreamt about it. Last night I had fantasized about kissing Philip, and here I was doing it! It felt like dozens of tiny explosions all over my body, and my face grew hot. Even my ears tingled.

Because I didn't back away, Philip moaned and kissed me again, harder this time. Suddenly I felt the hand that had been on my knee traveling up over my waist until his fingers settled around my breast. The moment they did, I pulled back and pushed him away at the same time. I couldn't help it. All the things I had heard about him flashed before my mind, especially Clara Sue's horrible threat.

"Easy," he said quickly. "I'm not going to hurt you."

My heart was pounding. I pressed my palm against my chest and took a deep breath.

"Are you all right?"

I nodded.

"Didn't you ever let a boy touch you there before?" he asked. When I shook my head, he tilted his skeptically. "Really?"

"Honest, no."

"Well, you're missing it all then," he said, inching toward me again. "There's nothing to be afraid of," he coaxed, bringing his hand back to my waist.

"Haven't you at least been kissed like that before?" he asked. His fingers started moving up my side. I shook my head. "Really?" He brought his hand firmly to the side of my breast. "Just relax," he said. "You don't want to be the only girl your age at Emerson Peabody who's never been kissed and touched like this, do you? I'll do it slowly, okay?" he said, barely inching forward over the top of my breast.

I took a deep breath and closed my eyes. Once again he pressed his lips to mine.

"That's it. Easy," he said. "See." The tips of his fingers surrounded a button on my blouse. I felt it open and then felt his fingers against my skin, moving like a thick spider in and under my bra. When the tips of his fingers found my nipple, I felt a surge of excitement that took my breath away.

"No," I said pulling back again. My heart was pounding so hard, I was sure he could hear it. "I . . . we'd better start back," I said. "I've got to help Momma with dinner."

"What? Help your mother with dinner? You're kidding. We just got here." He stared at me a moment.

"You don't have some other boyfriend already, do you?"

"Oh, no!" I said, nearly jumping out of my seat. He laughed and traced my collarbone with the tip of his forefinger. I felt his hot breath on my cheek. "Will you come back here with me one night?"

"Yes," I said with abandon. He was so handsome, and despite my fears, his touch had made my stomach feel like butterflies were flying around in it.

"Okay, I'll let you slip out of my hands this time then," he said and laughed. "You're really cute, you know." He leaned over and kissed me quickly again. Then he lowered his eyes to my opened blouse. I quickly buttoned it.

"Actually, I'm glad you're shy, Dawn."

"You are?" I thought he would hate me because I wasn't as sophisticated as most of the girls he knew at Emerson Peabody.

"Sure. So many girls are know-it-alls these days. There's nothing fresh and honest about them. Not like there is about you. I want to be the one who teaches you things, makes you feel things you've never felt before. Will you let me? Will you?" he pleaded with those soft blue eyes.

"Yes," I said. I wanted to learn new things and feel new things and be just as grown-up and sophisticated as the girls he knew at Emerson Peabody.

"Good. Now, don't bring any other boys up here behind my back," he added.

"What? I wouldn't."

He laughed and got back behind the steering wheel.

"You're definitely something else, Dawn. Something good," he added.

I gave him the directions to take me home and finished buttoning my blouse.

"Our section of town isn't very nice," I said, preparing him. "But we're only living there until Daddy can find something better."

"Yeah, well," he said, looking at the houses along the streets in my neighborhood, "for your sake I hope that's not much longer. Don't you have any family here?" he asked.

"No. Our family is all in Georgia, on farms," I replied. "But we haven't seen them for a while because we've been traveling a lot."

"I've taken trips here and there," he said, "but summers, when most of the other kids go off to Europe or to other parts of the country, I have to remain in Cutler's Cove and help with our hotel," he said, smirking unhappily. He turned to me.

"It's expected that someday I'll be the one to take it over and run it."

"How wonderful, Philip."

He shrugged.

"It's been in our family for generations. It was started as just an inn way back when there were whalers and fishermen from everywhere. We've got paintings and all sorts of antiques in the attic of the hotel, things that belonged to my great-great-grandfather. Our family's just about the most important one in town, founding fathers."

"It must be wonderful to have all of that family heritage," I said. He caught the note of longing in my voice.

"What were your ancestors like?"

What would I tell him? Could I tell him the truth—that I hadn't ever seen my grandparents, much less known what they were like? And how could I explain never seeing or knowing or ever hearing from any cousins, uncles, or aunts?

"They were . . . farmers. We used to have a big farm with cows and chickens and acres and acres," I said, but I looked out my window when I said it. "I remember riding on the hay wagon when I was just a little girl, sitting up front with my grandfather, who held me in his arm while he held on to the reins. Jimmy would be in the hay, looking up at the sky. My grandfather smoked a corncob pipe and played the harmonica."

"So that's where your musical talent comes from."

"Yes." I continued spinning the threads of my fantasy, nearly forgetting as I went on that my words were as false as false could be. "He knew all the old songs and would sing them to me, one after the other, as we went along in his wagon, and at night, too, on the porch of our big farmhouse, while he rocked and smoked and my grandmother crocheted. The chickens would run loose in the front yard, and sometimes I would try to catch one, but they were always too fast. I can still hear my grandfather laugh and laugh."

"I don't really remember too much about my grandfather, and I've never been very close to my grandmother. Life's more formal at Cutler's Cove," he explained.

"Turn here," I said quickly, already regretting my lies.

"You're the first girl I've driven home," he said.

"Really? Philip Cutler, is that the truth?"

"Cross my heart. Don't forget, I just got my license. Besides, Dawn, I can't lie to you. For some reason, it would be like lying to myself." He reached over and stroked my cheek so softly I could barely feel the tip of his finger. My heart dipped. Here he was being so thoughtful and truthful, and I was making up stories about my imaginary family, stories that made him sad about his own life, a life I was sure had to be a thousand times more wonderful than mine.

"Down this street," I pointed. He turned onto our block. I saw him grimace when he saw the cluttered lots and the sloppy front yards. "That's our apartment building just ahead, the one with the toy red wagon on the sidewalk."

"Thank you," I said as soon as he pulled up.

He leaned over to kiss me, and when I leaned toward him, he brought his hand up to my breast again. I didn't pull away.

"You taste real good, Dawn. You're going to let me take you for another ride soon, right?"

"Yes," I said, my voice barely above a whisper. I gathered my books into my arms quickly.

"Hey," he said, "what's your telephone number?"

"Oh, we don't have a phone yet," I said. When he looked at me strangely, I added, "We just didn't get around to it yet."

I got out of the car quickly and ran to my front door, positive he saw through my foolish lie. I was sure he never wanted to see me again.

Daddy and Momma were sitting at the kitchen table. Jimmy, who was on the couch, peered over a comic book at me.

"Where you been?" Daddy asked in a voice that made me start.

I looked at him. His eyes didn't soften, and there was that darkness around his face again, a darkness that made my heart pound hard and loud. "I went for a ride. But I got home early enough to help with dinner and Fern," I added in my own defense.

"We just don't like you riding around with boys yet, Dawn," Momma said, trying to calm the treacherous waters of Daddy's anger.

"But why, Momma? I bet the other girls my age at Emerson Peabody go for rides with boys."

"That don't matter none," Daddy snapped. "I don't want you riding around with this boy anymore." Daddy looked up at me and his handsome face was lit with a fiery rage—my mind raced, searching desperately for a reason for Daddy's anger.

"Please, Dawn," Momma said. It was followed with a cough that nearly took her breath away.

I looked toward Jimmy. He had the comic book up high, so I couldn't see his face and he couldn't see mine.

"All right, Momma."

"That's a good girl, Dawn," she said. "Now we can start on dinner." Her hands were shaking, but I didn't know what caused it—her coughing or the tension in the room.

"Aren't you home early, Daddy?" I asked. I had hoped to beat him and Jimmy home anyway.

"I left a little early. It don't matter. I ain't as crazy about this job as I thought I was," he said to my surprise. Had he found out what the girls had done to me? Did that turn him against the school?

"Did you have a fight with Mrs. Turnbell, Daddy?" I asked, suspecting his temper had reared its ugly head.

"No. There's just so much to do. I don't know. We'll see." He gave me a look that said there'd be no more talk about it. Since Daddy had started working at Emerson Peabody, these looks and his temper had disappeared. Suddenly it was all returning and I was frightened.

That night, after Fern had been put to sleep and Momma and Daddy went to bed, Jimmy turned to me after crawling under the covers.

"I didn't do anything to get them hot and bothered about you going for a ride with Philip." Jimmy's dark eyes begged me to believe him. "I just told Daddy. Next thing I knew, we were rushing home. Honest."

"I believe you, Jimmy. I guess they're just worried. We don't need any more problems," I said.

"Of course, it don't bother me all that much that you won't be going for rides with Philip," he said. "All those rich kids are spoiled and always get what they want," he said bitterly, staring at me, his dark gaze catching my own and holding it tightly.

"There are a lot of bad poor people, too, Jimmy."

"At least they got an excuse. Dawn"—he paused—"be careful." With that, Jimmy turned over, moving as far away from me as he could and still be in the same bed with me.

I didn't fall asleep for the longest time. All I could think about was not being able to go out with Philip—or even ride with him. The idea of it made me want to dig a well to cry my tears into—a well that would have been filled up in no time if Jimmy hadn't been there trying to sleep.

Why couldn't I have this one thing I wanted? I'd had little enough until now, my brain cried, and I'd tried so hard to keep my family happy—to make smiles appear on my Daddy's face. How could they take this away, too?

Philip was special. I relived his kiss, the way he brought his lips to mine, the deep blue in his eyes, the way my face glowed and the excitement that flashed through my body when his fingers touched my breast. Just thinking about it warmed me and made the butterflies in my stomach wake up all over again.

It would have been exciting parking with him on that hill at night with the lights below us and the stars above us. When I closed my eyes, I imagined him in the dark moving closer, bringing his hands back to my breasts and his lips to mine. The image was so vivid, I felt a wave of warmth travel up my body as if I had lowered myself gently into a tepid bath. When it reached my neck, I moaned. I didn't realize I had done so aloud until Jimmy spoke.

"What?" he asked.

"I didn't say anything," I said quickly.

"Oh. Okay. Night," he repeated.

"Night," I said and turned over so I could force myself to sleep and forget.

5
MY BROTHER'S KEEPER

Philip came to school extra early the next morning just so he could meet me before all the other students had arrived. Daddy went right to work on an electrical problem they were having in the gymnasium, and Jimmy and I went to his office as usual. A few minutes after we had arrived, Philip came to the door.

"Morning," he said and smiled at both Jimmy's and my look of surprise. "I had to get to the library early this morning and thought I'd see if you were here."

"The library don't open this early," Jimmy replied, busting Philip's flimsy excuse to bits.

"Sometimes it is," Philip insisted.

"I've got to go to the library, too," I said. "I'll join you."

Jimmy scowled as I got up.

"See you later, Jimmy," I said and walked upstairs with Philip.

"I was thinking about you a lot last night," Philip said. "I wanted to call you every five minutes last night to see how you were. Are you going to get a phone soon?"

"Oh, Philip," I said, spinning on him, "I don't think so. Jimmy would just hate me for saying all this, but I have to be truthful. We're a very poor family. The only reason Jimmy and I are in this school is on account of my daddy having this job. That's why I wear these plain clothes and Jimmy just wears a pair of dungarees and a shirt. He'll wear the same shirt twice a week at least. I've got to wash everything right away so we can wear it again. We're not just living in that ugly neighborhood temporarily. It's the nicest place we've ever lived!" I cried and started away.

Philip reached out quickly and seized my arm.

"Hey." He spun me about. "I knew all that."

"You did?"

"Sure. Everyone knows how you got into Emerson Peabody."

"They do? Of course they do," I realized bitterly. "I'm sure we're on everybody's gossip list, especially your sister's."

"I don't listen to gossip, and I don't care whether you're here because your father's rich or because your father works here. I'm just happy you're here," he said. "And as for belonging here—you belong here more than most of these spoiled kids. I know your teachers are happy you're here, and Mr. Moore is walking on a cloud because he finally has a very talented student to teach," Philip declared. He looked so sincere. His eyes shone bright with determination, and his gaze was so soft and warm upon me that I shivered.

"You're probably just saying all these nice things to make me feel better," I said softly.

"I'm not. Really." He smiled. "Cross my heart and hope to fall in a well full of chocolate sauce." I laughed. "That's better. Don't be so serious all the time." He looked around and then drew closer, practically pressing his body to mine. "When can you and I take a ride again?"

"Oh, Philip, I can't take any more rides with you." Uttering the words hurt so much, but I couldn't disobey Momma and Daddy.

"Why not?" His eyes grew small. "Did my sister or her friends say something else to you about me, because whatever they said, it's a lie," he added quickly.

"No, it's not that." I looked down. "I had to promise Momma and Daddy I wouldn't."

"Huh? How come? Someone say something to your father about me?" he demanded. I shook my head.

"It's not you, Philip. They think I'm too young yet, and I can't do anything about it right now. We have too many problems."

He stared hard at me and then suddenly smiled.

"Well, then," he said, refusing to be defeated. "I'll just wait until they give you permission. I might even speak to your father."

"Oh, no, Philip. Please don't. I don't want to make anyone unhappy, least of all Daddy."

Despite my words, part of me wanted Philip to talk to Daddy. I was so flattered that he wouldn't give up on me or take no for an answer. He was my knight in shining armor who wanted to whisk me off into the sunset and give me everything I had always dreamed of.

"Okay," he said. "Take it easy. If you don't want me to talk to him I won't."

"Even though Daddy won't let me ride with you now, I want you to know I will go for a ride with you as soon as they say it's all right," I added in a rush. I didn't want to lose Philip. He was becoming a special part of my life that I liked very much. When I saw that his eyes brightened hopefully, I felt much better.

We heard the doors opening and saw some other students beginning to arrive. Philip looked toward the library.

"I do have to get some research material for my term paper. It wasn't a total fib," he said, smiling. He started backing away. "See you later."

He kept backing up until he backed into a wall. We both laughed. Then he turned and hurried toward the library. I took a deep breath and turned to the front doors. The rest of the student body was charging in, and I caught sight of Louise. Louise waved, so I waited for her.

"Everyone's talking about you," she said, rushing over to me, her pale, freckled face flushed with excitement.

"Oh?"

"They all know you went for a ride with Philip after school. Linda just told me there's a lot of gossip at the dorms."

"What are they saying?" My heart was racing like a train at the thought of all these rich girls talking about me.

Louise looked back at the growing crowd of arriving students and nodded toward the girls' room. I followed her in.

"Maybe I shouldn't tell you," Louise said.

"Of course you should. If you want to be my friend, like you keep saying you want to be. Friends don't hide things from each other. They help each other."

"Clara Sue's telling everyone that her brother wouldn't be interested in a girl like you, a girl from such a poor family, if he hadn't found out that you have a reputation. . . ."

"Reputation? What kind of a reputation?"

"A reputation for going all the way on the first date," she admitted finally and bit her lower lip quickly as if to punish herself for permitting the words to fall out of her mouth. "She told the girls Philip told her you two . . . did it yesterday. She said her brother bragged."

I could see the way she eyed me that she wasn't convinced it was all a lie.

"It's a disgusting, hateful lie!" I shouted. Louise only shrugged.

"Now Linda and the other girls are saying the same things. I'm sorry, but you wanted to know."

"I never met a girl as horrible as Clara Sue Cutler," I said. I felt the fury in my face, but I couldn't help it. One moment the world was bright and beautiful. There were birds singing and the sky was blessed with soft, clean white clouds that made you feel happy to be alive and able to see them, and the next moment, a storm came rushing in, flooding the blue with dirty dark gray and drowning the sunlight and the laughter and the smiles.

"They want me to spy on you," Louise whispered. "Linda just asked me."

"Spy? What do they mean?"

"Tell them anything you tell me about things you do with Philip," she explained. "But I would never tell them anything you told me in confidence," she said. "You see you can trust me," she added, but I wondered if she had told me what the girls were saying because she really wanted to help me or because she wanted to see me made sad.

Jimmy was right about rich people, I thought. These rich, spoiled girls were much more conniving than the girls I had known at my other schools. They had more time to spend on intrigues and seemed to swim in a pool of jealousy. There were more green eyes here, and everyone was so conscious of what each wore and had. Of course, girls were proud of their nice clothes and their jewelry everywhere I had been, but here they flaunted it more, and if one had something special, the others tried to have something even better very quickly.

I was no threat to them as far as clothes and jewelry went; yet it must be bothering them a great deal that Philip Cutler cared about me. They couldn't get him to care about them, no matter how expensive their clothes were and how dazzling their jewels were.

"So what did happen yesterday?" Louise asked.

"Nothing," I said. "He was very polite. He took me for a ride and showed me wonderful scenery and then he took me home."

"He didn't try to . . . do anything?"

"No," I said and quickly swung my eyes away. When I looked back at her, I could see her disappointment. "So Clara Sue had better stop spreading her lies."

"She's just ashamed her brother likes you," Louise said rather nonchalantly.

How horrible, I thought, to be considered so much lower than someone else just because your parents weren't rich. It was on the tip of my tongue to say she could tell Clara Sue not to worry anymore anyway, since my parents had forbidden me to go riding with Philip, but before I could say anything, we heard the bell for homeroom.

"Oh, no," I said, realizing the time. "We're going to be late."

"That's all right," Louise said. "I've never been late before. Old Turnkey won't keep us after school for just one lateness."

"We had better get going anyway," I said, heading for the door. Louise stopped in the doorway when I opened it.

"I'll tell you what they say about you," she said, her watery eyes watching me from under her lashes, "if you want me to."

"I don't care what they say about me," I lied. "They're not worth caring about." I hurried on to homeroom with Louise right beside me, her shoes clicking as we flew down the hallway. My heart, which had been made of feathers, had suddenly grown as heavy as lead.

"You girls are late," Mr. Wengrow said the moment we came through the doorway.

"I'm sorry, sir," I said first. "We were in the bathroom and—"

"Gossiping and you didn't hear the bell," he concluded and shook his head. Louise hurried to her desk, and I slipped into mine. Mr. Wengrow made some notations and then slapped his yardstick on the desk in anticipation of the morning's announcements.

Another day at Emerson Peabody had only just begun, and already I felt as if I had been on a roller coaster for hours and hours.

A little more than halfway through the third period, I was called out of my social studies class to see Mrs. Turnbell. When I came to her office, her secretary glared at me and spoke curtly, telling me to take a seat. I had to wait at least another ten full minutes and wondered why I had been told to come right away if I couldn't go right in. I was missing valuable class time just sitting there. Finally Mrs. Turnbell buzzed her secretary, who then told me to go in.

Mrs. Turnbell was sitting behind her desk, looking down and writing. She didn't even look up when I entered. I stood there for a few moments, waiting, clutching my books to my chest tightly. Then, still without looking at me, she told me to take the seat in front of her desk. She continued to write for a few moments after I had sat down. Finally her cold gray eyes lifted from the papers before her and she sat back in her seat.

"Why were you late for homeroom today?" she demanded without any greeting first.

"Oh. I was talking to a friend in the bathroom, and we got so involved, I lost track of time until the second bell rang, but as soon as it had, I ran to my homeroom," I said.

"I can't believe I have another problem with you so soon."

"It's not a problem, Mrs. Turnbell. I—"

"Do you know that your brother has been late twice for classes since you two were entered in this school?" she snapped.

I shook my head.

"And now you," she added, nodding.

"It's my first lateness. Ever," I added.

"Ever?" She raised her dark and somewhat bushy eyebrows skeptically. "In any case this is not the place to begin developing bad habits. This is especially not the place," she emphasized.

"Yes, ma'am," I said. "I'm sorry."

"I believe I explained our rules to you and your brother on your first morning here. Tell me, Miss Longchamp, was my explanation adequate?" She kept on without allowing me to answer. "I told you that both of you had an extra burden and an extra responsibility since your father was employed here," she continued. Her words stung and made the tears that had flown into my eyes feel hot.

"When a brother and sister have the same bad habits," she went on, "it is not hard to determine that they have them because they come from the same background."

"But we don't have bad habits, Mrs. Turnbell. We—"

"Don't be insolent! Are you questioning my judgment?"

"No, Mrs. Turnbell," I said and bit down on my lower lip to keep myself from adding any words.

"You will report to detention immediately after school today," she snapped.

"But . . ."

"What?" She raised her eyes and glared at me.

"I have a piano lesson with Mr. Moore after school and—"

"You're going to have to miss this one, but you have only yourself to blame," she said. "Now, return to your class," she commanded.

"What happened?" Louise asked when I saw her on the way to the cafeteria.

"I got detention for being late to homeroom," I moaned.

"Really? Detention for being late only once?" She tilted her head. "I guess I'm next, only . . ."

"Only what?"

"Clara Sue and Linda have been late to class twice this week, and the Turnkey hasn't even called them down to reprimand them. Usually it's after three latenesses."

"I think she's clumped my brother's two and my one together," I reasoned sourly.

Philip was waiting for me at the entrance to the cafeteria. He saw the sad look on my face, and I told him what had happened.

"That's so unfair," he said. "Maybe you should have your father speak to her."

"Oh, I couldn't ask Daddy to do that. What if she got mad at him and had him fired and all on account of me!"

Philip shrugged.

"It's still not fair," he said. He looked down at the paper bag I had clutched in my hand. "And what gourmet sandwich did you make for yourself today?" he asked.

"I . . . ." All I had in my bag was an apple I had grabbed on the way out. Fern had gotten up earlier than usual, and between taking care of her and making breakfast, I had just forgotten to make any sandwiches until it was time to leave. I couldn't make Daddy late for work, so I made a sandwich quickly for Jimmy and threw an apple into a paper bag for myself. "I just have an apple today," I said.

"What? You can't just have an apple for lunch. Let me buy you lunch today."

"Oh, no, I don't have much of an appetite anyway and—."

"Please. I never bought a girl lunch before. All the girls I ever knew could buy me lunch twice over," he added, laughing.

"If I can't take you for rides, at least let me do this."

"Well . . . okay," I said. "Maybe just this once."

We found a table off to the side and got into the lunch line. The girls who sat with Louise and the older girls all gazed with curiosity, especially the ones at Clara Sue's table. I saw the way she nodded and whispered. Ironically, my being with Philip helped confirm the ugly rumors she was spreading about me. I knew all their eyes would be glued to Philip and me when we approached the cashier, and they would all know he had bought me lunch. The thought of what she'd say then made me feel like ripping those golden strands out of Clara Sue's head.

"So," Philip said, turning to me after we sat down and started to eat, "there's no chance of your getting out for a ride soon, huh?"

"I told you, Philip—"

"Yeah, yeah. Listen, how about this," he said. "I'll come by your place about seven tonight. You sneak out. Tell your parents you're going to study with a friend or something. They won't know the difference and—"

"I don't lie to my parents, Philip," I said.

"It won't be a lie, exactly. I'll study something with you. How's that?"

I shook my head.

"I can't," I said. "Please don't ask me to lie."

Before he could say anything else, we suddenly heard a commotion and turned in Jimmy's direction. Some boys had gone over to Jimmy's table and said something to him, and whatever they had said had set him off like a firecracker. In seconds he was up and at them, pushing and wrestling with boys bigger than him. It drew the attention of the entire cafeteria.

"They're ganging up on him," Philip said, and shot off to jump into the fray. Teachers rushed in; cafeteria staff came around the counter. It only took a few moments to break it up, but to me it seemed like ages. All the boys involved were marched out of the cafeteria just as the bell rang for the students to return to class.

I was on pins and needles most of the afternoon. Whenever the bell rang to change classes, I, along with most everyone else, walked past Mrs. Turnbell's office to see what was happening. Louise, who was as good as a news service, found out that four boys, as well as Jimmy and Philip, had been brought to the office and kept sitting in the outer office while Mrs. Turnbell questioned each of them privately. Daddy had been called into Mrs. Turnbell's office, too.

By the day's end the verdict was known. All the boys except Jimmy were assigned detention for roughhousing in the cafeteria. Jimmy was declared the cause of it all and was suspended three days and put on probation.

I had ten minutes before I had to report to detention, so I rushed down to Daddy's office looking for him and Jimmy. As soon as I reached the basement, I could hear Daddy's shouting.

"How do you think this looks—my son being suspended? I got to have the respect of my men. Now they'll be laughing at me behind my back!"

"It wasn't my fault," Jimmy protested.

"Not your fault? You're always in trouble. Since when's it not your fault? Here they're doing us a favor letting you and Dawn attend the school—"

"It ain't no favor to me!" Jimmy snapped back. Before he could say another word, Daddy's hand came flying up and slapped him across the face. Jimmy fell back and saw me standing in the doorway. He looked at Daddy and then rushed out past me.

"Jimmy!" I cried and hurried to catch up with him. He didn't stop until he reached the exit. "Where are you going?" I asked.

"Out of here and for good," he said, his face beet red. "I knew it wouldn't be any good. I hate it here! *I hate it!*" he screamed and ran off. *"Jimmy!"*

He didn't turn back, and the clock was ticking against me. I couldn't be late for detention, too, especially after all this. Feeling as if I were bound and gagged, more frustrated than I'd ever been in my life, I lowered my head and hurried up the stairs and to the detention room, my tears flowing freely.

Everything had started to look like it would work out—my music, piano lessons, Philip, and now, just as if it had all been made of soap bubbles, it burst around me, splashing alongside my tears on the floor.

As soon as detention ended, I hurried downstairs to Daddy, hoping that he had calmed down. Cautiously I entered the office. He was sitting behind his desk with his back to the door, staring at the wall.

"Hi, Daddy," I said. He turned around, and I tried to judge his mood.

"I'm sorry about what happened, Daddy," I said quickly, "but it's not all my and Jimmy's fault, either. Mrs. Turnbell has been out to get us. She didn't like us from the start. You must have seen that in her face the first day," I protested.

"Oh, I know it bent her out a whack to have her told my children get to go here, but it's not the first time Jimmy's been in a ruckus, Dawn. And he's been late to class, too, and snippy with some of his teachers! Seems no matter what you do for him, he's going to be bad."

"It's harder for Jimmy, Daddy. He hasn't had the chance to be a real student until now, and these rich boys have been picking on him something terrible. I know. Up until now, he's taken all they've thrown at him and held his temper, just because he wanted to please you . . . and me," I added. I wouldn't dare tell him what some of the nastier girls were doing to me.

"I don't know," Daddy said, shaking his head. "He's bound for trouble's doors, I think. Takes after my brother Reuben, who, the last time I heard, was in jail."

"In jail? For what?" I asked, astounded with this sudden bit of information. Daddy had never mentioned his brother Reuben before.

"Stealing. He was always into one thing or another all his life."

"Is Reuben older or younger than you, Daddy?"

"He's older, by little more than a year. Jimmy even looks like him and sulks just the way he used to." Daddy shook his head. "Don't look good," he added.

"He won't be as bad as Reuben!" I cried. "Jimmy's not evil. He wants to be good and do well in school. I just know he does. He just needs a fair chance. I can talk to him and get him to try again. You'll see."

"I don't know. I don't know," he repeated and shook his head. Then he rose with a great effort. "Shouldn't have come here," he mumbled. "It was bad luck."

I followed Daddy out, walking in the coolness of his shadow. Maybe it was bad luck to try to do things that are beyond you. Maybe we just belonged in the poor world, gazing dreamily at the rich people as they went by, and looking hungrily in store windows. Maybe we were meant to always struggle to make ends meet. Maybe that was our terrible destiny, and we couldn't do anything about it.

"How come you never told me about Reuben before, Daddy?"

"Well, he was in trouble so much, I just put him out of mind," Daddy explained quickly.

We stepped out into the dreariest day I had seen in a long time, I thought. The sky was a bitter gray with a layer of clouds moving rapidly under another, thicker layer. The wind was cooler and sharper.

"Looks like it's going to be a cold rain soon," Daddy said. He started the car. "Can't wait for spring."

"When did you hear about your brother Reuben, Daddy?" I asked as we started away.

"Oh, about two years ago or so," he said casually. Two years ago? I thought. But how could he? We weren't near the family then.

"Do they have phones on the farm?" I asked incredulously. From all I had been able to learn about the farms back in Georgia, they sounded too poor to afford phones, especially if we couldn't.

"Phones?" He laughed. "Hardly. They don't have running water or electricity. The homestead, if you can call it that, has a hand pump and there's an outhouse. At night they use oil lamps. Some of them crackers think a phone's the devil's own invention and never in their lives have put their ear against one or want to."

"Then how did you hear about your brother only two years or so ago, Daddy?" I asked quickly. "Did you get a letter?"

"A letter. Hardly. There ain't a one of them who can write more than his name, if that much."

"Then how did you learn about Reuben?" I asked again. For a moment he didn't respond. I didn't think he was going to, so I added, "You didn't go back there yourself one time without us, did you, Daddy?"

The way he looked at me told me I had hit the mark.

"You're getting pretty smart, Dawn. It's not easy keeping something under the covers when you're around. Don't say nothing about it to your ma, but I did go back one time for a few hours. I was working close enough to make the drive and return the same night and I did it without saying nothing."

"Well, if we were that close, why didn't we all go, Daddy?"

"I said *I* was close. I woulda had to go hours back to get you and then hours back to where I was and then hours to the farm," he explained.

"Who did you see on the farm, Daddy?"

"I saw my ma. Pa died a while back. Just keeled over in a field one day clutching his heart." Tears came into Daddy's eyes, but he quickly blinked them back. "Ma looked so old," he added, shaking his head. "I was sorry I went. It near broke my heart to look at her sitting there in her rocker. Pa's death and Reuben's going to jail and problems with some of my other brothers and sisters grayed her skin as well as her hair. She didn't even recognize me, and when I told her who I was, she said, 'Ormand's in the house churnin' up some butter for me.' I used to do that for her all the time," he added, smiling.

"Did you see your sister Lizzy?"

"Yeah, she was there, married with four of her own kids, two not a year apart. She's the one told me about Reuben. I didn't stay there long, and I never told your ma because it was all bad news, so don't you go blabbing now."

"I won't. I promise. I'm sorry I didn't get to see Grandpa, though," I said sadly.

"Yeah, you would have liked him. He probably would have got out his harmonica and stumped out something for you, and then maybe the two of you would have sung and played something together," Daddy said, dreaming aloud.

"You must have told me about his playing the harmonica before, Daddy, because that stuck in my mind."

"Must have," he said. He started to hum something I imagined his father played, and I didn't say anything and he didn't say anything until we were home, but I wondered about Daddy and what other secrets he had.

Jimmy hadn't been home yet, so Momma didn't know a thing about the troubles at school. Daddy and I looked at each other after looking at her and silently decided to keep it all to ourselves.

"Where's Jimmy?" she asked.

"He's with some new friends," Daddy said. Momma took a look at me and saw the lie, but she didn't question it.

But when Jimmy didn't come home for supper, we had to tell Momma about the fight and his getting into trouble. She nodded as we spoke.

"I knew it anyway," she said. "Neither of you are worth a pig's knuckle when it comes to telling white lies—or any lies for that matter." She sighed. "That boy's just not happy, might never be," she added with a tone of prophetic doom.

"Oh, no, Momma. Jimmy's going to be something great yet. I just know it. He's very smart. You'll see," I insisted.

"Hope so," she said. She started to cough again. Her cough had changed, become deeper, shaking her entire body silently sometimes. Momma claimed that meant she was getting better, driving it down and out, but I didn't feel good about it, and I still longed for her to go to a real doctor or a hospital.

After I cleaned the dishes and put everything away, I practiced a song. Daddy and Fern were my audience, with Fern very attentive whenever I sang. She clapped her little hands together whenever Daddy clapped his hands. Momma listened from her bedroom, calling out once in a while to tell me how good I sounded.

It grew dark and the cold rain Daddy had forecast came, the drops splattering our windows. They sounded like thousands of fingers being tapped against the glass. There was thunder and lightning, and the wind whipped around the apartment house, whistling through all the cracks and crannies. I had to put another blanket on Momma when her teeth started chattering. We decided we would let little Fern sleep in her clothes this night. I felt so sorry and worried for Jimmy because he was still out there somewhere, wandering about in the dark, stormy night—

I thought my heart might break. I knew he didn't have any money with him, so I was sure he had gone without any supper. I had wrapped him up a plate of food that was ready to be warmed up the moment he returned.

But the night wore on and he didn't come home. I stayed awake as long as I could, staring at the door and listening for Jimmy's footsteps in the hallway, but whenever I heard footsteps, they were going upstairs or into another apartment. Once in a while I went to a window and gazed out through the cloudy glass and into the rainy darkness.

I finally went to sleep, too, but sometime in the middle of the night, I awoke to the sound of the front door opening.

"Where were you?" I whispered. I couldn't see his eyes or much of his face in the darkness.

"I was going to run away," he said. "I even got as far as fifty miles outside of Richmond."

"James Gary Longchamp, you didn't?"

"I did. I hitched a couple of rides, and the second one letting me out at a roadside restaurant. All's I had on me was some change, so I got a cup of coffee. The waitress took pity on me and brought me a roll and butter. Then she started asking me questions. She has a boy about my age, too, and works all the time because her husband was killed in a car accident about five years ago.

"I was going to go out and keep hitchhiking, but it started to rain so hard, I couldn't get out. The waitress knew this truck driver who was heading back to Richmond, and she asked him to take me along, so I came back. But I ain't staying, and I ain't going back to that snob school, and you shouldn't either, Dawn," he said with determination.

"Oh, Jimmy, you've got a right to be upset. Rich kids aren't better than the poor kids we've known, and we've been treated unfairly just because we're not rich like the others, but Daddy didn't mean to harm us by getting us into Emerson Peabody. He was only trying to do something good for us," I said. "You have to admit that the school is beautiful and full of new things, and you told me yourself some of your teachers were very nice and very good. You've already started doing better schoolwork, haven't you, and you like playing on the intramural team, right?"

"We're still like fish out of water there, and those other kids are never going to accept us or let us live in peace, Dawn. I'd rather be in a regular public school."

"Now, Jimmy, you can't really mean that," I whispered. I touched his hand, which was still very cold. "You must have been freezing out there, James Gary. Your hair is soaked. And so are your clothes. You could have caught pneumonia!"

"Who cares?"

"I care," I said. "Now get out of those wet clothes quickly," I ordered and went for a towel. When I returned, he was wrapped in the blanket, his wet clothing on the floor. I sat beside him and began to wipe his hair dry. When I was finished, I saw the outline of his smile in the dark.

"I never met another girl like you, Dawn," he said. "And I'm not just saying that because you're my sister. I guess I came back because I didn't want to leave you all alone with this mess. I got to thinking about you having to go back to that school and how you'd have no one to protect you."

"Oh, Jimmy, I don't need protection, and besides, if I do, Daddy will protect me, won't he?"

"Sure," he said, pulling his hand back. "Just like he protected us today. I tried to tell him it wasn't my fault, but he wouldn't listen. All he could do was yell at me for being no good and letting him down. And then he goes and hits me."

He flopped back on his pillow.

"He shouldn't have hit you, Jimmy. But he said you reminded him of his brother Reuben, who's in jail now."

"Reuben?"

"Yes," I said, lowering myself to lie beside him. "He told me all about him and why he was so afraid when you got into trouble. He says you look like Reuben and even act like him sometimes."

"I don't remember him mentioning anyone named Reuben," he said.

"Me neither. Daddy's been back to his home," I whispered even lower, and told him what Daddy had said about his visit.

"I was thinking of heading for Georgia myself when I left here," he said, his voice full of wonder.

"Were you? Oh, Jimmy," I said, sitting up and looking down at him, "can't you try again, just once more, just for me? Ignore those nasty boys and just do your work."

"It's hard to ignore them when they get ugly and disgusting." He looked away from me.

"What did they say to you, Jimmy? Philip wouldn't tell me." Jimmy

was silent. "It had to do with me and Philip, didn't it?" There was a
long painful silence between us.

"Yeah," he finally said.

"They knew they could get you angry that way, Jimmy." And it was
all because of Clara Sue Cutler, I thought, and her vicious jealous
streak. I never disliked anyone as much as I disliked her. "They were
deliberately baiting you, Jimmy."

"I know, but . . . I can't help getting angry when anyone says bad
things about you, Dawn," he confessed, gazing at me with eyes so full
of hurt it made my heart ache. "I'm sorry if you're mad," he finished.

"I'm not mad at you. I like the way you look after me, only I don't
want to cause you any trouble."

"You didn't," he said. "But it's just like you to think it was all your
fault. All right," he said after a moment and after a deep sigh, "I'll sit
out my suspension and go back and try again, but I don't think it's
going to matter. We just don't belong there. At least, I don't," he added.

"Sure you do, Jimmy. You're just as smart and strong as any of
them."

"I don't mean I'm not as good as them. I'm just not their kind.
Maybe you are, Dawn. You can get along with anyone. I bet you could
make the devil repent."

I laughed.

"I'm glad you came back, Jimmy. It would have broken Momma's
heart if you hadn't, and Daddy's, too. Little Fern would have been
crying for you every day."

"And you?" he asked quickly.

"I was crying already," I admitted. He didn't say anything. After a
moment he took my hand and squeezed it gently. It seemed like it had
been so long since he had wanted to touch me. I brushed back the
strands of hair that had fallen over his forehead. I felt like kissing him
softly on the cheek, but I didn't know how he would react. We were so
close, my breast grazed his arm, but unlike all the other times, he didn't
jump as if he had been stuck with a pin. Suddenly I felt him shudder.

"Aren't you warm enough, Jimmy?"

"I'll be all right," he said, but I put my arm around him and held
him, rubbing his naked shoulder.

"You'd better get under the blanket yourself and go back to sleep,
Dawn," he said, his voice cracking.

"All right. Night, Jimmy," I whispered and risked kissing him on the
cheek. He didn't pull away.

"Good night," he said, and I lay back. For a long time I stared up into the darkness, my emotions in a turmoil. When I closed my eyes, I still saw Jimmy's naked shoulders glistening in the darkness, and the feel of his soft cheek still lingered on my lips.

6
OPENING NIGHT

Daddy started to yell at Jimmy first thing in the morning.

"Why'd you run away for?" he shouted.

"You always do," Jimmy shot back. They glared at each other, but when Momma came out, she was so happy Jimmy had come home that for once Daddy stopped.

"I'll go around and get all your schoolwork from your teachers, Jimmy," I said quickly. "In the meanwhile you'll be able to help Momma with Fern."

"Just what I wanted to be, a baby-sitter," he moaned.

"It's your own fault," Daddy said. Jimmy went into a sulk. I was glad when it was time for Daddy and me to go to school.

"Jimmy's going to try again, Daddy," I told him after we started off. "He promised me last night after he came home."

"Good," Daddy grunted. Then he turned to me and looked at me so strangely. "It's nice of you to care so much about your brother."

"Didn't your family care about each other, Daddy?" I asked.

"Nothing like you and Jimmy," he said, but I could see from the way his eyes narrowed that he didn't want to talk about it.

I couldn't imagine not caring about Jimmy. No matter how happy I could be, if Jimmy wasn't happy, I wasn't. So much had happened to us so quickly at Emerson Peabody, it left my head spinning. I thought the best thing I could do now was concentrate on my schoolwork and my music and put all the bad things behind me. Jimmy really did try harder, too. When he returned, he became more involved with his intramural sports and even did passingly well in his classes. It was beginning to look like we would be all right.

However, once in a while, when I was passing through the corridors,

I would see Mrs. Turnbell standing off to the side watching me. Jimmy said he felt as if she were haunting him, he saw her watching him so often. I smiled and greeted her politely whenever I could and she nodded back, but she looked like she was waiting for something to confirm her belief that we couldn't live up to the demands a school like Emerson Peabody made on its students, students who she believed were more special than us.

Of course, Philip was still upset that I couldn't go out on dates with him, and that I wouldn't sneak out to do it. He kept after me to ask Daddy or to meet him secretly. In my heart I hoped everything would improve when spring came. Unfortunately, winter held on stubbornly, keeping the floorboards cold, the skies gray, and the trees and bushes bare. But when the air finally turned warm and the trees and flowers budded, I was filled with a sense of renewed hope and happiness. I drew strength and pleasure from everything that blossomed around me. Bright sunshine and bright colors made even our poor neighborhood look special. Daddy wasn't talking about quitting his job anymore, Jimmy was doing well in school, and I was finally involved in music the way I had always dreamt I would be.

Only Momma's persistent illness depressed us, but I thought that with the coming of spring, with her walking outside on sunny days and keeping the windows open for more fresh air, she would surely improve. Spring had a way of renewing all faith. It always had for me, and now, more than ever, I prayed it would do wonders for us again.

One bright afternoon after I was finished with my piano lesson, I found Philip waiting for me at the door of the music suite. I didn't see him and almost bumped into him because I was walking with my books cradled in my arms and my eyes down. My body was still filled with the music. The notes I had played continued to play repeatedly in my head. When I played the piano, it was as if my fingers had dreams of their own. Ten minutes after I had gotten up from the piano stool, I could still sense how they held on to the feel of the piano keys. The tips tingled with the memory of the touch, and they wanted to repeat their movements over the keyboard, drawing out the notes and weaving them into melodies and tunes.

"Penny for your thoughts," I heard and looked up at Philip's smiling, gentle eyes. He was leaning against the corridor wall nonchalantly, his arms crossed over his chest. His golden hair was brushed back and shiny, still a little wet from the shower he had just taken after baseball practice. Philip was one of the starting pitchers on the school's varsity team.

"Oh, hi," I said stopping abruptly with surprise.

"I hope you were thinking about me," he said.

I laughed.

"I was just thinking about my music, about my piano lessons."

"Well, I'm disappointed, but how's it going?"

"Mr. Moore's pleased," I said modestly. "He just gave me the solo to sing at the spring concert."

"He did? Wow!" Philip said, straightening up. "Congratulations."

"Thank you."

"We had a shortened practice today, and I . . . I knew you would still be here."

The halls were practically empty. Once in a while someone came out of a room and walked off, but other than that, we were alone for what was really the first time in a long time.

He drew closer until he had my back to the wall and put his hands on the wall to cage me in.

"I wish I could drive you home," he said.

"So do I, but—"

"What if I come by your house tonight, and we don't go for a ride? We just sit in my car."

"I don't know, Philip."

"You won't be lying then, will you?"

"I'll have to tell them where I'm going and—"

"You tell them everything? All the time?" He shook his head. "Parents expect you to do secret things sometimes. They do," he said. "How about it?"

"I don't know. I . . . I'll see," I said. There was such frustration in his eyes. "Maybe one night."

"Good." He looked around and drew closer.

"Philip, someone could see us," I said when he brought his lips closer.

"Just a quick congratulations kiss," he said and brought his lips to mine. He even brought his hand to my breast.

"Philip," I protested. He laughed.

"All right. So," he said, standing straight again, "are you nervous about singing at the concert?"

"Of course. It will be the first time I've ever sung by myself in front of so many people, and so many well-to-do people who have heard and seen really talented performers. Louise told me your sister's going to be jealous and angry about it. She expected to get the solo."

"She had it last year. Besides, she sounds like a foghorn."

"Oh, no, she doesn't," I said, looking up quickly. "But I wish she would stop saying nasty things about me. If I do well on a test, she tells people I cheated. She hasn't let up on me since I arrived. One of these days I'm going to have it out with her." Philip started to laugh. "It's not funny."

"I was laughing at how bright and intense your eyes become when you're angry. You can't hide your true feelings."

"I know. Daddy says I would be a terrible poker player."

"I'd like to play strip poker with you someday," he said, smiling licentiously.

"Philip!"

"What?"

"Don't say things like that," I said, but I couldn't help imagining it. He shrugged.

"Can't help it sometimes. Especially when I'm around you."

Could he hear my heart pounding? I saw some students coming around the corner behind us.

"I've got to get down to Daddy's office. He and Jimmy are probably waiting for me," I added and started down the stairway.

"Dawn. Wait."

I turned back to him. He joined me on the stairs.

"Do you think . . . I mean, since it's such a special occasion and all . . . that you can get your father and mother to let me take you to the concert at least?" he asked hopefully.

"I'll ask," I said.

"Great. I'm glad I waited around to see you," he added and leaned forward to kiss me. I thought he was going to kiss me quickly on the cheek, but he kissed me on the neck instead. He did it and was on his way before I had a chance to respond. The students coming down the corridor saw him and the boys howled. My heart didn't seem to fit my chest. It beat too fast, too fierce, too loud, and my pulse raced too excitedly. I was afraid Daddy and Jimmy would see the redness in my cheeks and know I had been kissed.

Surely there was something very special between me and Philip, I thought, if his merely kissing me or looking at me or speaking softly to me could set my body on fire, make me tingle and make me dizzy. I took a deep breath and sighed. Daddy and Momma just had to let him take me to the concert; they just had to, I thought. I had done what they had wanted and not nagged them to go out on dates, even though girls my age all around me were allowed to do so. It wasn't fair; they had to understand.

I could understand them being a little afraid for me when I had first started at Emerson Peabody. But I believed I had grown considerably during these last few months anyway. Success with my music and my schoolwork had given me a new sense of confidence. I felt older, stronger. Surely if I saw that in myself, Momma and Daddy could see it as well.

Confident they would give me permission, I hurried down to the basement to meet Daddy and Jimmy and give them the news about my solo. I had never seen Daddy so excited and proud.

"You hear that, Jimmy boy!" he exclaimed, slapping his hands together. "Your sister's a star."

"I'm not a star yet, Daddy. I've got to do it well," I said.

"You will. What good news," Daddy said. "Something good to bring home to your momma."

"Daddy," I said as he gathered his things for us to leave. "Do you think since this is a special occasion that Philip Cutler could pick me up and take me to the concert?"

Daddy stopped in his tracks. His smile evaporated slowly and his eyes darkened for a moment and grew small. As I stared at him, hoping, a little warmth crept back into his gaze.

"Well, I don't know, honey. I . . . we'll see."

When we got home, Momma was lying in bed awake, one eye on Fern, who sat on a blanket on the floor playing with her toys. The late afternoon sunlight played peekaboo with some lazy clouds, but Momma had the shades drawn so even when the sun peeped out, it didn't drop any warm, happy rays into the room. When I entered, Momma sat up slowly and with great effort.

She had obviously not brought a brush to her hair all day. The strands hung down randomly on the sides and some curled up and spiraled about on top. She used to wash her hair almost every day, so that it had gleamed like black silk.

"A woman's hair is her crowning jewel," she had told me many times. Whenever she had been too tired to brush her hair herself, she always asked me to do it.

Momma never needed much makeup. She always had a smooth complexion with pink lips. Her eyes sparkled like polished black onyx. I

wanted so much to look like her and thought it was unfair of nature to
have skipped a generation while most other children looked exactly like
their parents.

Before she became sickly, Momma would stand perfectly straight and
walk with her shoulders back, as proud as the mythical Indian princess
Daddy always compared her to. She moved gracefully, swiftly, passing
through the day like a streak of ebony paint stroked through a milk-
white canvas. Now she sat hunched over, her head down, her arms
resting limply on her legs, and she looked at me with sad, glassy eyes,
the onyx dulled, the silk hair turned into a rough cotton, her complexion faded, pale, and her lips nearly colorless. Her cheekbones were far
more prominent and her collarbone looked as if it would pop right
through her thin layer of skin.

Before I could say anything about Philip, Fern reached up for me and
started to cry my name.

"Where's your daddy and Jimmy?" Momma asked, looking behind
me.

"They went to pick up some groceries. Daddy thought I should come
right in to help you with Fern."

"I'm glad," she said, fighting for a deep breath. "The baby tired me
out today."

"It's not just the baby, Momma," I chastised gently.

"It's coming along, Dawn," she replied. "Could you get me a glass of
water, honey? My lips feel parched."

I went out with Fern and got Momma her water. Then I handed her
the glass and watched as she drank. Her Adam's apple bobbed like a
float on a fishing line.

"For months you've been promising you would go to a real doctor
and not rely on backwoods medicines and such if you didn't get better
quickly. Well, you're not getting better that fast, and you're not living
up to your promise." I hated speaking to her so firmly, but I thought I
had to now.

"It's just one of them stubborn coughs. I had a cousin back in Georgia who had a cold for nearly a year before it upped and left her."

"Well, she suffered for a year for no reason," I insisted. "Just like
you're suffering, Momma."

"All right, all right. You're getting worse than Grandma Longchamp.
Why, when I was pregnant with Jimmy, she wouldn't let up on me a
minute. Everything I did was wrong. It was a relief giving birth, just so
I could get her off my back."

"Grandma Longchamp? But, Momma, I thought you gave birth to Jimmy at a farmhouse on the road."

"What? Oh, yeah, I did. I meant until I left the farm."

"But didn't you and Daddy leave right after you got married?"

"Not exactly right after. Soon after. Quit questioning me so closely, Dawn. I'm not thinking straight just yet," she snapped. It wasn't like her to be so short with me, but I imagined it was because of her illness.

I thought I should change the topic. I didn't want to make her unhappy while she was still suffering so.

"Guess what, Momma?" I said, bouncing Fern in my arms, "I'm going to sing the solo at the concert," I said proudly.

"Why, bless my soul. Bless my soul." She pressed her palms against her chest. Even when she wasn't coughing, she seemed to have trouble breathing every once in a while, especially when something caught her by surprise or she moved too quickly. "Ain't that wonderful. I knew you'd show those rich folks they ain't no better than you. Come here so I can give you a real hug," she said.

I put little Fern down on the bed, and Momma and I embraced. Her thin arms held me to her as tightly as she could, and I could feel her ribs through her shift dress.

"Momma," I said, the tears filling my eyes. "You've lost so much weight, much more than I realized."

"Not so much and I shoulda lost a few pounds here and there. It'll come back on faster than you can shake a stick, you'll see. One thing about women my age, when they wanna gain weight, they just gotta smell food. Sometimes just looking at it will add a pound here and there," she joked. She kissed me on the cheek. "Congratulations, Dawn honey. Did you tell your daddy?"

"Yes."

"I bet his chest blew out some," she said, shaking her head.

"Momma, I got something to ask about the concert."

"Oh?"

"Since it is a special occasion and all, do you think it would be all right for Philip Cutler to pick me up and take me? He promises to drive carefully and—"

"Did you ask your daddy?" she responded quickly.

"Uh-huh. He said we'll see, but I think if it's all right with you, it's all right with him."

Suddenly she looked so troubled and old staring back at me.

"It's not a long ride, Momma, and I really want to go with Philip.

Other girls my age go for rides and on dates, but I haven't complained. . . ."

She nodded. "I can't hold you back from growing up, Dawn. And I don't want to, but I don't want you to get serious with this boy . . . any boy yet. Don't be like me and give up your youth."

"Oh, Momma, I'm not getting married. I'm just going to the spring concert. Will it be all right?" I pleaded.

It was as if it took all her strength to do it, but she nodded.

"Oh, thank you, Momma." I hugged her again.

"Dawn, up," Fern called impatiently, jealous of all the affection Momma and I were passing between us. "Dawn, up."

"Her Highness is calling," Momma said, and then lay back against her pillow. I watched her with my heart in a turmoil: happy about my being about to go out on a date, but sad and aching with the sight of how slowly and painfully Momma spoke and moved.

Mr. Moore decided to double up my lessons for the rest of the week. Finally it was the day of the concert. At lunchtime Mr. Moore played the piano and I sang. Twice my voice cracked. He stopped playing and looked up at me.

"Now, Dawn," he said. "I want you to take a deep breath and calm yourself down before we go on."

"Oh, Mr. Moore, I can't do this!" I cried. "I don't know why I thought I could. But to sing a solo in front of all those people, most of whom go to the opera and to Broadway in New York City and know real talent—"

"*You* are real talent," Mr. Moore said. "Do you think I would put you out on that stage alone if I didn't think so? Don't forget, Dawn, when you go out there, I go, too. Now, you're not going to let me down, are you?"

"No, sir," I said, nearly in tears.

"Remember when you told me once you wished you could be like a bird, high on a tree, singing freely into the wind and not worrying about who hears it and who doesn't?"

"Yes. I still do."

"Well, then, close your eyes and see yourself perched on that branch and then sing into the wind. After a while, just like a baby bird, you'll get your wings and fly. You'll soar, Dawn. I just know it," he said. Gone was his cherub smile and his impish grin; gone was the playful happy twinkle in his eyes. Instead, his face was stone serious, and his words and eyes filled me with confidence.

"Okay," I said softly, and we began again. This time I sang my heart out, and when we were finished, his face was flushed with satisfaction. He got up and kissed me on the cheek.

"You're ready," he said.

My heart was pounding with excitement and happiness as I hurried out of the music suite.

As soon as the last bell rang, I ran to find Jimmy and Daddy. I was paralyzed with nervousness and wanted to go straight home to get ready for the concert, scheduled for 8:00 P.M.

When we arrived home, Momma was lying in bed, her face more flushed than usual, and shivering something terrible. Fern had gotten into some of the kitchenware, but I could see Momma didn't know. We all gathered around her bed, and I felt her forehead.

"She's shivering, Daddy," I said, "but she feels feverish."

Momma's teeth chattered, and she turned her eyes to me and forced a smile.

"It's . . . just . . . a cold," she claimed.

"No, it's not, Momma. Whatever's been eating at you is getting worse."

"I'll be all right!" she cried.

"You will if you go to a doctor, Momma."

"Dawn's right, Sally Jean. We can't let this go on anymore. We're going to wrap you up real good and take you over to that hospital so they can look at you and give you some medicine fast," he said.

"Nooo!" Momma cried. I tried to comfort her while Daddy gathered her warmest clothing. Then I helped him dress her. When I looked at Momma without her clothes, I was shocked at how thin she had gotten. Her ribs poked so hard against her skin, and all her bones looked like they were going to pop out. There were fever blotches all over her, too. I kept myself from crying and worked at getting her ready. When it came time to take her out, we discovered she couldn't walk on her own. Her legs ached too much.

"I'll carry her," Daddy said, barely holding back his own tears. I hurriedly dressed Fern. Momma didn't want us to, but we were all going to go along. Neither Jimmy nor I wanted to remain home and wait.

When we arrived I went in first and told the emergency room nurse about Momma. She had an attendant roll out a wheelchair, and we got

Momma into it quickly. The hospital security guard helped get Momma in. He looked at Daddy oddly, like someone trying to remember someone he had known years ago. Daddy didn't notice anything but Momma.

While we waited, Jimmy went to the gift store and brought back a lollypop for Fern. It kept her occupied, but it also smeared her face green. She had a baby's gibberish now, mixed with a real word or two, and often looked at other people waiting in the lobby and started blubbering at them. Some smiled; some were so worried about their loved ones, they could only stare blankly.

Finally, well over an hour later, a doctor sought us out. He had red hair and freckles and looked so young, I thought he couldn't bring anyone bad news. But I was wrong.

"How long has your wife had this cough and run fevers, Mr. Longchamp?" he asked Daddy.

"A while, on and off. She seemed to be getting better, so we didn't think much of it."

"She has consumption and very bad, too. Her lungs are so congested, it's amazing she can breathe," he said, not hiding his annoyance at Daddy.

But it wasn't Daddy's fault. Momma was the stubborn one, I wanted to shout. Daddy looked overwhelmed. He lowered his head and nodded. When I gazed at Jimmy, I saw him standing stiffly, his hands clenched into fists, his eyes burning with anger and sorrow.

"I've rushed her into intensive care," the doctor continued, "and put her on oxygen. She looks like she's lost a great deal of weight," he added and shook his head.

"Can we see her?" I asked, tears streaming down my face.

"Just for five minutes," he said. "And I mean five minutes."

How could a man so young be so firm? I wondered. However, it made me feel he was a good doctor.

Silently, with only little Fern repeating "lolly, lolly," and reaching for the rest of her lollypop, we walked to the elevator. Fern was intrigued with it as Jimmy pushed two and it lifted us up. Her eyes went from side to side. I pressed her closely to me and kissed her soft pink cheek.

We followed the sign that directed us to the intensive care unit. When we opened the door, the head nurse came around her desk quickly to greet us.

"You can't bring a baby in here," she declared.

"I'll wait out here, Daddy," I said. "You and Jimmy go in first."

"I'll come out after a minute or two," Jimmy promised. I saw how much he wanted and needed to see Momma. There was a small couch and a chair in a special waiting room outside of intensive care. I took Fern in there and let her crawl around on the couch while we waited. Just about two minutes later Jimmy appeared. His eyes were red.

"Go on," he said quickly. "She wants to see you."

I handed Fern to him and hurried into the room. Momma was lying in the last bed on the right. She was in an oxygen tent. Daddy stood at the right of the bed holding her hand. When I came up beside her, Momma smiled and reached out to take my hand, too.

"I'll be all right, honey," she said. "You just do a wonderful singing job tonight."

"Oh, Momma, how can I sing with you lying here in the hospital?" I cried.

"You sure better," she said. "You know how proud me and your daddy are, and it's gonna make me a whole lot better knowing my little girl's singing for all those fancy people. Promise me you'll do it, Dawn, and not let my getting sick stop you. Promise."

"I promise, Momma."

"Good," she said. Then she beckoned me closer. "Dawn," she said, her voice barely audible. I drew as close to the tent as I could. She was squeezing my hand as firmly as she was able to. "You must never think badly of us. We love you. Always remember that."

"Why should I think badly of you, Momma?"

She closed her eyes.

"Momma?"

"I'm afraid your five minutes are up, and the doctor was very explicit about that," the intensive care nurse said.

I looked back at Momma. She had her eyes closed tightly, and her face looked more flushed than before.

"Momma!" I cried under my breath. I looked at Daddy. Tears were flowing freely down his face now, and he was staring at me so hard, I felt terrible for him.

We obeyed the nurse and started away. As soon as we left the intensive care unit, I turned to Daddy.

"Why did Momma say that, Daddy? What did she mean by 'you must never think badly of us'?"

"Part of her fever, I guess," he said. "She's a bit delirious. Let's go home," he said, and we went to fetch Jimmy and little Fern.

When we got home, we didn't have time to worry about Momma, although she was on our minds. We were too busy getting ready for the concert and trying to find a baby-sitter for Fern.

As hard as I tried, I couldn't bear the thought of making my singing debut without Momma present. Yet I'd promised her I would do my best, and I wasn't going to let her down.

I didn't have time to take a shower or shampoo my hair. Instead I brushed my hair a hundred times, giving it a soft, silky sheen, adding a blue ribbon for a nice dash of color.

At least I didn't have to worry about what I should wear. One of the good things about being in the school band and chorus was that we got to wear uniforms when we performed. The school uniform consisted of a white and black wool sweater and black skirt. After I put it on, I stood up and straightened my skirt. Then I stood back and gazed at myself, imagining myself standing there before all those fine people. I knew I had developed a young girl's figure and I filled out the school sweater better than most girls my age. For the first time I thought my fair skin, blond hair, and blue eyes were attractive. Was it terrible to suddenly become infatuated with yourself? I wondered. Would this bring me bad luck? I was afraid, but I couldn't help it. The girl in the mirror smiled with satisfaction.

Daddy came in then and told me that Mrs. Jackson, an old lady who lived down the hall from us, would be willing to watch Fern tonight. He also told me that he had given the hospital Mrs. Jackson's number in case we needed to be reached. After telling me that, Daddy took a step back, giving me a long admiring look.

"You look real beautiful, honey," Daddy said. "Real grown-up."

"Thank you, Daddy."

He held something in his hand.

"Before we left the hospital, your momma asked me to give you these to wear tonight, since it's such a special occasion."

He held out the precious string of pearls.

"Oh, Daddy," I said, nearly breathless. "I can't; I shouldn't. That's our insurance policy."

"No, no, Sally Jean said you must wear them," he insisted and put them on me. I looked down at the pearls gleaming soft and white and perfect and then gazed at myself in the mirror.

"They'll bring you luck," Daddy said and kissed me on the cheek. We heard a knock on the front door.

"It's Philip," Jimmy called from the other room. Daddy stepped back, his face suddenly serious again.

Philip was dressed in a blue suit and matching tie and looked very handsome.

"Hi," he said. "Boy, you look great."

"Thank you. So do you. Philip," I said. "This is my father."

"Oh, yes, I know. I've seen you around the school, sir," Philip said. "Waved to you once in a while."

"Yes," Daddy said, his eyes growing smaller and smaller.

"How's Mrs. Longchamp?" Philip asked. "Jimmy just told me that you had to take her to the hospital earlier."

"She's very sick, but we're hopeful," Daddy said. He looked from him to me, his face so somber.

"Well, we'd better get started," Philip said softly.

"Okay," I said. I grabbed my coat, and Philip moved forward quickly to help me put it on. Daddy and Jimmy stared, Daddy looking very troubled. Just as Philip and I reached the front door, I heard Jimmy call my name.

"I'll be right with you, Philip," I said. Philip went out, and I waited for Jimmy.

"Just wanted to wish you luck," he said and leaned forward quickly to kiss me on the cheek. "Good luck," he whispered and hurried back to the apartment. I stood there a moment, bringing my fingers to my cheek, and then I turned and went out into the night. It was full of stars. I hoped one was twinkling just for me.

7
TWINKLE, TWINKLE LITTLE STAR

When the Emerson Peabody School came into view, my heart began to pound so hard, I thought I might faint. That's how nervous I was, and when we turned into the school driveway and we saw the lines of expensive cars arriving, I couldn't stop myself from trembling.

The parents and guests were dressed tonight as though they were attending a performance at the Metropolitan Opera House. The women wore magnificent furs and diamond earrings. Under their warm, extravagant coats they wore silk dresses in the most beautiful colors I'd ever seen. The men were all in dark suits. Some people arrived in long limousines and had their doors opened by uniformed chauffeurs.

Philip drove us around to the side entrance used by the students performing in the concert. He stopped near the door to let me out.

"Wait," Philip said when I reached for the door handle. I turned back, and he simply stared for a moment. Then he leaned forward, brought his lips to mine, and kissed me.

"Dawn," he whispered. "I spend every night dreaming of kissing you and holding you. . . ."

He started to kiss me again, but I heard the sound of the other students arriving. We were in the parking lot under the tall bright lights.

"Philip, they'll see us," I said and pulled back even though I was giddy with the nearness of him.

"Most of the girls around here wouldn't care," he said. "You're so bashful."

"I can't help it."

"It's all right. There's always later," he said, winking. "Good luck," he said.

"Thank you," I replied. It was barely a whisper.

"Wait!" he exclaimed. Then he jumped out and ran around the car to open my door for me as I gathered myself together.

"A star should be treated like a star," he said, reaching in to take my hand.

"Oh, Philip. I'm far from a star. I'm going to fall flat on my face!" I cried, looking at the crowd of impressed students who stared.

"Nonsense, Miss Longchamp. By the end of the evening we'll have to fight off the autograph seekers. Good luck. I'll be sitting out there rooting for you." He held on to my hand.

"Thank you, Philip." I took a deep breath and looked toward the doorway. "Here I go," I said. Philip didn't release my hand.

"See you right after the concert," he said. "We'll get something to eat and then . . . we'll go to my favorite spot and look at the stars. Okay?"

He pleaded with his eyes and held on to my hand tightly.

"Yes," I whispered and felt as if I had surrendered myself to him already, just by agreeing to go.

He smiled and let go. Then he started toward the auditorium. I watched him for a moment, my heart still pounding. All three of the men in my life had kissed me and filled me with confidence. Buoyed by their good wishes and affection, I turned toward the entrance. I suddenly felt a little like Sleeping Beauty awakened by the kiss of the prince.

I entered the school with some of the other members of the chorus. We all headed down the corridor toward the music suite and the backstage area. We were to put our coats in the music suite and then go prepare for the concert: warming up our instruments and our voices.

"Hi, Dawn," Linda said, approaching me. "Are those real pearls?" she asked as soon as I had taken off my coat. At the word *pearls* other girls gathered around us, including Clara Sue.

"Yes, they are. They're my mother's and they're our family heirloom," I emphasized, looking down at them myself. I was terrified the string would break and I would lose them.

"It's so hard to tell real pearls from fake pearls nowadays," Clara Sue said. "At least, that's what my mother told me once."

"These are real," I insisted.

"They really don't go with what you're wearing," Linda said, smirking, "but if they're some sort of family good-luck piece, I suppose it's all right."

"Why don't we go to the girls room and freshen up. We've got a few minutes yet," Clara Sue suggested. As usual, when Clara Sue made a suggestion, the others quickly agreed.

"What's the matter," Linda said to me as they started out, "you too good to join us?"

"I hardly think I'm the one who's stuck-up, Linda."

"So?"

"There's plenty of time," Melissa Lee said.

They all stared at me.

"Oh, all right," I said, actually surprised at their desire to include me. "I guess I should brush my hair."

The bathroom was crowded. Girls were making last-minute adjustments on their hair and freshening lipstick. Everyone was talking excitedly. There was an electricity in the air. I went to a mirror to check myself and suddenly realized all of Clara Sue's friends were around me.

"I love your hair tonight," Linda told me.

"Yes, I never saw it looking so radiant," Clara Sue said. The others nodded, these silly smiles on their faces.

Why were they all being so nice to me? I wondered. Did they always follow Clara Sue's lead like a bunch of sheep? Was it that Philip wanted me to be his girlfriend? Maybe he told Clara Sue once and for all to be nice to me.

"Do you smell something, girls?" Clara Sue suddenly asked. Everyone started sniffing. "Someone needs some perfume."

"What's that supposed to mean, Clara Sue?" I said, realizing all this friendliness was phony.

"Nothing. We're just thinking of you. Right, girls?" she said.

"Yeah," they replied in chorus, and on that cue everyone brought out a can of stink-bomb spray from behind her back and aimed it at me. A cloud of horrible putrescence hit me. I screamed and quickly covered my face and hair. The girls laughed and kept spraying over my uniform. They were in hysterics, some holding their stomachs, they were laughing so hard. Only Louise looked pained. She stepped back as if I might explode like a bomb.

"What's the matter?" Clara Sue asked. "Don't you like expensive perfume, or are you so used to cheap stuff you can't stand it?"

That made everyone laugh harder.

"What is this?" I cried. "How can I get it off?" Every time I spoke, it made the crowd of horrid girls laugh more. I rushed forward to the sink and started to wet a paper towel. Then I began wiping my sweater frantically.

"Who's the poor idiot who has to stand and sit beside her tonight?" Linda asked the dreadful audience. Someone screamed.

"That's not fair. Why should I be the one to suffer?"

The laughter continued.

"It's getting late," Clara Sue announced. "We'll meet you on the stage, Dawn," she called as they all started out, leaving me to my horrible fate at the sink. I scrubbed at my sweater and skirt so hard the paper towel tore into shreds, but mere water had no effect.

Becoming more frantic, I took off the pearls carefully and then pulled my sweater off and shook it out. I didn't know what to do. Finally I sat down on the floor and cried. Where would I get another school uniform now? How could I go on stage smelling like this? I would have to stay in the bathroom and then go home.

I cried until I had no more tears and my head and throat ached. I felt as if a heavy blanket of defeat had been thrown over me. It weighed far too much for me to simply throw it off. My shoulders shook with my sobs. Poor Daddy and Jimmy. They were probably already out there in their seats anxious for me. Poor Momma lying in her hospital room and watching the clock, thinking soon I would be out on that stage.

I looked up when someone came in, and I saw it was Louise. She gazed at me quickly and then looked down at the floor.

"I'm sorry," she said. "They made me do it, too. They said if I didn't, they would make up stories about me, just like they made them up about you."

I nodded.

"I should have expected something like this, but I was too excited to see through their false smiles," I said, standing up.

"Would you do me a favor? Would you go back to the music suite and get my coat for me? I can't put this back on," I said, indicating my sweater. "The odor is too strong."

"What are you going to do?"

"What can I do? I'll go home."

"Oh, no, you can't. You just can't," she said, nearly in tears herself. "Please, get me my coat, Louise."

She nodded and left, her head down. Poor Louise, I thought. She wanted to be different—she wanted to be nice—but the girls wouldn't let her, and she wasn't strong enough to stand against them.

Oh, why were girls like Clara Sue so cruel? They had so much—all the fancy clothes they wanted; they could get their hair done, their nails done, even their toenails! Their parents took them on wonderful trips, and they lived in big houses with enormous rooms of their own with big soft beds and floors of plush carpet. They never went to sleep in cold rooms, and they always had anything and everything they wanted to eat. If they ever got sick, they knew they had the best doctors and medical care available. Everyone respected their parents and their family names. They shouldn't be filled with jealousy. Why in the world did they resent me—me who'd had so little compared to them. My heart hardened against them as I stood there in the bathroom, became as small and as sharp as theirs.

A few moments later Louise returned, only she didn't have my coat; she had another school uniform.

"Where did you get that?" I asked, smiling through my tears.

"Mr. Moore. I found him in the hall and told him what had happened. He just went to the storage room quickly and got this out. It smells a little like mothballs, but—"

"Oh, that's far better than this!" I exclaimed, tossing the spoiled sweater aside and slipping out of my skirt as fast as I could. I slipped the new sweater on quickly and put on Momma's pearls. The sweater was a little tighter, clinging to my bosom and my ribs firmly, but as Momma always said, "Beggars can't be choosers."

"Does my hair smell? I don't think they got much spray on it." I leaned down so she could check.

"It's all right."

"Thank you, Louise." I hugged her to me. We heard all the instruments being tuned. "Let's hurry," I said and started out.

"Wait," Louise called. She picked up my smelly sweater and skirt with her right thumb and forefinger and held them away from herself. "I have an idea."

"What idea?"

"Follow me," she said. We left the bathroom. Everyone was in the backstage area warming up. Louise hurried back to the music suite. I followed, curious. "Keep your eyes on the hallway," she said.

She went to Clara Sue's beautiful soft blue cashmere coat and shoved my smelly sweater into it, closing the coat around it.

"Louise!" I couldn't help smiling. Louise was not usually this brave, and Clara Sue deserved it.

"I don't care. Besides, she won't blame it on me; she'll blame it on you," Louise said so nonchalantly, it made me laugh.

We hurried to the backstage area and our instruments. The girls who had been in the bathroom when I had been betrayed looked with curiosity as I entered. They soon realized I had another sweater and skirt on. Even so, Linda and Clara Sue pretended I still smelled awful.

Mr. Moore announced it was time for us to take our positions on the stage. We all marched out behind the closed curtains. I could hear the murmur of the audience as people took their seats.

"Ready, everyone?" Mr. Moore asked. He stopped beside me and squeezed my arm softly. "Are you all right?"

"Yes," I said.

"You'll do fine," he said and then took his position. The curtain was opened and the audience responded with loud applause. The stage lights made it hard to look out at the crowd and distinguish faces easily, but after a while my eyes got used to the lights and I could see Jimmy and Daddy gazing up.

The chorus sang three songs, and then Mr. Moore nodded toward me. I stepped out to the front of the stage, and Mr. Moore went to the piano. The hush in the audience was deep, and I felt the warm lights on my face.

I didn't even remember beginning. Everything came naturally. Suddenly I had my head back, and I was singing to the world, singing into the wind, and hoping my voice would be carried all the way to Momma, who would close her eyes and hear me, as far away as she was.

"Somewhere, over the rainbow, way up high . . ."

When I sang my final note, I closed my eyes. For a moment I heard nothing, just a great silence, and then there was a thunder of applause. It rolled in from the audience like a wave rushing to shore, building and building until it hit with a crescendo that overwhelmed me. I looked at Mr. Moore. He was smiling from ear to ear and had his hand out and toward me.

I curtsied and stepped back. Looking through the audience, I found Daddy again and saw him clapping so hard his whole body shook. Jimmy was clapping, too, and smiling up at me. Someone squeezed my arm and then someone else and soon everyone in the chorus was congratulating me.

The entire chorus sang another song, and then the band played three numbers. The evening ended with the band playing "The Star-Spangled Banner" and then the Emerson Peabody school song. The moment the last note was sounded, the band and the chorus cheered and everyone congratulated everyone else, but girls and boys were coming to me especially. Boys shook my hand and girls hugged me. Some of the girls who had been in the bathroom earlier hugged me, too, all looking sorrowfully guilty. I accepted their hugs and squeezed them just as hard. My heart was too full and had no room for hate and anger at this moment.

"I don't think that was anything special," Clara Sue said, coming up behind me. "I'm sure I would have done a lot better, but Mr. Moore took pity on you and gave you the solo."

"You're a despicable person, Clara Sue Cutler," I said. "Someday you'll have no one but yourself."

When we all emerged in the hallway, we were greeted by our parents and friends. Daddy and Jimmy were standing by, both smiling proudly.

"You did good, Dawn. Just like I thought." Daddy hugged me to him and held me tightly. "Your momma will be awfully proud of you."

"I'm glad, Daddy."

"You were great," Jimmy said. "Better than you sound in the shower," he kidded. He kissed me again on the cheek. I looked past him and saw Philip standing by, waiting for his chance. When Jimmy stepped back, Philip approached.

"I knew you were headed for stardom," he said. He looked at Daddy, who lost his smile again. "You've got a talented daughter, sir."

"Thank you," Daddy said. "Well, I guess we all better head home and relieve Mrs. Jackson."

"Oh, Daddy," I said after Philip had taken my hand, "Philip is taking me to have some pizza. Can you look after Fern until I get back? We won't be long."

Daddy looked uncomfortable. For a moment I thought he would say no. My heart pounded in anticipation, teetering on the brink of disaster. Philip looked as if he were holding his breath. Daddy gazed at him a moment and then looked at me and finally smiled.

"All right, sure," he said. "Jimmy, are you going with them?"

Jimmy stepped back as if he had been punched.

"No," he said quickly. "I'm going home with you."

"Oh." Daddy looked disappointed. "Well, okay then. Be careful and come home early. I just gotta check on how things are being cleaned up, Jimmy. And then we can go."

"I'll go with you, Daddy," he said. He looked at me and then at Philip. "See you later," he added quickly and followed Daddy down the hall.

"Come on," Philip said, pulling me along. "Let's beat the crowd out of here."

"I've got to get my coat," I said, and he followed me to the music suite. When we arrived, we found a small group of girls gathered around Clara Sue. I had forgotten what Louise had done to her coat. She looked up at me hatefully.

"This wasn't funny," she said. "This was an expensive coat, probably worth more than your entire wardrobe."

"What's she talking about?" Philip asked.

"Something stupid that happened earlier," I said. I just wanted to get away from all of them and their stupidity. Suddenly all that seemed so immature. I grabbed my coat and we left. After we got into his car and started away, Philip insisted I tell him all about the bathroom incident. As I did, he grew angrier and angrier.

"She's so spoiled, and she hangs around with spoiled girls," he said. "Jealous, spoiled girls. My sister has become the worst of all of them. When I get my hands on her . . ." He nodded and then he suddenly laughed. "I'm glad you gave it back to her."

"I didn't," I said and told him about Louise.

"Good for her," he replied. Then he looked at me and smiled. "But let's not let anything ruin this night, your night—your opening night, I should say.

"Dawn, you were so good. You've got the prettiest voice I've ever heard!" he exclaimed. I didn't know how to react to such lavish praise. It was all so overwhelming. I felt a warmth in my heart and sat back. It was wonderful . . . the applause, Daddy's happiness and Jimmy's pride, and now Philip's affection. I couldn't believe how lucky I was. If only my luck would spread to Momma, I thought, and help her get better quicker. Then we would have everything.

A number of students from Emerson Peabody came to the restaurant to get pizza. Philip and I had a booth toward the rear, but anyone entering the restaurant could see us. Most of the students who attended the concert came by to tell me how much they'd enjoyed my singing. They heaped so many compliments on me, I really did begin to feel like a star. Philip sat across from me smiling, his blue eyes twinkling with pride. Of course, the girls who came by all made it their business to say hello to him, too, and bat their eyelashes. Suddenly Philip looked at me with such longing.

"Why don't we order our pizza to go," he said. "We can eat it under the stars."

"Okay," I said, my heart pounding.

Philip told our waitress, who then brought our pizza in a box. I felt every other student's eyes on us as we got up and left the restaurant.

After we drove off, Philip decided we should have a piece of pizza on the way. The aroma was driving us crazy. I held his piece for him and fed him carefully as he drove. We laughed at the string of cheese he had to gobble. Finally we drove down his secret road and parked in the darkness with the stars blazing in the sky before us.

"Oh, Philip, it's everything you promised. I feel like I'm on top of the world!" I cried.

"You are and you should be," he said. He leaned toward me and we kissed, a very long kiss. Before it ended I felt the tip of his tongue press against mine. It shocked me at first and I started away, but he held me firmly and I let him continue.

"Didn't you ever French kiss?" he asked.

"No."

He laughed.

"I do have a lot to teach you. Did you like it?"

"Yes," I whispered, as if it were a sin to admit it.

"Good. I don't want to go too fast," he said, "or scare you like I did the last time we were here."

"I'm all right. My heart is just pounding," I confessed, frightened it would cause me to faint.

"Let me feel it?" he said, bringing his fingers to my breast slowly. But then suddenly his hand was at the bottom of my sweater, his fingers gliding underneath and coming up to my bra. I couldn't help getting tense.

"Easy," he whispered into my ear. "Relax. You'll enjoy it. I promise."

"I can't help being nervous, Philip. I never did this with any other boy but you."

"I understand," he said. "Easy," he whispered in a soothing voice. "Just keep your eyes closed and lean back. That's it," he said when I closed my eyes. He slipped his fingers under the elastic material and gently lifted it from my naked bosom. I felt a rush of heat just before he brought his lips to mine again.

I moaned and leaned back. Contradictory voices were crying out. One, sounding like my mother, demanded that I stop, that I push him away. For some reason Jimmy's angry eyes flashed before me. I recalled the way Daddy had gazed sadly at Philip when I had asked him if we could go for pizza.

Philip started to lift my sweater.

"Philip, I don't think—"

"Easy," he repeated, lowering his head so he could bring his lips to my breast. When they touched me, I felt as though I would burst with excitement. I felt the tip of his tongue begin to explore.

"You're delicious," he said, "so fresh, so soft."

His other hand began to make its way under my skirt. Wasn't this all happening too quickly? I thought. Did the other girls my age let boys touch them under their clothes like this? Or was I being the bad girl they gossiped and lied about?

I envisioned Clara Sue's hateful face before me when she said, "My brother makes girls like you mothers once a month."

Philip's fingers found the bottom of my panties. I twisted my legs away from him.

"Dawn . . . you don't know how long I've dreamt of this. This is my night . . . your night. Relax. I'll show you . . . teach you." He brought his lips to the nipple of my breast and I felt myself sinking back, giving in like someone losing consciousness. His other hand was in my panties. How do girls resist? How do they stop it once the feelings get so strong? I wanted to stop it, but I felt so helpless. I was drifting, losing myself in his kisses and his touch and the way it brought heat to my breasts and into my thighs.

"I want to teach you so much," he whispered, but just at that moment the light from another car's headlights exploded over us, and I screamed.

Philip pulled back instantly, and I sat up to straighten my clothing. We turned to see the second car pull very close to ours.

"Who is it?" I asked, unable to hide my fear. I rushed to bring down my sweater.

"Aw, it's just one of the other guys from the baseball team," Philip said. "Damn it." We could hear the radio playing in his friend's car, and we could hear the laughter of girls. Our precious, private place had been invaded; our moment violated. "They're probably going to bug us soon," Philip said angrily.

"I thought this was your special place, Philip," I said. "I thought you found it accidentally."

"Yeah, yeah," he said. "I made the mistake of telling one of the guys about it one day, and then he told someone else."

"It's getting late anyway, Philip, and with Momma sick . . . I'd better get back."

"Maybe we can go someplace else," he said, not hiding his disappointment and frustration. "I know other spots."

"We'll come back some other time," I promised and squeezed his arm. "Please. Take me home."

"Damn," he repeated. He started the car and backed away before his friends could bother us. They beeped their horn, but we didn't pay any attention. Philip drove me home quickly, barely looking at me.

"I should have come right up here instead of taking you for the pizza," he said, almost in a growl.

We made the turn on our street, but as we were approaching the house, I thought I saw Daddy and Jimmy rushing down the sidewalk toward our car. Drawing closer, I was sure of it and sat up quickly.

"It's Daddy! And Jimmy! Where are they going so late?" I cried. Philip sped up until he pulled alongside, just as Daddy got behind the steering wheel.

"What is it, Daddy? Where are you going this time of night?"

"It's Momma," he said. "The hospital called Mrs. Jackson just now. Momma ain't doin' so good."

"Oh, no!" I felt my throat close up and the tears come rushing over my eyes. I got out of Philip's car quickly and into Daddy's.

"I hope everything will be all right," Philip called out. Daddy just nodded and started away.

As soon as we reached the hospital, we rushed to the entrance, where the security guard came forward to stop us. I recognized him as the same one who had been at the emergency room when we had brought Momma in.

"Where you all heading?" he asked. He spoke gruffly, demanding an answer, and just like the first time, looked closely at Daddy.

"The hospital just phoned about my wife, Sally Jean Longchamp. They told us to come right over."

"Just a minute," the security guard said, holding his hand up. He went to the central desk and spoke to the receptionist. "All right," he said, returning. "Go on up. The doctor's waiting for you." He followed us to the elevator and watched us go in, still staring hard at Daddy.

When we arrived at the door to the intensive care unit, Daddy paused. The young-looking, red-haired doctor who had examined Momma in the emergency room was off to the side talking softly with a nurse. They both turned when we approached. I felt the lump crawl up in my throat, and I bit down on my lower lip. There were shadows deep and dark in the young doctor's eyes. Suddenly they looked more like the eyes of an old man, a more experienced doctor who had seen a great many more very sick patients. He stepped up to Daddy and shook his head as he came forward.

"Wha . . . what?" Daddy asked.

"I'm sorry," the young doctor said. The nurse he had been speaking to joined him.

"Momma!" My voice cracked. My tears were stinging.

"Her heart just gave out. We did the best we could, but she was so far gone with this lung congestion . . . the strain . . . it was all just too much for her," he added. "I'm sorry, Mr. Longchamp."

"My wife's . . . dead?" Daddy asked, shaking his head to deny whatever the young doctor would say. "She ain't . . ."

"I'm afraid Mrs. Longchamp passed away a little over ten minutes ago, sir," he replied.

"Nooo!" Jimmy screamed. "You're a liar, a dirty liar!"

"Jimmy," Daddy said. He tried to embrace him, but Jimmy pulled away quickly. "She ain't dead. She can't be dead. You'll see; you'll see." He started for the intensive care door again.

"Wait, son," the young doctor said. "You can't . . ."

Jimmy thrust open the door, but he didn't have to go in to see where Momma had been lying and see her bed was now empty, the mattress stripped. He stood there staring incredulously.

"Where is she?" Daddy asked softly. I embraced him around the waist and held on tightly. He had his arm around my shoulder.

"We have her down here," the doctor said, pointing to a door about halfway down the hall.

Daddy turned slowly. Jimmy came up beside him, and he reached for him. This time Jimmy didn't pull away. He drew closer to Daddy, and the three of us moved down the hallway slowly. The nurse led the way and stopped at the door.

I couldn't feel myself moving; I couldn't feel myself breathing. It was as if we had all slipped into a nightmare and were being carried away by it. We're not here, I hoped. We're not about to go into this room. It's a terrible dream. I'm home in bed; Daddy and Jimmy are home in bed.

But the nurse opened the door, and in the dimly lit room I saw Momma lying on her back, her black hair resting around her face, her arm at her sides, the palms up. Her fingers were curled inward.

"She's at peace," Daddy muttered. "Poor Sally Jean," he said and moved to the side of the gurney.

Everything in me broke loose. I cried harder than I had ever cried.

My body shook and my chest ached. Daddy took Momma's hand into his and held it and simply stared down at her. Her face looked so peaceful. No more coughing, no more struggle. When I looked at her more closely, I thought I saw a slight smile on her lips. Daddy saw it, too, and turned to me.

"She must've heard you singing, Dawn. Just before she passed on, she must've heard."

I looked at Jimmy. He was crying now, but he stood so still, his eyes firmly fixed on Momma. His tears ran down his cheeks freely and dripped off his chin. A part of him was fighting the show of emotion and a part of him was just letting go. The struggle dazed him. Then he wiped the tears away with the back of his hand and turned away. He started for the door.

"Jimmy!" I cried. "Where are you going?"

He didn't answer. He just kept walking.

"Let him be," Daddy said. "He's like my side of the family. He's got to be alone when he hurts real bad." He looked back at Momma. "Good-bye, Sally Jean. I'm sorry I wasn't more of a husband for you; sorry the dreams we started with never took shape. Maybe now you'll realize some of them." He leaned down and kissed Momma for the last time. Then he turned, put his hand around my shoulder, and started out. I wasn't sure whether he was leaning on me for support or I was leaning on him.

When we left the hospital, we looked for Jimmy, but he was nowhere in sight.

"He ain't here," Daddy said. "We might as well go home, Dawn."

Poor Jimmy, I thought. Where could he be? It wasn't right for him to be all alone now, I thought. No matter how strong the Longchamps were when it came to hard times, everyone needed comfort and love when he or she was cast so deeply into the pool of tragedy as we were. I was sure he was feeling the same deep pain I was, feeling as if his heart had been ripped out, as if he were made hollow and so weak and light, a gust of wind could wipe him away. He probably didn't care anymore, didn't care what happened to him or where he would go.

Despite his hard shell, Jimmy had always suffered something terrible whenever Momma was unhappy or sick. I knew that many times he ran off just so he wouldn't have to see her unhappy or exhausted. Perhaps he had become real acquainted with loneliness and solitude and had retreated to some dark spot to cry with his shadow. The thing was I needed him as much as I hoped he needed me.

After we had stepped out of the hospital, I noticed that all the stars were gone. Clouds had come rolling in and swept away the brightness and the light. The world was dismal, dark, somber, and unfriendly.

Daddy embraced me and we went on to the car. I rested my head against his shoulder and lay there with my eyes closed all the way home. We didn't say anything to each other until we drove down our street.

"It's Jimmy," he said as we pulled up in front of the apartment building. I sat up quickly. Jimmy was sitting on the stoop. He saw us, but he didn't get up. I got out of the car slowly and approached him.

"How did you get home, Jimmy?" I asked.

"I ran all the way," he said, looking up at me. The small light at the doorway threw enough illumination over him for me to see the redness in his face. His chest was still heaving. I could imagine just what it had been like for him running all those miles, pounding the pavement to drive away the blackbird of sorrow that had made a nest in his heart.

"We made all the arrangements, son," Daddy said. "You might as well come inside now. There ain't nothing else we can do."

"Please come inside, Jimmy," I pleaded. Daddy went to the door. Jimmy looked up at me, and then he stood up and we went into the apartment house.

Thankfully, Fern was fast asleep. Mrs. Jackson was very sympathetic and offered to come in early in the morning to help with Fern, but I told her I could do it all. I needed and wanted to keep myself busy.

After she left, the three of us stood there silently, almost as if none of us knew what to do next. Daddy went to his bedroom door, and then he broke into heavy sobbing. Jimmy looked at me and we both embraced him. We held each other tightly and cried until we were all too exhausted to stand. Never before had the three of us welcomed sleep as much.

Of course, we couldn't afford a fancy funeral. Momma was buried in a cemetery just outside of Richmond.

Some of the people Daddy worked with at the school attended, as well as Mrs. Jackson. Mr. Moore came and told me that the best thing I could do for my mother's memory was continue with my music. Philip brought Louise.

I had no idea what we would do now. The school gave Daddy a week off with pay. Daddy went over his accounts and said with a little tightening here and there we could afford to give Mrs. Jackson something to watch Fern while Jimmy and I were at school, just so we could finish off the year, but Jimmy, more than ever, didn't want to return to Emerson Peabody. We didn't have many more days to go to complete the semester. I begged Jimmy to reconsider and at least finish up, and I think he might have relented and done it, too, if we hadn't woke up one morning a few days later to a loud knocking on our door. There was something in the way the knocking echoed through our apartment that sent chills up and down my spine and made my heart pound.

It was a knocking that would change our lives forever and forever, a knocking at the door that I would hear in a thousand dreams to come, a knocking that would always wake me, no matter how deeply I slept or how comfortable I was.

I was just getting up and had put my robe on to go out to the kitchen and make breakfast. Little Fern was stirring in her crib. Although she was too young to understand the nature of the tragedy that had befallen us, she sensed some of it in our voices, in the way we moved about, and in the expression in our faces. She didn't cry as much or want to play as much, and whenever she looked for Momma and didn't find her, she would turn toward me and look at me with sad, inquisitive eyes. It made my heart sick, but I tried not to cry. She had seen enough tears.

The knocking at the door frightened her, and she pulled herself up in her crib and began to cry. I hoisted her up and into my arms.

"There, there, Fern," I cooed softly. "It's all right." I could hear Momma saying the same words to her time and time again. I squeezed Fern tightly to me and started out, just as Daddy came to his doorway. Jimmy sat up in the pull-out. We all looked at one another and then at the door.

"Who can that be this early?" Daddy muttered and ran his hand through his messed hair. He scrubbed his face with his dry palms to wake himself a bit more and then started across the living room to the doorway. I stood back beside Jimmy and waited. Fern stopped crying and turned toward the door, too.

Daddy opened the door, and we saw three men—two policemen and a man I recognized as the security guard at the hospital.

"Ormand Longchamp?" the taller of the two policemen said.

"Yeah?"

"We have a warrant for your arrest."

Daddy didn't ask what for. He stepped back and sighed as if something he had always expected had finally taken place. He lowered his head.

"I recognized him the first time I seen him at the hospital," the security guard said. "And when I heard the reward still stood—"

"Recognized who? Daddy, what is this?" I cried, my voice filled with panic.

"We're arresting this man on the charge of kidnapping," the taller policeman said.

"Kidnapping?" I looked to Jimmy.

"That's stupid," Jimmy said.

"Kidnapping? My daddy didn't kidnap anyone!" I cried. I turned back to Daddy. He still hadn't responded in his own defense. His silence frightened me. "Who could he have kidnapped?" I asked.

The security guard spoke up first. He was proud of his achievement. "Why, he kidnapped you, honey," he said.

8
DADDY . . . A KIDNAPPER?

Chilled with fear, I sat alone in a small room without windows in the police station. I couldn't stop shivering. Once in a while my teeth chattered. I embraced myself and gazed around the room. The walls were a faded beige, and there were ugly scuff marks along the bottom of the door. It looked like someone had been kicking at it, trying to get out. The room's light came from a single bulb in a silver-gray fixture dangling at the end of a chain from the center of the ceiling. The bulb threw a pale white glow over the short, rectangular light metal table and chairs.

The police had brought all of us here in two cars: a car for Daddy and a car for Jimmy, Fern, and me; but once we arrived, they separated all of us. Jimmy and I were sure this was all a terrible mistake, and soon they would realize it and return us to our home, but this was the first time I had ever been inside a police station, and I was more afraid than I'd ever been before.

Finally the door opened and a short, plump policewoman entered. She wore a uniform jacket with a dark blue skirt, a white blouse, and a dark blue tie. Her reddish-brown hair was cut short and she had bushy eyebrows. Her eyelids drooped so that she looked sleepy. She was carrying a notepad under her arm and went around the table to the other side. She sat down, put the pad on the table, and looked up at me without smiling.

"I'm Officer Carter," she said.

"Where's my little sister and where's my brother?" I demanded. I didn't care who she was. "I want to see my daddy, too," I added. "Why did you put us all into separate rooms?"

"Your daddy, as you call him, is in another room being questioned and booked for kidnapping," she said sharply. She leaned forward with both her arms on the table. "I'm going to complete our investigation, Dawn. I have some questions to ask you."

"I don't want to answer questions. I want to see my sister and my brother," I repeated petulantly. I didn't like her, and I wasn't going to pretend I did.

"Nevertheless, you will have to cooperate," she proclaimed. She straightened up sharply in her seat, bringing her shoulders back.

"It's all a mistake!" I cried. "My daddy didn't kidnap me. I've been with my momma and daddy forever and ever. They even told me how I was born and what I was like as a baby!" I exclaimed. How could she be so stupid? How could all these people make such a horrible error and not see it?

"They kidnapped you as a baby," she said and gazed down at her pad. "Fifteen years, one month and two days ago."

"Fifteen years?" I started to smile. "I'm not fifteen yet. My birthday isn't until July tenth, so you see—"

"You were born in May. They changed it as part of the cover-up of their crime," she explained, but so nonchalantly it turned my blood cold. I took a deep breath and shook my head. I was already fifteen? No, I couldn't be, none of this could be true.

"But I was born on a highway," I said, hot tears burning into my eyes. "Momma told me the whole story a hundred times. They didn't expect it, I was delivered in the back of the pickup truck. There were birds and—"

"You were born in a hospital in Virginia Beach." She gazed at her pad again. "You weighed seven pounds and eleven ounces."

I shook my head.

"I have to confirm something," she said. "Would you please unbutton your blouse and lower it."

"What?"

"No one will intrude. They know why I am in here. Please," she repeated. "If you don't cooperate," she added when I didn't move, "you will only make things harder on everyone, including Jimmy and the baby. They have to remain here until this investigation is completed."

I lowered my head. The tears were escaping now and zigzagging down my cheeks.

"Unbutton your blouse; lower it," she commanded.

"Why?" I looked up, grinding the tears away with my small fists.

"There is a small birthmark just below your left shoulder, isn't there?"

I stared at her, the cold wave rushing over me and streaming down my body, turning me into a statue made of ice.

"Yes," I said, my voice barely audible.

"Please. I have to confirm that." She stood up and came around the table.

My fingers were cold and stiff and far too clumsy to manipulate the buttons on my blouse. I fumbled and fumbled.

"Can I help you?" she offered.

"No!" I said sharply and succeeded in opening my blouse. Then I lowered it over my shoulders slowly, closing my eyes. I sobbed and sobbed. I jumped when she put her finger on my birthmark.

"Thank you," she said. "You can button your blouse again." She went back to her seat. "We have footprints to match . . . just to finish the confirmation, but Ormand Longchamp has confessed anyway."

"*No!*" I cried. I buried my face in my hands. "I don't believe it, none of it. *I can't believe it!*"

"I'm sure it's a shock to you, but you're going to have to believe it," she said firmly.

"How did all this happen?" I demanded. "How . . . Why?"

"How?" She shrugged and looked at her pad again. "Fifteen years ago, Ormand Longchamp and his wife worked at a resort in the Virginia Beach area. Sally Jean was a chambermaid, and Ormand was a handyman at this hotel. Soon after you were brought home from the hospital, Ormand and"—she looked at the pad again—"Sally Jean Longchamp stole you and a considerable amount of jewelry."

"They wouldn't do such a thing!" I moaned through my tears.

She shrugged again, her pale face indifferent, her dull eyes unfeeling, as if she had seen this happen time after time and was used to it.

"No . . . no . . . no . . ." I'm in the middle of a nightmare, I told myself. Soon it will end and I will wake up in my bed back at our apartment. Momma won't be dead, and we will all be together again. I'll hear Fern squirming in her crib, and I'll get up and make sure she's warm and comfortable. Maybe I'll peek out at Jimmy and see his head silhouetted in the darkness as he sleeps soundly on the pull-out. I'll just count to ten slowly, I told myself, and when I open my eyes . . . one . . . two . . .

"Dawn."

"Three . . . four . . . five . . ."

"Dawn, open your eyes and look at me."

"Six . . . seven . . ."

"I'm supposed to prepare you for your return to your real family now. We are going to leave the station shortly and . . ."

"Eight . . . nine . . ."

"Get into a police car."

"Ten!"

I opened my eyes, and the unobstructed harsh light burned away all hope, all dreams, all prayers. Reality came thundering down over me.

"*No!* Daddy!" I screamed. I stood up.

"Dawn, sit down."

"I want Daddy! I want to see Daddy!"

"Sit down this moment."

"Daddy!" I screamed again. She had her arms around me, holding my arms down at my sides and forcing me back into the chair.

"If you don't stop this, I'll have a straitjacket put on you and deliver you that way, do you hear?" she threatened.

The door opened and two police officers stepped in.

"Need any help?" one asked. I gazed up at them, my eyes on fire with the terror and the anger and the frustration. The younger officer looked sympathetic. He had blond hair and blue eyes and reminded me of Philip.

"Hey," he said. "Take it easy, honey."

"I've got this under control," Officer Carter replied. She didn't ease her embrace, but I let my arms relax.

"Yeah, you look like you're doing a terrific job," the younger policeman said.

She released me and stood up.

"You want to do this, Dickens?" she asked the young policeman.

I caught my breath and subdued my sobs, my shoulders heaving as I gasped for air. The young policeman looked down at me with his soft blue eyes.

"It's a raw deal for a kid this age. She's about my sister's age," he said.

"Oh, boy," Officer Carter said. "A social worker in disguise."

"We'll be right outside when you're ready," Patrolman Dickens said, and they left the room.

"I told you," Officer Carter said, "that if you aren't cooperative, you will just prolong the difficulties, especially for your stepbrother and stepsister. Now, are you going to behave, or do I have to leave you in here for a few hours thinking about it?"

"I want to go home," I moaned.

"You are going home, to your real home and your real parents."

I shook my head.

"I need to do that footprint now," she said. "Take off your shoes and socks."

I sat back in my chair and closed my eyes.

"Damn," I heard her say and a moment later felt her taking off my shoes. I didn't resist, nor did I open my eyes. I was determined to keep them closed until all this had ended.

Some time later, when it was all over, the two policemen who had been waiting outside returned and stood by as Officer Carter completed her report. She looked up from her notepad.

"The captain wants us to get started," Patrolman Dickens announced.

"Terrific," Officer Carter said. "You want to go to the bathroom, Dawn? This is the time."

"Where are we going?" I asked, my voice seemingly drifting away from me. I felt as if I were floating. I was in a daze, time and place were lost. I had even forgotten my name.

"You're going home, to your real family," she replied.

"Come on, honey," Patrolman Dickens said, taking my arm gently and helping me to my feet. "Go on. Use the bathroom and wash your face. You have funny little streaks across your cheeks from crying, and I know once you wash them off, you'll feel better."

I looked at his warm smile and kind eyes. Where was Daddy? Where was Jimmy? I wanted to hold Fern in my arms and kiss her soft, pudgy cheeks until they were red. I would never complain about her whining and crying again. In fact, I wanted to hear her whine. I wanted to hear her chanting: "Dawn, up. Dawn, up," and see her reaching for me.

"This way, honey," the patrolman said. He directed me toward the bathroom. I washed my face. The cold water on my cheeks did restore some of my energy and awareness. After I had used the bathroom, I came out and looked at the policemen expectantly.

Suddenly another door across the hall opened, and I saw Daddy sitting in a chair, his head down to his chest.

Daddy! I screamed and ran toward the opened door. Daddy lifted his head and gazed out at me, his eyes vacant. It was as though he were hypnotized and didn't see me standing there. "Daddy, tell them this isn't true; tell them it's all been a horrible mistake." He started to speak to me, but shook his head and looked down instead.

"Daddy!" I screamed again when I felt someone's hands on my shoulders. *"Please, don't let them take us all away!"*

Why wasn't he doing anything? Why didn't he show some of his temper and strength? How could he let this go on?

"Come on, Dawn," I heard someone say behind me. The door to the room Daddy was in started to close. He looked up at me.

"I'm sorry, honey," he whispered. "I'm so sorry."

Then the door was closed.

"Sorry?" I pulled out of the grip on my shoulders and pounded on the door. *"Sorry? Daddy? You didn't do what they said, you didn't!"*

The grip on my shoulders was firmer this time. Officer Dickens pulled me back.

"Let's go, Dawn. You've got to go."

I turned and looked into his face, the tears streaming down my own.

"Why didn't he help me? Why did he just sit there?" I asked.

"Because he's guilty, honey. I'm sorry. You've got to go now. Come on."

I looked back at the closed door once. It felt as if I had a hole in my chest where my heart had been. My throat ached and my legs felt wobbly. Officer Dickens practically carried me to the front door of the police station, where Officer Carter was waiting with my little suitcase.

"I threw whatever I thought was yours into this suitcase," she explained. "There didn't seem to be that much."

I stared down at it. My little suitcase, how I used to take such care packing it so I could get everything I owned into it for our frequent journeys from one world to another. Suddenly panic seized my heart. I went to my knees and opened it to search the little compartment. When my fingers found Momma's picture, I breathed relief. I cradled it in my hands and then pressed it to my bosom. Then I stood up. They started me forward again.

"Wait," I said stopping. "Where's Jimmy?"

"He's already gone to a home for wayward children until he gets placed," Officer Carter said.

"Placed? Placed where?" I asked frantically.

"With a foster family who might adopt him," she said.

"And Fern?" I held my breath.

"Same thing," she said. "Let's go. We have a long ride."

Jimmy and little Fern must be so frightened, not knowing what lay

ahead of them. Was this all my fault—all because of me? Fern had been
calling out for Momma, and now she would be calling out for me.

"But when will I see them? How will I see them?" I looked to Patrolman Dickens. He shook his head. "Jimmy . . . Fern . . . I must see
them . . . please."

"It's too late. They're gone," Patrolman Dickens said softly. I shook
my head. Officer Carter moved me forward to the waiting patrol car.
Patrolman Dickens took my suitcase from her and put it into the car
trunk. Then he got in behind the steering wheel quickly, and the other
policeman opened the rear door for me and Officer Carter. He didn't
say anything.

Officer Carter directed me into the backseat. Between the backseat
and the front seat was a metal grate, and the doors had no handles on
them. I couldn't get out until someone opened the doors. I was like a
criminal being transported from one jail to another. Officer Carter was
on my right and the second patrolman was on my left.

The speed with which it was all happening kept me in a daze. I didn't
start to cry again until the patrol car shot off and I realized Daddy,
Jimmy and Fern were really gone and I was all alone, being carried off
to another family and another life. A panic came over me when I understood what was about to happen. When would I ever see Daddy again,
or Jimmy, or little Fern?

"It isn't fair," I muttered. "This isn't fair." Officer Carter heard me.

"Imagine how your real parents must have felt when they discovered
you were missing—that their employees had taken you and run off?
Think that was fair?"

I stared at her and shook my head. "It's a mistake," I muttered.

How could my daddy and mommy have done such a terrible thing to
someone? Daddy . . . steal me from another family? Not care about
that mother's sorrow and that father's pain?

And Momma with all her stories and memories of us growing up
. . . Momma working so hard so that we would have enough . . .
Momma getting sicker and thinner, but not caring about herself as long
as Jimmy and I and Fern had clothes to wear and food to eat. Momma
knew sorrow and tragedy from her own life. How could she hurt some
other Momma?

"There's no mistake, Dawn," Officer Carter said dryly. Then she
repeated, "Dawn," and shook her head. "I wonder what they'll do
about that?"

"What?" My heart started to pound again. It was thumping like a drum in a marching band, the throb pulsating all through my body.

"Your name. That's not your real name. They stole you after you had been brought home and you had already been named."

"What's my name?" I asked. I felt like an amnesiac slowly regaining her memory, returning from a world where everyone's face was blank, just eyes, a nose, and a mouth, like faces etched on white paper.

Officer Carter opened her notebook and turned a few pages.

"Eugenia," she replied after a moment. "Maybe you're better off being Dawn," she added dryly and started to close her notebook again.

"Eugenia? Eugenia what?"

"Oh, how stupid of me to not give you all of it." She opened her notebook again. "Eugenia Grace Cutler," she declared.

My thumping heart stopped.

"Cutler? You didn't say Cutler?"

"Yes, I did. You're the daughter of Randolph Boyse Cutler and Laura Sue Cutler. Actually, honey, you're going to be pretty well off. Your parents own a famous resort, the Cutler's Cove Hotel."

"Oh, no!" I cried. It couldn't be! It just couldn't be!

"Don't be so upset. You could be a lot worse off."

"You don't understand," I said, thinking of Philip. "I can't be a Cutler. I can't!"

"Oh, yes, you can and yes, you are. It's about as confirmed as it could be."

I couldn't speak. I sat back, feeling as if I had been punched in the stomach. Philip was my brother. Those resemblances between us that I had thought were wonderful, that I had thought had been planted by destiny to bring us together as boyfriend and girlfriend instead were brother and sister resemblances.

And Clara Sue . . . horrible Clara Sue . . . was my sister! Fate was forcing me to trade Jimmy and Fern for Philip and Clara Sue.

So much of what had been a mystery to me in the past was now falling in place. No wonder Momma and Daddy never wanted to return to their families. They knew they were being hunted as criminals and must have expected the police would search for them there. And now I understood why Momma cried out to me from her hospital bed after I told her Philip was taking me to the concert. I could see why she said, "You must never think badly of us. We love you. Always remember that."

It was all true. My stubborn insistence that it was not would have to

be put aside. I would have to face it, even though I could not understand it. Would I ever?

I sat back and closed my eyes again. I was so tired. The crying, the
pain, the agony of leaving Jimmy and Fern and Daddy behind, Momma's death, and now this news weighed down on me. I felt drained,
listless, a shell of myself. My body had been turned into smoke, and I
was caught in a breeze that was carrying me wherever it wanted.

Jimmy's face and Fern's face fell away, peeling off like leaves blown
from tree limbs. I could barely see them anymore.

The patrol car rushed on, carrying us toward my new family and my
new life.

The trip seemed to take forever. By the time we arrived in Virginia
Beach, the cloudy night sky had cleared a little bit. Stars peeked out
through every available opening, but I took no comfort in their twinkling. Suddenly they seemed more like frozen tears, tiny drops of ice
melting very slowly out of a black and dismal sky.

For most of the ride the police officers had talked to each other and
rarely said anything to me. They barely looked at me. Never had I felt
so alone and lost. I dozed on and off, but I welcomed sleep because it
was a short escape from the horror of what was happening. Every time
I woke, I held on to some hope for an instant, hope this had all been a
dream. But the dreary sound of the car tires, the dark night washing
past the windows, and the quiet conversation of the police officers
brought home the terrible reality time after time.

I couldn't help but be curious about the new world I had been liter-
ally dragged into, but they were going so fast, buildings and people
whizzed by before I could absorb what I had seen. In moments we were
on a highway and away from the busier areas. I knew the ocean was just
out there in the darkness somewhere, so I studied the scenery until the
land gave way to a vast mirrored sea of dark blue. In the distance I
could see the tiny lights of fishing boats and even pleasure ships. Shortly
after that the coastline of Virginia Beach itself was announced by a road
sign and in moments, we were driving through the seaside resort with
its neon lights, its restaurants, motels and hotels.

Soon I caught sight of a large road sign that indicated we were about
to enter Cutler's Cove. It wasn't much of a village, just a long street
with all sorts of small stores and restaurants. I couldn't see much because we passed through it so quickly, but what I did see looked quaint
and cozy.

"According to our directions, it's just up here," Officer Dickens said.

I thought about Philip, who was still back at school, and wondered if he had been told any of this yet. Perhaps his parents had phoned him. How had he taken the news? Surely he was just as confused by the lightning revelations.

"Looks real nice for a new start," the policeman next to me said, finally acknowledging what we were doing and why we were in the car heading for the Cutler's Cove Hotel.

"That's for sure," Officer Carter said.

"There it is," Officer Dickens announced, and I sat forward.

The coastline curved inward at this point, and I saw that there was a beautiful length of sandy white beach that sparkled as if it had been combed clean. Even the waves that came up came up softly, tenderly, as if the ocean were afraid of doing any damage. As we passed the entrance to the beach, I spotted a sign that read, RESERVED FOR CUTLER COVE HOTEL GUESTS ONLY. Then the patrol car turned right up a long drive, and I saw the hotel ahead, sitting on a little rise, the manicured grounds gently rolling down before it.

It was an enormous three-story Wedgwood blue mansion with milk-white shutters and a large wraparound porch. Most of the rooms were lit up, and there were Japanese lanterns along the top of the porch and above the spiraling stairway built out of bleached wood. The foundation was made from polished stone. Bathed in the ground lights, it sparkled as if it had been built out of pearls. Guests were meandering about the beautiful grounds upon which there were two small gazebos; wooden and stone benches and tables; fountains, some shaped like large fish, some simple saucers with spouts in the middle; and gardens full of beautiful flowers capturing almost all the colors of the rainbow. The walkways were bordered with short hedges and lit by well-spaced footlights.

"Somewhat better than what you've been used to, huh?" Officer Carter said. I just glared at her. How could she be so callous? I didn't answer her; I turned away and gazed out the window as the patrol car wound its way around the circular drive.

"Keep going," Officer Carter said. "Round back. That's where we were told to go."

Round back? I thought. Where were my new parents, my real parents? Why hadn't they rushed to Richmond to claim me instead of having policemen bring me as if I were a criminal? Weren't they excited about meeting me? Perhaps they were as nervous about it as I was. I wondered if Philip had told them things about me. Had Clara Sue? She would get them to hate me for sure.

The patrol car stopped, but my heart wouldn't stop pounding, thumping against my chest as if there were a tiny little drummer inside me beating his drumsticks against my bones. I could barely breathe, and I couldn't stop trembling. Oh, Momma, I thought, if you hadn't gotten sick and been taken to the hospital, I wouldn't be here now. Why was fate so cruel? This can't be happening; you and Daddy just couldn't have been baby kidnappers. There has to be another explanation, one my true parents might know and be willing to tell me. Please let it be so, I prayed.

As soon as we stopped, Officer Dickens got out quickly and opened the door for us.

"After I get them to sign this," Officer Carter said, indicating papers on her clipboard, "I'll come right out."

Sign this? I thought, looking at the document. I was being treated as if I were something delivered and actually taken to the delivery entrance.

I stood there, staring at the back entrance of the hotel. All it was was a small door with a screen door. There were four wooden steps leading up to it. Officer Carter started toward the door, but I didn't follow. I stood there holding my suitcase.

"Come along," she commanded. She saw my hesitation and put her hands on her hips. "This is your home, your real family. Let's go," she snapped and reached out to take my hand.

"Good luck, Dawn," Officer Dickens called.

Officer Carter tugged me, and I followed her to the door. Suddenly it was opened and a nearly baldheaded, tall man, with skin so pale he could be an undertaker, stood looking out at us. He was dressed in a dark blue sport jacket, matching tie, white shirt, and slacks. He stood at least six feet tall. As we drew closer, I saw he had bushy eyebrows, a long mouth with thin lips, and a nose that was an eagle's beak. Could this be my real father? He looked nothing like me.

"Please come right this way," he said, stepping back. "Mrs. Cutler is awaiting you in her office. My name is Collins. I'm the maître d'," he added. He looked at me with curious dark brown eyes, but he did not smile. He gestured ahead with his long arm and long, slightly brown fingers, moving so gracefully and quietly it was as if he moved in slow motion.

Officer Carter nodded and headed down the short, narrow entryway that brought us to what was obviously the rear of the kitchen where the storage rooms were. Some doors were opened, and I saw cartons of canned goods and boxes of grocery items. Collins pointed to the left when we reached the end of the corridor.

Why were they sneaking me in? I wondered. We turned a corner and moved down another long hallway.

"I hope we get there before I have to retire from the police force," Officer Carter quipped.

"Just right down here," Collins replied.

Finally he stopped at a door and knocked softly.

"Come in," I heard a firm female voice say. Collins opened the door and peered inside.

"They've arrived," he announced.

"Show them in," the woman said. Was it my mother?

Collins stepped back so we could enter. Officer Carter walked in first, and I followed slowly. We were in an office. I looked around. There was a pleasant lilac scent, but I saw no flowers. The room had an austere and simple look. The floor had hardwood slats that were probably the original floor. There was a tightly woven dark blue oval rug in front of the aqua chintz settee, which was at right angles to the large, dark oak desk on which everything was neatly arranged. Presently, the only light in the room came from a small lamp on the desk. It cast an eerie yellowish glow over the face of the elderly woman who gazed at us.

Even though she was seated, I could see that she was a tall, stately looking woman with steel-blue hair cut and styled in soft waves that curled under her ears and just at the base of her neck. Pear-shaped diamond earrings dangled from each lobe. She wore a matching pear-shaped diamond necklace set in gold. Although she was thin and probably didn't weigh more than one hundred and fifteen pounds, she looked so stern and secure, she seemed much larger. Her shoulders were pulled back in the bright blue cotton jacket she wore over her white frilly collar blouse.

"I'm Officer Carter and this is Dawn," Officer Carter said quickly.

"What has to be done?" the elderly woman, who I thought must be my real grandmother, demanded.

"I need this signed."

"Let me see it," my grandmother said and put on her pearl-framed glasses. She read the document quickly and then signed it.

"Thank you," Officer Carter said. "Well." She looked at me. "I'll be on my way. Good luck," she muttered and left the office.

Without speaking to me, my grandmother rose and came around her desk. I saw she wore an ankle-length matching blue skirt and eggshell-white leather shoes designed for someone who had to do a great deal of walking. They looked more like men's shoes. The only imperfection in her appearance, if it could be called that, was a slight roll in her nylon stocking on her right foot.

She turned on a pole lamp in the corner, so that there was more light, and then with her stone-cold gray eyes she stood staring at me for a long moment. I searched her face for evidence of myself and thought my grandmother's mouth was firmer and longer than mine and her eyes didn't show a trace of blue.

Her complexion was almost as smooth and as perfect as a marble statue's. There was just a tiny brown age spot on the top of her right cheek. She wore a touch of rose-red lipstick and just a brush of rouge on her cheeks. Not a strand of her hair was out of place.

Now that there was more light in the room, I gazed about and saw the walls were paneled in rich wood. There was a small bookcase behind and to the right of the desk. But above the rear wall was a large portrait of who I thought had to be my real grandfather.

"You have your mother's face," she declared. Queenly stiff, she moved behind her impressively wide desk. "Childlike," she added, disdainfully, I thought. There was just the slightest lift in the corner of her mouth when she ended her sentences. "Sit down," she snapped. After I had done so, she crossed her arms over her small bosom and leaned back in her chair, but kept her posture so straight I thought her back was a sheet of cold steel.

"I understand your parents have been drifters all these years and your father never settled on a solid job anywhere," she declared harshly. I was surprised she had called them my parents, and had referred to Daddy as my father.

"Worthless," she continued. "I knew it the day I set eyes on him, but my husband had a soft spot for lost souls and hired him and his ragtag wife," she said with disgust.

"Momma wasn't a ragtag wife!" I snapped back.

She didn't reply. She stared at me again, delving into the depths of my eyes as if to drink up my essence. I was beginning to get very upset with the way she glared at me, studying me as if she were searching for something in my face, looking me over with very interested gimlet eyes.

"You don't have the nicest manners," she finally replied. She had a habit of nodding after saying anything she thought was absolutely true. "Weren't you ever taught to respect your elders?"

"I respect people who respect me," I said.

"You have to earn respect. And I must say you have not yet earned it. I can see you will have to be retrained, redeveloped; in a word, brought up properly," she proclaimed with a power and an arrogance that made my head spin. As small-framed as she was, she had the strongest gaze I had ever seen a woman have, much sterner and stronger than even Mrs. Turnbell's frightening green look. These eyes were piercing, cold, so sharp they could cut and draw blood.

"Did the Longchamps ever tell you anything about this hotel or this family?" she demanded.

"No, nothing," I replied. The tears in my eyes burned, but I wouldn't let her see how painful they were or how horrible she was making me feel. "Maybe this is all a mistake," I added, even though I harbored little hope after seeing Daddy at the police station. I sensed if it were somehow a mistake, she would be able to correct it. She looked like she had the power to rearrange time.

"No, no mistake," she said, sounding almost as sad about it as I was. "I'm told you're a good student in school despite the life you've been leading. Is that so?"

"Yes."

She sat forward, resting her hands on the top of the desk. She had long thin fingers. A gold watch with a large face dangled loosely on her tiny wrist. It, too, looked like something a man would wear.

"Since the school year is just about over, we won't bother to send you back to Emerson Peabody. It's all been somewhat embarrassing for us anyway, and I don't think it would do either Philip or Clara Sue any good if you returned under these conditions. We have time to decide what to do about your schooling. The season has begun and there is much to do here," she said. I glanced at the door, wondering where my real father and mother were and why they were leaving all these decisions up to her.

I had always dreamt about meeting my grandparents, but my real grandmother didn't fit any of my visions. This wasn't the kind of grandmother who made cookies and comforted me when life was hard. This wasn't the soft and lovable grandmother of my dreams, the grandmother I had imagined would teach me things about life and love and cherish me as much as she did her own daughter, love me even more.

"You will have to learn all about the hotel, from the ground up," my grandmother lectured. "No one is permitted to be lazy here. Hard work makes good character, and I'm sure you need hard work. I have already spoken to my house manager about you, and we have let one of our chambermaids go to provide a position for you."

"Chambermaid?" That's what Momma had done here, I thought. Why did my grandmother want me to do the same thing?

"You're not a long-lost princess, you know," she said curtly. "You're to become part of this family again, even though you were part of it only for a short while, and to do so properly you will have to learn all about our business and our way of life. Each one of us works here, and you will be no exception. I expect you're a lazy thing," she continued, "considering—"

"I am not lazy. I can work just as hard as you can or anyone can," I declared.

"We'll see," she said. She nodded slightly, staring at me intently again. "I've already discussed your living arrangements with Mrs. Boston. She is in charge of our quarters. She will be here momentarily to show you your room. I will expect you to keep it neat and tidy. Just because we have a servant looking after our rooms doesn't mean we can be sloppy and disorganized."

"I've never been sloppy, and I've always helped Momma clean and organize our apartments," I said.

"Momma? Oh . . . yes . . . well, let that be the rule and not the exception." She paused, almost smiling, I thought, because of the way she lifted the corners of her mouth.

"Where are my father and mother?" I asked.

"Your mother," she said, making the word sound obscene, "is having another one of her emotional breakdowns . . . conveniently," Grandmother Cutler said. "Your father will see you shortly. He's very busy, very busy." She sighed deeply and shook her head. "This situation is not easy for any of us. And it has all occurred at the wrong time," she said, making me feel as if I were to blame for Daddy having been recognized and the police finding me. "We are right in the middle of the start of a new season. Don't expect anyone to have time to cater to you. Do your work, keep your room clean, and listen and learn. Do you have any questions?" she asked, but before I could respond, there was a knock on the door.

"Come in," she called and the door was opened by a pleasant-looking black woman. She had her hair pinned up neatly and tied in a bun. She wore a white cotton chambermaid's uniform with white stockings and black shoes. She was a small woman, barely my height.

"Oh, Mrs. Boston. This is . . ." My grandmother paused and looked at me as if I had just come in. "Yes," she said, listening to a voice only she could hear, "what about your name? It's a silly name. We'll have to call you by your real name, of course . . . Eugenia. Anyway, you were named after one of my sisters who had passed away from smallpox when she was no older than you are."

"My name is not silly, and I don't want to change it!" I cried. Her eyes shifted quickly from me to Mrs. Boston and then back to me.

"Members of the Cutler family do not have nicknames," she replied firmly. "They have names that distinguish them, names that bring them respect."

"I thought respect was something that had to be earned," I whiplashed. She pulled herself back as if I had slapped her.

"You will be called Eugenia as long as you live here," she declared firmly. Her voice was cold and uncaring, as if I were without ears to hear.

"Show *Eugenia*," my grandmother said, "her room, Mrs. Boston. And"—she gazed at me quickly, a look of disgust on her face—"take her the back way."

"Yes, ma'am." Mrs. Boston looked to me.

"My name fits me," I said, unable to hold back my tears now and recalling how many times Daddy had told me about my birth, "because I was born at the break of day." Surely that couldn't have been a lie, too, not the story about the birds and the music and my singing.

My grandmother smiled so coldly it sent a chill up my spine.

"You were born in the middle of the night."

"No," I protested. "That's not true."

"Believe me," she said. "I know what is true and what is not true about you." She leaned forward, her eyes appearing long and catlike. "For your whole life you've lived in a world of lies and fantasy. I told you," she continued, "we don't have time to cater to you and pretend. We're in the middle of the season. Now, pull yourself together immediately. Members of the family do not show their emotions or their problems to the guests. As far as the guests are concerned, everything is always wonderful here. I don't want you going out and through the lobby crying hysterically, Eugenia.

"I have to return to the dining room," my grandmother said, rising. She came around her desk and paused before Mrs. Boston. "After you show her to her room, take her to the kitchen and get her something to eat. She can eat with the kitchen staff," she said. "Then take her to Mr. Stanley so he can find her a chambermaid's uniform. I'd like her to begin work tomorrow."

She turned back to me, pulling her shoulders back and holding her head so high, it was as if she were looking down at me from a great height. Despite my desire to do so, I couldn't look away. Her eyes pulled and held mine fixed in her glare.

"You are to get up at seven A.M. promptly, Eugenia, and go to the kitchen for your breakfast. Then report directly to Mr. Stanley, our house manager, and he will assign you your duties. Is that all clear?" she asked. I didn't respond. She turned to Mrs. Boston. "See that she remembers all this," she added and walked out.

Although the door clicked softly closed, it sounded like a gunshot to me.

Welcome to your real family and real home, Dawn, I told myself.

9
MY NEW LIFE

"Grab your suitcase and follow me, Eugenia," Mrs. Boston commanded in a tone of voice my grandmother had been using.

"My name is Dawn," I declared firmly.

"If Mrs. Cutler wants you called Eugenia, that's what you'll be called here. Cutler's Cove is her kingdom and she's the queen. Don't expect nobody to go against her wishes, not even your daddy," Mrs. Boston added and then widened her eyes and leaned toward me to whisper, "And especially not your mother."

I turned away and quickly wiped the tears from my eyes. What sort of people were my real parents? How could they be so afraid of my grandmother? Why weren't they dying of curiosity about me and making it their business to see me right away?

Mrs. Boston led me out the rear door and down the dimly lit corridor that ran behind the kitchen.

"Where are we going now?" I asked. I was tired of being dragged around like some stray dog.

"The family lives in the old section of the hotel," Mrs. Boston explained as we walked.

When we paused at the end of the corridor, I was able to see the hotel lobby. It was lit by four large chandeliers and had a light blue carpet and pearl-white papered walls with a blue pattern. Behind the reception counter were two middle-aged women greeting guests. All were quite well dressed, the men in suits and jackets, the women in pretty dresses and bedecked with jewels. Once they entered the lobby, they milled about in small groups chatting.

I caught sight of my grandmother standing by the dining room entrance. She glanced our way once, her eyes like ice, but as soon as some guests approached, her face brightened and softened. One woman held on to her hand as they spoke. They kissed each other, and then my grandmother followed all the guests toward the dining room, throwing a gaze like a snowball back at us before disappearing into the dining room herself.

"Let's move along . . . quickly," Mrs. Boston said urgently, stung by my grandmother's sharp, cold look. We turned down a long corridor and finally reached what was clearly the older section of the hotel.

We passed a sitting room that had a fieldstone fireplace and warm-looking antique furniture—soft cushion chairs in hand-carved wood frames, a dark pine rocking chair, a thick cushioned couch with pine-wood end tables and a thick, eggshell-white rug. I saw that there were many paintings on the walls, and there were pictures and knickknacks on the mantel above the fireplace. I thought I glimpsed a picture of Philip standing beside the woman who must be our mother, but I couldn't pause long enough to see her clearly. Mrs. Boston was practically trotting.

"Most of the bedrooms are on the second floor, but there is one bedroom downstairs off the small kitchen. Mrs. Cutler told me that one's to be yours," she said.

"What was it, a servant's bedroom?" I asked. Mrs. Boston didn't respond. "After I earn respect, I will be able to sleep upstairs," I grumbled. I don't know if Mrs. Boston heard me or not. If she had, she didn't acknowledge it.

We went through the small kitchen and then passed through a short hallway to my bedroom on the right. The door was opened. Mrs. Boston turned on the light as we entered.

It was a very small room with a single bed against the wall on the left. The bed had a simple light-brown headboard. At the foot of the bed was a slightly stained cream-colored oval rug. There was a single-drawer night table beside the bed with a lamp on it. To the right was a dresser and a closet, and directly ahead of us was the room's only window. Right now I couldn't tell what the window looked out on, for it was dark and there were no lights at this side of the hotel grounds. The window had no curtains, just a pale yellow shade.

"Do you want to put your things away now, or would you rather go to the kitchen and get something to eat?" she asked. I placed my little suitcase on the bed and looked around sadly.

There were many times we had moved into an apartment so small that Jimmy and I didn't have much more room than this to share, but somehow, because I was with a loving family, because I was with people who cared about me and about whom I cared, the size of my room didn't matter as much. We made do, and besides, I had to keep a cheerful face to help keep Jimmy cheerful and Daddy happy. But there was no one to keep happy here, no one to care about right now but myself.

"I'm not hungry," I said. My heart felt like an iron weight, and my stomach was all twisted and tight.

"Well . . . Mrs. Cutler wanted you to eat," she said and looked troubled. "I'll stop by later and take you to the kitchen," she decided, nodding. "But don't forget, I got to bring you to Mr. Stanley and get you a uniform. Mrs. Cutler told us."

"How could I forget?" I said. She stared at me a moment and pressed her lips together firmly. Why was she so annoyed with me? I wondered. Then it occurred to me—my grandmother had said she had let someone go to make a position for me.

"Who was fired so I could have this job?" I asked quickly. The expression on Mrs. Boston's face confirmed my suspicions.

"Agatha Johnson, who had been working here five years."

"I'm sorry," I said. "I certainly didn't want her fired."

"Nevertheless, that poor girl is gone and walking the streets looking for something new. And she got a little boy to raise," she said with disgust.

"Well, why did she have to fire her? Couldn't she keep her on along with me?" I asked. My grandmother had put me in a horrible position, fixing it so the help would resent me for being discovered and returned as much as she apparently did.

"Mrs. Cutler runs a very tight ship," Mrs. Boston said. "No excess, no waste. Whoever don't pull his load goes. She got just as many chambermaids as she needs, just as many waiters and busboys, just as many kitchen help and service people. Not a single one more. That's why this hotel goes on and on while other places have peeled off over the years."

"Well, I'm sorry," I repeated.

"Um," she said, still without much sympathy. "I'll be back in a while," she added and left.

I sat down on the bed. The mattress was old and had lost any firmness it might have had and the springs squeaked with complaint. Even my little weight was too much. I took a deep breath and opened my suitcase. The sight of my simple belongings brought back a flood of memories and feelings. How my heart ached. The tears started to flow. I sat there and let them run down my cheeks and drip off my chin. Then I saw something white peeking out of the cloth pocket inside my suitcase. I reached inside and pulled out Momma's wonderful string of pearls. They had been in my dresser drawer at home—because of the confusion after the concert and Momma's death, I had never given them back to Daddy to put away. The policeman who had packed my bag must have thought they were mine. Now I hugged them to me, crying ten oceans of tears as memories came crashing over me, dragging me down to drown within their depths. How I longed for Momma now to hold me and stroke my hair, to see Jimmy's face full of pride and anger, to have Fern's eyes light up at the sight of me and her little arms reach up to be held. The pearls brought back all of this and more till my heart was an aching ruin.

Daddy, how could you do this? How could you do this? I screamed inside.

Suddenly there was a knock on my door. I quickly hid the pearls in a drawer, wiped my face with the back of my hands, and turned.

"Who is it?"

The door opened slowly and a handsome man dressed in a tan sport jacket and matching slacks peered in. His light brown hair was brushed back neatly at the sides, but he had a small, soft wave in the front. There was a tinge of gray at his temples. His rich, dark tan emphasized the blue in his eyes. I thought he looked as debonair and as elegant as a movie star.

"Hello," he said, gazing in at me. I didn't respond. "I'm your father," he said as if I should have known. He stepped in. "Randolph Boyse Cutler." He held out his hand for me to shake. I couldn't imagine ever being introduced to Daddy and shaking his hand like a stranger. Daddies were supposed to hug their daughters, not shake their hands.

I gazed up at him. He was tall, at least six feet two or three, but he was slim. He had Philip's gentle smile and soft mouth. Everyone was telling me that the man standing before me was my real father, so I searched for resemblances to myself. Had I inherited his eyes? His smile?

"Welcome to Cutler's Cove," he said squeezing my fingers gently. "How was your trip?"

"My trip?" He was acting as though I had been away for a holiday or something. I was about to say, "Horrible," when he spoke.

"Philip has already told me a lot about you," he said.

"Philip?" Just pronouncing his name brought tears to my eyes. It took me back to the world I had been ripped from, a world that had begun to be friendly and wonderful before Momma's death, a world full of stars and hope and kisses that carried promises of love.

"He told me about your beautiful singing voice. I can't wait to hear you sing," he said.

I couldn't see myself ever singing again, for my singing came from my heart, and my heart had been shattered into so many pieces, it would never be strong again and certainly it would never be filled with music.

"I'm glad to see you're such a pretty girl, too. Something else Philip warned me about. Your mother's going to be pleased," he said and looked at his watch as if he had a train to catch.

"Naturally, this has all been something of an emotional shock for her, so I'll have to take you to see her tomorrow sometime. She's under some medication, in her doctor's care, and he advises us to go slowly. You can imagine what it was like for her to learn that the baby she had lost fifteen years ago had been found, but I'm sure she's as excited about finally seeing you as I have been," he added quickly.

"Where is she now?" I asked, thinking she might be in a hospital. Even though I hated being here, I couldn't help but be curious about her and what she looked like.

"In her room, resting."

She was in her room? I thought. Why wasn't she excited about seeing me? How could she put it off?

"In a day or so, when I get some free time, I would like to spend some of it with you and let you tell me what your life has been like up until now, okay?"

I looked down so he wouldn't see the way my eyes had filled with tears.

"I imagine all this must have come as a terrible shock, but in time we'll make it all up to you," he said.

Make it up to me? How could anyone do that?

"I want to find out what happened to my baby sister and my brother," I heard myself say before I even realized I was going to say the words. He pressed his lips in and shook his head.

"That's out of our hands. They're not really your brother and sister, so we don't have any right to demand information about them. I'm afraid you will have to forget them."

"I'll never forget them! Never!" I cried. "And I don't want to be here.

I don't, I don't . . ." I started to sob. I couldn't help it. The tears overflowed my lids and my shoulders shook.

"There, there. Everything will be fine," he said, touching my shoulder tentatively and then pulling back as if he had done something forbidden.

This man, my real father, was suave and handsome, but he was still a stranger. There was a wall between us, a thick wall, not only built out of time and distance, but built out of two entirely different ways of life. I felt like a visitor in a foreign land with no one to trust and no one to help me understand the strange new customs and ways.

I took a deep breath and fumbled through my purse for a tissue.

"Here," he said, obviously anxious to do something. He handed me his soft silk handkerchief. I wiped my eyes quickly.

"Mother has told me about your first meeting and how she intends to take a special interest in you. With all she has to do around here, you should be flattered," he added. "When Mother takes personal interest in someone, he or she usually succeeds."

He paused, maybe to hear me say how grateful I was, but I wasn't and I wouldn't lie.

"My mother was the first to learn about you, but she's usually the first to learn about anything around here," he continued. Perhaps he's as nervous as I am, I thought, and has to keep talking. He shook his head and widened his smile. "She never thought she would have to pay out the reward money and, like the rest of us, had given up all hope long ago."

"Well," he said, looking at his watch again. "I've got to return to the dining room. Mother and I visit with the guests at dinner. Most of our guests are regulars who return year after year. Mother knows them all by name. She has a wonderful memory for faces and names. I can't keep up with her."

Whenever he spoke about his mother, his face brightened. Was this the same elderly woman who had greeted me with eyes of ice and words of fire?

There was a knock on the door, and Mrs. Boston appeared.

"Oh," she said, "I didn't know you was here, Mr. Cutler."

"That's all right, Mrs. Boston. I was just leaving."

"I come to see if Eugenia wanted something to eat yet."

"Eugenia? Oh, right. I had forgotten your real name for a moment," he said, smiling.

"I hate it!" I cried. "I don't want to change my name."

"Of course you don't," he said. I breathed relief until he added, "Right now. But after a while I'm sure Mother will convince you. One way or another she usually gets people to see what would be best."

"I won't change my name," I insisted.

"We'll see," he replied, obviously unconvinced. He looked around the room. "Do you need anything?"

Need anything? I thought. Yes. I need my old family back. I need people who really love me and really care about me and who don't look at me as if I were some unwashed and polluted person who could contaminate them and their precious world. I need to sleep where my family sleeps, and if the woman upstairs is my real mother, I need her to treat me like her real daughter and not have to have doctors and medicine before she can face me.

I need to go back to the way things were, as bad as they seemed. I need to hear Jimmy's voice and be able to call him through the darkness and share my fears and my hopes with him. I need my little sister calling for me, and I need a daddy who comes to greet me with a hug and a kiss—not one who stands in the doorway and tells me I have to change my name.

But there was no point in telling my real father any of this. I didn't think he would understand.

"No," I said.

"Okay, then, you should go with Mrs. Boston and eat something. Take her right along, Mrs. Boston," he said, heading out. He turned back to me. "I'll speak to you again soon," he said and left.

"I'm not hungry," I repeated as soon as he was gone.

"You got to eat something, child," she said. "And you got to do it now. We have a schedule to meet. Mrs. Cutler, she cracks a whip around here."

I saw she wasn't going to leave me alone, so I stood up and followed her back to the hotel and to the kitchen. When we reached the stairway, I looked up. My real mother was up there somewhere, in her room, unable to face seeing me yet. The very idea made it sound like I was a monster with fangs and claws. What would she be like when we finally did meet? Would she be more loving and thoughtful than my grandmother? Would she insist I be moved upstairs immediately so I could be near her?

"Come along," Mrs. Boston said, seeing I had paused.

"Mrs. Boston," I said, still gazing up the stairs, "if you call my

grandmother Mrs. Cutler, what do you call my mother? Doesn't everyone get confused?"

"No one gets confused."

"Why not?"

She gazed upstairs to be sure no one was near us and could overhear.
Then she leaned toward me and whispered.

"They call your mother little Mrs. Cutler," she said. "Now, let's go.
We got lots to do."

The kitchen seemed like bedlam to me. The waiters and waitresses
who served the guests in the dining room were lined up in front of a
long table to pick up their trays of food.

The food was delicious, but Mrs. Boston stood behind me waiting
impatiently for me to finish. As soon as I rose from the table, we were
off to see Mr. Stanley.

He was a slim man about fifty with thin brown hair and a narrow face
with small eyes and a long mouth. There was something birdlike about
him and the way he moved in short, jerky motions. He stood back with
his arms folded and considered me after Mrs. Boston had introduced
us.

"Hmm," he said, his head bobbing. "She could fit into Agatha's old
uniform."

I wanted Agatha's old uniform even less than I wanted her job, but
Mr. Stanley was very efficient and didn't wish to carry on any conversation. He chose the uniform, found me some white shoes my size with
white socks, and distributed it all to me as though I were entering the
army. I even had to sign for it.

"Whatever anyone breaks here, they pay for," he said. "What they
lose, they pay for, too. Things don't walk away from this hotel as easily
as they do from the others. That's for sure," he said proudly.

"When you get here in the morning, you'll go to the east wing with
Sissy."

"You know how to get back to your room?" Mrs. Boston asked as we
left. I nodded. "Okay, then, I'll see you in the morning," she said. I
watched her walk off and then I started back.

After I reached the old wing, I paused at the living room and entered
so I could look at the family pictures on the mantel. There was Clara
Sue when she was a little girl, and there was Philip, standing together in
front of one of the small gazebos. I found the picture of Philip and our
mother I had only glimpsed before, but just as I reached up to bring it

closer to me, my grandmother appeared in the doorway. I jumped when she spoke.

"If I were you, Eugenia, I would get a good night's rest," she said, her eyes moving from me to the pictures. "You have to get yourself into the daily schedule."

I put the picture back quickly.

"I told you," I said defiantly, "my name is Dawn." I didn't wait for her response. I hurried away and to my little room, shutting the door after I entered. I stood there listening to see if she had followed me, but I heard no footsteps. Then I let out the breath I was holding and turned to my little suitcase.

I took out the picture of Momma as a young girl and placed it on the little table. As I looked at her, I recalled her final words to me.

"You must never think badly of us. We love you. Always remember that."

"Oh, Momma!" I cried. "Look what has happened to us! Why did you and Daddy do this?"

I reached into the drawer where I had hidden the pearls and removed them. Holding them made me feel closer to Momma, but I couldn't wear them. I just couldn't. Not here. Not in this horrible place that was my new home. The pearls had been meant to be worn on happy occasions, and my current situation certainly didn't qualify. I looked at the pearls one last time and then hid them away again. No one at Cutler's Cove would know about their existence. The pearls were my last link to my family. They were the only thing that gave me some feeling of comfort, and they would be my secret. If I ever felt lonely or needed to remember happier times, I'd just take them out of their drawer and hold them. Maybe one day I'd wear them again.

Finally, exhausted from what had to be one of the worst days of my life, I put away the rest of my things and dressed for bed. I crawled under the cover that smelled clean, but felt rough, and the pillow was too soft. I hated this room more than any of the awful apartments we had lived in.

I stared up at the cracked white ceiling. The cracks zigzagged across, looking like threads pasted up there. Then I turned over and switched off the light. With the night sky now overcast and no lights outside my window, it was pitch dark in my room. Even after my eyes grew used to it, I could barely make out the dresser and the window.

It was always hard to get used to a new place when we were traveling and moving from one town to another. First nights were scary, only then Jimmy and I had each other to comfort each other. Now, alone, I couldn't help but listen to every creak in the antique wing of the old hotel and shudder. I had to get used to every sound until nothing surprised me.

Suddenly, though, I thought I heard someone crying. It was muffled, but it was clearly the sound of a woman crying. I listened hard and heard my grandmother's voice, too, although I couldn't make out any words. The crying stopped as suddenly as it had started.

Then the silence and the darkness became heavy and ominous. I strained to hear the sounds of the hotel, just so I would have the comfort that came from hearing other people's voices. I could hear them, but they seemed so distant, like voices on a radio far, far away, and they didn't make me feel any safer or any more comfortable. But after a while my exhaustion overcame my fear, and I fell asleep.

I had arrived at what was my real home, only I didn't feel any sense of belonging. How long, I wondered, would I be a stranger in my own house and to my own family?

My eyes snapped open when I heard someone at the door. For a moment I forgot where I was and what had happened. I expected to hear Fern cry out and see her bounce up and down impatiently in her crib. But instead, when I sat up, I confronted my grandmother. Her hair was brushed back as perfectly as it had been when I had first met her, and she was wearing a dark gray cotton skirt with a matching blouse and jacket. Pearl earrings dangled from her lobes, and she wore the same rings and watch. She smirked with disapproval.

"What is it?" I asked. The look on her face and the way she had burst in my room jumped my heart right up against my throat.

"I had a suspicion you were still in bed. Didn't I make clear what time you were to get up and dressed?" she asked sharply.

"I was very tired, but I didn't fall right asleep because I heard someone crying," I told her. She drew her shoulders up and made her eyes small.

"Nonsense. No one was crying. You were probably already asleep and dreaming."

"It wasn't a dream. I heard someone crying," I insisted.

"Must you always contradict me?" she snapped. "A young girl your age should learn when to speak and when to be quiet."

I bit down on my lower lip. I wanted to snap back at her. I wanted to demand she stop treating me this way, but fate had pulled me through a knothole and stretched me out thin and flat. I trembled. It was as if I had lost my voice and everything would be trapped forever inside me, even tears. She glanced at her watch.

"It's seven," she said. "You must get dressed and go to the kitchen immediately if you want any breakfast. If any member of the staff wants breakfast, he or she has to eat it earlier than the guests. See to it that you get yourself up in the morning from now on," she commanded. "At your age, you shouldn't be dependent upon others to fulfill your responsibilities."

"I always get up early, and I always fulfill my responsibilities," I shot back at her. My anger finally exploded like a balloon filled with too much air. She stared a moment. I remained in bed, holding my blanket against my chest to keep down the pounding of my broken heart.

She studied me for a moment, and then her glance went to my little nightstand. Suddenly her face grew fiery red.

"Whose picture is that?" she demanded stepping forward.

"It's Momma," I said.

"You brought Sally Jean Longchamp's picture into my hotel and put it out for anyone to see?"

In a flash, far faster than I ever imagined someone as old as she could move, she seized my precious photograph.

"How dare you bring this here?"

"No!" I cried, but in an instant she tore it in two. "That was my picture, my only picture!" I cried through my tears. She pulled herself up to her full height.

"These people were kidnappers, child-stealers, thieves. I told you," she said through her clenched teeth, her lips pulled back until they were pencil thin, "I don't want any contact with them. Wipe them from your memory."

She threw Momma's picture into the small wastebasket. "Be in the kitchen in ten minutes. The family must set a good example for the staff," she added and stepped back out, closing the door as she did so.

The tears flowed down my cheeks.

Why was my grandmother being so horrible to me? Why couldn't she see the pain I was in having been ripped from the family I thought was mine? Why wasn't I given a little time to adjust to a new home and a new life? All she could do was treat me as if I were someone who had been brought up to be wild and useless. It made me furious. I hated this place; I hated being here.

I got up and quickly got dressed in a pair of jeans and a blouse. Not thinking about anything else but getting away from this horrible place, I ran out of my room and out the side entrance. I didn't care about breakfast; I didn't care about being late for my new work. All I could think of was my grandmother's hateful eyes.

I walked on, my head down, not caring where I ended up. I could walk off a cliff, for all I cared. After a while I did look up, however, and found myself standing in front of a tall, stone archway. The words carved into it read CUTLER'S COVE CEMETERY. How appropriate, I thought. I felt as though I'd rather be dead.

I gazed through the dark portal at the stones gleaming like so many bones in the morning sunlight and found myself drawn in like someone who had been hypnotized. I discovered a path to the right and walked down it slowly. It was a well-cared-for cemetery, with the grass neatly cut and trimmed and the flowers well weeded. Before long I found the Cutler section and looked upon my ancestors' stones: the graves of the people who had to be my great-grandfather and great-grandmother, aunts and uncles, cousins. There was a large monument marking my grandfather's grave, and right behind that and to the right was a very small stone.

Curious, I walked over to the small stone and then stopped in my tracks as I was able to read what it said. I blinked disbelieving eyes. Was I reading correctly, or was the morning light playing tricks on me? How could this be? Why would this be? It didn't make sense. It just didn't make sense!

Slowly I knelt at the tiny monument, running my fingers over the carved letters as I read the few words.

EUGENIA GRACE CUTLER
INFANT
GONE BUT NOT FORGOTTEN

My stomach tightened even further as I looked at the dates which fit my own birth and disappearance. There was no denying the fact. This grave was *mine*.

Suddenly the ground beneath my knees felt as though it were burning. I felt icicles dripping down the back of my neck. I stood up quickly on trembling legs, tearing my eyes away from the evidence of my nonexistence. There wasn't any doubt in my mind as to who had had that grave created: Grandmother Cutler. She'd certainly be happier if my little body was really in there. But why? Why was she so anxious to have me buried and forgotten?

Somehow I had to face up to this hateful old woman and show her I was not a lowly creature to be spit upon and tormented. I wasn't dead. I was alive, and nothing she could do would deny my existence.

When I returned to the hotel and my room, I reached into the waste-basket and took out Momma's torn picture. It had been ripped through her beautiful smile. It was as if my grandmother had ripped through my heart. I hid the torn pieces under my underwear in the dresser. I would try to tape it together, but it would never be the same.

I changed into my uniform and went directly to the kitchen. By the time I arrived, it was already filled with waiters, other chambermaids, kitchen help, and the bellhops and receptionists. The conversations stopped and every face turned my way. I felt just the way I used to feel whenever I entered a new classroom. I imagined most of them knew who I was by now.

Mrs. Boston called to me, and I joined her and the other chamber-maids. I could see they resented me for taking someone's job, someone who really needed it. Nevertheless, she introduced me to everyone and pointed out Sissy. I sat down beside her.

She was a black girl who was five years older than I was even though she didn't look a day older. I was an inch or so taller. She had her hair chopped short, cut evenly around as if someone had put a bowl over her head and snipped it.

"Everyone's chattering about you," she said. "People always knew about the missing Cutler baby, only everyone thought you was dead. Mrs. Cutler even had that memorial put up on the family cemetery," she added.

"I know," I said. "I've seen it."

"You have?"

"Why did they do it?"

"I heard that Mrs. Cutler had it made years later after she came to the conclusion you weren't going to be found alive. I was too little to go to the service, of course, but my grandmother told me no one but the family went anyway. Mrs. Cutler told everyone the day you was kid-napped was the same as if it was the day you died."

"No one mentioned it to me," I said. "I just came upon it by accident when I wandered into the cemetery and found the family section."

"I suppose they'll be digging it up now," Sissy said.

"Not if my grandmother has her way," I mumbled.

"What's that?"

"Nothing," I said. I was still shaking from the sight of the small stone with that name on it. Even though it wasn't the name I accepted, it was meant to be me it was the same thing. I was glad to get to work and put my mind on other things.

After breakfast we went with the other chambermaids to Mr. Stanley's office. He gave out the assignments, new rooms that had to be prepared, rooms that had to be cleaned because guests were checking out. Sissy and I had to do what was called the east wing. We had fifteen rooms. We alternated rooms down the corridor. Just before lunch my father came to get me.

"Your mother is ready to meet you, Eugenia," he said.

"I told you . . . my name's Dawn," I retorted. Now that I had seen the gravestone, the other name was even more despicable.

"Don't you think Eugenia has a more distinguished sound to it, honey?" he asked as we walked. "You were named after one of my mother's sisters. She was only a young girl when she died."

"I know, but I didn't grow up with that name, and I don't like it."

"Maybe you will. If you give it a chance," he suggested.

"I won't," I insisted, but he didn't seem to hear or care.

We turned into the old section of the hotel and headed for the stairway, my pulse throbbing harder and harder with each forward step.

The upstairs had new-looking wallpaper with light blue polka dots, and the corridor had a plush cream carpet. A large window at the far end made it airy and bright.

"This is Philip's room," my father explained as we came to a door on the right, "and the next door is Clara Sue's. Our bedroom suite is right down here on the left. Your grandmother's suite is just around the corner."

We paused outside the closed door to his and my mother's bedroom, and my father took a deep breath, closing and opening his eyes as if he had a weight on his chest.

"I must explain something to you," he began. "Your mother is a very delicate woman. The doctors say she has frayed nerves, and so we try to keep tension and pressure away from her. She comes from a fine old southern family, aristocrats, and she was well protected all her life. But that's why I love her. To me she's like . . . a work of art, fine china, fragile, beautiful, exquisite," he said. "She's someone who needs to be protected, cherished, and held dearly. Anyway, you can imagine what all this has done to her. She's a little afraid of you," he added.

"Afraid of me? Why?" I asked.

"Well . . . bringing up our two children has been a strain on her as it is. To suddenly be confronted by a long-lost child who has lived an entirely different sort of life . . . it frightens her. All I ask is that you be patient.

"All right," he said, taking another deep breath and reaching for the doorknob, "here we go."

It was like entering another world. First we stepped into a sitting room with a burgundy velvet carpet. All of the furniture, although shiny, clean, and new-looking, was obviously antique. Later I would learn how valuable it was. It was all original and dated back to the turn of the century.

On the left was a fieldstone fireplace with a long, wide mantel. Atop it at the center was a silver frame with a picture of a young woman holding an umbrella and standing on the beach. She was dressed in a light-colored dress with a long hem. On both ends of the mantel were slim vases with a single rose in each.

Above the mantel was a painting of what must have been the original Cutler's Cove Hotel. There were people gathered on the lawn and people sitting on the wraparound porch. A man and a woman stood together at the front door. I wondered if they weren't supposed to be my grandparents. The sky behind and above the hotel was dotted with small puffy clouds.

To my immediate left was a piano. There was a sheet of music on it, but it looked as though it had been placed there simply for show. In fact, the entire sitting room looked unused, untouched, like a room in a museum.

"Right this way," my father said, indicating the double doors before us. He took hold of both handles and opened both doors with one graceful motion. I stepped forward into the bedroom and nearly gasped in astonishment. It was so big, I thought it was larger than most of the apartments I had lived in. The thick sea-blue carpet rolled on forever until it reached an enormous canopy bed at the far end. There were large windows on each side of the bed, with white lace curtains draped over them. The walls were covered with dark blue velvet. To the right was a long milk-white marble vanity table with cherry-red streaks running through it. There were two high-back matching cushioned chairs. Vases filled with jonquils were spaced along the table. A floor-to-ceiling mirror ran the entire wall behind the vanity table, which made the bedroom look even longer and wider.

A door on the left opened to a walk-in closet bigger than the room I now slept in. There was another closet down from that. The bathroom was on the right. I had only a glimpse of it, but I was able to see the gold fixtures in the sinks and the enormous tub.

My mother was almost lost in the enormous bed. She sat up against two jumbo fluffy pillows. She was wearing a bright pink silk robe with a lace cotton nightie. As we drew closer, she looked up from her magazine and put a chocolate back into the box that was beside her on the bed. Even though she was still in bed, she wore pearl earrings and lipstick and eyeliner. She looked as if she could get out of bed, slip into a fancy dress, and go dancing.

"Laura Sue, we're here," my father sang, stating the obvious. He stopped and turned to me, gesturing for me to come farther forward. "Isn't she a pretty girl?" he added when I stepped up beside him.

I looked at the woman I had been told was my real mother. Yes, there were resemblances, I thought. We were both blondes, my hair the same shade of yellow and as bright as the morning sun. I had her blue eyes, and I had her peaches-and-cream complexion. She had a graceful neck and slight shoulders, and her hair rested softly on those shoulders and looked as if it had been brushed a thousand strokes, it was so soft and shiny.

She looked me over quickly, her eyes darting from my feet to my head, and then she gasped deeply as if trying to catch her breath. She brought her hand to the heart-shaped locket between her breasts and fingered it nervously. There was an enormous diamond ring on her hand, the stone so large it looked awkward and out of place on her slim, short finger.

I took a deep breath, too. The room was permeated with the scent of the jonquils, for there were vases of them on the end tables and one on the table in the far corner.

"Why is she in a chambermaid's uniform?" my mother asked my father.

"Oh, you know Mother. She wanted her to get used to the hotel life immediately," he replied. She grimaced and shook her head.

"Eugenia," she finally said in a whisper, directing herself to me. "Is it really you?" I shook my head, and she looked confused. She turned quickly to my father. A worried frown drew his eyebrows together.

"I must tell you, Laura Sue, that Eugenia has known only Dawn as

her name, and she is a little uncomfortable being called anything else,"
he explained. A puzzled expression flashed through her face and
creased her brow. She battered her eyelashes and pursed her lips.

"Oh? But Grandmother Cutler named you," she said to me, as if that
meant it had been written in stone and could never be changed or
challenged.

"I don't care," I said. Suddenly she looked frightened, and when she
looked to my father this time, it was to ask for help.

"They named her Dawn? Just Dawn?"

"However, Laura Sue," my father said, "Dawn and I did just agree
she would give Eugenia a chance."

"I never said I agreed," I said quickly.

"Oh, this will be so difficult," my mother said, shaking her head. Her
hand hovered near her throat; her eyes darkened. Something frightening burgeoned in my heart just from watching her reactions. Momma
had been deathly ill, but never looked as weak and helpless as my real
mother did.

"Whenever anyone calls her Eugenia, she won't know they're calling
her. You can't call yourself Dawn now," she said to me. "What would
people think?" she moaned.

"But it's my name!" I cried. She looked as if she would cry herself.

"I know what we will do," she said suddenly, clapping her hands
together. "Whenever we introduce you to anyone who is important, we
will introduce you as Eugenia Grace Cutler. Around here, in the
family's quarters, we will call you Dawn, if you like. Doesn't that sound
sensible, Randolph? Won't Mother think so?"

"We'll see," he replied, not sounding happy. But my mother put on a
pained expression, and he relaxed and smiled. "I'll speak to her."

"Why can't you just tell her that's what you want?" I asked my
mother. At this point I was more curious than angry. She shook her
head and brought her hand to her breast.

"I . . . can't stand arguments," she said. "Must there be arguments,
Randolph?"

"Don't concern yourself with this, Laura Sue. I'm sure Dawn and I
and Mother will work it all out."

"Good." She took a deep breath. "Good," she repeated. "That's settled," she said.

What was settled? I glanced at my father. He smiled at me as if to say
let it be. My mother was smiling again, looking like a little girl who had

been promised something wonderful like a new dress or a day at the circus.

"Come closer, Dawn," she said. "Let me get a real good look at you. Come, sit by the bed." She indicated a chair I should bring up with me. I did so quickly and sat down. "You are a pretty girl," she said, "with beautiful hair and beautiful eyes." She reached out to stroke my hair, and I saw her long, perfect pink fingernails. "Are you happy to be here, to be home?"

"No," I said quickly, perhaps too quickly, for she blinked and brought herself up as if I had slapped her. "I'm not used to it," I explained, "and I miss the only people I ever knew as my family."

"Of course," she said. "You poor, poor thing. How horrible this all must be for you." She smiled, a very pretty smile, I thought, and when I looked up at my father, I saw how much he adored her. "I knew you only for a few hours, held you in my arms for only a little while. My nurse, Mrs. Dalton, knew you longer than I did," she whined. She turned her sad eyes toward my father, and he nodded sadly.

"Whenever I am able to see you, you must spend as much time with me as you can, telling me all about yourself, where you have been, and what you have done. Did they treat you well?" she asked, grimacing as if preparing to hear the worst things: stories about being locked in closets or starved and beaten.

"Yes," I said firmly.

"But they were so poor!" she exclaimed.

"Being poor didn't matter. They loved me and I loved them," I declared. I couldn't help it. I missed Jimmy and little Fern so much it made me tremble inside.

"Oh, dear," my mother said turning to my father. "This is going to be just as difficult as I imagined it would be."

"It will take time," he repeated. "Don't work yourself into a panic, Laura Sue. Everyone will help, especially Mother."

"Yes, yes, I know." She turned back to me. "Well, I'll do what I can for you, Dawn, but I'm afraid my strength hasn't returned yet. I hope you will understand."

"Of course she will," my father said.

"After a while, when you've learned how to behave in society, we will have a little party to celebrate your homecoming. Won't that be nice?" she asked, smiling.

"I know how to behave in society," I replied, wiping the smile from her face.

"Well, of course you don't know how, dear. It took me ages and ages to learn the proper etiquette, and I was brought up in a nice home surrounded by nice things. People of position were continually coming and going. I'm sure you don't know the proper way to greet someone, or how to curtsy and look down when someone gives you a compliment. You don't know how to sit at a formal dinner table, what silverware to use, the proper way to eat soup, butter your bread, reach for things. There is so much for you to learn now. I'll try to teach you as much as I can, but you must be patient, okay?"

I looked away. Why were these things important to her now? What about us really getting to know each other? What about a true mother-daughter relationship? Why wasn't she more interested in what I wanted and needed?

"And we can talk about womanly things, too," she said. I raised my eyes with interest.

"Womanly things?"

"Of course. We can't have you looking like this all the time."

"She's working in the hotel this summer, Laura Sue," my father reminded her gently.

"So? She can still look like a daughter of mine should look."

"What's wrong with the way I look?" I asked.

"Oh, dear, honey, your hair should be cut and styled. I'll have my beautician look at you. And your nails," she said, grimacing. "They need a proper manicure."

"I can't make beds and clean rooms and worry about my nails," I declared.

"She's right, Laura Sue," my father said gently.

"Does she have to be a chambermaid?" my mother asked my father.

"Mother thinks it's the best place to begin."

She nodded with a look of deep resignation as if whatever my grandmother thought or said was gospel. Then she sighed and contemplated me again, shaking her head gently.

"In the future please change into something pleasant before coming to see me," she told me. "Uniforms depress me, and always shower and wash your hair first. Otherwise, you will bring in the dust and grime."

I guess I was a windowpane, easy to read, for she saw the pain in my heart.

"Oh, Dawn dear, you must forgive me if I sound insensitive. I have not forgotten how hard this is for you, too. But just think of all the wonderful and new things you will have and be able to do. You will be a

Cutler in Cutler's Cove and that's an honor and a privilege. Someday there will be a line of proper suitors begging for your hand in marriage, and all that has happened to you will seem like a bad dream.

"Just like it seems to me," she added and took another deep breath. It was more like she was gasping for air.

"Oh, dear, it's getting hot," she announced, practically in the same breath. "Could you turn on the fan, please, Randolph?"

"Of course, dear."

She fell back against the pillow and fanned herself with her magazine. "This is all so overwhelming," she said. "Randolph, you've got to help me with this!" she cried, her voice thin and high, sounding as if she were on the verge of hysterics. "It's hard enough for me to look after Clara Sue and Philip."

"Of course I will, Laura Sue. Dawn will not be a problem."

"Good," she said.

How could she think I would be a problem for her? I wondered. I wasn't a baby who needed constant care and watching.

"Does everyone know about her, Randolph?" she asked, staring up at the ceiling. When she spoke about me like this, it was as if I weren't in the room with her.

"It's getting around Cutler's Cove, if that's what you mean."

"Heavens. How will I go about? Everywhere I go, people will have questions and questions. I can't stand the thought of that, Randolph," she moaned.

"I'll answer the questions, Laura Sue. Don't worry."

"My heart is pounding so, Randolph. It just started and I feel my pulse throbbing in my neck," she said, bringing her fingers to her throat. "I can't catch my breath."

"Now, take it easy, Laura Sue," my father advised. I looked at him in anticipation. What was happening? He nodded and tilted his head toward the door.

"I'd better be going," I said. "I've got to get back to work."

"Oh . . . oh, yes, sweetheart," she said, turning back to me. "I need a little nap now anyway. Later we will talk again. Randolph, please ask Dr. Madeo to come back."

"Now, Laura Sue, he was just here not an hour or so ago and—"

"Please. I think I need him to change my medicine. It's not helping."

"All right," he said with a sigh. He followed me out. I looked back once and saw her lying back with her eyes closed, her hands still pressed to her bosom.

"She'll be all right," my father assured me as we stepped out. "Just one of her spells. They come and go. It's part of her nervous condition. Why, in a day or two, she will be up and about, dressed in one of her beautiful dresses and standing in the dining room doorway alongside Mother, greeting guests. You'll see," he said, patting me on the shoulder.

My father assumed my sad and troubled look came from my worrying about my mother, but she was still a stranger to me. True, we looked somewhat alike, but I did not feel any warmth between us and couldn't imagine calling her Mother. She hadn't even made an effort to kiss me. Instead, she had made me feel dirty and unschooled, a wild thing brought in from the streets, someone to be made over and trained like a stray dog.

I looked away. Not money, not power and position, not all the honor associated with being a Cutler could replace one loving moment I had lived as a Longchamp. But no one wanted to see this or understand, least of all my real parents.

Oh, Momma! Oh, Daddy! I cried in the darkness of my tormented thoughts. Why did you do this? I had been better off not knowing the truth. It would have been better for all of us if that memorial stone to a stolen baby remained untouched, lingering forever in the darkness on a quiet cemetery, just another lie.

But to me the world was full of lies, and one more now seemed not to matter.

10
A NEW BROTHER, A LOST LOVE

For the next few days I barely saw my father. Every time I did see him, he appeared frenzied, rushing from one place to another like a worker bee while my grandmother sauntered coolly about the hotel like the queen. Whenever my father saw me, he promised to spend more time with me. I felt like a pebble in his shoe. He would pause to shake me out and then hurry off, forgetting from one time to the next that he had seen me and said the same things.

My mother didn't come down from her room for days. Then one day she appeared at the dining room door, greeting the guests as they entered. She was dressed in a beautiful turquoise gown and had her hair brushed and curled so it lay just over her shoulders. She wore a diamond necklace that glittered so brightly it was blinding in the light from the overhead chandelier, and I thought she was one of the most beautiful women I had ever seen. She looked as if she had never been sick a single day in her life. Her complexion couldn't have been more rosy, her eyes brighter, her hair more healthy and rich.

I stood off in a corner of the lobby and watched how she and my grandmother greeted people, both of them smiling warmly, patting hands, accepting kisses on the cheeks, and kissing other women and men. It seemed as though everyone who stayed at the hotel was an old friend. Both my mother and my grandmother looked radiant and alive, energized by the crowd of guests filing past them.

But when it was over, when all the guests had entered, my grandmother gave my mother a strange, stern look and then walked into the dining room. My mother didn't see me watching her at first. She looked as though she would burst into tears. My father came out to fetch her.

Just before she turned to accompany him into the dining room, she looked my way.

I thought she had the oddest expression, one that even frightened me a bit. She looked as though she didn't recognize me. Her eyes were filled with curiosity, and she tilted her head slightly. Then she whispered something to my father. He turned, saw me, and waved. My mother continued into the dining room, but my father came across the lobby.

"Hi," he said. "How are you doing? You getting enough to eat?"

I nodded. He had asked me the same question three times in two days.

"Well, tomorrow you will have more to do and more fun. Philip and Clara Sue are coming home. School's out."

"Tomorrow?" I had forgotten the date. Time had lost its meaning for me.

"Uh-huh. I'd better get back in there. Lunch is about to begin. As soon as I get that free moment, we'll talk," he added and left me quickly.

Tomorrow Philip was coming, I thought. I was afraid of seeing him. How would he feel about all this? Would he be embarrassed? Maybe he wouldn't be able to look me in the face. How many times had he recalled kissing me, touching me? Did it disgust him now? None of this was his fault, nor was it mine. We didn't deceive each other; we had been deceived.

And then there was Clara Sue to think about. I would never be able to face the reality of her being my sister, I thought, and with the way she hated me . . . tomorrow . . . just the thought of it made me sweat and tremble.

Later that day I went exploring through the hotel. After I finished working with Sissy, afternoons usually belonged to me. The only problem was that there was usually nothing to do. I was all alone, without anyone to talk to. Sissy always had other jobs to do, and there was no one else my age among the guests since the summer season hadn't started yet. Part of me was looking forward to Philip and Clara Sue's arrival. Granted, things would be awkward at first, but we'd all adjust. We had to. After all, we were a family.

Family. It was the first time the word had entered my mind with regards to the new people in my life. We were a *family.* Philip, Clara Sue, Grandmother Cutler, my real mother and father, and *me,* were a family. There would never be any changing of that. We belonged to each other, and no one would ever be able to take them away from me.

Although the thought of the Cutlers as my real family gave me a sense of comfort and security I had never thought possible, it also made me feel guilty. I instantly envisioned Daddy and Momma, Jimmy and Fern. They were my family, too, no matter what anyone said. I would always love them, but that didn't mean I couldn't learn to love my real family, too, did it?

Not wanting to dwell on my two families anymore, at least for the moment, I concentrated on my exploration trek. I went from room to room, floor to floor, really paying attention to my surroundings. The extravagance and opulence of Cutler's Cove was dazzling. There were plush carpets, Oriental rugs, rich tapestries, sleek leather sofas and chairs, lamps with glittering shades of Tiffany glass, polished bookshelves with rows upon rows of books.

There were paintings and sculptures; delicate figurines and vases overflowing with lush, fragrant flowers. The beauty of it all left me speechless, but the most amazing thing of all was that I belonged here. This was my new world. I had been born into the wealth of the Cutler family, and now I had been returned to it. It was going to take some getting used to.

Each room outshined the next one that I stepped into, and soon I lost track of where I was. Trying to get my bearings so that I could return to the hotel's lobby, I rounded a corner. Yet instead of stairs, there was only a door in the wall. There were no other rooms. Intrigued by my discovery, I opened the door. It creaked on its hinges, and a musty smell drifted out. Darkness stretched before me. I reached out a hand, searching for a light switch. Finding one, I turned it on. The bath of light put me at ease and gave me the courage to walk down what seemed to be an unused corridor.

I reached the end and another door. Biting my lip I opened it and stepped inside. Surrounding me were packed boxes, trunks, and covered piles of furniture. I was in some sort of storage room. Suddenly I became excited. The perfect place to learn about one's family—one's past —was by going through what was left behind by one's ancestors.

Eagerly I knelt before a trunk, not caring about the dust on the floor, consumed only by thoughts of what I would discover. I couldn't wait!

Trunk after trunk was opened as the afternoon flew by. There were photos of Grandmother Cutler as a young woman, looking just as stern as ever. There were photos of my father from the time he was a child until he married my mother. There were photos of my mother, too, but for some reason she didn't look happy. In her eyes there was a sad faraway look. I turned to the back of the photos of her, noting the dates. The photos had been taken after I had been kidnapped. No wonder she looked the way she did.

There were photos of Clara Sue and Philip and photos of the hotel in its various stages of growth as Cutler's Cove became more and more prosperous.

A look at my watch showed me that it was six o'clock. Dinner would be in half an hour and I was a mess! A mirror across the room provided a reflection of my dusty self. I'd have to hurry to get myself ready. Gathering up the folders the photos had been in, I prepared to put them back in the trunk I had opened. As I was about to replace the folders, I noticed a folder I had missed in the bottom of the trunk. Although I knew I was cutting things close timewise, I couldn't resist taking a peek. Putting aside the other folders, I scooped up the one I had missed. After pouring out the contents, I was stunned.

There were newspaper clippings . . . newspaper clippings of my kidnapping!

Forgetting about having to be ready for dinner, I pored over the clippings. Each account was exactly the same, telling no more and no less than what was already known. Photos of Daddy and Momma, along with my real mother and father, accompanied the articles. I looked into their young faces, searching for answers, trying to understand how they all felt.

Reading about myself . . . about my kidnapping . . . was strange. A part of me still hadn't wanted to believe that Momma and Daddy had done such a terrible thing. Yet in my hands, in black and white newsprint, I held the proof. There was no longer any denying what had happened.

"So there you are! Just what do you think you're doing up here?" a steely whisper demanded.

There was no mistaking that voice. Startled, I fell to the floor, the newspaper clippings scattering from my hand. I turned around and my blood chilled as I stared up into the angry wrath of Grandmother Cutler.

"I asked you a question," she hissed. "What are you doing up here?"

"I was just looking," I managed to answer.

"Looking? Only *looking*? Don't you mean *snooping!* How dare you rummage through things that don't belong to you." She gave an indignant snort. "I shouldn't be surprised. You were raised by a thief and kidnapper."

"Don't you say such things about Momma and Daddy," I said, instantly coming to their defense.

Grandmother Cutler ignored me. "Look at this mess!"

Mess? What mess? The trunks were only open . . . their contents as neatly arranged as when I had found them. All that needed to be done was a closing of the trunk lids.

I felt like contradicting her, but one look at her face made me change my mind. Her face was turning red; she was barely controlling herself.

"I'm sorry," I said, nervously playing with the pearls I had chosen to wear around my neck that morning. When I had woken up this morning, I had suddenly missed Momma more than I ever had. Putting on the pearls had made me feel better. I knew I had broken my promise to myself, but I had been unable to help it. Besides, I'd kept the pearls hidden under my blouse. Momma would have liked seeing me wear them.

Grandmother Cutler's eyes suddenly bulged. *"Where did you get those?"*

Shocked, I looked up at her, shivering as she drew closer. "Get what?" I didn't know what she was talking about.

"Those pearls," she hissed.

Puzzled, I looked at the pearls. "These? I've always had them. They belonged to my family."

"*Liar!* You stole them, didn't you? You found those pearls in one of the trunks."

"I did not!" I hotly answered. How dare she accuse me of stealing. "These pearls belonged to my momma. My daddy gave them to me to wear on the night of the concert." I gave Grandmother Cutler a defiant look, despite the fact that I was quivering inside. She wasn't going to scare me. "These pearls are mine."

"I don't believe you. You've never worn them before. If they're so *special,*" she sneered, "then why is this the first time I'm seeing them around your neck?"

I was about to answer when Grandmother Cutler raced forward. With lightning speed she reached for the pearls, ripping them from my neck. Momma's beautiful pearls, each one individually knotted, didn't scatter or break. But they were still gone. She held them up in one hand, triumphantly tightening a fist. "They're *mine* now."

"No!" I protested, jumping to my feet and grabbing for her fist. "Give them back!" I couldn't lose Momma's pearls. I couldn't! They were all I had left of her after Grandmother Cutler had hatefully torn up her photo. "I'm telling you the truth. I swear I am."

Grandmother Cutler gave me a vicious shove, pushing me to the floor. I landed on the dusty attic floor with an "oomph," my bottom aching with soreness.

"Don't you ever raise a hand to me again! Do you understand?"

Glaring at her defiantly, I refused to answer. My silence only infuriated her further.

"Do you understand?" she repeated, snatching up a handful of my hair and twisting it painfully. "When I ask you a question, I expect an answer."

Tears sprang to my eyes, desperate to be free, but I wouldn't release them. I wouldn't give Grandmother Cutler the satisfaction. I wouldn't!

"Yes," I said, gritting my teeth. "I understand."

Amazingly, my answer returned her to some semblance of normalcy. She let go of my hair, and I rubbed my aching head. "Good," she purred. "Good." She gave a look at the open trunks. "Fix this place as you found it." She swept up the fallen newspaper clippings. "These will be burned," she stated, sending me a glare I had already become familiar with.

"You know I'm telling the truth," I told her. "You know those pearls belonged to Sally Jean Longchamp."

"I know nothing of the sort. All I know," she spat out, "is that I haven't seen these pearls since the day you disappeared."

"What are you saying?" I gasped.

She gave me a smug look. "What do you think I'm saying?"

"Those pearls belonged to my momma!" I cried out. "They did! I won't believe what you're insinuating. I won't!"

"I've always believed in the truth, Eugenia. Sally Jean and Ormand Longchamp stole these pearls. There's no escaping that fact, just like there's no escaping the fact that they stole you."

What she was saying couldn't be true. It couldn't! How could I bear this final stain against Momma and Daddy's memory? It was just too much to bear!

With her final words Grandmother Cutler left, taking away my last connection to my past. I waited for my tears to fall, but they didn't. That was because I had realized something. It didn't matter what had come with me from my former life. I had my memories and my memories of life with Daddy and Momma, Jimmy and Fern, were something that Grandmother Cutler could never take away.

The following morning I threw myself into my work, trying desperately not to think about what was soon to come or what had happened the previous day. I didn't linger around the other chambermaids and staff at lunch, either. Most of them were still very incensed about my taking Agatha's job. If I tried to speak or act friendly, one of them brought up Agatha and asked if anyone had heard anything about her. A few times I felt like standing up and shouting at them: "I didn't fire her! I didn't ask to be made a chambermaid! I didn't even ask to be brought back here! You're all so cruel and heartless. Why can't you see that?"

The words were tickling the tip of my tongue, but I was afraid to scream them, for I knew the moment I did, I would be even more isolated than I was now. Not even Sissy would speak to me, and my grandmother would have another reason to chastise me and make me feel lower than an insect. Not that I could feel much lower being stuffed away in some cubbyhole of a room in a distant part of the hotel as if I were a disgrace and an embarrassment my grandmother wanted hidden and forgotten.

I was beginning to feel like someone caught in limbo—not really accepted as a Cutler yet, and not accepted by the staff. My only real companion was my own shadow. Loneliness draped itself over me like a shroud. I felt invisible.

I was spending my break after lunch in my room alone when there was a knock on my door and Mrs. Boston appeared, her arms laden with a pile of clothing and a bag of shoes and sneakers.

"Little Mrs. Cutler asked me to bring this down to you," she said as she entered my bedroom.

"What is it?"

"I just finished getting Miss Clara Sue's room in order. That girl's the worst when it comes to being neat and organized. You would think a young lady from a good family like this would take a little more pride in her things and her living quarters, but that girl . . ." She shook her head and dropped everything at the foot of my bed.

"This here is everything Clara Sue don't use no more. Some of it is from a year or so back, so even though she's a mite bigger than you everywhere, this stuff might fit.

"Some of it she never even wore. That's how spoiled she is. Why, just look here," she added, reaching into the pile. She lifted a blouse up. "See, this still has the tag on it."

It did look brand-new. I began to sift through the things. It would certainly not be the first time I had worn used clothing. It was just the idea that it was Clara Sue's clothing, Clara Sue's hand-me-downs, that disturbed me. I couldn't help remembering all the terrible things she had done to me at school.

On the other hand, my mother, whom I really hadn't spoken to since our first meeting, was thinking about me. I supposed I should be grateful.

"My mother picked all this out for me?" I asked. Mrs. Boston nodded and raised her hands.

"She didn't pick it out exactly. She asked me to gather all the things I knew Clara Sue didn't use or want and see if you could make use of it."

I tried on one of the sneakers. Clara Sue was a year younger than me, but she was a lot bigger. The old sneakers and shoes were a perfect fit. All of the blouses and skirts would fit, too. There was even a bag of underwear.

"Everything in that is far too small for her now," Mrs. Boston said. I was sure all the panties would fit, but the year-old bra was still too big for me.

"You can sort out what works and what don't. Let me know what you don't want. There are plenty of poor people I know who would really appreciate most of this," she said, raising her eyebrows. "Especially Agatha Johnson."

"Well, I don't have time to work on this right now," I snapped. "I have to go to the card room. I'm supposed to clean it up between one and two while most of the guests are away." I put the clothing aside. Mrs. Boston grimaced and then left. I followed her out and went to do my afternoon chores.

I had just finished polishing the last table in the card room and put back the chairs when I heard Philip call, "Dawn." I turned and found him standing behind me in the doorway. He wore a light blue shirt with a button-down collar and khaki-colored slacks. With his hair brushed neatly, every strand in place, he looked his usual unperturbed self.

I had lost interest in my own appearance from the day I had arrived at Cutler's Cove. In the morning I would simply pin up my hair and then tie a bandanna around it the way the other chambermaids did. My uniform was dirty from cleaning the card room.

It was the first dark rainy day since I had arrived at the hotel. The brooding sky had made this particular day even more dreary and tedious for me. The air was cool and clammy, and I worked harder and faster to keep the chill out of my bones.

"Hello, Philip," I said, turning about completely.

"How are you?" he asked.

"All right, I guess," I replied, but my lips began to tremble and my shoulders started to shake. When I looked at him now, it made me think that my days at Emerson Peabody were all part of some dream, a dream that had turned into a nightmare the day Momma died.

"I set out looking for you as soon as I arrived," Philip said, not taking a step closer. "I haven't even unpacked. I just threw down my things and asked Mrs. Boston where I could find you. She told me Grandmother put you downstairs and started you working as a chambermaid," he added. "That's my grandmother—I mean, *our* grandmother—for you."

He paused again. The silences between our sentences were deep, and the small distance between us seemed like miles. Rapid and dramatic events had made him feel like a stranger to me. I was having trouble thinking of things to say and how to say them.

But suddenly he smiled the same way he always had with that twinkle in his eyes, that impish grin on his face. He shook his head.

"I can't think of you as my sister. I can't. This is too much," he said.

"What can we do, Philip? It's true."

"I don't know." He kept shaking his head. "So," he said, stepping closer, "how do you like the hotel? It's quite a place, isn't it? The grounds are beautiful. When it's not raining like this," he added.

"I've only been able to explore the inside of the hotel. I haven't had much of a chance to explore outside," I said. "Mostly, I've been working and spending time alone in my room."

"Oh." His smile widened. "Well, now that I've arrived, you will have more to do. I'll show you every nook and cranny. I'll re-explore everything with you, show you my favorite places, my old hiding places . . ."

For a moment we let our gazes lock. My face felt hot, my heart raced. What did he see when he looked at me? Did he still think me the nicest and prettiest girl he had met?

"On your day off," he continued quickly, "we'll walk along the beach and look for seashells and—"

"I don't have a day off," I said.

"What? No day off? Of course you do. Everybody gets a day off. I'll speak to Mr. Stanley right away about it."

I shrugged and put my polishing cloth and polish in my little cart. He came closer.

"Dawn," he said, reaching for my hand. When his fingers touched mine, I pulled away instinctively. I couldn't help it. What had once been thrilling now seemed as soiled as the linens I changed every morning. It felt wrong to look deeply into his eyes, wrong to hear him speak softly to me, wrong to have him care about me. I even felt guilty talking to him alone in the card room.

"Not a day has passed when I didn't think about you and what a horror you've been going through. I wanted to call you, even to leave school and come home to see you, but Grandmother thought it would be better to wait," he said, and I looked up at him sharply.

"Grandmother?"

"Yes."

"What did you tell her about us?" I asked quickly.

"Tell her?" He shrugged as if it had all been so simple and so harmless. "Just how you and I had become such good friends and what a wonderful person you were and how beautifully you sang. She asked me about your mother and father, and I told her about your mother's illness and death and how surprised I was to learn what they had done."

"I don't know why they did what they did or why any of this happened," I said, shaking my head. I looked away to hide the tears in my eyes.

"Grandmother felt the same way. It had been a terrible surprise to her, too, when it happened," he said. I spun around.

"Why . . . why did you call your grandmother? Why didn't you speak with . . . your father or mother?" It was still hard for me to think of them as my parents, too.

"Oh, I've always gone to Grandmother for most things," he replied, smiling. "She's always been in charge. At least, as long as I can remember, and . . . you've met Mother," he said, raising his eyes toward the ceiling. "She's having a hard enough time about it all as it is. Father would only ask Grandmother for advice anyway if I had called him. She's quite a woman, isn't she?"

"She's a tyrant," I snapped.

"What?" He kept his smile.

"She wants to change my name from Dawn to Eugenia, only I won't agree. She's insisting everyone in the hotel call me Eugenia, and they're all afraid to do otherwise."

"I'll talk to her. I'll get her to understand, you'll see."

"I don't care if she understands or not. I won't change my name to please her," I declared firmly.

He nodded, impressed with my determination. We stared at each other again.

"Don't worry," he said, moving closer. "It will be all right."

"It will never be all right," I moaned. "I try to keep busy so I won't think about Jimmy and Fern and what's happened to them." I looked up at him hopefully. "Have you heard anything? Do you know anything?"

"No. Sorry. Oh, before I forget, regards from Mr. Moore. He says no matter what, you must continue with your music. He said to tell you he wants to come hear you sing at Carnegie Hall someday."

I smiled for the first time in a long time.

"I haven't felt much like singing or playing piano these days."

"You will. After a while. Dawn," Philip said, this time seizing my hand and holding on to it tightly. He went on, his eyes soft as they saw my distress. "It's not all that easy forgetting about you the way you were, even when I see you here."

"I know," I said, looking down.

"No one can blame me, can blame you for feeling the way we do about each other. Let's just keep it our secret," he said. I looked up surprised. His eyes darkened with sincerity. "As far as I'm concerned, you're still the most beautiful girl I have ever met."

He pressed my hand more firmly and drew close as though he wanted me to kiss him on the lips. What did he expect me to do? To say?

I pulled my hand out of his and stepped back.

"Thank you, Philip, but we have to try to think of each other differently now. Everything's changed."

He looked disappointed.

"This isn't easy for me, either, you know," he said sharply. "I know you've suffered, but I've suffered, too. You can't imagine what it was like at school," he added, his forehead creasing. Then, easy as a mask to take off, he threw away his anger and put on his dreamy-eyed romantic look.

"But whenever I grew sad about it, I forced myself to think about all the wonderful things you and I could do here at Cutler's Cove. I meant what I said before. I want to show you the hotel and the grounds and the town and catch you up on our family history," he said, his voice full of energy and excitement.

"Thank you," I said. "I'll look forward to that," I added. He stepped back, still holding that sexy smile, but for me it was as if we were gazing at each other over a great valley, the distance between us widening and widening until the Philip I had known dwindled into a memory and burst like a soap bubble. He was gone. Then the gap dwindled, and he was replaced by this new Philip, my older brother.

Good-bye to my first and what I thought would be my most wonderful romantic love, I thought. Good-bye to being swept off my feet and floating alongside warm, soft white clouds. Our passionate kisses shattered and fell with the raindrops, and no one could tell which were my tears and which were the drops of rain.

Four elderly men came in and took up seats at a corner table. They were there for their daily game of gin rummy. Philip and I watched them for a moment and then turned back to each other.

"Well, I'd better get to my unpacking. I haven't even seen Mother yet. I can just imagine how this has all left her—headaches, nervous breakdowns." He shook his head. Then he laughed. "I wish I was here when she first set eyes on you. That must have been something. You can tell me all about it later, when we're alone," he said, his eyebrows rising.

"I'll start working with dinner tonight. Everybody's a slave driver around here. I'll come looking for you as soon as I get free," he said as he backed away, "and we'll go for a walk or something. Okay?"

"Okay."

He turned and hurried off. I stared after him a moment and then returned to my work.

Afterward I returned to my room as usual to rest. The rain had settled into a steady drizzle, and my room was dingy and dark, even though I had the lamp on. I waited for Philip and listened keenly for footsteps in the corridor. Soon I heard some and looked up expectantly when the door was opened. It was Clara Sue. For a moment we just glared at each other. Then she brought her hands to her hips and smirked, shaking her head.

"I can't believe it. I just can't believe it," she said.

"Hello, Clara Sue." Accepting her as my sister was a hard pill to swallow, but what choice did I have?

"You don't know how embarrassing all this was for me and Philip at school!" she exclaimed, widening her eyes.

"I've already spoken to Philip. I know about the gossip he had to endure, but—"

"Gossip?" She laughed, hard and mirthless; then her face turned hard, determined. "That was only part of it. He sat in a corner by himself and refused to have anything to do with anybody. But I wasn't going to let this spoil my fun," she said, coming a little farther into the room. She looked at the bland walls and the window without any curtains to warm them. "This used to be Bertha's room, my black nanny. Only it was a lot nicer then."

"I haven't had a chance to decorate," I said dryly. She stepped back quickly when she saw some of her hand-me-downs on my bed.

"Hey, isn't that one of my blouses and one of my skirts?"

"Mrs. Boston brought it to me after she cleaned up your room."

"What kind of people did you live with? Ugh. Stealing babies. No wonder you looked so . . . unwashed and Jimmy was so goofy."

"Jimmy wasn't goofy," I snapped. "And I never looked unwashed. I admit we were poor, but we were not dirty. I said I didn't have much clothing, but what I did have, I cleaned and washed regularly." She shrugged as if I couldn't say anything that would dispute her statements.

"Jimmy was weird," she insisted. "Everyone said so."

"He was shy and gentle and loving. He wasn't weird. He was just afraid, that's all. Afraid of not being accepted by a school full of snobs." I couldn't stand talking about Jimmy this way, acting as if he were dead. That made me more angry than the things she was saying.

"Why are you defending him so strongly? He wasn't really your brother," she retorted. Then she embraced herself and shook her head. "It must have been horrible and disgusting, like being forced to live with strangers."

"No, it wasn't. Momma and Daddy were always—"

"They weren't your momma and daddy," she snapped. "Don't call them that. Call them what they were—kidnappers, baby snatchers!"

I looked away, the tears stinging behind my eyes. I wouldn't let her see me cry, but what could I say? She was right, and she enjoyed driving the nails of ridicule into me.

"The worst thing of all was you and Philip," she said grimacing and twisting her mouth as if she had gulped castor oil. "No wonder he sat alone, sulking. He felt so dirty and stupid wanting to be his sister's boyfriend. And everybody knew!" She grimaced again, her face much chubbier than mine, ballooning in the cheeks. We shared hair color and eyes, but our mouths and our figures were so different.

"He can't be blamed for something he didn't know," I said softly.

How long would we have to make excuses and defend our actions? I wondered. Who else would bring it up here?

"So what? It was still disgusting. How far did you two go?" she asked, stepping closer again. "You might as well tell me. Besides, I warned you about Philip, so I won't be surprised by anything you say. I'm your sister now, and you don't have anyone else you can trust," she added and swung her eyes to me. They were full of expectation.

I stared at her. Could I ever trust her? Did she mean it? She saw the hesitation in my face.

"I'm glad Mrs. Boston brought you all my old clothing," she said. "I'd much rather you have it than throw it out or give it to the help. And I'm sorry about the things I did to you," she added quietly, "but I didn't know who you were, and I didn't think it was right then that Philip should like you so much. I must have had a prem . . . prem . . ."

"Premonition?"

"Yes," she said. "Thank you. I know you're smart and I'm glad." She pushed aside some of the clothing and sat on my bed. "So, you can tell me," she said, her face lighting with anticipation. "I know he took you to his favorite spot. You must have kissed and kissed, right?"

"Not exactly, no," I said, sitting down beside her. Maybe it would be wonderful to have a sister close to my age, I thought. Maybe I could forgive her for all the terrible things she had done, and we could learn to really get to like each other and share thoughts and dreams as well as clothes and other things. I had always wanted a sister near my age. Girls needed other girls to confide in.

She looked at me with inquisitive eyes, urging me on with her soft, sympathetic look.

"Was Philip your first boyfriend?" she asked. I nodded. "I haven't had a real boyfriend yet," she said.

"Oh, you will. You're a very pretty girl."

"I know that," she said, shaking her head. "It's not that I couldn't have a boyfriend. There have been a number who have wanted to be, but I didn't like any one enough. And none of them were as nice as Philip or as good-looking as he is. All my friends have crushes on him and were jealous of you."

"I thought so," I said.

"You know Louise had a terrible crush on Jimmy." She laughed. "I found this love letter she wrote to him but never had the nerve to mail. It was full of 'I love you' and 'You're the nicest boy I have ever met and the best-looking.' And she even wrote love words in French! I stole it and showed it to all the other girls."

"You shouldn't have done that. It must have been painful for her," I said. She blinked her eyes quickly and sat back on her hands.

"She's a freak anyway. You were the only one who ever paid her any attention. And anyway," she said, sitting up, "I used the letter to make her do things, like spy on you and get her to cooperate when we sprayed you with that stuff."

"It was a horrible trick, Clara Sue, no matter how much you didn't like me."

She shrugged.

"I said I was sorry. Look, you ruined one of my best coats," she retorted. "I had to throw it out."

"You threw it out? Why didn't you just clean it?"

"What for?" She smiled slyly. "It's easier to get Daddy to buy me a new one. I just told him someone stole it, and he sent me money for a new one." She sat forward eagerly. "But let's forget about all that and talk about Philip and you. What else did you two do besides kiss?"

"Nothing," I said.

"You don't have to be afraid to tell me," she urged.

"There's nothing to tell."

She looked very disappointed.

"You let him touch you and stuff, right? I'm sure he wanted to. He did it to one of my friends last year, slipped his hand right under her sweater, even though he denies it."

I shook my head quickly. I didn't want to hear these things about Philip, and I couldn't imagine him doing anything to a girl that she didn't want him to do anyway.

"I don't blame you for being embarrassed about it, now that the truth is out," Clara Sue said. She narrowed her eyes, eyes which became as cold metallic gray as our grandmother's eyes. "Look, I saw him kiss you in the car the night of the concert. It was a movie star kiss, a long kiss, with tongues touching, right?" she asked, her voice nearly a whisper. I shook my head vehemently, but she nodded, believing what she wanted to believe.

"He came looking for you as soon as he got here, didn't he? I heard him drop his suitcases and go rushing out of his room. Did he find you?" I nodded. "Well, what did he say? Was he angry? Did he feel like a fool?"

"He's understandably upset."

"I'll bet. I hope he doesn't forget you are his sister now," she added curtly. She gazed at me a moment. "He didn't kiss you again on the lips, did he?"

"Of course not," I said, but she looked skeptical. "We both understand what's happened," I added.

"Um." Her eyes brightened with a new thought. "What did my father say when he met you?"

"He said . . . he welcomed me to the hotel," I said, "and he told me he would have a long talk with me, but he hasn't yet. He's been very busy."

"He's always very busy. That's why I get whatever I want. He'd rather give it to me than be bothered.

"What do you think of Mother?" she asked. "You must have quite an opinion of her." She laughed anticipating. "If one of her fingernails breaks or Mrs. Boston leaves a hairbrush out of place, she has a breakdown. I can just imagine what she was like when she heard about you."

"I'm sorry she's so nervous and sick so often," I said, "because she is very beautiful."

Clara Sue nodded and folded her arms under her bosom. She was becoming a full-figured girl quickly, her baby fat already softening into what I knew most boys would consider a voluptuous look.

"Grandmother says she got sick right after you were kidnapped, and the only thing that saved her and made her happy at all again was my birth," she said, obviously proud of that. "They had me as quickly as they could to overcome their grief about losing you, and now you're back," she added, not disguising her note of disappointment. She gazed at me a moment and then smiled again.

"Grandmother made you into a chambermaid, huh?"

"Yes."

"I'm one of the receptionists now, you know," she boasted. "I get dressed up and work behind the counter. I'm letting my hair grow longer this year. Grandmother told me to go to the beautician tomorrow and have it styled," she said, gazing at herself in the mirror. She glanced quickly at me. "All the chambermaids usually cut their hair short. Grandmother likes them to."

"I'm not cutting my hair short," I said flatly.

"If Grandmother tells you to, you will. You'll have to, otherwise your hair will be dirty every day anyway. It looks dirty right now."

I couldn't argue with that. I hadn't washed it for days, not caring about my looks. It was easier to wear the bandanna.

"That's why I don't do menial jobs," Clara Sue said. "I never did. And now Grandmother thinks I'm pretty enough to be at the front desk and old enough to handle the responsibilities."

"That's very nice. You're very lucky," I said. "But I'd rather not be meeting a lot of people and forcing smiles anyway," I added. It wiped the condescending leer from her face.

"Well, I'm sure everyone's embarrassed about all this, and for now they're just trying to hide you from the public," she said curtly.

I shrugged. It was a very good theory, but I didn't want to show her that what she said might be true.

"Maybe."

"I still can't believe it." She stood up and looked down at me sharply. "Maybe I'll never believe it," she said. She tilted her head to one side and thought for a moment. "Maybe there's still a chance it's not so."

"Believe me, Clara Sue, I wish more than you that it wasn't."

That took her back a pace. Her eyebrows lifted.

"What? Why not? You certainly weren't better off living like a pauper. Now you're a Cutler and you live in Cutler's Cove. Everybody knows who we are. This is one of the finest hotels on the coast," she bragged with what I was beginning to recognize as a family arrogance she had inherited from Grandmother Cutler.

"Our lives were hard," I admitted, "but we cared about each other and loved each other. I can't help missing my little sister Fern and Jimmy."

"But they weren't your family, dummy," she said, shaking her head. "Whether you like it or not, we're your family now." I looked away. "Eugenia," she added. I spun around on her self-satisfied smile.

"That's not my name."

"Grandmother says it is, and whatever Grandmother says around here, goes," she crooned, moving toward the door. "I've got to get dressed and start my first shift at the front desk." She paused at the door. "There are a number of kids our age who come to the hotel every season. Maybe I'll introduce you to one or two of the boys, now that you can't chase after Philip anymore. After work change into something nice and come to the lobby," she added, throwing her words out as someone would throw a bone to a dog. Then she left, closing the door behind her. It clicked shut, sounding more like the door of a prison cell to me.

And when I looked around my dull and tedious room with its bland walls and worn furniture, I felt so empty and alone, I thought I might as well have been placed in solitary confinement. I folded my hands in my lap and dropped my head. Talking about family with Clara Sue made me wonder about Jimmy. Had he been given to a foster family yet? Did he like his new parents and where he had to live? Did he have a new sister? Maybe they were kinder people than the Cutlers, people who understood how terrible it had been for him. Was he worrying about me, thinking about me? I knew he must be, and my heart hurt for the pain he was surely feeling.

At least Fern was still young enough to make a quicker adjustment, I thought, even though I couldn't help but believe she missed us terribly. My eyes filled with tears just thinking about her waking up in a strange new room and calling for me, and then crying when a complete stranger came to pick her up. How terrified she must be, I thought.

Now I understood why we had always left so quickly in the middle of the night and why we'd moved so often. Daddy must have been spooked or thought he or Momma had been recognized. Now I knew why we couldn't go too far South those times and why we couldn't return to Daddy's and Momma's families. All the time we were fugitives and never knew it. But why had they taken me? I couldn't stand not knowing everything.

An idea came to me. I opened the top drawer of my night table and found some hotel stationery and began to write a letter I hoped would find its way.

Dear Daddy,

As you know by now, I have been returned to my rightful home and real family, the Cutlers. I do not know what has become of Fern and Jimmy, but the police told me that they would be farmed out to foster families, most likely two different families. So now we are all apart, all alone.

When the police came for me and accused you of kidnapping me, my heart sank because you did nothing to defend yourself, and at the police station all you could say was you were sorry. Well, being sorry is not enough to overcome the pain and the suffering you have caused.

I do not understand why you and Momma would have taken me from the Cutlers. It couldn't have been because Mommy wasn't able to have any more children. She had Fern. What possessed you to do it?

I know it doesn't seem all that important to know the reason anymore, since it has been done and is over with now, but I can't stand living with this mystery and pain, a pain I am sure Jimmy feels as well wherever he is. Won't you please try to explain why you and Momma did what you did?

We have a right to know. Keeping secrets can't mean anything to you anymore now that you are locked in prison and Momma is gone.

But it matters to us! Please write back.

Dawn

I folded it neatly and put it in a Cutler's Cove envelope. Then I left my room and went to the one person I hoped would be able to get this letter to Daddy: my real father.

I knocked on my father's office door and opened it when I heard him call. He was seated at his desk, a pile of papers and a stapler before him. I hesitated in the doorway.

"Yes?" The way he squinted at me, I thought for a moment he had forgotten who I was.

"I must talk to you. Please," I said.

"Oh, I haven't got much time at the moment. I have fallen behind on my paperwork, as you can see. Grandmother Cutler gets so upset when things aren't running on time."

"It won't take long," I pleaded.

"All right, all right. Come in. Sit down." He lifted the pile of papers and moved them to the side. "So, have you seen Philip and Clara Sue yet?"

"Yes," I said. I took the seat in front of the desk.

"Well, I imagine it will be quite an experience for the three of you to get to know each other as brother and sisters, now that you knew each other as school chums, eh?" he asked, shaking his head.

"Yes, it will."

"Well," he said, sitting up. "I'm sorry I don't have more time to spend with you right now . . ." He gestured at his office as if the responsibilities and the work were hanging on his walls. "Until we get things rolling in their proper rhythms, there is always so much to do.

"However," he said, "I've planned a night out for all of us. I'm just waiting on Laura Sue to decide which night. Then your mother and I, and Philip and Clara Sue and you will go to one of the finest seafood restaurants in Virginia. Doesn't that sound nice?"

"Yes, it does," I said.

"Well," he said, laughing softly, "you don't sound very excited about it."

"I can't help it. I know that in time, I'm supposed to get used to my new life, my real family, and forget all that has happened. . . ." I looked down.

"Oh, no," he said, "no one expects you will completely forget the past. I understand. It will take time," he said, sitting forward and stroking his ruby pinky ring as he spoke.

"So, what can I do for you?" he asked. His understanding tone of voice encouraged me.

"I can't understand why they did it. I just can't."

"Did it? Oh, you mean the Longchamps. No, of course not," he replied, nodding. "It's hard enough for other adults to understand these things, much less young people."

"And so I wrote a letter," I added quickly and produced the envelope.

"A letter?" His eyes widened and his eyebrows jumped. "To whom?"

"To my daddy . . . I mean, to the man I always thought was my daddy."

"I see." He sat back, thoughtful, his eyes narrowing and taking on some of that metallic tint I saw so often in my grandmother.

"I want him to tell me why he and Momma did this. I've got to know," I said with determination.

"Uh-huh. Well, Dawn." He grinned and lowered his voice to a loud whisper. "Don't tell my mother I keep calling you that," he said, half in jest and half seriously, I thought. His grin faded and his eyes turned severe. "I was hoping you would not try to keep in contact with Ormand Longchamp. It will only make things more difficult for everyone, even for him."

I looked down at the envelope in my hands and nodded. Tears blurred my vision. I rubbed at my eyes as a child would, feeling a child in a crazy adult world. My heart began to feel like a fist made of stone clenched in my chest.

"I just can't start a new life without knowing why they did it," I said. I looked up sharply. "I just can't."

He gazed at me quietly for a moment.

"I see," he said, nodding.

"I was hoping you would find out where they sent him and get this letter to him for me."

My suggestion surprised him. He raised his eyebrows and gazed quickly at the door as if he feared someone might be listening at the keyhole. Then he brought his left forefinger and thumb to his pinky ring and began to turn it and turn it as he nodded and thought.

"I don't know," he muttered. "I don't know whether or not that would create complications with the authorities," he said.

"It's very important to me."

"How do you know he will tell you the truth anyway?" he asked quickly. "He lied to you, told you terrible stories. I don't mean to be the one who hardens your heart against him," he added, "but what is true is true."

"I just want to try," I pleaded. "If he doesn't write back or if he doesn't tell me, I'll put it aside forever and ever. I promise."

"I see." Suddenly he picked up his pile of papers and put it down in front of him again, practically blocking me out of his vision. "Well, I don't know," he mumbled. "I don't know. I have all this work . . . Grandmother Cutler wants things running smoothly," he repeated. He started to staple papers. It seemed to me he wasn't even looking at what he was putting together.

"We shouldn't just run off doing things, half-cocked. There are responsibilities, obligations . . . preparation," he chanted.

"I don't know who else to ask, who else could do it for me," I said, my voice full of pleading. "Please!" I cried vehemently.

He stopped and looked at me.

"Well . . . all right," he said, nodding. "I'll see what I can do."

"Thank you," I said, handing him the envelope. He took it and looked at it. I had already sealed it. He put it in his top desk drawer quickly. As soon as it was gone, his face changed. The worried look disappeared and he smiled.

"Well, now," he said, "I've been meaning to talk to you about your wardrobe. Laura Sue and I discussed it last night. There are a number of things Clara Sue doesn't wear anymore that might fit you. Mrs. Boston will bring them down to your room later today, and you can go through them and see what's good and what's not."

"She already has," I said.

"Oh, good, good. Laura Sue wants to take you shopping in a day or so for whatever else you need. Is there anything else I can do for you right now?"

I shook my head. "Thank you," I said and stood up.

"It's a blessing, a miracle that you have been returned to us," he said.

Then he rose from his chair and came around his desk to walk me to the door.

"Oh. Philip told me how well you play the piano," he said.

"I just started to learn. I'm not that good."

"Still, it would be nice if you came up and played something for Laura Sue and me on the piano."

I was just getting ready to answer him when he looked back down at his desk and said, "I'm sorry, I'm just so busy. Soon I'll spend lots of time with you."

Busy with what, I wondered, stapling papers? Why didn't he have a secretary do that? "Everything will be fine. Just give it time," he advised and opened the door for me.

"Thank you," I said.

And then he leaned over and kissed me on the cheek. It was a tentative, quick peck. He squeezed my hand in his, too, and then he closed the door between us quickly as if he were afraid someone would see that he had kissed me and spoken with me.

His bizarre manner, my grandmother's unexpected harshness, my mother's strange infirmities, all left me in a daze, floundering in despair. How was I ever going to swim in this new ocean of turmoil and confusion?

And who would be my raft and keep me afloat now?

11
BETRAYED

At first I wasn't going to wear any of Clara Sue's hand-me-downs, but I wanted to look pretty again and feel like a girl instead of a tired, haggard maid. I expected Philip might come looking for me to take me for a walk through the hotel as soon as he finished his work in the dining room; so after dinner I returned to my room and tried on different blouse and skirt combinations, finally settling on a light blue, short-sleeved cotton blouse with pearl buttons and a dark blue pleated skirt. There was a pair of pretty white flat-heeled shoes in the bag. They had some slight smudges on the sides, but other than that, they looked nearly new.

Then I unpinned my hair and brushed it down. It really had to be washed and trimmed; there were a lot of split ends. I thought about Clara Sue going to a beautician, having all the brand-new clothes she wanted whenever she wanted them, and always being treated as though she were someone special. Would Grandmother Cutler eventually accept me and treat me the same way? I couldn't help imagining myself going to a beautician and wearing a new dress. I, too, would rather be working behind the reception desk than cleaning rooms.

I decided to tie a ribbon under my hair to lift it in the back. Momma used to say I shouldn't cover my ears. I could hear her even now. "You got beautiful ears, baby. Let the world see 'em." It brought a smile to my face, recalling. My eyes brightened. I was glad that Philip's arrival had made me long to be pretty again. It was good to have something to look forward to and not live in a dismal dark state all the time.

Even after getting into nice clothes and brushing my hair, however, I thought I still looked pale and sickly. My eyelids drooped and the brightness that had once radiated down from my light hair and warmed my smile had been dulled by sorrow, pain, and torment. All the expensive clothing, even a professional beautician, couldn't make the outside cheerful, if the inside was still melancholy, I thought. I pinched my cheeks as Momma used to pinch her own sometimes to make them look rosy.

When I looked at myself in the mirrors now, however, I suddenly wondered why I was doing all this. Philip wasn't my boyfriend anymore. Why did it matter how pretty I looked? Why was it still so important to please him? If anything, I was playing with forbidden fire. Just then I heard footsteps in the corridor. I went to the door and peered out, surprised to see someone in a staff uniform approaching.

"Your father asked me to have you come upstairs to your parents' rooms and play the piano for your mother." With that the short clerk hurried away. Well, I thought, being commanded to appear before them and perform isn't the loving attention I've been hoping for, but it's a start. Maybe by the end of the summer we'd be a close family, I hoped as I wandered through the hotel toward the section where the rest of my family lived.

I found Philip and Clara Sue at our mother's bedside, sitting in chairs they had brought up close. My mother was propped up against two large fluffy pillows. She had unpinned her hair, and it lay softly over her petite shoulders. She wore a gold nightie under her robe and still wore her earrings and diamond necklace, as well as all her makeup. I saw that Philip held her hand in his. Clara Sue sat back, her arms folded, her face in a smirk.

"Oh, how pretty you look, Dawn!" my mother exclaimed. "Clara Sue's clothes are a perfect fit."

"That skirt is so out of style, it isn't funny," Clara Sue inserted.

"Nothing that fits well and looks good is out of style," Father said in my defense. Clara Sue shifted her feet and squirmed in her seat. I could see she didn't like the way Father was gazing at me. "Aren't we lucky to have two pretty daughters?" he remarked. "Clara Sue and Dawn."

When I looked at Philip, I saw him staring at me intently, a slight smile on his face. Clara Sue looked at him, too, and then looked quickly at me, her eyes flashing with envy.

"I thought we weren't supposed to be calling her Dawn," Clara Sue reminded. "I thought we were supposed to call her Eugenia. That's what Grandmother said."

"When we're alone, it's all right," Mother replied. "Isn't it, Randolph?"

"Of course," he said and squeezed my hand gently after flashing a look at me that said, "Please, humor her for now."

"Grandmother's not going to like it," Clara Sue insisted. She glared at me. "You were named after her dead sister. It was a sacred gift. You should be grateful that you have a name like that instead of something stupid."

"My name is not stupid."

"Dawn for a name?" Clara Sue responded. Her laughter mocked me.

"Shut up," Philip snapped.

"Oh, please, Clara Sue!" Mother cried. "No controversy tonight. I'm so exhausted." She turned to me to explain. "It's always overwhelming when the summer people first come and we have to remember every-one's name and make them feel at home. None of us are permitted to be tired, or unhappy, or sick when Grandmother Cutler requires us to be present," she added, a note of bitterness in her voice. She tossed an icy glance at Father, but he rubbed his hands together and smiled as if he hadn't heard her.

"Well, now," he said. "Here we are, all of us, finally together. We have a great deal for which to be thankful. Isn't it wonderful? And what better way to make Dawn part of the family than to have her play something for us," Father said.

"Something soothing, please, Dawn," Mother pleaded. "I couldn't stand any rock and roll right now," she moaned, swinging her eyes at Clara Sue, who looked uncomfortable and very unhappy about being here.

"I don't know any rock and roll," I said. "There's a piece Mr. Moore, my music teacher, taught me. It was one of his favorites. I'll try to remember it," I said.

I was happy that they were all going to remain in the bedroom with Mother while I went out to the piano in the sitting room. At least I didn't have to play with Clara Sue glaring at me, I thought. But when I sat down, Philip came in and stood by my side, staring at me so intently, I felt myself begin to tremble.

I tested the notes the way Mr. Moore had instructed and I found the piano in tune.

"That's quite a song," Clara Sue quipped, hoping to make fun of me; but no one laughed.

"Relax," Philip said. "You're with your family now," he added, touching my shoulder. He gazed back at the doorway and quickly planted a kiss on my neck. "For good luck," he said quickly when I looked up surprised.

Then I closed my eyes and tried to shut the world out just the way I used to back at Emerson Peabody. With the first note I slipped softly into my musical kingdom, a land where there were no lies and sickness, no dreary skies and hateful days, a world full of smiles and love. If there was a wind, it was gentle, just strong enough to caress the leaves. If there were clouds, they were mushy white and as soft as downy silk pillows.

My fingers touched the ivory and began to move over the keyboard as though they had a mind of their own. I felt the notes flow from the piano up my arm, the music circling about me protectively, creating a cocoon of security. Nothing could touch me, not jealous eyes or ridiculing laughter. Resentment, bitterness, derogatory words of any kind were forgotten for the moment. I even forgot Philip was standing nearby.

When I was finished, it was a letdown. The music lingered like a shadow calling to me to go on. My fingers tingled and hovered over the keys, my eyes remained closed.

I opened them at the sound of the ovation. Father had come into the doorway to clap, and Philip applauded beside me. I heard my mother's gentle applause, too, and Clara Sue's quick salvo.

"Wonderful," my father said. "I'll speak to Mother. Maybe we'll have you play for the guests."

"Oh, I couldn't."

"Sure you could. What do you think, Laura Sue?" he called.

"It was beautiful. Dawn!" she cried. I got up. Philip was beaming, his eyes dancing with happiness. I returned to my mother's bedroom, and she surprised me by holding her arms out. I approached her and let her embrace me. She kissed me softly on the cheek, and when I pulled back, I saw tears in her eyes, but there was something in the way she gazed at me that made me tremble and hesitate. I sensed she saw something else in me, something I did not know existed. She was looking at me, but not exactly at me.

I questioned her with my eyes, searching her face for understanding. Now that I was this close to her, I saw how tiny her eyelashes were, how diminutive were her facial features, features I had inherited. Her eyes were dazzling, I thought, unable to take my gaze from the soft blue that twinkled with mystery as well as jeweled beauty. I spotted some faint freckles under them, just where mine were. Her skin was so translucent, I could see the tiny blue veins at the corners of her eyes, mapped out along her temples.

How delightfully sweet she smiled—her hair filled with the fragrance of jasmine. And how silky and soft her cheek had felt against mine. No wonder my father loved her so, I thought. Despite her nervous condition, she maintained a healthy, vibrant appearance, and she was as precious and lovely as any woman could be.

"That was so beautiful," she repeated. "You must come up often and play for me. Will you?"

I nodded and then glanced at Clara Sue. Her face was red and swollen with envy, her eyes burning, her mouth firm, her lips so taut they caused little patches of whiteness to appear in the corners. She clenched her fingers into puffy little balls in her lap and continued to glare at me.

"I've got to see Grandmother," she said, standing up quickly.

"Oh, already?" Mother cried mournfully. "You've just returned from school, and we haven't had time to gossip like we do. I so enjoy hearing about your friends at school and their families."

"I don't gossip," Clara Sue snapped unexpectedly, swinging her eyes at me and then back to Mother quickly.

"Well, I just meant—"

"Grandmother says we're very busy now, and we don't have time to lollygag around."

"Oh, how I hate those expressions," Mother said, grimacing. "Randolph?" she appealed.

"I'm sure Grandmother didn't mean for you to hurry right back. She knows you're up here visiting with us."

"I promised," Clara Sue insisted. Father sighed and then shrugged slightly at Mother. She took a deep breath and fell back against the pillow as if she had heard a death sentence. Why did she take everything so tragically? Had her condition begun when I had been stolen away? I felt sorry for her and terribly saddened, for it made Daddy and Mommy's action seem that much more terrible.

"I'm tired anyway," Mother suddenly said. "I think I'll retire for the evening."

"Very good, honey," Father said. Philip stepped forward.

"I can show you around a bit now," he told me. Clara Sue turned on us sharply, her eyes blazing.

"She's been here for days; you don't have to show her around," she complained.

"She's been working constantly and hasn't had time to really look over the hotel. Right, Dad?"

"Oh, yes, yes. We've all been so busy. Anyway, I'm making plans for our family outing—dinner at the Seafood House in Virginia Beach next week. If your mother feels up to it, that is," he added quickly.

"I'm working Tuesday night," Clara Sue interjected.

"Well, I'll speak to the boss and see if I can't get your schedule adjusted," Father said, smiling, but Clara Sue didn't return his smile.

"Grandmother hates when we do that. She wants the hotel to run like a clock," Clara Sue insisted, her hands on her hips. Whenever she nagged or whined, she scrunched up her nose, widening her nostrils and making herself look like a little hog.

"We'll see," Father said, still not showing any fluster. I couldn't imagine why not. Clara Sue needed discipline if anyone ever did, I thought.

"I've got to go," Clara Sue repeated and stormed out.

"Oh, how I hate the summer season," Mother said. "It makes everyone so tense. I wish I could go to sleep and wake up in September." She actually had two small tears shining in the corners of her eyes.

"Now, now, dear," Father said, going to her side. "Don't let anything bother you this summer, remember? Remember what Doctor Madeo said: You've got to develop a tougher skin, ignore things that disturb you and think about only pleasant things. Now that Dawn is back and she is so talented and beautiful, we have even nicer things to think about."

"Yes," Mother said, smiling at him through her tears. "I did enjoy her piano playing."

"We've had some talented performers play here over the years, Dawn," Father said. "It will be wonderful to add you to the list someday soon."

I looked from his smiling face to my mother's and saw that hers had become serious, even sorrowful again as she gazed intently at me. Once more I saw something confusing in her eyes, but I didn't give myself a chance to think about it.

The next day there was an air of excitement running throughout the hotel. Everywhere I looked the staff was busy working, taking extra care to make the hotel look spic and span. In the kitchen the cook, Nussbaum, was cooking up a feast, and outside the gardeners were tending to the grounds with meticulous care.

"What's going on?" I asked Sissy as I saw her zoom by with an armful of fine lace tablecloths.

Sissy stopped dead in her tracks. She stared at me, her eyes widening. "Don't you know?" she asked. "Don't you know what day today is?"

"No, I don't," I honestly admitted. "Is today a special day?"

"It sure is!" Sissy proclaimed. "Today is Mrs. Cutler's birthday. Tonight there's going to be a big party with decorations, a birthday cake, and tons of guests and presents."

After delivering the news Sissy continued on her way, leaving me to grapple with a dilemma. Today was Grandmother Cutler's birthday, and I hadn't even known. But even if I had, what difference would it have made? I knew how she felt about me—her feelings were obvious. Why should I care that today was her birthday? Yet suddenly I remembered Momma always telling me to treat others the way you would like them to treat you. Although I wanted to be just as mean and thoughtless to Grandmother Cutler as she had been to me, I kept remembering Momma's words. I sighed. I suppose I could turn my cheek the other way just this once. Maybe this was the chance I had been waiting for. Maybe this could be the first step in making things right between myself and Grandmother Cutler. I had hardly any money saved up to buy her a nice present. What was I going to do?

I supposed I could ask my father for some money to buy a present, but that wouldn't be the same as getting Grandmother Cutler something myself. Besides, knowing her, she'd be awfully suspicious if I bought something I really couldn't afford. Then I came up with a solution. A brilliant solution! I would give Grandmother Cutler a gift from my heart and upon which a price tag could never be placed.

I would sing her a song. This would be a step toward smoothing things out between us. Yes, my song would make everything right!

I eagerly dashed off to my room to practice, unable to wait for Grandmother Cutler's birthday party that evening.

That night I dressed with extra special care. First, I took a long, luxuriating shower, shampooing my hair and then conditioning it. When my hair was finally dry it was soft and fluffy, falling down my back in silky, cascading waves.

Surveying my wardrobe, I chose to wear a white pleated skirt with a pink silk blouse and a sweater vest of pink and white. Taking a look at myself in a mirror, I thought I looked very nice and hurried down to the hotel lobby. That's where Grandmother Cutler would be greeting her guests and accepting her gifts.

The lobby was already decorated with colorful streamers and balloons. A sign that read HAPPY BIRTHDAY stretched from one end of the lobby to the other. A line of guests was already waiting to meet with my grandmother. At its end were Clara Sue and Philip. Each had a gaily wrapped package in their hands. Philip's was tiny while Clara Sue's was huge. For a moment I felt embarrassed being empty handed. Then I reminded myself that I had a gift for Grandmother Cutler, too.

"What are you doing here?" Clara Sue sniffed disdainfully. She inspected me from head to toe. "Why does that outfit look so familiar? Oh, yes!" she laughed gaily. "It was mine before I decided to throw it out. Shall we call you 'Second-Hand Dawn' from now on? It seems like you're always settling for seconds. Clothing, family." She laughed cruelly.

Philip gave Clara Sue a dark look. "You sound jealous, Clara Sue. Could it be that your outfit looks much better on Dawn than it ever did on you?" he said, coming to my defense.

"Thank you," I said to Philip. "And thank you, Clara Sue." I was determined not to let Clara Sue's pettiness bother me. "I never owned anything so pretty before."

"It must be hard getting used to silk when you've only worn burlap for years," Clara Sue said sweetly.

I bit my tongue and turned to Philip. "What did you buy for Grandmother?"

"Perfume," he proudly boasted. "It's her favorite. It costs a hundred dollars a bottle."

"I bought her a handmade vase," Clara Sue threw in, shoving herself between me and Philip. "It was made in China. What did you get her?"

"I didn't have enough time or money to buy her a present," I admitted, "so I'm going to sing her a song."

"A song?" Clara Sue looked at me blandly. "A song? You've got to be kidding!"

"Yes, a song. What's wrong with that?" I could feel myself turning red. Maybe I should have brought Grandmother Cutler something. There was still time. I could get a bouquet of flowers in the hotel gift shop.

"You can't be serious!" Clara Sue exclaimed. "What's the matter? You too cheap?"

"I'm not cheap!" I told her. "I told you why I don't have a present. Besides, it's the thought that counts."

"Some thought," Clara Sue snorted. "An off-key tune. Whooppee!"

"That's enough, Clara Sue," Philip ordered sharply. "Dawn's right. It's the thought that counts."

I gave Philip a grateful smile as we moved closer up. "Thanks for the vote of confidence."

He gave me a wink. "Don't worry. You'll knock her socks off."

After half an hour we reached Grandmother Cutler. Both my parents were at her side, looking exceptionally nice. My father gave me a smile while my mother stared at me nervously.

Philip was the first to approach Grandmother. She opened his present slowly, being careful not to rip the paper. After finding the bottle of perfume, she dabbed some on her wrists and neck, inhaling the scent while giving Philip a big smile.

"Thank you, Philip. You know how much I adore this scent."

Clara Sue was next, and Grandmother once again opened the package slowly, removing a very pretty vase with an Oriental design from a mass of pink tissue paper.

"It's exquisite, Clara Sue," she raved. "Exquisite! It will look lovely in my bedroom."

Clara Sue nudged me in the side. "Let's see you top that with your dinky little song," she whispered before heading to kiss Grandmother Cutler on the cheek.

Now it was my turn. Butterflies fluttered around my stomach, but I ignored them as I stepped up to Grandmother Cutler, a tentative smile on my face.

"This is a surprise," she said, looking down at me from the ornately carved chair she sat upon. She held out her hands, expecting a gift to be placed in them. "Well?" she coldly asked.

I nervously cleared my throat. "My gift isn't wrapped, Grandmother."

She looked at me strangely. "It isn't?"

"No." I took a deep breath. "I'm going to sing you a song. That's my present to you."

Taking a deep breath, I launched into the song I had chosen to sing. It was my very favorite, "Over the Rainbow," the song I felt I sang with the most confidence. Suddenly I was no longer in Cutler's Cove, but over the rainbow. In the land of *my* dreams. I was back with Momma and Daddy, and Jimmy and Fern. We were all together, safe and happy. Nothing would ever tear us apart.

When I finished the song, there was a tear in my eye. The crowd broke into applause and I smiled at everyone. My parents and Philip were even clapping, although Clara Sue wasn't. I turned to Grand-mother Cutler. She was also clapping, but it wasn't because she was proud of me. Oh no! She was only doing this for appearance, because others were around. Her eyes glared at me icily and although there was a smile on her lips, her face was devoid of emotion. Frozen solid and as sleek as a chunk of granite.

The guests started heading to the dining room, talking among them-selves. Many of them complimented me as they walked by. Soon only my family was left.

"What did you think of my song?" I asked Grandmother Cutler meekly.

"Is that all?" she asked in her iciest tone as she rose from her seat. "If so, please step to one side. I have guests to entertain."

"That's all," I whispered. I stood still, speechless. How could every-thing have gone so wrong? I looked to my parents, to Philip and Clara Sue, but no one came to my defense. No one. Once again I was all alone.

Grandmother Cutler turned to the rest of my family. "Shall we ad-journ to the dining room?" She led the way out, not even looking at me.

Not able to say anything, fearing I would break down and cry, I turned away and fled. As long as I lived I would never, ever forget this horrible evening.

The following day Philip found me alone in the lobby, still feeling sorry for myself.

"Shake away that frown and forget about last night," he said. "You'll win over Grandmother. Wait and see. In the meantime, you need some cheering up." He grabbed my hand, pulling me after him as he headed outside.

The clouds had parted, and the sunlight was now streaming down in warm rays and making everything look bright and new. The grass smelled fresh and was Kelly green, as were the leaves on bushes and trees.

I did look at everything as though for the first time. Up until now I had spent most of my time in the hotel working or sitting in my room.

Philip's excitement opened my eyes and made me realize just how beautiful and big the Cutler's Cove Hotel and grounds were.

To the left was a huge sparkling blue swimming pool with a bright white and blue cabana at the far end and a children's wading pool at the near end. A number of guests had come out to greet the returning sun and were bathing and sunning themselves on the lounge chairs that were set up along the sides of the pool. Pool boys were circulating about, setting up the cushions and providing guests with towels or whatever they needed. The lifeguard sat in his high chair at the far end overseeing the swimmers.

There were pretty little walkways off to the right, circling through gardens and fountains. At the center was a large bright green gazebo. Some guests were seated at a table playing cards, and others were simply relaxing on the benches, talking softly, enjoying the afternoon.

We walked down one of the fieldstone pathways. I paused to smell the scent of the tulips, and Philip broke off a white gardenia and put it into my hair.

"Perfect," he said, standing back.

"Oh, Philip, you shouldn't do that," I said gazing about quickly to see if anyone had noticed. No one was looking our way particularly, but my heart fluttered beneath my breast.

"No big deal. We own the place, remember?"

He took my hand again, and we continued down the pathway.

"We have a baseball field over there," Philip said, pointing to the extreme right. I could see the high-back stop fence. "There's a staff softball team. Sometimes we play the guests; sometimes we play the staffs from other hotels."

"I didn't realize how beautiful and spacious it was back here," I said. "When I arrived at the hotel, it was already dark, and I haven't done much exploring on my own."

"Everyone's jealous of how much land we own and what we've been able to do with it over the years," he said proudly. "We offer guests much more than the average beach resort can," he added, sounding like a true son of a hotel family. He saw the smile on my face. "I sound like an advertising brochure, huh?"

"That's all right. It's good to be excited about your family's business."

"It's your family's business now, too," he reminded me. I looked about again. How long would it take before I had such a feeling? I had to keep telling myself that if I hadn't been stolen right after my birth, I would have grown up here and been used to it.

We stopped at one of the fountains. He stared at me a moment, his blue eyes growing darker and more thoughtful and then suddenly lighting up with the exciting thought that had occurred behind them.

"Come on," he said, seizing my hand again, "I want to show you something secret." He tugged me so hard, I nearly fell over.

"Philip!"

"Oh, sorry. You all right?"

"Yes," I said laughing.

"Come on," he repeated, and we ran around the side of the old section until we came to a small cement stairway that led down to a faded white and chipped wooden door with a black iron handle. The door's hinges were rusted, and it was so off kilter that when he scurried down the steps and started opening it, it scraped along the cement and he had to jiggle and lift it to get it to open.

"Haven't been here since school began," he explained.

"What is it?"

"My hideaway," he said with furtive eyes. "I used to come here whenever I was unhappy or just when I wanted to be alone."

I gazed through the doorway into a pitch-dark room. A whiff of cold, damp air came out to greet us.

"Don't worry, there's a light. You see," he said, entering slowly. He reached back for my hand. This time a tingle traveled through my fingers when they became laced with his. I followed.

"Most buildings in Cutler's Cove don't have basements, but ours, because it was built up here, does," he explained. "Years and years ago, when Cutler's Cove was just a rooming house, this was where the caretaker lived." He stopped and reached up through the darkness for a cord that dangled from the sole light fixture. When he pulled it, the naked bulb cast a pale white glow over the room, revealing cement walls and a cement floor, some shelving, a small wooden table with four chairs, two old dressers, and a bed in a metal frame. There was only a stained old mattress on the bed.

"There's a window here," Philip said, pointing, "but it's kept boarded up to keep field animals out. Look," he said, indicating the shelves, "there are still some of my toys down here." He went to the shelves and showed me little trucks and cars and a cap pistol quite rusted. "There's even a bathroom down here," he said and pointed to the right rear of the underground room.

I saw a narrow doorway and went to it. There was a small sink, toilet, and tub. Both the tub and sink had ugly brown stains, and there were cobwebs everywhere.

"Needs a good cleaning, but everything works," Philip declared, coming up beside me. He knelt down and turned the water on in the tub. Brown, rusted liquid came gushing out. "Hasn't been used for some time, of course," he explained. He let the water run until it began to clear up.

"So," he said, standing. "How do you like my hideaway?"

I smiled and gazed around. It wasn't that much worse than some of the places Momma and Daddy, Jimmy and I had lived in before Fern had been born, I thought, but I was too embarrassed to tell Philip.

"Use it whenever you want, whenever you want to get away from the turmoil," he said as he walked over to the bed and flopped down on the mattress. He bounced on it, testing the springs. "I'm going to bring down some bedding and some clean dishes and towels." He lay back on the mattress, his hands behind his head, and gazed up at the beams in the ceiling. Then he swung his eyes to me, gazing intently, his full sensual lips open.

"I couldn't help thinking about you all the time, Dawn, even after I had found out about us and I knew it was wrong to think of you this way." He sat up quickly. I couldn't take my eyes from his. They were so magnetic, demanding. "I like to think of you as two different people: the girl with whom I had found magic and . . . my new sister. But I can't just forget the magic," he added quickly.

I nodded and looked down.

"I'm sorry," he said and got up. "Am I embarrassing you?"

I looked into his soft blue eyes again, unable to stop myself from recalling that first day at school when he had come to sit with me in the cafeteria, when I had thought him the handsomest boy I had ever met.

"How am I ever going to get used to the idea that you're my sister?" he complained.

"You'll have to." Standing this close to him made me shiver. Those were the lips that had pressed so warmly against mine. If I closed my eyes, I could feel his fingers traveling gently over my breasts. The memory made them tingle. He was right about one thing—our new relationship was so surprising and so new, it was hard to accept it yet.

"Dawn," he whispered. "Can I just hold you, just for a moment, just to—"

"Oh, Philip, we shouldn't. We should try to—"

He ignored me and brought his hands to my shoulders to pull me toward him. Then he gathered me in his arms and held me there against him. His breath was warm on my cheek. He clutched me as if I were the only one who could save him. I felt his lips graze my hair and forehead. My heart pounded as he held me tighter, my breasts brought firmly to his chest.

"Dawn," he whispered again. I felt his hands coming around my shoulders. Electric tingles seized madly up and down my arms, and all those nerves that a girl my age wasn't supposed to have burned with fire. I must stop him, I thought. This is wrong. I screamed inside myself, but suddenly he seized my wrists and held them against my sides. Then he kissed my neck and started to travel down to my breasts.

He let go of my wrists and brought his hands to my bosom quickly. As soon as he did, I stepped back.

"Philip, stop. You mustn't. We'd better go." I started toward the door.

"Don't go. I'm sorry. I told myself I wouldn't dream of doing that when I was alone with you, but I couldn't help it. I'm sorry," he said.

When I looked back at him, he did look like someone in torment.

"I won't do it again. I promise," he said. He smiled and stepped toward me. "I just wanted to hold you to see if I could hold you the way a brother should hold a sister, to comfort you or greet you, but not . . . to touch you that way."

He bowed his head remorsefully.

"I guess I shouldn't have brought you here so soon."

He waited, his eyes hopeful that I would disagree and want to forget the truth.

"Let's leave, Philip," I said. When his arms had encircled me and held me fast, I had become an instrument of desire for romantic fulfillment. Now I was scared, too, of what was inside me.

He reached up quickly and pulled the light cord dropping a sheet of darkness over us. Then he seized my arm.

"In the darkness we can pretend we're not brother and sister. You can't see me; I can't see you." His grip tightened.

"Philip!"

"Just kidding," he said and laughed. He released his hold on me, and I retreated to the door.

I hurried out and turned to wait for him to close the door and follow. As soon as he did, we started up the cement stairs. But just as we did so, a shadow moved over us, and we both looked up into the disapproving eyes of Grandmother Cutler.

Bloated with anger, she glared down at us and looked so much bigger and taller.

"Clara Sue thought you two would be here," she spat. "I'm returning to my office. Eugenia, I want to see you there within five minutes. Philip, Collins needs you in the dining room immediately."

She spun on her heels and walked off briskly.

My heart felt as if it would crack open my chest, and my face felt so hot and flushed, I thought my cheeks would burn. Philip turned back to me, his face filled with fear and embarrassment. What had happened to the strong, confident look he had worn so often back at school? He looked so feeble and weak. He gazed after Grandmother and then back at me.

"I . . . I'm sorry. I'd better get going," he stammered.

"Philip!" I cried, but he lunged up the remaining steps and rushed off.

I took a deep breath and continued up the stairs. A heavy-looking, bruised gray cloud slipped over the warm afternoon sun, putting a chill in my heart.

Clara Sue smiled smugly at me from the receptionist's desk as I walked through the lobby toward Grandmother Cutler's office. She was obviously still jealous and upset by the way Father and Mother had reacted to my playing the piano the other day, I thought, as well as to the crowd's applause for my singing at Grandmother Cutler's birthday party. I knocked on Grandmother's office door. I found her seated behind her desk, her back straight, her shoulders stiff, and her arms on the arms of the chair. She looked like a high court judge. I stood before her, a tight wire inside, stretched so taut I thought I might break and cry.

"Sit down," she commanded icily and nodded toward the chair before her desk. I slipped into it, clutching the arms tightly in my palms, and gazed nervously at her.

"Eugenia," she said, only moving her head slightly forward, "I'm going to ask you this just once. Just what is there between you and your brother?"

"Between us?"

"Don't force me to define every one of my words and speak unspeakable things," she snarled and then quickly relaxed again. "I know that when you were at Emerson Peabody, before Philip learned the truth of your identity, he fancied you one of his girlfriends, and you, understandably, were attracted to him. Did anything happen for which this family should feel shame?" she asked, raising her eyebrows inquisitively.

It was as if my heart stopped beating and waited for my mind to stop reeling. A gush of heat rushed up my stomach and over my breasts, circling my throat in a fiery ring that choked me. I felt feverish. At first my tongue refused to form words, but as the silence stretched and became uncomfortably thick, I vanquished my throat lumps and caught my breath.

"Absolutely nothing," I said with a voice so deep I hardly recognized it as my own. "What a horrible thing to ask!"

"It would be far more horrible if you had something to confess," she retorted. Her sharp, penetrating gaze rested on me with deep concentration.

"Philip is a healthy young man," she began, "and like all young men, he is not unlike a wild horse just finding his legs. I think you have the worldly experience to understand my point." She waited for me to acknowledge her, but I simply stared, my heart pounding, my teeth coming down on my lower lip. "And you are not without attractive feminine characteristics, the sort most men find irresistible," she added disdainfully. "Therefore," she concluded, "most of the responsibility for proper behavior will depend on you."

"We've done nothing wrong," I insisted, now unable to keep the tears that burned behind my eyelids from emerging.

"And that's the way I want to keep it," she replied, nodding. "I am forbidding you from this day forward to spend any time alone with him, do you hear? You are not to go into any hotel rooms by yourselves or invite him into your room without a third party present."

"That's not fair. We're being punished when we haven't done anything wrong."

"It's for preventative purposes," she said and in a little more reasonable tone added, "until you are both able to conduct yourselves more like a normal brother and sister. You must keep in mind how unusual the circumstances have been and are. I know what's best."

"You know what's best? Why do you know what's best for everyone else? You can't tell everyone how to live, how to act, even when to speak to each other," I stormed, my anger now rising like an awakened giant. "I won't listen to you."

"You will only make things more difficult for yourself and for Philip," she threatened.

I gazed about the room frantically and wondered where were my mother and my father? Why wasn't at least my father here to participate in this discussion? Were they merely puppets? Did my grandmother pull their strings and run their lives, too?

"Now, then," she said, shifting herself in the seat and shifting her tone of voice as if the issue had been settled, "I have given you sufficient time to adjust yourself to your new surroundings and your new responsibilities, yet you persist in hanging on to some of your old ways."

"What old ways?"

She leaned forward and uncovered something on her desk.

"That silly name, for one," she said. "You have succeeded in confusing my staff. This nonsense has got to end. Most girls who had lived the kind of hand to mouth existence you were forced to live would be more than grateful for all you have now. I want to see some signs of that gratitude. One way you can do that is to wear this on your uniform; it's something most of my staff does anyway."

"What is it?" I leaned forward, and she turned the nameplate toward me. It was a tiny brass plaque with EUGENIA written boldly in black. Instantly my heart became a thumping heavy lead drum in my chest. My cheeks became so inflamed, it felt as if my skin were on fire. All I could think was that she was trying to brand me, to make me a conquest, a possession, to prove to everyone in the hotel that she would have her way whenever she wanted.

"I'll never wear that," I said defiantly. "I'd rather be sent to live with some foster family."

She shook her head and pulled the corners of her mouth in as if I were some pitiful creature.

"You'll wear it; you won't go live with any foster family, though goodness knows, I would gladly send you if I thought that would end the turmoil.

"I was hoping that by now you had seen that this is your life and that you should live according to the rules set down for you. I was hoping that in time you would somehow fit in here and become part of this distinguished family. Because of your squalid background and upbringing, I see now that you will not fit in as quickly as I'd wished—particularly since despite some qualities and talents to recommend you, you cling to your wild and unrefined ways."

"I'll never change my name," I said resolutely. She glared at me and nodded.

"Very well. You are to return to your room and remain there until you change your mind and agree to put this nameplate on your uniform. Until then you will not report to work and you will not go to the kitchen to eat. No one will bring you anything to eat, either."

"My father and mother won't let you do this," I said. That made her smile. "They won't!" I cried through my tears. "They like me; they want us to be a family," I bawled. The hot drops streaked down my face.

"Of course we will be a family; we are a family, a distinguished family, but in order for you to become part of it, you must cast off your disgraceful past.

"Now, after you put on your nameplate and accept your birthright—"

"I won't." I ground the tears out of my eyes with my fists and shook my head. "I won't," I whispered.

She ignored me.

"After you put on your nameplate," she repeated, hissing through clenched teeth, "you will return to your duties." She stopped talking and scrutinized me.

"We'll see," she said with such cold confidence, it made my knees shake. "Everyone in the hotel will know you are being insubordinate," she added. "No one will talk to you or be friendly until you conform. You can save yourself and everyone else a great deal of grief, Eugenia." She held out the nameplate. I shook my head.

"My father won't let you do this," I said, half in prayer.

"Your father," she said with such vehemence it widened my eyes. "That's another problem you cling to stubbornly. You have learned what terrible things Ormand Longchamp has done, and yet you want to remain in contact with him." I looked up sharply. She sat back and opened her desk drawer to take out the letter I had written to Daddy and had given to my father to send. My heart jumped and then plunged. How could my father have given it to her—I'd told him how important it was to me. Oh, was there no one I could trust in this hateful place?

"I forbid you to communicate with this man, this child stealer." She tossed the letter across her desk. "Take this and yourself back to your room. Don't even come out to eat. When you are ready to become part of this family, this hotel, and this great heritage, return and ask for your nameplate. I don't want to set eyes on you again until you do that. You're excused," she said and turned to some papers on her desk.

For a long moment my legs wouldn't respond to my command to stand. I felt paralyzed in the chair. Her strength seemed so formidable. How could I hope to defeat such a person? She ruled the hotel and the family like a queen, and I, still the most lowly family member, had been returned to her kingdom, in many ways more of a prisoner than Daddy, who was in jail.

I rose slowly, my legs shaking. I wanted to run out of her office and charge out of the hotel, but where would I run to? Where would I go? Who would take me in? I never knew any of Daddy or Momma's relatives in Georgia, and they, as far as I knew, never even heard of me or Jimmy or Fern. If I just ran off, Grandmother would send the police after me, I thought. Or maybe she wouldn't; maybe she would be glad. Still, she couldn't help but inform the police, and a girl like me in a strange place would soon be found and returned.

Everyone would consider me the ungrateful one, too, the unwashed wild thing who had to be trained, broken, and forced to be a young lady. Grandmother would look like the abused yet loving matriarch of the family. No one would want anything to do with me until I obeyed her and changed into what she wanted me to be.

I started out of her office, my head down. Who could I turn to?

Never did I miss Jimmy more than I did at this moment. I missed the way he narrowed his eyes when he gave something deep thought. I missed the confident smile he had when he was sure what he was saying was right. I missed the warmth in his dark eyes when he looked at me lovingly. I remembered the way he promised to always be there whenever I needed him, and how he swore he would always protect me. How I missed the security that came from the feeling that he was nearby watching over me.

I opened the office door and without looking back walked out. The hotel lobby was growing crowded. People were coming in from their afternoon activities. Many milled about talking excitedly. I saw some children and teenagers standing with their parents. Like all of the guests, they were well dressed, happy, affluent-looking people. Everyone was bubbly and cheerful. They were enjoying their holiday together. For a moment I stood there and looked longingly and enviously at these happy families. Why were they so lucky? What had they done to be born into that sort of world, and what had I done to be tossed and turned about in a storm of confusion: mothers and fathers who were not real parents, brothers and sisters who were not real brothers and sisters.

And a grandmother who was a tyrant.

With my head down I walked through the lobby and did the only thing that I could do: return to my room, which had now become my prison. But I was determined. I would rather die than give up my name, even though it was a lie.

Sometimes we need our lies more than we need the truth, I thought.

12
ANSWERED PRAYERS

On the way to my room I paused when I reached the stairway that led up to my parents' suite. I was still feeling cold because of my father's betrayal, but I thought my mother should at least know what my grandmother was doing to me. After only a short hesitation, I scampered up the steps and met Mrs. Boston, who had just brought my mother her supper.

"Doesn't she feel well?" I asked, and Mrs. Boston looked at me as if to say, "When does she?"

After she left I knocked softly and entered my mother's bedroom.

"Dawn. How nice," she said, looking up from her tray of food. It had been placed on a bed table, and she was propped up against her pillows as usual; and as usual, she had her face all made up as though she were going to throw off her covers and jump into a pair of shoes to attend a party or a dance. She wore a soft-looking silk nightgown with a silver lace collar. Her fingers and wrists were laden with rings and bracelets. Gold drop earrings dangled from her lobes.

"Did you come to play me some dinner music on the piano?" she asked, smiling softly. She did have an angelic face with eyes that betrayed just how fragile she was. I was tempted to do only what she asked—play the piano and leave without telling her about the horrible events.

"I was going to come down and join everyone for dinner, but when I began to get dressed, I was suddenly stricken with an ugly headache. It's diminished some now, but I don't want to do anything that would bring it back," she explained.

"Come, sit by me a moment and talk to me while I eat," she said and nodded toward a chair.

I brought the chair closer to the bed. She continued to smile and began to eat, cutting everything up into tiny pieces and then pecking at the food like a small bird. She rolled her eyes as if the effort it took to chew exhausted her. Then she sighed deeply.

"Don't you sometimes wish you could skip eating, just go to sleep and wake up nourished? Meals can be such ordeals, especially in a hotel. People are so involved with their food. It's absolutely the most important thing for most of them. Have you noticed?"

"I will be skipping my meals," I began, taking a cue from her complaint. "But not because I want to skip them."

"What?" She started to widen her smile, but saw the intensity in my eyes and stopped. "Is something wrong? Oh, please, don't tell me something's wrong," she pleaded, dropping her fork and pressing her palms to her bosom.

"I have to tell you," I insisted. "You're my mother, and there just isn't anyone else."

"Are you sick? Do you have some obnoxious stomach cramps? Your time of month?" she said, nodding hopefully, and continued pecking at her food with her fork, scrutinizing each piece before stabbing it quickly to bring it to her mouth. "Nothing bores me more and disgusts me so much. During my period, I don't budge from this bed. Men don't know how lucky they are not to have to go through it. If Randolph gets impatient with me then, I just remind him of that, and he shuts right up."

"It's not my period. I wish it were only that," I replied. She stopped chewing and stared.

"Did you tell your father? Has he sent for the doctor?"

"I'm not sick, Mother. Not in that sense, anyway. I just came from a meeting with Grandmother Cutler."

"Oh," she said, as if one sentence explained everything.

"She wants me to wear a nameplate on my uniform with the name Eugenia on the plate," I said. I skipped the part about Philip, not only because I didn't want to confuse her, but I couldn't stand talking about it myself.

"Oh, dear." She looked down at her food and then dropped the fork again and pushed the tray away. "I can't eat when there is so much controversy. The doctor says it would damage my digestion, and I would have bad stomachaches."

"I'm sorry. I didn't mean to ruin your dinner."

"Well, you did," she said with surprising sharpness. "Please, don't talk about these things anymore."

"But . . . Grandmother Cutler has told me to remain in my room until I wear the nameplate, and she has forbidden me to eat. The kitchen staff certainly won't serve me if she tells them not to."

"Forbidden you to eat?" She shook her head and looked away.

"Can't you speak to her for me?" I pleaded.

"You should have gone to your father," she said, still not looking at me.

"I can't. He won't do anything to help me anyway," I moaned. "I gave him a letter to mail to . . . to the man who had pretended to be my daddy, and he promised he would, but instead, he gave the letter to Grandmother Cutler."

She nodded, slowly, and turned back to me, now a different sort of smile on her face. It was more like a smirk of disgust.

"It doesn't surprise me," she said. "He makes promises easily and then forgets he made them. But why did you want to mail a letter to Ormand Longchamp after you learned what he had done?"

"Because . . . because I want him to tell me why he did it. I still don't understand, and I never had a real chance to speak with him before the police scooted me off and brought me back here. But Grandmother Cutler won't let me have any contact with him," I said and held up the envelope.

"Why did you give it to Randolph?" Mother asked, her eyes suddenly small and suspicious.

"I didn't know where to send it, and he promised he would find out and do it for me."

"He shouldn't have made such a promise." She was thoughtful for a moment, her eyes taking on a glazed, far-off look.

"What should I do?" I cried, hoping she would assume her role as my mother and be in charge of what happened to me. But instead, she looked down in defeat.

"Wear the nameplate and take it off when you're not working," she replied quickly.

"But why should she be able to tell me what to do? You're my mother, aren't you?" I cried.

She looked up, her eyes sadder, darker.

"Yes," she said softly. "I am, but I am not as strong as I used to be."

"Why not?" I demanded, frustrated by her weakness. "When did you become sick? After I was kidnapped?" I wanted to know more.

She nodded and fell back against her pillows.

"Yes," she said, looking up at the ceiling. "My life changed after that." She sighed deeply.

"I'm sorry," I said. "But I don't understand. That's why I wrote to the man I grew up thinking was my daddy. Where was I kidnapped from? The hospital? Had you brought me home?"

"You were here. It happened late at night when we were all asleep. One of the suites that we keep shut up across the hall was your nursery. We had set it up so nicely." She smiled at the memory. "It was so pretty with new wallpaper and new carpet and all the new furniture. Every day during my pregnancy, Randolph bought another infant's toy or something to hang on the walls.

"He had hired a nurse, of course. Her name was Mrs. Dalton. She had two children of her own, but they were fully grown and off making their own lives, so she was able to live here."

Mother shook her head.

"She lived here only three days. Randolph wanted to keep her on duty after you were stolen. He was always hopeful you would be found and returned, but Grandmother Cutler discharged her, blaming her for being so negligent. Randolph was heartbroken over it all and thought it was wrong to blame her, but there was nothing he could do."

She took a deep breath, closed her eyes, and then opened them and shook her head.

"He stood right there in that doorway," she said, "and cried like a baby himself. He loved you so." She turned to me. "You never saw a grown man act so silly over a baby when you were born. If he could have spent twenty-four hours a day with you, he would have.

"You know, you were born with nearly a full head of hair, all golden. And you were so small, almost too small to take right home. For a long time afterward, Randolph used to say he wished you had been too small. Then maybe we'd still have you.

"Of course, he wouldn't give up searching and hoping. False alarms sent him traveling all over the country. Finally Grandmother Cutler decided to put an end to the hope."

"She made the memorial stone," I said.

"I didn't think you knew about that," Mother said, her eyes wide with surprise.

"I saw it. Why did you and Father let Grandmother Cutler do such a thing? I wasn't dead."

"Grandmother Cutler's always been a strong-willed woman. Randolph's father used to say she was as tenacious as tree roots and as hard as bark.

"Anyway, she insisted we do something to face facts and go on with our lives."

"But wasn't it terrible for you? Why would you do such a thing?" I repeated. I couldn't imagine a mother agreeing to bury her own child symbolically without knowing for sure that the child was dead.

"It was a quick, simple ceremony. No one but the family, and it worked," she said. "After that, Randolph stopped hoping, and we went on to have Clara Sue."

"You let her force you to give up," I said. "To forget me," I added, not without some note of accusation.

"You're too young to understand these things, honey," she replied in her own defense. I glared at her. There were some things that didn't require you to be old to understand and appreciate. One of them was a mother's love for her child, I thought. Momma wouldn't have let someone force her to go to the funeral of her missing child.

It was all so strange.

"If I was so small, wasn't it dangerous for them to kidnap me?" I asked.

"Oh, sure. That's why Grandmother Cutler insisted you were probably dead," she replied quickly.

"If you had a sleep-in nurse, how did they get me anyway?" I still couldn't believe I was talking about something terrible Daddy and Momma had done.

"I don't remember all the details," Mother said and rubbed her forehead. "My headache's coming back. Probably because you forced me to recall so many horrible memories."

"I'm sorry, Mother," I said. "But I have to know."

She nodded and sighed.

"But let's not talk about it anymore," she suggested and smiled. "You're here now; you've been returned. The horror is behind us."

"The monument is still there," I said, remembering what Sissy had told me.

"Oh, dear, how morbid you can be."

"Why did they steal me, Mother?"

"No one has told you that?" She looked at me slyly, her head tilted. "Grandmother Cutler didn't tell you?"

"No," I said. My heart paused. "I was afraid to ask her anything like that."

Mother nodded understandingly.

"Sally Longchamp had just given birth to a stillborn baby. They simply substituted you for the dead baby.

"That's another reason why Grandmother Cutler wants your name changed so much, I guess."

"What is?" I asked, my voice so weak it was barely audible.

"Not many people remember anymore. Randolph never knew. I just happened to know because . . . I just happened to know. And of course your grandmother knew. There wasn't much she didn't know if it happened anywhere near or on the hotel grounds," she added acridly.

"What?" I repeated.

"The dead Longchamp baby was a girl, too. And they were going to name it Dawn."

I could see there wasn't much point to my continuing to plead for my mother to intercede between me and my grandmother. Mother's attitude was to do what Grandmother Cutler wanted because in the long run that was the easiest route to take. She told me that somehow Grandmother Cutler always managed to get her way anyway. It was futile to fight.

Of course, I didn't agree. The things she had told me about Momma and Daddy and my kidnapping left me stunned. No matter how terrible it must have been for Momma to give birth to a stillborn, it was still horrible of them to steal me from my real parents. What they had done was selfish and cruel, and when my mother described my father crying in the doorway, my heart ached for him.

I returned to my little room and plopped down on the bed to stare up at the ceiling. It had begun to rain, another summer storm rushing in from the ocean. The staccato beats on the building and windows were military drums to take me into dreams, into nightmares, to exactly where I didn't want to go. I envisioned Momma and Daddy sneaking up the stairs at night when everyone was asleep. Although I had not met her, I imagined Nurse Dalton dead asleep in the nursery suite, perhaps her back to the door. I pictured Daddy tiptoeing into the suite and scooping me up in his arms. Perhaps I had just started to cry when he handed me to Momma, who pressed me dearly to her bosom and kissed my cheeks, giving me the sense of comfort and security again.

Then, with me wrapped firmly in my blanket, they stole down the stairs and through the corridor outside my room to the rear door. Once out in the night they easily made their way to their awaiting vehicle, with infant Jimmy asleep in the backseat, unaware that he was soon to have a new sister.

In moments they were all in the car and off into the night.

I pressed my eyelids tightly shut when I then imagined Nurse Dalton finding the crib empty. I saw my parents come rushing out of their room, my grandmother charging out of hers. Philip was awakened by the shouting and sat up terrified. Surely, he had to be comforted, too.

The hotel was in an uproar. My grandmother was shouting orders at everyone. Lights were snapped on, the police were called, staff members were ordered out and about the grounds. Moments after the little beach town of Cutler's Cove came to life, all the inhabitants discovered what had happened. Sirens were sounded. Police cars were everywhere. But it was too late. Momma and Daddy were some distance away by then, and I, just a few days old, didn't know the difference.

My heart felt as if it would split in two. The ache traveled up and down my spine. Maybe I should give up, I thought. My name was a lie; it belonged to another little girl, one who had never had the chance to open her eyes and see the dawn, one who had been taken from one darkness to another. My body shook with my sobs.

"You don't have to lie there crying," Clara Sue said. "Just do what Grandmother tells you to do."

I spun around. She had come sneaking into my room, not knocking, but opening the door as softly as a spy. She stood there with a terribly satisfied grin of self-satisfaction on her face and leaned against the door-jamb. Obviously intending to tease and torment me, she nibbled on a chocolate-covered pastry.

"I want you to knock before you come into my room," I snapped and ground the tears out of my eyes quickly. I wiped my cheeks with the back of my hands as I sat up.

"I did knock," she lied, "but you were crying so loud, you couldn't hear me. You don't have to go hungry," she lectured and took another bite of her pastry, closing her eyes to telegraph how delicious it was.

"That stuff will make you even fatter," I said in a sudden burst of nastiness. Her eyes popped open.

"I'm not fat," she insisted. I only shrugged.

"Pretend what you want, if it makes you happy," I said casually. My tone infuriated her more.

"I'm not pretending. I have a full figure, a mature woman's figure. Everyone says so."

"They're just being polite. How many people have the nerve to tell someone she's fat, especially the owner's daughter?"

She blinked, finding it hard to refute the logic.

"Look at all the clothing you've outgrown, and some of it you hadn't even worn yet," I said, nodding toward my closet. She stared at me, her eyes growing smaller with anger and frustration, making her cheeks look even fuller. Then she smiled.

"You just want me to give you the rest of this so you won't be hungry."

I shrugged again and pulled myself up in the bed to lean back against my pillow. "Of course not," I said. "I wouldn't eat sweets instead of real food."

"You'll see. After a day you're going to be so hungry your stomach will growl and ache," she promised.

"I've been hungry, far hungrier than you've ever been, Clara Sue," I retorted. "I'm used to going without food for days and days," I said, relishing the effect my exaggeration was having on her. "There were days when Daddy couldn't find any work, and we had only a few crumbs left for all of us. When your stomach starts to ache, you just drink loads of water and the ache goes away."

"But . . . this is different," she insisted. "You can smell the food being cooked, and all you have to do to get it is wear the nameplate."

"I won't do it and I don't care anyway," I said with unexpected sincerity. It made her eyebrows lift. "I don't care if I waste away in this bed."

"That's stupid," she said, but she backed up as if I had some infectious disease.

"Is it?" I shifted my eyes to her and glared. "Why did you tell Grandmother Cutler stories about Philip and me? You did, didn't you?"

"No. I just told her what everyone at school knew—that Philip was your boyfriend for a little while, and you and he went on a date."

"I'm sure you told her more."

"I didn't!" she insisted.

"It doesn't matter anyway," I said and sighed. "Please leave me alone." I lowered myself down onto the bed and closed my eyes.

"Grandmother sent me to see if you had changed your mind before she makes a big announcement about you to the staff."

"Tell her . . . tell her I won't change my name, and she can bury me right where she put up the monument," I added. Clara Sue's eyes nearly bulged. She backed into the doorway.

"You're just being a stubborn little brat. No one's going to help you. You'll be sorry."

"I'm sorry already," I said. "Please close the door on your way out."

She stared at me in disbelief and then shut the door and was gone.

Of course, she was right. It would be harder to go hungry here, where there was so much and where the aromas of the wonderful foods threaded their way through the hotel, drawing the guests like flies to the dining room for delicious entrées and sumptuous desserts. Just the thought of it made my stomach churn in anticipation. I thought the best thing to do was to try to sleep.

I was emotionally and mentally exhausted anyway. The rainstorm continued and the musty, damp scent chilled me. I slipped out of my uniform, wrapped my blanket around my body, and turned away from the tear-streaked window. I heard the growl of thunder. The whole world seemed to tremble, or was it just me? After a few moments I fell asleep and didn't wake up until I heard shouting in the hall followed by many loud footsteps. A moment later my door was thrown open, and my grandmother burst in, followed by Sissy and Burt Hornbeck, chief of the hotel's security.

I pulled my blanket around myself and sat up.

"What is it?" I gasped.

"All right," my grandmother snapped and tugged Sissy forward by the wrist so she could stand at her side and face me. Burt Hornbeck stepped up on the other side of her and stared at me. "I want you to say it all in her presence with Burt as a witness." Sissy looked down and then looked up at me slowly, her eyes wide and bright with fear. Yet there was a glint of sadness and pity in them, too.

"Say what?" I asked. "What is this?"

She turned on Sissy.

"You alternated rooms, correct?" my grandmother demanded with a prosecutor's clipped, sharp tone of voice. Sissy nodded. "Speak up," my grandmother commanded.

"Yes, ma'am," Sissy said quickly.

"You took the odd number and she took the even?"

"Uh-huh."

"Then she would have been the one to clean room one-fifty?" she pursued. I looked from her to Burt Hornbeck. He was a stout, forty-year-old man with dark brown hair and small brown eyes. Whenever I had seen him before, he had always smiled warmly at me. Now he looked stern, angry, a moon locked in orbit around my grandmother's blazing face of fury and anger.

"Yes, ma'am," Sissy said.

"So we alternated rooms and I did the even numbers. What does this mean?" I asked.

"Get out of bed," she ordered. I looked at Burt. I was wearing only my bra and panties. He understood and directed his gaze at the window while I rose, keeping the blanket as tightly wrapped around me as I could.

"Are you naked?" my grandmother asked, as if to be so was a sin in her hotel.

"No. I'm wearing underwear. What do you want?"

"I want the return of Mrs. Clairmont's gold necklace, and I want it now," she said, her eyes fixed on me with such fire. She stuck out her palm, her long thin fingers straight.

"What necklace?" I looked at Burt Hornbeck, but he didn't change expression.

"There's no point in denying it now. I have managed to keep Mrs. Clairmont, one of my lifelong guests, I might add, quiet about this entire matter, but I have promised her the return of her necklace. She will get it back," she insisted, her shoulders hoisted, her neck so stiff it looked carved out of marble.

"I didn't take her necklace!" I cried. "I don't steal."

"Sure you don't steal," she said with ridicule and a birdlike nod. "You lived with thieves all your life and you don't steal."

"We never stole!" I cried.

"Never?" She twisted her lips into a cold, sharp mocking smile. My eyes fled before the onslaught of hers. My knees began to click together nervously even though I had nothing to fear. I was innocent. Swallowing first, I repeated my innocence and looked at Sissy. The poor, intimidated girl swung her eyes away quickly.

"Tear this place apart, Burt," she ordered, "from top to bottom until you locate that necklace."

Reluctantly he moved toward the small dresser.

"It's not here. I told you . . . I swear . . ."

"Do you realize," she said slowly, her eyes now like two hot coals in a stove, "how embarrassing this can be for Cutler's Cove? Never, never in the long and prestigious history of this hotel, has a guest had anything stolen out of his or her room. My staff has always consisted of hardworking people who respect other people's property. They know what it is to work here; they think of it as an honor."

"I didn't steal it," I moaned, the tears now streaming down my cheeks. Mr. Hornbeck had everything out of my drawers and was turning the drawers over. He looked behind them in the dresser, too.

"Sissy," my grandmother snapped, "take her bed apart. Strip off the sheets and pillowcase and turn that mattress over."

"Yes, ma'am," she said and moved instantly to carry out my grandmother's orders. She gazed up at me, her eyes asking my forgiveness as she began to tear off my bed sheet.

"I won't leave here until I have that necklace back," my grandmother insisted, folding her arms under her small bosom.

"Then you will sleep here tonight," I said. Mr. Hornbeck turned to me, surprised at my defiance, his eyebrows raised in a question mark. I could see the doubt flash across his brow—perhaps I was innocent. He turned to my grandmother.

Her puckered, now prune-colored mouth drew up like a drawstring purse. I watched and waited for her sardonic smile to come and break her parchment skin. I expected her voice to crackle, cackle, witchlike.

"You won't fool anyone with this defiance," she finally said. "Least of all me."

"I don't care what you or anyone else thinks—I didn't steal any gold necklace," I insisted.

Sissy had the bed stripped down. She pulled off the mattress, and Mr. Hornbeck searched under the bed. He looked up at my grandmother and shook his head.

"Look in those shoes," my grandmother told Sissy. She got down on her knees and searched every pair. My grandmother made her sift through all my garments and look in socks and pants pockets while Mr. Hornbeck searched the remainder of the room. When both came up empty-handed, she scrutinized me closely with her suspicious eyes. Then she turned to Mr. Hornbeck.

"Burt, step outside a moment," she said. He nodded and left quickly. At this point I was shivering from the fright and the indignity. My grandmother stepped toward me.

"Drop that blanket," she commanded.

"What?" I looked at Sissy, who was standing on the side looking as frightened as I was.

"Drop it!" she snarled.

I released the blanket and she gazed upon me, giving my body such close scrutiny, I couldn't help from blushing. Her eyes lifted to mine, and I felt as if she were delving the depths of my soul, trying to absorb my very being into her own so she could control me.

"Take off your brassiere," she said. I stepped back, my heart pounding. "If you don't do it now, I'll have to have the police from town come here and take you down to the station for an even more embarrassing strip search. Do you want that?"

Memories of the police station where I had been questioned and told of Daddy's crime returned vividly. I shook my head and my tears flowed again, but she was unfeeling, unsympathetic, her metallic eyes cold and determined.

"I'm not hiding any necklace," I said.

"Then do what I say," she snapped back.

I looked at Sissy, and she looked down, ashamed for me. Slowly I brought my hands behind my back and unfastened my bra. Then I slipped it down my arms and quickly folded my arms across my bosom to shield it from her probing eyes. I stood there trembling. She stepped forward and checked the inside of my bra, of course finding nothing.

"Lower those panties," she said, not satisfied. I took a deep breath. Oh, the horror of her, I thought. I couldn't stop crying. My body shook with sobs.

"I can't stand here all day and wait," she said.

I closed my eyes to block out the embarrassment, and I brought my panties to my knees. As soon as I did so, she demanded I turn around.

"All right," she said. I pulled up my panties and put on my bra. Then I wrapped the blanket around myself again. I was shaking as much as I would had I been left out naked in the middle of a winter storm. My teeth wouldn't stop clicking against each other, but she didn't appear to notice or care.

"If you have hidden this necklace somewhere in this hotel, I will eventually know about it," she said. "Nothing, absolutely nothing happens here without my knowing about it one way or another, one time or another. And this is a unique necklace with rubies and small diamonds. You can't hope to sell it without it being known."

"I didn't take the necklace," I said, holding my sobs back and keeping my eyes closed. I shook my head vehemently. "I didn't."

"If I leave here now, and we discover you have the necklace, I will have to turn you over to the police. Do you understand? Once I leave, I can no longer cover for your crime," she warned.

"I didn't steal it," I repeated.

She pivoted and seized the door handle.

"You can't imagine the embarrassment I have to face now. You are defiant and stubborn, refusing to listen and do the things I have told you. Now thievery has been added to the list. I won't forget it," she threatened. She gazed at Sissy. "Let's go," she said.

"I'm sorry," Sissy mumbled quickly and rushed out after her. I collapsed on my naked mattress and cried until my tears dried up. Then I remade my bed and crawled under the blanket, stunned by the events that had just occurred. It all seemed much more like a nightmare than reality. Had I been dreaming?

The emotional tension exhausted me. I must have drifted off into a sleep of escape, because when I opened my eyes, I saw the rain had stopped, although there was still a wet chill in the air and the world outside was pitch dark—no stars, no moon, just the sound of the wind rushing in and over the hotel and grounds, swishing around the building.

I sat up with my back to the headboard, keeping the blanket wrapped around me. Then I decided to get up and get dressed. I needed to talk to someone and Philip was the first person who came to mind. But when I went to open the door, I found it locked. I pulled on the handle, disbelieving.

"No!" I cried. *"Open this door!"*

I listened, but all I heard was silence. I turned the handle and pulled. The door wouldn't budge. Being locked in this small room suddenly filled me with panic. I was sure my grandmother had done it to add salt to my wounds, to punish me this way because she hadn't found the necklace in my room as she had expected.

"Someone open this door!"

I pounded the door with my small fists until they grew red and my arms ached. Then I listened. Someone had heard me. I could hear footsteps in the hallway. Maybe it was Sissy, I thought.

"Who's there?" I called. *"Please, help me. The door is locked."*

I waited. Although I didn't hear anyone speak, I sensed someone was there. I could feel someone's presence on the other side of that door. Was it my mother? Or Mrs. Boston?

"Who's there? Please."

"Dawn," I finally heard my father say. He spoke through the crack between the door and the jamb.

"Please, unlock the door and let me out," I said.

"I told her you didn't take the necklace," he said.

"No, I didn't."

"I didn't think you would steal."

"I didn't!" I cried. Why wasn't he opening the door? Why was he speaking through a crack? He must be standing right up against it, I thought, with his lips to the opening.

"Mother will get to the bottom of it," he said. "She always does."

"She's a very cruel person," I said. "To do what she did and then lock me in my room. Please, open the door."

"You mustn't think that, Dawn. Sometimes she appears hard to people, but after she makes her point, people usually see she's right and fair and they're happy they've listened to her."

"She's not a god; she's just an old lady who runs a hotel!" I cried. I waited, expecting him to unlock the door, but he said nothing and did nothing. "Father, please open the door," I pleaded.

"Mother just wants to do the right things, bring you up the right way, correct all the wrong things you've been taught."

"I don't have to be locked up in here," I moaned. "I didn't live like some animal. We weren't thieves, dirty, and stupid," I said.

"Of course you weren't, but there is much you have to learn that's new. You're part of an important family now, and Grandmother Cutler just wants you to adjust.

"I know it's hard for you, but Mother's been in this business for more years than even I've been alive, and her instincts about people and things are excellent. Look what she's built here and how many people come back every year," he said in a soft, reasonable tone of voice through the crack.

"I'm not going to wear that dumb nameplate," I insisted, my eyes burning with determination.

He was silent again, this time for so long that finally I thought he had left.

"Father?"

"When you were stolen away from us, you weren't just taken away from your mother and me; you were also taken away from Grandmother Cutler," he said, his voice now louder. "When you were stolen, her heart broke, too."

"I can't believe that," I declared. "Wasn't she the one who decided to put a monument in the cemetery with my name on it?" I couldn't believe I was talking to him through a door, but in a way it made it easier for me to say what I wanted.

"Yes, but she did that only to save my sanity. I thanked her for it later on. I couldn't work; I was no good to Laura Sue or to Philip. All I did was call police departments and chase around the country whenever there was a slight lead. So you see, it wasn't such a terrible thing."

Not a terrible thing? To symbolically bury a child who wasn't dead? What sort of people were these? What kind of family had I inherited?

"Please, open the door. I don't like being locked in."

"I have an idea," he said instead of opening the door. "People who don't know me well call me Mr. Cutler and other people, close friends and family, call me Randolph."

"So?"

"Think of Eugenia the way I think of Mr. Cutler and Laura Sue thinks of Mrs. Cutler. How's that? Your friends are always going to call you by your nickname."

"It's not a nickname; it's my name."

"By your informal name," he said, "but Eugenia could be your . . . your hotel name. How's that?"

"I don't know." I stepped back from the door, my arms folded under my breasts. If I didn't agree, they might never open the door, I thought.

"Just do this little compromise, and you'll bring peace and tranquillity back. We're right in the middle of the season, and the hotel is full, and—"

"Why did you give her my letter to Ormand Longchamp?" I snapped.

"She still has that letter?"

"No," I said. "I have it. She returned it and forbid me to have anything to do with him. She likes to forbid things," I said.

"Oh, I'm sorry, I . . . I thought she was going to get the letter delivered. We had discussed it, and although she wasn't happy about it, she said she would get the police chief of Cutler's Cove to take care of it. I guess she got so upset, she—"

"She was never going to have the letter delivered," I said. "Why couldn't you do it yourself?"

"Oh, I guess I could. It's just that Mother and the police chief are good friends, and I thought . . . I'm sorry," he said. "I'll tell you what," he said quickly. "If you agree to wear the nameplate, I'll take the letter to the chief myself and see to it that it's delivered. How's that? Is it a deal? I'll even make sure there's a receipt so you can see that it was delivered."

For a moment I was caught in a storm of confusion raging through my mind and heart. The kidnapping had put an ugly stain on Momma and Daddy. I could never forgive them for what they had done, but deep inside I still clung to the hope that there was some explanation. I had to have Daddy tell me his side of it.

Now I had to pay a price to have any contact with him. One way or another Grandmother Cutler got her way at Cutler's Cove, I thought. But this time I was going to get something, too.

"If I agree, will you find out what has happened to Jimmy and Fern?"

"Jimmy and Fern? You mean the Longchamps' real children?"

"Yes."

"I'll try. I promise, I'll try," he said, but I recalled what Mother had said about his promises and how easily he made them and then forgot them.

"Will you really try?" I asked.

"Sure."

"All right," I said. "But people who want to can call me Dawn."

"Sure," he said.

"Will you open the door?"

"Where's the letter?" he replied.

"Why?"

"Slip it under the door."

"What? Why won't you open the door?"

"I don't have the key," he said. "I'll go get it and tell Mother about our agreement."

I slipped the letter under, and he took it quickly. Then I heard him walk off, leaving me feeling as though I had just made a deal with the devil.

I sat down on the bed to wait, but suddenly I heard the turning of the key in the lock. The door opened and I faced Philip.

"How come your door's locked?"

"Grandmother did it. She thinks I stole a necklace."

He shook his head.

"You better get out of here. Grandmother doesn't want us to be alone together. Clara Sue told her stories and—"

"I know," he said, "but I can't help it this time. You must come with me."

"Come with you? Where? Why?"

"Just trust me," he said in a loud whisper. "Hurry."

"But—"

"Please, Dawn," he pleaded.

"How come you had the key to my room?" I demanded.

"Had the key?" He shook his head. "It was in the door."

"It was? But . . ."

Where had my father gone? Why did he lie about the key? Did he have to get permission before opening the door to let his own daughter out?

Philip seized my hand and pulled me out of the room. He started down the corridor to the side exit.

"Philip!"

"Quiet," he ordered. We rushed out and around the building. When I saw he was leading me to the little cement stairway, I stopped.

"Philip, no."

"Just come, will you. Before someone sees us."

"Why?" I demanded, but he tugged me forward.

"Philip, why are we going in there?" I demanded.

Instead of answering, he opened the door and dragged me into the darkness with him. I was about to shout angrily when he reached up and pulled the light cord.

The contrast between pitch darkness and blazing brightness hurt my eyes. I closed them and then opened them.

And there, standing before us, was Jimmy.

13
A PIECE OF THE PAST

"Jimmy! What are you doing here?" I asked, half in shock, half in delight. I had never been so happy to see anyone as I was to see him. He stared at me, his dark eyes twinkling impishly. I could see just how happy he was to set his eyes on me, too, and that warmed my heart.

"Hi, Dawn," he finally said.

We both faced each other awkwardly for a moment, and then I embraced him. Philip watched us with a half smile on his face.

"You're drenched to the bone," I said, pulling back and shaking out my palms.

"I got caught in it just outside of Virginia Beach."

"How did you get here?"

"Hitched all the way. I'm getting to be real good at it," he said, turning to Philip.

"But how . . . why?" I squealed, unable to cloak my joy.

"I ran away. Couldn't take it anymore. I'm on my way to Georgia to find our . . . to find my relatives and live with them. But I thought I'd stop by here and see you one more time."

"One of the guys came into the hotel looking for me," Philip explained. "They said someone from Emerson Peabody wanted to see me outside. I couldn't imagine . . . anyway, there he was."

"I thought I should get a hold of Philip and have him find you. I didn't want to take any chances. I'm not going back," he declared firmly, pulling back his shoulders.

"I told him he could stay here in the hideaway for a few days," Philip said. "We'll get him some food, warm clothing, and some money."

"But, Jimmy, won't they just come after you?"

"I don't care if they do, but they probably won't. No one really

cares," he said, his eyes small and determined and full of anger. "I
didn't know when you and I would ever see each other again, Dawn. I
had to come," he said.

Our gazes locked warmly on each other's, and in that gaze I saw all
our happier times together, saw his smile, and something inside me
became warm. Suddenly I felt safer here at Cutler's Cove.

"I'm going back to the hotel and sneak into the kitchen to get him
something to eat," Philip said. "I'll also get him some dry clothes and a
towel. We've just got to be careful that no one discovers him," Philip
emphasized. He turned to Jimmy. "My grandmother would blow her
stack. Don't go out without checking carefully to see that no one's
around, okay?"

Jimmy nodded.

"Give me about fifteen minutes to get the food and the clothing," he
said and hurried out.

"You'd better start taking off those wet clothes, Jimmy," I advised. It
was as if we had never been apart and I was still looking after him.

He nodded and pulled off his shirt. His wet skin gleamed under the
light. Even in the short time we had been apart, he looked changed—he
was older, bigger, with broader shoulders and thicker arms. I took his
shirt and draped it over a chair as he sat down to take off his soaked
sneakers and socks.

"Tell me what happened to you after we were taken to the police
station, Jimmy. Do you know anything about Fern?" I added quickly.

"No, I never saw her after we were brought to the station. They took
me to what they called a holding house where there were other kids
waiting to be assigned to foster homes. Some were older, but most were
younger than me. We slept on bunk beds not much bigger or nicer than
this one," he said, "and we were crowded four in a room. One little boy
kept whimpering all night. The others continually shouted at him to
shut up, but he was too frightened. I got into a fight with them because
they wouldn't stop terrorizing the kid."

"Why doesn't that surprise me?" I said, smiling.

"Well, it made them feel big to bully him," he said angrily. "Anyway,
one thing led to another, and I was put in the basement of the house to
sleep. It had a dirt floor and lots of bugs and even rats!

"A day later I was told they had already found a home for me. I
think they were determined to get rid of me first. The others were
jealous, but that was only because they didn't know where I was going.

"I went home with this chicken farmer, Leo Coons. He was a stout, grouchy man with a face like a bulldog, and he had a scar across his forehead. It looked like someone had hit him with an ax. His wife was half his size, and he treated her like another kid. They had two daughters. It was his wife who encouraged me to run away. Her name was Beryle, and I couldn't believe she was only in her thirties. She had gray hair and looked as worn down as an old pencil. Nothing she did made Coons happy. The house was never clean enough; the food never tasted right. Complain, complain, complain was all he did.

"I had a nice room, but he had come to the holding house to get a foster kid my age to make into a slave. First thing he did was show me how to candle eggs and had me up before dawn working alongside his two daughters, both older than me, but both as skinny as scarecrows and both with big, sad dark eyes that reminded me of frightened puppy dogs.

"Coons moved me from one job to the next—shoveling chicken manure, lugging feed. We worked before the sun rose until an hour or so after it went down.

"At first I didn't care what happened to me; I was that depressed, but after a while I got so tired of the work and hearing Coons shouting this and shouting that . . .

"What did it, I suppose, was the night he hit me. He was complaining about the supper, and I said I thought it was pretty good, too good for him. He hit me with the back of his hand, but so hard, I fell off the chair.

"I was going to just punch and kick at him, but Dawn, this guy is big and he's as hard as bricks. Later that night Beryle came to me and told me the best thing I could do for myself was run away like the others. Seems he's done this before—go fetch a foster kid and make him work until he drops. They don't care back at the home, because they get so many kids, they're glad anyone comes to get one."

"Oh, Jimmy . . . if Fern was given to mean people . . ."

"I don't think so. It's different with babies. Lots of good people want babies because they can't have their own for one reason or another. Don't look so glum," he said, smiling. "I'm sure she's all right."

"It's not that, Jimmy. What you just said reminded me of something terrible. They tell me that's why Momma and Daddy stole me—she had a baby right before, and the baby was born dead."

His eyes widened, and then he nodded as if he had always known it.

"So Daddy talked her into taking you," he concluded. "It was just

like him. I don't doubt any of it. Now look what a mess he got us all in.
I mean, I'm in. You ain't in such a mess, I guess."

"Oh, Jimmy," I said, sitting beside him quickly. "I am. I hate it
here."

"What? With this big, fancy hotel and all? Why?"

I began by describing my real mother and her continuous nervous
condition. Jimmy listened intently, his eyes full of wonder as I related
the story of my kidnapping and how it had affected her and made her
into some kind of invalid soaked in luxury.

"But weren't they glad to see you when you were brought here?" he
asked. I shook my head.

"As soon as I arrived here, I was made a chambermaid and put into a
little room away from the family. You won't have much trouble imagining how mean Clara Sue has been," I said. Then I told him about being
accused of stealing and related the horrible search I had been put
through.

"She made you take off your clothes?"

"Strip to the bone. Afterward, she locked me in my room."

He stared at me in disbelief.

"What about your real father?" he asked. "Did you tell him what she
did?"

"He's so strange, Jimmy," I said and told him how he had come to
the door and refused to do anything until I had agreed to the compromise over my name. "Then he left, claiming he had to get the key, but
Philip said the key was in the door when he came to fetch me to bring
me to you."

He shook his head.

"And here I thought you were living high on the hog."

"I don't think my grandmother's ever going to let up on me. For
some reason she hates me, hates the sight of me," I said. "I just can't
get it through my head that Daddy did this. I can't." I shook my head
and stared down at my hands in my lap.

"Well, I can," Jimmy said sharply, drawing my eyes to his. Fiery
anger filled his eyes. "You don't want to believe it; you never liked
believing bad things about him, but you gotta now."

I told Jimmy about my letter to Daddy.

"I hope he writes back and tells me his side of it."

"He won't," Jimmy insisted. "And even if he does, it'll be all lies."

"Jimmy, you can't go on hating him like this. He's still your real
father, even if he's not mine."

"I don't want to ever think of him as my father. He's dead with my mother," he declared, his eyes burning with such fury, it brought an ache to my heart. I couldn't keep the tears trapped under my eyelids; they burned so.

"No sense in crying about it, Dawn. There's nothing we can do to change things. I'm going down to Georgia and maybe live with Momma's side of the family, if they'll have me. I don't mind working hard, as long as it's for my own family."

"I wish I was going with you, Jimmy. I still feel those people are more my family than these people, even though I never met them."

"Well, you can't. If you came with me, we'd be hunted down for sure."

"I know." My tears kept coming. Now that Jimmy was here, I couldn't help myself.

"I'm sorry you're not happier, Dawn," he said and slowly brought his arm up and around my shoulders. "Whenever I lay awake thinking about how terrible all this was, I would cheer myself a bit by thinking you were safe and comfortable in a new and richer life. I thought you deserved it and maybe it was good it all happened. I didn't mind what happened to me as long as it meant you would have better things and be with better people."

"Oh, Jimmy, I could never be happier if you were unhappy, and just thinking about poor little Fern in a strange place—"

"She's little enough to forget and start new," he said, his eyes dark with a wisdom beyond his years, a wisdom forced upon him by hard times. He was older in mind and body. Hard, cruel times had dragged him out of childhood.

He sat inches from me, his arm still around my shoulders, his face so close I could feel his breath on my cheeks. It made me dizzy, confused. I was trapped on a runaway merry-go-round of emotions. Jimmy, whom I had thought to be my brother, was now just a boy who cared for me, and Philip, a boy who had cared for me, was now my brother. Their kisses, their smiles, and the way they touched and held me had to have different meaning.

Just a little while ago I would have felt strange and guilty about the feelings that passed through me when Jimmy touched me. Now, when the tingle traveled up and down my spine and made me shudder pleasantly, I didn't know what to do, what to say. He cupped my face between his palms and tenderly kissed away my tears. I felt so warm all over. Before this I would have forced that warmth to stop its journey to my heart. Now it rushed over the highways along my skin and curled up comfortably inside my breast.

His face remained close to mine, his serious eyes so delving, worried, and intense. A lump came in my throat as I wondered where the boy was I used to know. Where was that brother, and who was this young man staring so long into my eyes? Greater than any pain or ache or hurt I had ever felt before or since was the pain caused me by the suffering I saw in his tortured eyes.

We heard Philip's footsteps on the cement stairway, and Jimmy pulled his arm off my shoulders and continued to take off his sneakers and socks.

"Hi," Philip said, coming in. "Sorry the food's not hot, but I wanted to rush in and out of the kitchen before someone caught me and wondered what I was doing."

"Food's food. I don't care whether it's hot or cold at this point," Jimmy said, taking the covered dish from Philip. "Thanks."

"I brought you some of my clothes—should fit—and this towel and blanket."

"Get the wet clothes off and dry yourself before you eat, Jimmy," I advised. He went into the bathroom and slipped out of his pants and underwear, wiped himself down, and returned in Philip's clothes. The shirt was a little big and the pants too long, but he rolled up the cuffs. Philip and I stood by and watched him gobble the food, scooping one mouthful into his mouth before he had swallowed the one he already had.

"Sorry, but I'm starving," he said. "I didn't have any money to stop to eat."

"That's all right. Look, I'm going to have to get back to the hotel. Grandmother saw me go in before and probably will be keeping an eye out for me to be sure I'm mixing with the others.

"In the morning I'll put aside some food as I serve breakfast, and later, as soon as I can get loose, I'll bring it down to you, Jimmy."

"Thanks."

"Well," Philip said, standing and looking at us. "See you later. Have a good night."

We watched him go.

"I don't understand," Jimmy said almost as soon as Philip disappeared up the cement stairway. "Why was he worried about his grandmother seeing him in the hotel?"

I told him what Clara Sue had told Grandmother Cutler and what she had forbidden. Jimmy lay back in the bed, his hands behind his head, listening. His eyes grew small and the tight smile around his lips became a serious and intense look.

"Of course, I was worried about all that, too," he said. "I was wondering what it was going to be like for you. You were starting to get stuck on him in school."

I was going to tell him how it was harder for Philip to adjust, how he still wished I could be his girlfriend, but I thought it might make Jimmy upset and cause more problems. "It hasn't been easy," I simply said. Jimmy nodded.

"Here you have to work at thinking about him as your brother, and here I was your brother and you got to work at forgetting I was," he said.

"I don't want to forget, Jimmy."

He looked sad, disappointed.

"Do you want me to forget? Do you want to forget me?" Perhaps he did; perhaps it was the only way he could start new, I thought mournfully.

"I don't want you to feel dirty about it or ever let anyone make you feel that way," he said firmly.

I nodded and sat beside him on the bed. Neither of us said anything for a few moments. This old section of the hotel creaked and moaned as the sea breeze poked and prodded, slipping itself into every crack and cranny, and we could hear music from the jukebox in the recreation room spilling out into the night and being carried off by the same sea breezes.

"I'll tell the relatives that Momma and Daddy are both dead. They don't have to know all the ugly details, and I'll try to start a new life," Jimmy said with a far-off look in his eyes.

"I hate thinking about you being in a new life without me, Jimmy."

He smiled the soft and gentle smile I recalled so fondly.

"Let's just lie here together one more time like we used to lie together," he said. "And you talk me to sleep like you always did by telling me about all the good things we're going to have someday." He shifted over to make room for me.

I lowered myself beside him, resting my head against his arm and closed my eyes. For a moment I threw myself back through time, and we were lying together on one of our poor pull-out beds in one of our run-down apartments. Rain pounded the dilapidated building, and the wind scratched at the windows, threatening to poke them in.

But Jimmy and I cuddled together, taking solace in the warmth and closeness of our bodies. We closed our eyes, and I began to spin the rainbows. I did it now.

"We will have good things happen to us, Jimmy. We've been through a storm of trouble, but after every storm, the clouds part and the sun returns with its warmth and its promise.

"You'll go off and find Momma's relatives like you planned, and they'll welcome you with open arms. You'll meet uncles and aunts and cousins.

"And maybe they're not as bad off as we always thought. Maybe they got a good farm. And you're a strong, willing worker, Jimmy, so you'll be a great help to them. Before you know it, the farm will become something special, and people from all around will ask: Who's that new young man who came to help and made your farm so good?

"But you'll have to promise to write to me and . . ."

I turned to him. His eyes were closed, and he was breathing softly. How tired he had been. He must have walked miles and miles and been in the rain for the longest time, suffering just to get down here to see me one more time.

I leaned over and pressed my lips to his warm cheek.

"Good night, Jimmy," I whispered as I had done so many nights before. I hated to leave him all alone in so strange a place, but from what he had described to me, he had been in more horrible places.

I paused in the doorway and looked back. It did seem more like a dream to see Jimmy lying there. It was almost like a wish come true. I slipped out of the hideaway and up the stairs, checking carefully to be sure no one was looking my way. It looked all clear so I made my way around the building. Just as I entered and started down the corridor, I saw the door to my room open, and Clara Sue stepped out.

"What are you doing in there?" I demanded, approaching quickly.

She looked flustered for a moment and then smiled.

"Grandmother sent me to unlock your door," she said. "Who did it?"

"I don't know," I said quickly. She smirked.

"If I find out and tell Grandmother, she'll fire her."

"I don't know who did it," I repeated. "I shouldn't have been locked in there anyway."

She shrugged.

"If you weren't such a brat, Grandmother wouldn't have to do these things," she said and hurried off. I thought she was in quite a rush to get away from me. After I watched her go, I went into my room.

I got undressed, put on my robe, and went to the bathroom. I really was very tired and looked forward to crawling under the covers. But when I returned and pulled back my blanket to slip in and under, I discovered what Clara Sue had been doing in my room. It was as if I had been made to swallow a glassful of ice water. It sent a painful shiver through my heart.

There on my sheet was a gold necklace with rubies and diamonds. Clara Sue had taken it out of Mrs. Clairmont's room and placed it here so I would be blamed. Now what would I do? If I returned it, everyone was sure to think I had stolen it originally and my grandmother had frightened me into returning it. No one would believe Clara Sue had done this, I thought.

The sound of footsteps drove me into a panic. What if she had gone and told Mr. Hornbeck she had seen me with the necklace and was returning with my grandmother? I looked about frantically for a place to hide it and realized that this was just what Clara Sue would want me to do. They would search again and find it hidden and be convinced I had stolen it.

I froze, unable to decide on anything. Fortunately, the sound of the footsteps died away. I let out my breath and scooped up the necklace. It felt hot and forbidding in my hands. I had the urge to open the window and heave it out into the night, but then, what would happen if someone found it the next morning near my window?

Should I take it to my father? My mother? Maybe I should find Philip and give it to him. He would certainly believe me when I told him what Clara Sue had done, I thought, but merely walking through the hotel with it in my possession frightened me. I could be stopped if Clara Sue had gone to tell someone.

It should be returned to Mrs. Clairmont somehow, I thought. Perhaps it was a very precious, meaningful piece of jewelry for her, a necklace with special memories. Why should she suffer just because Clara Sue was so jealous and spiteful?

I decided to get dressed and take a chance of carrying it through the hotel. I slipped it into my uniform pocket and hurried out. It wasn't that late. Guests were enjoying the grounds, playing cards, visiting in the lobby, some listening to a string quartet in the music suite. There was a good chance Mrs. Clairmont wasn't in her room, I thought. I went directly to the linen closet and got the master key for the section Sissy and I worked in. Then I hurried to the corridor.

My heart was pounding so hard, I was sure I would faint just after entering Mrs. Clairmont's room. I envisioned them finding me on the floor with the necklace in my palm. I brushed the sweat off my forehead and walked quickly to her door. Fortunately, there was no one around. I knocked and waited. If she were in there, I thought I would pretend I had knocked on the wrong door. No one answered, so I slipped the master key into the lock and turned. The small clicking sound never seemed so loud. In my mind I thought it had echoed throughout the hotel and was surely going to bring people running.

I waited, listening. It was quiet and dark within. I didn't want to take any more chances than I had to, so I simply leaned in and tossed the necklace at the dresser. I heard it land safely, and then I quickly closed the door and locked it, my fingers trembling so badly as I did so, I had to do it twice.

Just as I turned and started down the corridor, I heard voices. Terrified of being discovered on the floor, I spun around and headed in the opposite direction, never looking back to see who it was. I rushed away, but this path took me back into the lobby of the hotel.

It took my father three times to call "Eugenia" before I realized he was calling me. I stopped midway across the lobby and turned to see him beckoning. Had Clara Sue reported seeing me with the necklace? I approached him slowly.

"I was just on my way to see you," he said. "I wanted to be sure Clara Sue went directly to your room with the key and unlocked your door."

"There was a key in the door," I said pointedly.

"There was? I didn't see it. Well," he said, smiling quickly, "at least that unpleasantness is all over. You'll be happy to know your grandmother likes our little compromise," he added, smiling. And then he reached into his jacket pocket and produced my hateful nameplate. I stared down at it.

It hadn't looked as large when my grandmother first showed it to me. It wouldn't have surprised me to learn that she had had it redone so she could make it bigger. It would be her way of showing me that she always got her way and if I challenged her, I would only suffer more for it.

I plucked it out of his palm slowly. It felt like a small block of ice in my hands.

"You want me to pin it on for you?" he asked when I hesitated.

"No, thank you. I can do it myself." I did so quickly.

"And that's that," he said beaming. "Well, I've got to get back to work. See you tomorrow. Have a good night's sleep," he said and left me standing there, feeling as if I had just been branded.

But it didn't bother me as much as it ordinarily might have. Just knowing that Jimmy was close by brought me comfort. In the morning right after I had done my work, I would go to him and we would talk and spend almost the whole day together. Of course, I would have to show myself around the hotel every once in a while so no one would come looking for me.

For the first night since I had arrived at Cutler's Cove, I went to sleep easily and looked forward eagerly to the once familiar sunrise.

The next morning Grandmother Cutler made an appearance in the kitchen while the staff was having its breakfast. She greeted everyone as she crossed the room to come toward the table I was at. After she reached us, she paused to be sure I was wearing her precious nameplate. When she saw it pinned on my uniform, she pulled herself up and her eyes twinkled with satisfaction.

I didn't dare look defiant or upset. If she confined me to my room again, I wouldn't be able to see Jimmy, or if I snuck out against her wishes, I might cause him to be discovered. I went on with Sissy, and we did our assignments. I worked so hard and fast that even Sissy remarked about it. As I came out of my last room, I found Grandmother Cutler waiting. Oh, no, I thought, she is going to give me another assignment, and I won't be able to go to Jimmy. I held my breath.

"Apparently, Mrs. Clairmont's necklace has miraculously turned up," she said, her metallic eyes glued to me.

"I never took it," I said firmly.

"I hope nothing is ever taken from here again," she retorted and continued down the corridor, her shoes clicking.

I didn't return to my room to change out of my uniform. Taking great care, I made my way out the back of the hotel and scurried around to Philip's hideaway.

It was such a bright warm summer's day, I wished I could take Jimmy out of the dark basement room and walk with him through the gardens with their rainbow colors of flowers and sparkling fountains. He had looked so pale and tired to me the night before. He needed to be in the warm sunlight. Bright sunshine on my face always cheered me, no matter how hard and troubled the day was.

Just as I reached the cement stairway, I saw some guests standing and talking nearby, so I waited for them to wander off before descending. When I opened the door and slipped in, I found Jimmy well rested and eagerly waiting for me. He was sitting on the bunk bed and beamed a wide, happy smile.

"Philip was already here with some breakfast, and he gave me twenty dollars for my trip to Georgia," he told me and then sat back and laughed.

"What?"

"You look funny in that uniform and bandanna. Your nameplate looks like a medal your grandmother pinned on you."

"I'm glad you like it," I said. "I hate it," I added and shook my hair loose as soon as I pulled off the bandanna. "Did you sleep all right?"

"I don't even remember your leaving, and when I woke up this morning, I forgot where I was for a moment. Then I fell asleep again. Why did you sneak away?"

"You fell asleep pretty quickly, so I decided to let you get your rest."

"I didn't wake up again this morning until Philip arrived. That's how tired I was. I'd been traveling all day and all night for two days. I slept on the side of the road for a couple of hours night before last," he admitted.

"Oh, Jimmy, you could have been hurt."

"I didn't care," he said. "I was determined to get here. So what does a chambermaid do? Tell me about this hotel. I didn't see much of it last night. Is it a nice place?"

I described my work to him and the layout of the hotel. I went on to tell him about some of the staff, especially Mrs. Boston and Sissy, but he was mostly interested in my mother and father.

"What's exactly wrong with her?"

"I don't know for sure, Jimmy. She doesn't look sick. Most of the time she looks beautiful, even when she's in bed with her headaches. My father treats her like a fragile little doll."

"And so your grandmother really runs the hotel?"

"Yes. Everyone is afraid of her, but they're afraid to say anything bad about her even to each other. Mrs. Boston says she's tough but fair. I don't think she's been very fair to me," I said sadly. I told him about the memorial stone. He listened wide-eyed as I described what I knew of my symbolic funeral.

"But how do you know the stone's still there?" he asked.

"It was as of the time I arrived. No one's told me otherwise."

"They wouldn't. They'd just remove it, I'm sure."

He sat back on the bed with his shoulders against the wall and looked thoughtful.

"It took a lot of nerve for Daddy to steal a baby right out from under the nurse's eyes," he said.

"That's what I thought," I said, happy he found trouble believing it, too.

"Of course, he might have been drinking—"

"Then he wouldn't have been as careful, and he would surely have been heard."

Jimmy nodded.

"You don't believe he would do such a thing, either, do you, Jimmy? Not deep down in your heart."

"He confessed. They had him cold, Dawn. And he didn't try to deny it to us." He lowered his eyes sadly. "I guess I should be getting on my way."

My heart stopped, my thoughts taking frantic flight, wanting to go off with Jimmy and escape this prison. I felt trapped and needed to seek out the wind so it could fan my hair and sting my skin and make me feel free and alive again.

"But, Jimmy, you were going to stay here a few days and rest up."

"I'll just get caught here and make trouble for you and Philip."

"No, you won't!" I cried. "I don't want you to go yet, Jimmy. Please stay." He lifted his eyes to gaze into mine. Swelling up in both of us was a turmoil of whirling emotions.

"Sometimes," Jimmy said in the softest, warmest voice I ever heard him speak, "I used to wish you weren't my sister."

"Why?" I said and held my breath.

"I . . . thought you were so pretty, I wished you could be my girl-friend," he confessed. "You were always after me to choose this friend of yours or that to be my girlfriend, but I didn't want anybody else but you." He looked away. "That's why I was so jealous and angry when you started getting interested in Philip."

For a moment I didn't know what to say. My first impulse was to put my arms around him and lavish a million kisses on his face. I wanted to draw his head down against my breast and cuddle it there.

"Oh, Jimmy," I said, my eyes tearing something awful again, "it just isn't fair. All this mix-up. It's not right."

"I know," he said. "But when I learned that you were not really my sister, I couldn't help feeling happy as well as sad. Of course, I was unhappy about your being taken away, but what I was hoping . . . aw, I shouldn't hope," he added quickly and looked away again.

"No, Jimmy. You can hope. What do you hope? Please tell me." He looked down, his face red. "I won't laugh."

"I know you wouldn't laugh, Dawn. You would never laugh at me; I just can't help feeling ashamed thinking it, much less saying it."

"Say it, Jimmy. I want you to say it," I replied in a much more demanding tone. He turned and looked at me, his gaze moving up and down my face as if he wanted to capture me in his mind forever and ever.

"I was hoping that if I ran away and stayed away long enough, you would stop thinking of me as your brother, and someday I would come back and you might think of me as . . . as a boyfriend," he said, all in one breath.

For a moment it was as if the world had stopped on its axis, as if every sound in the universe had died, as if birds were frozen in midair, and cars and people. There was no wind; the ocean became like glass, the waves up and ready to fall, the tide stuck just at the shore. Everything waited on us.

Jimmy had uttered the words that had lingered unspoken in both our hearts for years and years, for our hearts knew the truth long before we did, and kept feeding us feelings we thought were unclean and forbidden.

Could I ever do what he dreamt I would: look into his face and not see him as my brother, not see every touch, every kiss as a sin?

"You can see now why I have to get going," he said sternly and stood up.

"No, Jimmy." I reached out and seized his wrist. "I don't know whether or not I can ever do what you hope, but we're not going to find out if we're apart. We're just going to always wonder and wonder until the wondering becomes too much and we stop caring."

He shook his head.

"I'll never stop caring about you, Dawn," he said with such firmness, it washed away any shred of doubt. "No matter how far away I am or how much time passes. Never."

"Don't run off, Jimmy," I pleaded. I held on to his wrist, and his body finally relaxed. He lowered himself back to the bunk, and we sat there beside each other, neither speaking, me holding his wrist, him staring ahead, his chest lifting and falling with his own excitement.

"My heart's pounding so much," I whispered and lowered my forehead against his shoulder. Now, whenever we touched, it sent a streak of warmth through my body. I felt feverish.

"Mine, too," he said. I brought my palm to his chest and pressed it against his heart to feel the thumping; and then I lifted his hand and brought it to my breast so he could feel mine.

The moment his fingers were pressed to my bosom, he closed his eyes tightly, just like someone in pain.

"Jimmy," I said softly, "I don't know whether I could ever be your girlfriend, but I don't want to wonder forever."

Slowly, almost a millimeter at a time, he turned his face to mine. Our lips were inches apart. It was I who moved toward him first, but then he moved toward me, and we kissed on the lips for the first time like any boy and girl might kiss. All our years as brother and sister came raining down around us, threatening to drown us in dark and gloomy guilt, but we held on to each other.

When we parted, he stared at me with a face sculptured in seriousness, not a line creasing softly, his dark eyes searching mine quickly for some sign. I smiled and his body relaxed.

"We haven't been properly introduced," I said.

"Huh?"

"I'm Dawn Cutler. What's your name?" He shook his head. "Jimmy what?"

"Very funny."

"It isn't funny, Jimmy," I replied. "We are meeting for the first time in a way, aren't we? Maybe, if we pretend—"

"You always want to pretend." He shook his head again.

"Try it, Jimmy. Just try it once. For me. Please."

He sighed.

"All right. I'm James Longchamp of the renowned southern Longchamps, but you can call me Jimmy."

I giggled. "See? It wasn't that hard to do." I lay down on my side and looked up at him. His smile widened, spreading through his face and brightening his eyes.

"You're so crazy, but so special," he said, running his fingers up my arm. He touched my neck, and I closed my eyes. I felt him lean over, and then I felt his lips on my cheek and a moment later pressing against mine again.

His hands moved over my breasts. I moaned and reached up to bring him down to me. All the while as we kissed and caressed, I kept smothering the voice that tried to scream out that this was Jimmy, my brother, Jimmy. If he had similar thoughts about me, they were driven down, too, held underwater by the building passion and excitement as our bodies touched and our hands and arms held us tightly to each other.

I was back on that merry-go-round of emotions, only it was spinning faster than ever, and I was getting so dizzy, I thought I would become unconscious. I never even realized he had unbuttoned my uniform and his fingers had traveled under my bra until I felt the tips slip over my firming nipples. I wanted him to stop, and I wanted him to go on.

I opened my eyes and looked into his face. His eyes were closed; he looked lost in a dream. A smothered groan escaped his lips—more like a moan. As the skirt of my uniform traveled up my thighs, he slipped himself between my legs, and I felt that male part of him grow hard against me. It sent a panic up through my bosom.

"Jimmy!"

He stopped and opened his eyes. Suddenly they were filled with shock as he realized what he had done and what he was doing. He pulled back quickly and turned away. My heart was drumming against my chest, making it hard for me to catch my breath. As soon as I had, I put my hand on his back.

But he pulled away as if my hand were on fire, keeping his back to me.

"It's all right, Jimmy," I said softly. He shook his head.

"I'm sorry."

"It's all right. I just got frightened. It wasn't because of who we were to each other. I would have gotten frightened no matter who you were."

He turned and looked at me skeptically.

"Really," I said.

"But you can't stop thinking of me as your brother, can you?" he asked, his anticipation of disappointment making his eyes darker and bringing creases to his forehead.

"I don't know, Jimmy," I said honestly. It looked as though he might cry. "It's not something that I can do quickly, but . . . I'd like to try," I added. That pleased him and his smile returned. "Will you stay a little longer?"

"Well," he said, "I do have some pressing engagements with my business associates in Atlanta, but I suppose I could manage a few more days. . . ."

"See," I said quickly, "pretending isn't so hard for you either."

He laughed and lay back beside me again.

"It's the effect you have on me, Dawn. You always kept the gloom and doom out of my eyes." He traced my lips with his forefinger and grew serious again. "If only something good could come out of all this. . . ."

"Something good will, Jimmy. You'll see," I promised. He nodded.

"I don't care what your real parents and your grandmother say, Dawn has to be your name. You bring sunshine into the darkest places."

We both closed our eyes and started to bring our lips toward each other's again, when suddenly the hideaway door was thrust open and we turned to see Clara Sue standing in the hideaway doorway, her hands on her hips, a gleeful smile of satisfaction on her twisted lips.

14
VIOLATIONS

"Well, isn't this a pleasant surprise," Clara Sue purred, sauntering farther in. "I came here expecting to find you with Philip, but instead it's your . . ." She stared a moment and then smiled. "What should we call him? Brother? Boyfriend?" She laughed. "Maybe both?"

"Shut up," Jimmy snapped, the blood rushing to his face.

"Clara Sue, please," I pleaded. "Jimmy's had to run away from a terrible foster father. He's had a horrible time, and now he's on his way to Georgia to live with relatives."

She whipped her eyes to me and flared them with hate. Then she put her hands on her hips.

"Grandmother sent me to find you," she said. "Some kids had a food fight in the coffee shop, and we need all the chambermaids to help clean up." She gazed again at Jimmy, a sly smile returning to her twisted lips. "How long are you going to keep him hidden here? Grandmother would sure be angry if she knew," she said, her threatening note clear.

"I'm leaving," Jimmy said. "You don't have to worry."

"I'm not the one who has to be worried," she sneered.

"Jimmy, don't go yet," I said, pleading with my eyes for him not to leave.

"It's all right," Clara Sue suddenly said in a much softer, kinder tone of voice. "He can stay. I won't tell anyone. It might be fun."

"It's not fun," Jimmy said. "I don't want to get people in trouble on account of me."

"Does Philip know about all this?" Clara Sue demanded.

"He brought him down here," I said, replacing the sneer on her face with a look of indignation. Her hands flew back to her hips.

"Nobody tells me anything," she moaned. "You come and everyone forgets I'm part of the family. You better get inside before Grandmother sends someone else to look for you, too," she warned, her eyes turning cold and hard again.

"Jimmy, you won't run off, will you?" I said. He looked at Clara Sue and then shook his head.

"I'll wait," he said. "As long as she promises not to tell and get you in trouble."

I looked imploringly at Clara Sue. I wanted to tear into her for trying to get me into trouble with the necklace, but I had to keep my tongue glued to the roof of my mouth. In order to protect Jimmy, I had to remain under her thumb.

"I said I wouldn't tell, didn't I?"

"Thank you, Clara Sue." I turned back to Jimmy. "I'll return as soon as I can," I promised and started out. Clara Sue lingered behind me, staring at Jimmy. He ignored her and returned to the bunk.

"Boy, wouldn't Louise Williams like to know he's here. She would come right away." She laughed, but Jimmy didn't look at her or say anything, so she turned and followed me out.

"Please help us, Clara Sue," I pleaded as we walked up the cement stairway. "Jimmy's had a terrible time living with a cruel man. He hitched rides and didn't eat for days. He needs to rest up."

She didn't say anything for a moment, and then she smiled.

"Lucky Mrs. Clairmont found her necklace," she said.

"Yes, lucky." There was no love lost between us as we stared hatefully at each other.

"All right, I'll help you," she said, her eyes narrowing. "As long as you help me, too."

"What can I do for you?" I asked, surprised. Mother and Father bought her anything she wanted. She lived upstairs in a warm, cozy suite, and she had a nice job in the hotel and could dress up and be pretty and clean all day.

"I'll see. You better hurry to the coffee shop before Grandmother blames me for not finding you and demands to know what kept me."

I started obediently toward the front of the building, feeling like a puppet whose strings were in Clara Sue's hateful fingers.

"Wait!" she cried. "I know something you can do for me right away."

I turned back with dread.

"What?"

"Grandmother's upset about the way I keep my room. She thinks I make too much work for Mrs. Boston and I'm too messy and disorganized. I don't know why she worries so much about Mrs. Boston. She's just another one of the help around here," she said, wagging her head. "Anyway, when you're finished in the coffee shop, go up to my room and straighten it up. I'll be there later and see how you did.

"And don't take anything!" she added, smiling. "No necklaces." She pivoted on her heels as if she were my drill instructor and went in the opposite direction. I felt the heat rise in my neck. How could she think to make me her personal maid? I wanted to chase after her and pull out her hair, but I gazed toward the hideaway and thought about poor Jimmy. All I would do was create a commotion and drive him away. Frustrated and fuming, I plodded on to help the others clean up the coffee shop.

Clara Sue hadn't exaggerated. It was a mess with ketchup and French fries, milk and mustard, ice cream and soda all splattered on the walls and tables. I had seen a food fight at a cafeteria in one of the schools Jimmy and I attended, but it didn't seem as bad a mess as this. Of course, I didn't have to clean the school mess up, but now I could feel sorry for the custodial staff.

"It's some of those spoiled rich kids who come here," Sissy muttered as soon as I arrived and began washing down one of the tables. There were pieces of food everywhere. I had to step around puddles of milk and ketchup splashed on the floor. "They thought it was funny, even after it was all over and there was this mess. They run off through the hotel laughing and giggling. Mrs. Cutler was fit to be tied. She says the younger families ain't what the older ones used to be. The older ones is more classy and wouldn't have children this bad. That's what she told us."

Grandmother appeared in the doorway shortly afterward and watched us work. When we were finished, she and Mr. Stanley inspected the coffee shop to be sure it had been restored properly. I thought I would go up and do Clara Sue's room right away, but Mr. Stanley told Sissy and me to go right to the laundry and help wash and dry linens. That took more than two hours. I worked as hard and as fast as I could, realizing Jimmy was all alone, shut up in the hideaway, waiting for my return. I was afraid he might leave before I arrived.

As soon as we finished in the laundry, I started out to visit him, but Clara Sue caught me going down the corridor toward the exit. She had come looking for me.

"You've got to go right to my room," she demanded urgently.

"Grandmother is coming up later this afternoon to see how I fixed it up."

"Well, why can't you do it?"

"I have to entertain the children of some important guests. Besides, you're better at cleaning up. Just do it. Unless you don't want me to help you and Jimmy," she said, smiling.

"Jimmy needs something for lunch!" I cried. "I won't leave him without food all day."

"Don't worry. I'll see that he gets it," she said.

"You have to be careful no one sees you sneak food to him," I warned.

"I think I'm better at being careful than you are, Eugenia," she commented and walked off laughing.

Grandmother Cutler was right about one thing—Clara Sue was a slob. Her clothing was scattered all about—panties and bras draped over chairs, shoes under the bed and in front of the closet instead of inside it, skirts and blouses on the floor, blouses hanging on the headboard and on the back of the vanity table chair. And the vanity table! Makeup and creams were left open. There were streaks of cream and powder over the table. Even the mirror was spotted.

Her bed was unmade and covered with fashion and fan magazines. I found an earring under the bedspread and searched everywhere in vain for its mate. She had her jewelry strewn about, some of it on her desk, some on her vanity table, and some on the top of the dresser.

All the dresser drawers were open, and some had panties and stockings leaking out. When I started to put things into the drawers, I saw they were all mixed up—stockings with panties, T-shirts with stockings. I shook my head. There was so much to do. No wonder Grandmother Cutler was angry.

And when I opened the closet door! Clothing hadn't been properly hung, so skirts and pants, blouses and jackets were half on and half off hangers, some of the clothing fallen to the floor in heaps. Clara Sue had no respect for her possessions, I thought. It all came too easily.

It took me more than two more hours to do up her room, but when I was finished, it was clean, organized, and spotless. I was exhausted, but I headed out quickly and snuck around the back of the hotel to see Jimmy.

When I entered the hideaway, however, he wasn't there. The bathroom door was open, so I could see he wasn't in it. He had gotten disgusted waiting for me, I thought mournfully, and he had run off again. I flopped down on the bunk bed. Jimmy was gone; perhaps I would never see him or hear from him again. I couldn't keep the tears from rushing out—all my frustrations, fatigue, and unhappiness ganged up on me. I cried hysterically, my shoulders heaving, my chest aching. The dark, damp room closed in on me as I bawled. All our lives we were trapped in small, run-down places. I didn't blame Jimmy for fleeing from this one. I made up my mind I wouldn't come here again.

Finally, exhausted from crying, I stood up and wiped my tear-streaked cheeks with the back of my hands, which were dusty and dirty from all the cleaning I had done. Head bowed, I started for the door, but just before I reached it, Jimmy came in.

"Jimmy! Where were you? I thought you had run off for Georgia without saying good-bye!" I cried.

"Dawn, you should have known I wouldn't do that to you."

"Well, where were you? You could have been seen and . . ." There was a strange look in his eyes. "What happened?"

"Actually, I was running away," he said, lowering his head with a look of embarrassment. "I was running away from Clara Sue."

"What?" I followed him to the bunk bed. "What did she do? What happened?"

"She came down with some lunch for me and stayed while I ate, talking nonsense to me about Louise and the other girls and asking me all sorts of nasty questions about you and me and how we lived together. I got angrier and angrier, but I kept my temper down because I didn't want her to make any more trouble for you.

"Then . . ." He shifted his eyes from me and sat down.

"What then?" I asked sitting beside him.

"She got cute."

"What do you mean, Jimmy?" My heart started to race.

"She wanted me to . . . kiss her and stuff. I finally told her I had to get out for a while and ran out. I hid out by the baseball field until I was sure she would be gone and then I snuck back. Don't worry. No one saw me or paid any attention to me."

"Oh, Jimmy."

"It's all right," he said, "but I think I'd better go before she does make things worse."

I looked down, my tears building again.

"Hey," he said, reaching out to lift my chin. "I don't remember you ever being this unhappy."

"I can't help it, Jimmy. After you go, I'm just going to feel so terrible. When I first came in here and I thought you had left—"

"I can see." He laughed and got up to go into the bathroom. He ran the water over a washcloth and returned to clean my cheeks. I smiled at him, and he leaned forward to plant a soft kiss on my lips. "All right," he said, "I'll stay one more night and leave sometime tomorrow."

"I'm glad, Jimmy. I'll sneak back and eat dinner with you," I said excitedly, "and later I'll come down and . . . stay with you all night. No one will know," I quickly added when he took on a look of worry. He nodded.

"Be careful. I feel like I'm making so much trouble for you, and you've got more than your share because of us Longchamps."

"Don't ever say that, Jimmy. I know I'm supposed to be happier here because I'm a Cutler and my family's well off, but I'm not and I'll never stop loving you and Fern. Never. I don't care. I'll never stop," I insisted. Jimmy had to laugh.

"All right," he said. "Don't stop."

"I'm going to go get washed and changed and show my face about the hotel, so no one suspects anything," I said. "I'll eat with the staff, but I won't eat much. I'll save my appetite to eat with you." I stood up and looked down at him. "Are you going to be all right?"

"Me? Sure. It gets a little stuffy in here, but I'll keep that door partly open. And later, after it gets good and dark, I might sneak over to that big pool and jump in."

"I'll jump in with you," I said. I headed for the door and turned back just as I reached it. "I'm glad you came, Jimmy, so glad."

He beamed the widest, brightest smile at me, which wiped away all the frustration and fatigue I had to suffer to keep him here. Then I hurried out and away, cheered by the promise of once again spending a night with Jimmy. But as soon as I entered the old section of the hotel, I heard my grandmother and Mrs. Boston talking in the corridor. They had just come down from upstairs where they had inspected Clara Sue's room. I stood just outside the doorway and waited until I saw Grandmother walk by, her face so firm, it looked like a chiseled bust of her. How straight she stood, I thought, her posture so perfect when she walked. She radiated so much confidence and authority, I was sure not even a fly would cross her path.

As soon as she passed, I reentered and started down the corridor, but just as I went by the sitting room, Mrs. Boston stuck her head out and called to me.

"Now, you tell me the truth," she said as I approached. She lifted her eyes toward the family suites above. "It was you who cleaned and fixed up Miss Clara Sue's room, right?"

I hesitated. Would she get me into more trouble now?

"She never did nothing that good, not that child." Mrs. Boston folded her arms under her bosom and peered at me suspiciously. "Now, what she give you to get you to do that, or what she promise you, huh?"

"Nothing. I just did her a favor," I said, but shifted my eyes too quickly. I was never a very good liar and hated trying.

"Whatever it is she promised you, you shouldn't have done it. She's always getting someone to do things for her. Mrs. Cutler is trying to get her to take more responsibility for herself. That's why she ordered her to fix up her room before dinner."

"She told me Grandmother Cutler was mad because she was leaving too much for you to do."

"Well, goodness knows, that's true, too. That girl makes enough of a mess for two of me. Always has, from the day she was born," she said. It made me think.

"Mrs. Boston, you were here when I was stolen away, right?" I asked quickly.

Her eyes grew smaller, and there was a slight tremble in her lips.

"Yes."

"Did you know the woman who had been my nurse for that short time . . . Nurse Dalton?"

"I knew her before and knew her after. She's still living, but she needs a nurse herself these days."

"Why's that?"

"She's an invalid, suffering from diabetes. She lives with her daughter just outside of Cutler's Cove." She paused and looked at me askance. "Why you asking questions? There's no sense dragging up bad times."

"But how could my daddy . . . I mean Ormand Longchamp steal me right out from under my nurse's nose? Don't you remember the details?" I pursued.

"I don't remember no details. And I don't like dragging up bad times. It happened; it's over and done. Now I got to get going and finish up my work." She started away.

Puzzled by the way she reacted to my questions, I stood there and watched her walk off.

How could she forget the details of my kidnapping? If she once knew and still knew Nurse Dalton, she surely knew the way it had happened. Why was she so nervous when I asked her questions? I wondered.

If anything, it made me want to pursue the answers even harder.

I hurried on to get out of my dirty uniform and clean up. I wanted to take a long, hot shower and wash my hair so it smelled fresh and clean for Jimmy. I'd choose one of the nicer outfits from Clara Sue's hand-me-downs and brush out my hair so it shone the way it used to before all this happened. This could be the last night Jimmy and I spent together for years, I thought. What I wanted to do was bring back happier memories, help him to recall the times when we were all cheerful and hopeful. I needed to bring back the memories as much for myself as for him.

As soon as I got into my room, I stripped off my uniform and tossed it in the corner. I took off my underthings and my shoes and socks. Then I wrapped a towel around my body and went to the little bathroom. It always took a few minutes to get the water hot, so I turned it on and stood back to wait when all of a sudden the bathroom door was thrust open behind me.

I gasped and quickly scooped up the towel to wrap around myself again. Philip, smiling coyly, eyes big and bright, stepped in and closed the door behind me.

"Philip, what are you doing? I'm taking a shower!" I cried.

"So? Go ahead. I don't mind." He folded his arms across his chest and leaned back against the door provocatively.

"You get out of here, Philip, before someone comes along and hears you in here."

"No one's coming along," he said calmly. "Grandmother's busy with guests; Father's in his office, Clara Sue's with her friends, and Mother . . . Mother is debating whether or not she is well enough tonight to come to the dining room. We're safe," he said, smiling again.

"We're not safe. I don't want you in here. Please . . . go," I begged.

He continued to gaze at me, his eyes moving from my feet to my head, drinking me in with pleasure. I tightened the towel around my body, but it was too small to be an adequate covering. When I brought it higher to cover my breasts, it came up too far on my thighs, and when I lowered it, most of my bosom was revealed.

Philip's tongue moved across his lips as if he had just finished eating something delicious. Then he grinned wickedly and took a step toward me. I backed up until I was against the wall.

"What are you doing, getting all cleaned and dressed for Jimmy?"

"I'm . . . getting ready for dinner. I did a lot of work today, and I'm not very clean. So go. Please."

"You're clean enough for me," he said. I cringed as he drew closer. In a moment he had me pinioned in his arms, with his palms flat against the wall to prevent my escape. His lips brushed my cheek.

"Philip, are you forgetting who we are now and what has happened?"

"I'm not forgetting anything, especially," he said, kissing my forehead and moving his lips toward mine, "our night under the stars when we were rudely interrupted by my idiot friends. I was about to teach you things, things you should know by your age. I'm a very good teacher, you know. You'll be grateful, and you don't want to learn these things from just anybody, do you?" He dropped his right hand to my shoulder.

"You've had a taste of what it's like," he said softly, his eyes fixed on me. "How can you not want more?"

"Philip, you can't. We can't. Please . . ."

"We can as long as we know when to stop, and I promise I know that. I keep my promises, too. I'm keeping my promise to help you with Jimmy, aren't I?" he said, raising his eyebrows to drive home his point.

Oh, no, I thought. Not Philip, too. Both he and Clara Sue were taking advantage of Jimmy's troubles to get me to do things.

"Philip, please," I pleaded. "This doesn't feel right anymore. I can't help it. I'm just as sorry as you are that it's turned out this way, believe me; but there is nothing we can do about it but accept it."

"I accept it. I accept it as another challenge," he said, slipping his hand farther down to run his fingers along the top of my towel. I clutched it desperately.

"But it's not fair," he said, his face suddenly turning dark and angry. "You knew how much I wanted to touch you and hold you, and you led me to believe it would happen."

"But it's not my fault."

"It's nobody's fault . . . or maybe it's your other father's fault, but who cares right now? As I said," he continued, working his forefinger in and under the top of my towel, "we don't have to go as far as ordinary, unrelated men and women do. It won't mean anything then, but I had promised you I would show you—"

"I don't need to be shown."

"But I do," he said, forcing the towel down against my inadequate grip. I tried twisting away, but that only helped him get a better grip and the towel slipped off my breasts. His eyes widened with appreciation.

"Philip, stop!" I screamed. He gripped the inside of my elbows, pinning my arms back.

"If anyone hears you, we'll all get into trouble," he warned, "you, me, and Jimmy especially." He brought his lips to my nipples, moving quickly from one to the other and then back again.

I closed my eyes to try to deny this was happening. Once I had dreamt of him holding me and loving me, but this was twisted and harsh. My poor confused body responded to his caresses—stirred in places it had not been stirred before, but my mind screamed *No!* I felt like someone sinking into warm, soothing quicksand. For a few seconds it felt good, but it promised only trouble.

I continued to twist and squirm under his pincerlike fingers. The tip of his tongue drew a line from one breast to another and then he began to lower his body, kissing his way down my stomach until he reached the towel that was barely around my waist. I held it in the tip of my fingers. He bit the towel and tugged at it like a mad dog.

"Philip, stop, please," I pleaded.

With one strong pull, he drew the towel away from my body and dropped it at my feet. Then he gazed up at me, his eyes mad with desire. The glint in them was enough to set my heart racing even faster and pounding even harder than it already was.

Unable to get around him because he had me trapped against the wall, I brought my hands to my face as soon as he released my arms to embrace my thighs and draw them to his face. I felt my legs crumble and slid down the wall to the floor, keeping my face covered.

"Dawn," he said, his breathing heavy and hard. "It feels so good holding you. We don't have to think about anything else."

All I could do was cry as his hands moved over my body, exploring, caressing.

"Doesn't this feel good? Aren't you happy?" he whispered. I took my hands off my face when he took his hands from me and started unbuttoning his pants. It sent an electric bolt of fear up my spine. With all my strength, I tried pushing him away so I could drive him back enough for me to lunge for the door and make a quick exit. But he seized my wrists and turned them until I was on my back on the wooden floor.

"Philip!" I cried. "Stop before it's too late."

In one swift motion he slipped himself between my legs.

"Dawn . . . don't be so frightened. I can't help wanting to be with you. I thought I could, but you're too pretty. It doesn't have to mean anything," he said, gasping his words.

I clenched my hands into small fists and tried to pummel his head, but it was like a small bird slapping its wings against the snoot of a fox. He didn't even acknowledge it; instead, he moved himself more comfortably against me, his lips catching the soft flesh of my breast between them and nibbling his way over my bosom.

Suddenly I felt his hardness press itself firmly against me until he forced in that swollen, rigid male sex part of him that had to be satisfied. It drove into my tight and resisting flesh, which tore and bled.

I screamed, not caring anymore if we were discovered and if Jimmy were found. The shock of feeling him inside me drove away any concern for anything but my own violated being. My piercing screech was enough to cause his retreat.

"All right," he pleaded. "Stop. I'll stop." He drew back and stood up, quickly pulling up his underwear and pants and buckling his belt. I turned over on my stomach and cried into my arms, my body shaking.

"Wasn't it good for you?" he asked softly, kneeling beside me. I felt his palm on my lower back. "At least now you have an idea of what it will be like."

"Go away. Leave me alone, Philip. Please!" I cried through my tears.

"It's just the shock of it all," he said. "All girls have the same reaction." He stood up. "It's all right," he repeated, more to convince himself, it seemed, than to convince me.

"Dawn," he whispered. "Don't hate me for wanting you."

"Just leave me alone, Philip," I demanded in a much sterner tone. There was another long pause and then I heard him open the bathroom door and leave.

I turned over to be sure he was gone. This time I made sure the door was locked. Then I gazed down at myself. There were red blotches over my breasts and stomach where he had nibbled and sucked on me. I shuddered. His violation of me, although short, left me feeling unclean. The only way I could stop myself from sobbing was to step into the shower and let the now hot water run over my body, practically scalding my flesh. I endured the heat, feeling it was cleansing me and washing away the memory of Philip's fingers and kisses. I scrubbed myself with such intensity, I brought about new red blotches, making my skin scream with pain. All during my shower my tears mixed in with the water, seeming to fall as freely. What had once held the promise of romantic ecstasy and wonder had now turned sordid and depraved. I scrubbed and scrubbed.

Finally, exhausted from the effort to wash away what had just happened, I stepped out of the shower and dried myself. I returned to my bedroom and, feeling more tired than I could ever remember, lay down. I couldn't cry anymore. I closed my eyes and fell asleep, awakening when I heard a gentle rapping at my door.

He's returned, I thought, my heart racing again. I decided to remain still and see if he would believe I was already gone. The knocking got louder, and then I heard, "Dawn?"

It was my father. Had Philip, upset about my rebuffing him gone to him and told him about Jimmy? I got up slowly, my arms and legs as sore as they would be had I been working out in a farm field all day. I put on my robe and opened the door.

"Hi," he said. His smile quickly wilted. "Aren't you feeling well?"

"I'm . . ." I wanted to tell him all of it, wanted to shout it out as a way of getting rid of the memory. I wanted to scream about all my violations, this sexual one only being the most recent. I wanted to demand retribution, demand love and concern, demand to be treated like a human being at least, if not a member of the family. But I could only look down and shake my head.

"I'm very tired," I said.

"Oh. I'll see about getting you a day off."

"Thank you."

"I have something for you," my father said and reached into his breast pocket to pull out an envelope.

"What's that?"

"The receipt of delivery from the prison. Ormand Longchamp has your letter," he said. "I did what I promised."

I took the receipt slowly from his hand and gazed upon the official signature. Daddy had received my letter and most likely had already set his eyes upon my words. At least now I could look forward hopefully to receiving his reply.

"But you mustn't be upset if he doesn't write back," my father advised. "I'm sure by now he's ashamed and would have a hard time facing you. Most likely, he doesn't know what to say."

I nodded, staring down at the official receipt.

"It's still hard for me to understand," I said, squeezing back my tears. I looked up at him sharply. "How could he have stolen me right out from under my nurse's nose?"

"Oh, he was very clever about it. He waited until she had left the nursery to go visit Mrs. Boston in her room. It wasn't that she neglected you. You had fallen asleep, and she had taken a break. She and Mrs. Boston were good friends. He must have been hiding in the corridors, watching and waiting for his opportunity. When it came he went in and took you and snuck out the back way."

I looked up sharply.

"Nurse Dalton had gone to Mrs. Boston's room?" He nodded. But why didn't Mrs. Boston tell me this when I asked her how Daddy could have taken me right out from under Nurse Dalton's eyes? I wondered. That was such an important detail; how could she forget it?

"We didn't know you had been taken until Mrs. Dalton returned and discovered you gone," my father continued. "At first she thought we had taken you into our room. She came to our door, frantic.

" 'What do you mean?' I said. 'We don't have her.' We didn't think Grandmother Cutler would take you to her suite, but Mrs. Dalton and I ran out to see, and then the realization hit me, and I went running through the hotel. But it was far too late.

"One of the staff members had seen Ormand Longchamp in the family section of the hotel. We put two and two together and came to the realization about what he had done. By the time we contacted the police, he and his wife were gone from Cutler's Cove, and of course, we had no idea in what direction they had headed.

"I jumped into my car and went tearing about, hoping to be lucky and come upon him, but it was futile." He shook his head.

"If he should write you, whatever he tells you in a letter," my father said, his face turning as sour and angry as I imagined it could, "it can't justify the terrible thing he did. Nothing can.

"I'm sorry his wife died and he's had such a hard life, but perhaps they were being punished for the horrible crime they committed."

I turned away because the tears had begun to sneak out the corners of my eyes and zigzag down my cheeks.

"I know it's been especially difficult for you, honey," he said, putting his hand softly on my shoulder, "but you're a Cutler; you'll survive and become all you were meant to become.

"Well," he continued, "I've got to get back to the job. You should try to eat something," he said, and I remembered Jimmy. I had to get food to him. "Tell you what," my father said. "I'll stop by the kitchen and have someone fix you a plate and send it on down. Okay?"

I could bring that food to Jimmy, I thought.

"Yes, thank you."

"If you still don't feel too well later, let me know, and I'll have the hotel doctor look in on you," he said and left.

I gazed in the mirror to see how bad I looked. I couldn't let Jimmy know what had happened between Philip and me. If he found out, he would become enraged and go after him, only getting himself into terrible trouble. I had to make myself look good for him so he couldn't sense that anything terrible had happened to me. There were still some blotches on my neck and right around my collarbone.

I went to the closet and found a pretty blue skirt and white blouse that had a wide collar and would hide most of the blotches. Then I brushed out my hair and tied a ribbon around it. I put on a little lipstick, too. I wished I had some rouge to make my pale cheeks look healthier, I thought.

I heard a knock on my door and opened it to accept my tray of food from one of the kitchen staff. I thanked him and closed the door, waiting to hear his footsteps disappear. Then I opened the door slowly and peered out. When I was certain all was clear, I hurried down the corridor and out the exit, carrying the warm tray of food to Jimmy.

"I'm stuffed," Jimmy announced and then looked up from his plate. "One thing you have here is great food, huh?" He sighed. "But I feel like a cooped-up chicken in here, Dawn. I can't stay much longer."

"I know," I said sadly and looked down. "Jimmy . . . Why can't I go with you?"

"Huh?"

"Oh, Jimmy, I don't care about the food or the beautiful grounds. I don't care how important my family is in this community or how wonderful people think the hotel is. I'd rather go with you and be poor and live with people I can love.

"Daddy's and Momma's relatives won't know anything if we don't tell them. We'll tell them about Momma dying, but we'll make up another reason for Daddy's being in prison."

"Oh, I don't know, Dawn . . ."

"Please, Jimmy. I can't stay here."

"Oh, things are bound to get better for you, a whole lot better than they would be in Georgia. Besides, I told you, if you ran off with me, they'd surely send someone after us, and we'd only be caught."

I nodded and looked into his soft, sympathetic eyes.

"Doesn't all this seem like one long, terrible nightmare sometimes,

Jimmy? Don't you just hope you will wake up and it will all have been a horrible dream? Maybe if we wish hard enough . . ."

I closed my eyes.

"I wish I could lock out all the bad things that had happened to us and put us in a magical place where we could live out our deepest, most secret dreams, a place where nothing ugly or sordid could touch us."

"So do I, Dawn," he whispered. I felt him lean toward me, and then I felt his breath on my lips before I felt his lips. When we kissed, my body softened, and I thought how right it would have been for Jimmy to be the one to have taken me from girlhood innocence into a woman's world. I had always felt safe with him, no matter where we went or what we did, because I sensed how much he cared for me and how important it was to him that I be happy and secure. Tragedy and hardship had tied us together as brother and sister, and now it seemed only right, even our destiny, that romantic love bind us even tighter.

But Philip's attack had stolen away the enchantment that comes when a girl willingly casts off her veil of innocence and enters maturity hand in hand with someone she loves and someone who loves her. I felt stained, polluted, spoiled. Jimmy felt me tense up.

"I'm sorry," he said quickly, thinking it was his kiss that had done it.

"It's all right, Jimmy," I said.

"No, it's not all right. I'm sure you can't stop seeing me beside you on one of our pull-out couches. I can't stop seeing you as my sister. I want to love you; I do love you, but it's going to take time—otherwise we won't feel clean and right about it," he explained.

He tried to look away, but slowly he was drawn back to me, his eyes so full of torment. It made my heart pound to see how much he loved and wanted me and yet his deep sense of morality kept him chained back. My impulses, my unleashed sexuality thrashed about like a spoiled child, demanding satisfaction, but the wiser part of me agreed with Jimmy and loved him more for showing his wisdom. He was right —if we rushed into things, we would suffer regret. Our confused consciences could turn us away from each other afterward, and our love would never grow to be pure and good.

"Of course you're right, Jimmy," I said, "but I always loved you as much as a sister could love her brother, and now I promise to learn to love you the way a woman should love a man, no matter how long it takes me and how long I have to wait."

"Do you mean that, Dawn?"

"I do, Jimmy."

He smiled and kissed me softly again, but even that short, gentle peck on the cheek sent an electric thrill through my body.

"I should leave tonight," he said.

"Please don't, Jimmy. I'll stay with you all night," I said. "And we'll talk until you can't keep your eyelids open."

He laughed.

"All right, but I should leave early in the morning," he said. "The truckers get started early, and they're the best chance I got to get rides."

"I'll get you breakfast when I go to eat with the rest of the staff. That's early. And we'll have a little more time together.

"But do you promise that when you get to Georgia, you'll write and tell me where you are?" I asked. Just the thought of his leaving and being so far away from me now made me feel sick inside.

"Sure. And as soon as I earn enough money on my own, I'll come back to see you."

"Promise?"

"Yes."

We lay together on the bunk, me snuggled in his arm, and talked about our dreams. Jimmy had never had his mind set on being anything before, but now he talked about joining the air force when he was old enough and maybe becoming a pilot.

"But what if there was a war, Jimmy? I'd feel terrible and worry all the time. Why don't you think about being something else, like a lawyer or a doctor or—"

"Come on, Dawn. Where am I going to get enough money to go to a college?"

"Maybe I'll get enough money to send you to college."

He was quiet and then he turned to me with his dark eyes so sad and heavy.

"You won't want me to be your boyfriend if I'm not somebody big and important. Is that it, Dawn?"

"Oh, no, Jimmy. Never."

"You won't be able to help it," he predicted.

"That's not true, Jimmy," I protested.

"Maybe it's not true now, but after you've been living here a while, you'll get to feel that way. It happens. These rich, old southern families plan their daughters' lives—what they will be, who they will marry—"

"It won't happen to me," I insisted.

"We'll see," he said, convinced he was right. He could be so stubborn sometimes.

"James Gary Longchamp, don't tell me what I will and will not be like. I am my own person, and nobody—not a tyrant grandmother or anybody else—is going to mold me into someone else. She can call me Eugenia until she gets red in the face."

"All right," he said, laughing. He kissed me on the cheek. "Whatever you say. I don't think she's going to be a match for your temper anyhow. I wonder who you get that from? Your mother got a temper?"

"Hardly. She whines instead of yells. And she gets everything she wants anyway. She doesn't have to be mad at anyone."

"What about your father?"

"I don't think he's capable of getting angry. Nothing seems to bother him. He's as smooth as fresh butter."

"So then you inherited your grandmother's temperament. Maybe you're more like her than you think."

"I don't want to be. She's not what I imagined my grandmother would be like. She's . . ."

We heard the sets of footsteps on the cement stairway before the door was thrust open. A moment later the hideaway was illuminated, and we looked up at two policemen. I grabbed Jimmy's hand.

"See," Clara Sue said from behind them, "I told you I wasn't lying."

"Let's go, kid," one of the policemen said to Jimmy. He stood up slowly.

"I ain't going back there," he said defiantly. The policeman moved forward. Jimmy stepped to the side. When the policeman reached out to grab him, Jimmy ducked and scooted to the side.

"Jimmy!" I cried.

The other policeman moved swiftly and seized him around the waist, lifting him off the ground. Jimmy flared out, but the second policeman joined the first, and they restrained him quickly.

"Let him go!" I screamed.

"You can come along quietly, or we'll put handcuffs on you, kid," the policeman holding him from behind said. "What's it going to be?"

"All right, all right," Jimmy said, his face red with embarrassment and anger. "Let go."

The policeman loosened his grip, and Jimmy stood by, his head lowered in defeat.

"Move on out," the other policeman commanded.

I turned to Clara Sue, who stood in the doorway.

"How could you do this?" I screamed. "You mean, selfish . . ."

She stepped back to let the policemen and Jimmy pass. Just as Jimmy reached the door, he turned back to me.

"I'll come back, Dawn. I promise. Someday I'll come back."

"Move it," the policeman commanded, pushing him. Jimmy stumbled forward through the door.

I ran after them.

"Jimmy!" I cried. I started running up the steps and stopped when I reached the top.

My father stood beside my grandmother, and Clara stood just behind them both.

"Go directly to your room, Eugenia," my grandmother commanded. "This is a terrible disgrace."

"Go on," my father said a little softer, but his face dark with disappointment. "Go to your room."

I looked after Jimmy and the policemen. They were nearly at the front of the building.

"Please," I said. "Don't let them take him back. He had a horrible time living with a mean man. Please—"

"It's not our problem," my grandmother said.

"We can't do anything," my father confirmed. "And it's against the law to harbor a fugitive."

"He's not a fugitive. No," I said, shaking my head. "Please . . ." I turned in Jimmy's direction, but he had already gone around the building. *"Jimmy,"* I called. I started after him.

"Eugenia!" my father cried. "Get back here."

I ran, but by the time I had reached the front of the hotel, the policemen had shoved Jimmy into the back of the patrol car and slammed the door. I stood by watching as they got in. Jimmy peered out the window.

"I'll be back," he mouthed.

The roof light began, and the patrol car was started up.

"Jimmy!"

I felt my father's hand on my shoulder, restraining me.

"How utterly embarrassing," my grandmother said from somewhere behind me. "That my guests should see this."

"You'd better get inside," my father advised.

My body shook with sobs as the police car pulled away, taking Jimmy back into the night.

15
SECRETS REVEALED

I felt my father's fingers grip my shoulders softly as the lights from the police patrol car disappeared on the street below. My grandmother stepped forward to face me. Her lips were tight and thin, and her eyes were wide and maddening with rage. Under the lanterns and the bright porch lights, her skin was ghostly white. With her shoulders raised and her neck lowered between them, she looked like a hawk about to pounce on a mouse, and right now I felt like some sort of trapped creature.

"How could you do such a thing?" she hissed. She turned sharply to my father. "I told you she was no better than a wild animal brought in from the streets. She's sure to bring them all here if we don't put an immediate stop to it. She has to be sent away to some private school that specializes in this sort of person."

"I'm not a wild animal! You're a wild animal!" I screamed.

"Eugenia," my father snapped. I spun out of his hands.

"I'm not Eugenia! I'm not! I'm Dawn, Dawn!" I insisted, pounding my sides with my own small fists.

I looked up and saw the guests who had gathered at the front entrance and on the porch gawking down at me, some of the elderly women shaking their heads and the men nodding their agreement. Suddenly Philip pushed his way through and gazed at us in confusion.

"What's happening?" he cried. He turned to Clara Sue, who was off to the side looking very content with herself. She flashed a smile of satisfaction up at him.

"You'd better get yourself inside," my father advised in a strong, loud whisper. "We'll talk about all this when everyone's a bit calmer."

"No," I said. "You shouldn't have let them take him," I added and began to sob. "You shouldn't have."

"Eugenia," he said softly, stepping toward me.

"Get her inside," my grandmother commanded through her teeth. "Now!" She turned away and smiled up at her guests. "It's all right, everyone. Just a misunderstanding. Nothing to alarm anyone."

"Please, Eugenia," my father said, reaching out to take my hand. "Let's go inside," he pleaded.

"No!" I backed farther away. "I'm not going inside. I hate it; I hate it!" I screamed and turned and ran down the driveway.

"Honestly, Daddy, you're always treating Dawn with kid gloves," I heard Clara Sue say. "She's a big girl. She's made her bed! Now let her lie in it."

Her words put more force into my stride. Clara Sue was such a liar. As I ran, the tears streamed down and blew off my cheeks. I felt as though my chest would explode, but I didn't stop running. I reached the street and turned right, running down the sidewalk, half the time with my eyes closed, sobbing.

I ran and ran until the pain in my side became a sharp knife cutting deeper and deeper, forcing me to slow down to a trot and then a walk, my hand on my ribs, my head down, gasping for breath. I had no idea where I was headed or where I was. The street had turned to the left, bringing me closer to the ocean, and the pounding surf seemed right beside me. Finally I stopped by some large rocks and leaned against them to rest and catch my breath.

I gazed out at the moonlit sea. The sky was dark, deep, even cold, and the moon looked sickly yellow. Occasionally the spray from the surf reached me and sprinkled my face.

Poor Jimmy, I thought, spirited off into the night like some common criminal. Would they force him to return to that mean farmer? What had we done to deserve this? I bit down on my lower lip to prevent myself from sobbing any more. My throat and chest ached so much from crying.

Suddenly I heard someone calling. It was Sissy wandering through the streets looking for me.

"Your daddy sent me after you," she said.

"He's not my daddy," I spat out hatefully. "He's my father, and I'm not going back. I'm not."

"Well, what'cha going to do?" she asked, looking around. "You can't stay out here all night. You gotta come back."

"They dragged Jimmy away like some hunted animal. You should have seen."

"I did see. I seen it all from the side of the porch. Who was he?"

"He was my . . . the boy I thought was my brother. He had run off from a cruel foster parent."

"Oh."

"And there was nothing I could do to help him," I wailed helplessly, standing back and wiping my cheeks. "Nothing." I sighed deeply and lowered my head. How frustrated and defeated I felt. Sissy was right: I had to return to the hotel. Where else would I go?

"I hate Clara Sue," I said through my clenched teeth. "She told my grandmother Jimmy was hiding out here and got her to call the police. She's a mean, spiteful . . . She's the one who stole Mrs. Clairmont's necklace just so I'd be blamed. Afterward, I saw her sneak into my room and put it in my bed."

"But I thought Mrs. Clairmont found it."

"I snuck into her room and put it back, but Clara Sue did it," I repeated. "I know no one will believe me, but she did."

"I believe you. That's one spoiled child for sure," Sissy agreed. "But she will get hers someday. That kind always does, because they hate themselves too much. Come on, honey," Sissy said, putting her arm around my shoulders, "I'll walk you back. You're shivering something terrible."

"I'm just upset, not cold."

"Still, you're shivering," Sissy said, rubbing my arm. We started back to the hotel. "Jimmy's a handsome boy."

"He is handsome, isn't he? And he's very nice. People don't see that at first because he seems so standoffish. That's because he's really shy."

"Ain't nothing wrong with being a little shy. It's the other type I don't like much."

"Like Clara Sue?"

"Like Clara Sue," she agreed, and we both laughed. It felt good to laugh, like finally letting out a breath you had to hold for the longest time. And then an idea came to me.

"Do you know the woman who was my nurse when I was first born —Mrs. Dalton?"

"Uh-huh."

"She lives with her sister, right?" Sissy nodded. "Does she live nearby?"

"Well, back there about four blocks," she said, indicating behind us.

"In a little Cape Cod house on Crescent Street. Once in a while my granny sends me over with a jar of this or a jar of that. She's a sick woman, you know."

"Mrs. Boston told me. Sissy, I want to go see her."

"What for?"

"I want to ask her questions about my kidnapping. Will you take me there?"

"Now?"

"It's not that late."

"It's too late for her. She's very sick and would be asleep by now."

"Will you take me in the morning after we do our work? Will you?" I asked. "Please," I begged.

"Okay," she said, seeing how important it was to me.

"Thank you, Sissy," I said.

When we returned to the hotel, my grandmother was nowhere to be seen, but my father greeted us in the lobby.

"Are you all right?" he asked. I nodded and looked down at the carpet. "I think you should just go to your room. We'll have a chance to talk about all this tomorrow when everyone is calmer and can think clearly."

As I was crossing the lobby, I decided what I was going to do. It was time to deal with Clara Sue. She wasn't going to get away with what she had done.

Without even bothering to knock, I stormed into Clara Sue's bedroom, slamming the door behind me.

"How could you?" I angrily demanded. "How could you tell them about Jimmy?"

Clara Sue was on her bed, flipping through a magazine. By her side was a box of chocolates. Despite my angry words, she didn't look up. Instead she continued reading, reaching into the box of chocolates, nibbling one after another and discarding them after one or two bites.

"Aren't you going to say anything?" I asked. I still received no answer, and it infuriated me the way she was so blatantly ignoring me. I swooped down on her and swatted the box of chocolates. It flew off the bed and into the air before crashing to the floor, chocolates scattering everywhere.

I waited for Clara Sue to look up at me. I couldn't wait to confront her about the treacherous thing she had done. But she didn't look up. She only continued reading, ignoring me as though I wasn't there. For some reason this infuriated me even more. I tore her magazine out of her hands, ripping it to shreds, tossing the pieces in the air.

"I'm not leaving, Clara Sue Cutler. I'm staying right here until you look at me."

Finally she looked up, her blue eyes sending me a warning look. "Didn't anyone ever teach you to knock? It's the polite thing to do."

I chose to ignore the look in Clara Sue's eyes. "And didn't anyone ever teach you about trust? About keeping a secret sacred? Jimmy and I trusted you. Why did you do it? Why?"

"Why not?" she purred softly. Then more angrily and with a burst of force as she jumped off her bed, "*Why not?* Making your life miserable gives me pleasure, Dawn. It makes me happy."

I stared at her in outrage. Without even thinking about it, I brought up my hand and slapped her across the face. "You're nothing but a spoiled selfish brat! I'll never forgive you for this. *Never!*"

Clara Sue laughed at me, massaging her cheek. "Who wants your forgiveness?" she sneered. "You think you're doing me a favor?"

"We're sisters. Sisters are supposed to be best friends. You didn't want me a friend, Clara Sue, and now you don't want me as a sister. Why? Why are you so intent on hurting me? What did I ever do to you? Why do you keep doing these nasty things?"

"Because I hate you!" Clara Sue screamed at the top of her lungs. "I hate you, Dawn! I've hated you all my life!"

I was shocked by her anger. It threw me off guard, and I didn't know how to respond. There was such ferocity in her words and her face was bright red, her eyes bulging like the eyes of a madwoman. I'd seen such a look before—on Grandmother Cutler's face. Clara Sue's look chilled me the way Grandmother's had. But I couldn't understand it. Why did they both hate me so? What had I ever done to this family to warrant such ugly emotions?

"How can that be?" I whispered. Part of me wanted to understand Clara Sue's feelings. "How can that be?"

"How can that be?" Clara Sue mimicked cruelly. *"How can that be? I'll tell you how. I'll tell you!* You've been a part of my life without even being in it! From the day I was born I've lived in your shadow, and I've hated every minute of it!"

"But that wasn't my fault." Part of me was starting to understand. The aftermath of my kidnapping had become a permanent part of life at Cutler's Cove, and Clara Sue had been born into it.

"Oh, wasn't it? I wasn't the first-born, like Philip, or the first daughter, like you. I wasn't even considered the baby of the family. Oh, no! *I was nothing but the baby born to replace you!*" Clara Sue closed the distance between us. "Get out of my room. *Get out!* The sight of you sickens me. But before you go, Dawn, here's a promise. A very special promise that I intend to keep. I will *never* accept you as a part of this family. I will *never* welcome you with open arms or make your life easier. *Never!* Instead I will do everything humanly possible to make your life a living hell. And when that isn't enough, I'll do even more. I will go out of my way to bring you sorrow and heartache. Your unhappiness will bring a smile to my face and make the sun even shinier. I will shatter your dreams until they're nothing more than twisted remnants of your hopes and will bring you only nightmares. *Nothing less will do!*"

I was speechless. "You can't be serious!" I cried. Clara Sue's reasons for turning in Jimmy were now crystal clear, and although I was still very angry at her, part of me pitied her. With everything she had, Clara Sue was miserable. I wanted to help her overcome her unhappiness. Maybe then she wouldn't hate me so much.

Clara Sue's eyes glinted wildly as she stared at me with open amazement. "I don't believe you! I honestly don't believe you! You just don't give up, do you? This isn't some sappy movie where we pour out our hearts to each other, have a good cry, and then kiss and make up. Get your pretty little head out of the clouds, Dawn. Didn't you hear a word I said? We will never be friends, and we will certainly never be sisters. *Ever!*" Clara Sue inched closer, and I backed away from her into the bedroom door. "Never let your guard down with me, Dawn," she warned. "Watch out for me. Always."

With those final words she turned her back on me. I fumbled with the doorknob, anxious to escape from my sister because in my heart I knew that what she had promised was true.

Neither my father nor my grandmother had time to see me the following morning since it was the day of a big check-in and checkout. I was busy with Sissy anyway because we had an additional five rooms to clean and remake. Nevertheless, I anticipated my grandmother's appearance in the kitchen when the staff had its breakfast. I hadn't slept well the night before, and I wasn't in the mood to be yelled at or embarrassed in front of the other workers. I made up my mind to stand up to her, even if it meant being confined to my room without food again.

Because Clara Sue had the early evening shift at the front desk, she always slept late, so I didn't have to face her, but Philip was up and with the other waiters, of course. He avoided me until it was time to go to work. Then he followed me out and called to me.

"Please," he begged when it looked like I wouldn't stop. I turned on him abruptly.

"I have work to do, Philip," I said. "I have to earn my keep," I added bitterly. "And I don't believe Grandmother. I'm not learning the business from the bottom up. I'll always be on the bottom as far as she is concerned." I gazed at him. He looked so different to me now, so cheap and pathetic since he had attacked me. To think I had almost been in love with him!

"Dawn, you have to believe me. I had nothing to do with my grandmother's finding out about Jimmy. She doesn't know I brought him down there to hide him when he first arrived," he said, his eyes showing his fear. So that was it, I thought.

"You're afraid I'll tell her?" He didn't reply, but his face answered. "Don't worry, Philip. I'm not like our precious younger sister. I won't deliberately get you in trouble just to get revenge, although I should," I snapped and pivoted to catch up with Sissy.

During the rest of the morning, whenever I heard footsteps in the corridor, I expected my father or my grandmother. After our work was completed and neither had arrived, I pulled Sissy aside.

"Take me right to Mrs. Dalton's daughter's house, Sissy. Please, before my grandmother finds more work for us."

"I don't know why you want to go see that woman. She don't remember things that well," Sissy said, looking away quickly.

"Why do you say that, Sissy?" I sensed the change in her attitude.

"My granny says so," she said, looking up quickly and then looking down again.

"You told her you were taking me and she didn't like it?" Sissy shook her head. "You don't have to go in with me, Sissy. Just point out the house. And I won't tell anyone you showed me. I promise."

She hesitated.

"My granny says people who dig up the past usually find more bones than they expected, and it's better to let bygones be bygones."

"Not for me, Sissy. I can't. Please. If you don't help me, I'll just go looking anyway until I find the house," I said, screwing my face into a look of determination to impress her.

"All right," she said and sighed. "I'll show you the way."

We left the hotel through a side entrance and quickly went down to the street. It was strange how everything looked different to me in daylight, especially the cemetery. Gone was its foreboding and ominous atmosphere. Today it was just a pleasant, well-manicured resting place, easy to pass.

It was a bright, nearly cloudless day with a soft, warm ocean breeze. The sea looked calm, peaceful, inviting, the tide gently combing the beach and falling back into small waves. Everything looked cleaner, friendlier.

There was a constant line of traffic in the street, but it moved lazily. No one seemed to be in a rush; everyone was mesmerized by the glitter of the sunlight on the aqua water and the flight of terns and sea gulls that floated effortlessly through the summer air.

This might very well have been a wonderful place in which to grow up, I thought. I couldn't help wondering what I might have been like had I been raised in the hotel and Cutler's Cove. Would I have turned out as selfish as Clara Sue? Would I have loved my grandmother, and would my mother have been an entirely different person? Fate and events beyond my control had left these questions forever unanswered.

"There it is, straight ahead of us," Sissy said, pointing to a cozy little white Cape Cod house with a patch of lawn, a small sidewalk, and a small porch. It had a picket fence in front. Sissy looked at me. "You want me to wait here for you?"

"No, Sissy. You can go on back. If anyone asks you where I am, tell them you don't know."

"I hope you're doing the right thing," she said and turned back, walking quickly with her head down as if she were afraid she would set eyes on some ghost in broad daylight.

I couldn't help trembling myself as I approached the front door and rang the buzzer. At first I thought no one was home. I pushed the buzzer again and then I heard someone shout.

"Hold your water. I'm coming; I'm coming."

The door was finally opened by a black woman with completely gray hair. She was in a wheelchair and peered up at me with big eyes, magnified under her thick lenses. She had a soft, round face and wore a light blue housecoat, but her feet were bare. Her right leg was wrapped in a bandage from her ankle up until the bandage disappeared under her dress.

Curiosity brightened her eyes and drew deep creases in her forehead. She pressed her lips together and leaned forward to peer out at me. Then she raised her glasses and wiped her right eye with her small fist. I saw a gold wedding band on her finger, but other than that, she wore no jewelry.

"Yes?" she finally said.

"I'm looking for Mrs. Dalton, the Mrs. Dalton who was a nurse."

"You're looking at her. What do you want?" she asked leaning back in her wheelchair. "I don't work no more, not that I don't wish I could."

"I want to talk to you. My name's Dawn, Dawn Lon . . . Dawn Cutler," I said.

"Cutler?" She studied me. "From the hotel family?"

"Yes, ma'am."

She continued to stare at me.

"You ain't Clara Sue?"

"Oh, no, ma'am."

"Didn't think you was. You're prettier than I remember her to be," she said. "All right, come on in," she added and finally backed her wheelchair up.

"I'm sorry I can't offer you anything. I'm having enough trouble taking care of myself these days," she said. "I live with my daughter and her husband, but they got their own lives and problems. Spend most of my time alone," she mumbled, looking down at the floor and shaking her head.

I paused and looked into the entryway. It was a small one with hardwood floors and a blue and white throw rug. There was a coatrack on the right, an oval mirror on the wall, and a globular overhead light fixture.

"Well, come in if you're coming in," Mrs. Dalton said when she looked up and saw I was still standing in the doorway.

"Thank you."

"Go on into the living room there," she said, pointing after I entered. I went through the doorway on the left. It was a small room with a rather worn dark brown rug. The furniture was vintage, too, I thought. The flower-pattern covering on the couch looked thin in the arms. Across from it was a rocking chair, an easy chair, and a matching settee, all equally tired-looking. There was a square-shaped dark maple table at the center. Against the far wall were paintings—seascapes and pictures of seaside houses. To the left was a glass-door bookcase filled with knickknacks as well as some novels. Over the small fieldstone fireplace hung a ceramic cross, but I thought the nicest thing in the room was an old dark pine grandfather's clock in the left corner.

The room had a pleasant lilac scent. Its front windows faced the sea, and with the curtains drawn back it provided a nice view and made the room bright and cheery.

"Sit down, sit down," Mrs. Dalton commanded and wheeled herself in behind me. I chose the couch. The worn cushions sank in deeply under me, so I sat as far forward as I could. She turned her wheelchair to face me and put her hands in her lap. "Now, then, what can I do for you, honey? There ain't much more I can do for myself," she added dryly.

"I'm hoping you can tell me more about what happened to me," I said.

"Happened to you?" Her eyes narrowed. "Who'd you say you were?"

"I said I was Dawn Cutler, but my grandmother wants me to go by the name I originally had been given when I was born—Eugenia," I added, and I might as well have reached out to slap her across the face. She snapped back in her chair and brought her hands to her sagging bosom. Then she crossed herself quickly and closed her eyes. Her lips trembled, and her head began to shake.

"Mrs. Dalton? Are you all right?" What was wrong with her? Why had my words caused such a reaction? After a moment she nodded. Then she opened her eyes and gazed at me with wonder, her lips still trembling.

She shook her head softly. "You're the lost Cutler baby. . . ."

"You were my nurse, weren't you?"

"Only a few days. I should have known someday I'd set eyes on you. . . . I should have known," she mumbled. "I need a drink of water," she decided quickly. "My lips feel like parchment. Please . . . in the kitchen." She gestured toward the doorway.

"Right away," I said, getting up quickly. I went out to the hallway and followed it to the small kitchen. When I brought back the water, she was slumped to the side in her wheelchair, looking as if she had gone unconscious.

"Mrs. Dalton?" I cried in a panic. "Mrs. Dalton!"

She straightened up slowly.

"It's all right," she said in a loud whisper. "I'm all right. My heart's still strong, although why it still wants to beat in this broken, twisted body is beyond me."

I handed her the water. She sipped some and shook her head. Then she looked up at me with big searching eyes.

"You turned out to be a very pretty girl."

"Thank you."

"But you've been through a few things, haven't you, child?"

"Yes, ma'am."

"Ormand Longchamp was a good father and Sally Jean was a good mother to you?"

"Oh, yes, ma'am," I said, happy to hear their names from her lips. "You remember them well?" I took my seat on the couch again quickly.

"I remember them," she admitted. She swallowed some more water and sat back. "Why did you come here? What do you want from me?" she asked. "I'm a sick woman, advanced diabetes. I'm going to have to have this leg amputated for sure, and after that . . . I might as well be dead anyway," she added.

"I'm sorry for your trouble," I said. "My momma . . . Sally Jean . . . became a sick woman and suffered something terrible."

Her face softened.

"Well, what can I do for you?"

"I want you to tell me the truth, Mrs. Dalton," I said, "every last detail of it you remember, for my daddy . . . the man I called my daddy, Ormand Longchamp, sits in prison, and my mother Sally Jean is dead, but I can't think of them as being the evil people everyone tells me they were. They were always good to me and always took care of me. They loved me with all their hearts, and I loved them. I can't allow such bad things to be said about them. I just can't. I owe it to them to find the truth."

I saw a slight nod in Mrs. Dalton's face.

"I liked Sally Jean. She was a hardworking woman, a good woman who never looked down on nobody and always had a pleasant smile no matter how hard things were for her. Your daddy was a hardworking man who didn't look down on nobody. Never saw me without saying hello and asking how I was."

"That's why I can't think of them as bad people, Mrs. Dalton, no matter what I'm told," I insisted.

"They did take you," she said, her eyes turning glassy.

"I know that, but why . . . how is what I don't understand."

"Your grandmother doesn't know you're here, does she?" she asked, nodding because she anticipated the answer.

"No."

"Nor your real father or mother?" I shook my head. "How is your mother these days?" she asked, pulling the corners of her mouth in.

"Nearly always locked up in her room for one reason or another. She suffers from nervous ailments and gets everything brought to her, although she doesn't look sick to me." I refused to feel sorry for my mother. In her own way she was just as selfish as Clara. "Occasionally she accompanies my grandmother at dinner and greets guests."

"Whatever your grandmother wants," Mrs. Dalton muttered, "she's sure to do."

"Why? How do you know so much about the Cutlers?" I asked quickly.

"I was with them a long time . . . always worked special duty for them when any of them were sick. I liked your grandfather. He was a sweet, gentle man. I cried as much when he died as I did when my own father died. Then I was a maternity nurse for your brother, for you, and for your sister."

"You cared for Clara Sue, too?" She nodded. "Then my grandmother certainly wasn't mad at you for what happened and didn't blame you for my abduction."

"Heavens, no. Who told you that?"

"My mother."

She nodded again. Then she widened her eyes.

"If your grandmother don't know you're here and neither does your parents, who sent you? Ormand?"

"Nobody sent me. Why would my daddy send me?" I asked quickly.

"What do you want?" she asked again, this time more sharply. "I told you I'm sick. I can't sit up and talk long."

"I want to know what really happened, Mrs. Dalton. I spoke to Mrs. Boston—"

"Mary?" She smiled. "How is Mary doing these days?"

"She's fine, but when I asked her about what happened, she didn't tell me you were visiting with her when I was abducted, and she didn't want to talk about it."

"I was with her; she just forgot, that's all. There's nothing more to tell. You were asleep, comfortably. I left the nursery; Ormand took you and then he and Sally Jean run off. You know the rest."

I looked down, the tears building quickly.

"They ain't treating you so good since you been returned, is that it?" Mrs. Dalton asked perceptively. I shook my head and wiped away the tears that had escaped my eyes.

"My grandmother hates me; she's upset I was found," I said and looked up. "And she was the one who put up the money for the reward leading to my recovery. I don't understand. She wanted me found, but she was upset when I was, and it wasn't just because all this time has passed. There's something else. I feel it; I know it. But no one wants to tell me, or no one knows it all.

"Oh, Mrs. Dalton, please," I begged. "My daddy and momma just weren't bad people. Even you just said so. I can't understand them stealing a baby from someone, even if my momma had suffered a stillborn. No matter what I'm told, I can't learn to hate them, and I can't stand thinking about my daddy locked up in some prison.

"My little sister, Fern, and my brother, Jimmy, have been sent to live with strangers. Jimmy just ran away from a mean farmer and hid out in the hotel until Clara snitched on him. The police took him away last night. It was just terrible."

I took a deep breath and shook my head.

"It's like some curse was put on us, and for what? What did we do? We're no sinners," I added vehemently. That widened her eyes again. She brought her hands to the base of her throat and looked at me as if I were a ghost. Then she nodded slowly.

"He sent you," she muttered. "He sent you to me. This is my last chance at redemption. My last chance."

"Who sent me?"

"The Lord Almighty," she said. "All my good churchgoing days don't matter none. It ain't been enough to wash me clean." She leaned forward and grasped my hand firmly into hers. Her eyes were wide, wild. "That's why I'm in this wheelchair, child. It's my penance. I always knew it. This hard life is my punishment."

I sat absolutely still as she stared into my face. After a moment she nodded and released her grip on my hand. She sat back, took a deep breath and looked at me.

"All right," she said. "I'll tell you everything. You was meant to know and I was meant to tell you. Otherwise, He wouldn't have sent you to me."

"Your mother comes from a rich and distinguished old family in Virginia Beach," Mrs. Dalton began. "I remember your father and mother's wedding. Everybody does. It was one of the most gala affairs in Cutler's Cove, and everyone in society was invited, even people from Boston and New York. People thought it was the perfect marriage—two very attractive people from the best families. Why, people here went around comparing it to the marriage of Grace Kelly, the movie star, and that prince in Europe.

"Your father was like a prince here anyway, and there was a number of suitors after your mother's hand. But even back then I heard stories."

"What kind of stories?" I asked when she looked like she wouldn't continue.

"Stories about your grandmother being unhappy about the marriage, not thinking your mother was right for your father. Say what you want about your grandmother, she's a powerful woman with eyes like a hawk. She sees things other people close their eyes to, and she goes and does what has to be done.

"Yes, she's a distinguished lady who wouldn't do anything to embarrass the family. Your grandfather liked your mother. Any man would have. I don't know if she's still as beautiful as she was, but she was like some precious little doll, her features tiny but perfect, and when she batted her eyelashes . . . men would turn into little boys. I seen that firsthand," Mrs. Dalton added, lifting her eyes to me and raising her eyebrows.

"So your grandmother kept her opposition quiet, I guess. I don't know all that went on behind closed doors, mind you, although some of the older staff, people who had been with the Cutlers a long time, people like Mary Boston, had a good idea what was going on and said there was a struggle.

"Not that Mary is the type who goes around gossiping, mind you. She don't. I was always close with Mary, so she told me what she knew. I was already a nurse and had done some special duty at the hotel, taking care of guests who got sick occasionally, and then, as I told you, taking care of Mr. Cutler Senior when he got sick.

"It wasn't no big secret then how your grandmother felt about your mother. She thought she was too flighty and self-centered to be a good hotel man's wife, but your father was head over heels. There was nothing he wanted more.

"Anyway, they got married, and for a while it seemed your mother might make a good hotel man's wife. She behaved, did what your grandmother wanted, learned how to be nice to the guests and be a host . . . She really enjoyed getting all dressed up and wearing all her expensive jewelry so she could be the Princess of Cutler's Cove, and in those days, as it still is, Cutler's Cove was a very special hotel catering to the richest, most distinguished families from up and down the East Coast . . . even Europe!"

"What happened to change things?" I asked, unable to contain my impatience. I knew all about the hotel and how famous it had become. I wanted her to get to the parts I didn't know.

"I'm getting to it, child. Don't forget, I'm not spry, and my mind wanders something awful because of this ailment, this curse, I should say." She waved her hand and then took on a far-off look. I sat obediently, waiting until she turned back to me.

"Where was I?"

"You were telling me about my mother, the wedding, how good things were in the beginning . . ."

"Oh, yeah, yeah. Well, it wasn't long after your brother was born . . ."

"Philip."

"Yeah, Philip, that your mother started to stray a bit."

"Stray?"

"Don't you know what stray means, child? You know what it is when a cat strays, don'tcha?" she asked, leaning toward me.

"I think so. Flirting?" I guessed.

She shook her head.

"She was doing more than just flirting. If your father knew, he didn't let on. 'Least as far as anyone knew, but your grandmother knew. Nothing happens at that hotel, she doesn't know about it the same minute or minutes afterward. It always looked like your grandfather was in charge, but she's the strength, always was, 'least as long as I can remember," she added, blinking quickly.

"I know," I said sadly.

"Anyway, from what I know about it, there comes this entertainer, piano player and singer, as handsome a man as could be. All the young women drooled over him, and he and your mother . . ." She paused and then leaned toward me again as if there were other people in the room and she didn't want to be overheard.

"There was this chambermaid, Blossom, who told me she come upon them out behind the pool house one night. She went out there herself with a man called Felix, who was a handyman. Nothing to look at," she added, twisting her nose, "but Blossom, she'd make love to any man who paused long enough to notice her.

"Anyway, she knew it was your mother, and she got frightened and pulled Felix away. Blossom didn't tell but one or two of her close friends besides me about what she saw, and your mother and her lover didn't know Blossom had been there at the same time, but it wasn't much longer after that, your grandmother found out all of it. She had ears and eyes working for her everywhere in that place, if you know what I mean," Mrs. Dalton said, nodding.

"What did she do?" I asked in a voice barely audible.

"The singer was let go and shortly afterward . . . well, your mother was pregnant."

"With me?"

" 'Fraid so, child. And your grandmother, she got your mother into her office and whipped her with words so bad, she had her begging for mercy. Of course, your mother swore up and down that you was her and Randolph's, but your grandmother was too sharp and knew too much about what went on. She knew dates, times . . . your mother finally confessed and admitted you was most likely not Randolph's child. Besides," she said, her eyebrows up again, "I don't think things was running that smooth between your mother and your father, as smooth as they're supposed to be running between a man and a woman. You understand?"

I shook my head. I didn't.

"Well," she said, "that's another story. Anyway, the only reason I found out about all this was your grandmother was going to force your mother to have an abortion on the sly. She wanted me to take her to someone."

I shook my head, dazed. Randolph Cutler wasn't my father. Once again what I believed to be the truth wasn't. When would this all end? When would the lies stop?

"What was the singer's name?"

"Oh, I don't remember. In those days entertainers came through here like hurricanes. Some stayed a season; some stayed a week on their way to New York or Boston or Washington, D.C. And as I said, he wasn't the first one your mother took behind the pool house."

I couldn't believe what I was hearing about my mother. My poor, sick mother. Ha! What an elaborate farce she had managed to create. How could she have done such a thing to Randolph? How could she have betrayed their love and marriage vows by sleeping with other men? It disgusted me. *She* disgusted me, for her actions were nothing more than those of a selfish woman thinking only of herself and what she wanted.

"Didn't Randolph find out?" I asked.

"He found out your mother was pregnant," she replied. "And that's what saved her from getting an abortion. You see, he thought you were his baby. So Laura Sue begged your grandmother to let her keep the child, go through with the pregnancy, and keep Randolph from knowing of her infidelity.

"Your grandmother didn't want no scandal, but she wasn't happy about keeping another man's child and calling that child a Cutler. She's too proud of her blood and no one *ever* gets the upper hand with her.

"But I was born. She let it happen," I said.

"Yeah, you was born, but right before you was, your grandmother decided she couldn't live with the lie in the hotel after all. I guess it was eating away at her seeing Laura Sue grow bigger and bigger with child, and seeing people fawn over her and talk about a new grandchild, while she knew that child wasn't truly her grandchild. Plus, your mother took every chance she could to gloat in front of your grandmother. That was her big mistake."

"What did she do?" I asked, my heart beginning to pound. I was afraid to breathe too loudly for fear Mrs. Dalton would stop or go off on another subject.

"She confronted Laura Sue. I was already working at the hotel, taking care of her in her last month and staying where I would stay in the nursery after you was born. So I was close by," she added, pulling herself up in the wheelchair and raising her eyebrows.

"You mean you overheard what was said?" I asked. I didn't want to say "eavesdropped." I could see she was sensitive about it.

"I would have found out most of it anyway. They needed me and had to tell."

"Needed you?" I was confused. "Why?"

"Your grandmother had come up with the plan. She rescinded her original agreement with your mother and told her she had to give up the baby. As long as she did that, your grandmother would keep her infidelity a secret, and she could continue to be Princess of Cutler's Cove."

"What did my mother say? There must have been a terrible argument." Despite my mother's illusion of illness, I suspected she could be quite strong-willed when she wanted. When it suited her advantage.

"No argument at all. Your mother was too self-centered and pampered. She was afraid to lose the good life, so she agreed to the ruse."

"Ruse? What ruse?"

"The plan, child. Sally Jean Longchamp had just given birth to a stillborn, as you know. Your grandmother went to her and to Ormand and made a deal with them—they were to abduct the newborn baby. She gave them jewelry and money to help them afford an escape.

"Sally Jean was upset about just losing a child, and here was Grandmother Cutler offering her another one, a child nobody seemed to want anyway. Laura Sue had agreed, and I think they were told that Randolph had too. I can't say for certain about that.

"Your grandmother worked it all out with them and promised to cover their escape well and send the police off in the wrong directions.

"Then she come to me," Mrs. Dalton said and looked down. "I couldn't disagree with her when she said Laura Sue would make a terrible mother. I could see how she was with Philip. She never had any time for him. Too busy lunching or shopping or sunning by the pool. And your grandmother was very upset about the child not being a true Cutler.

"Anyway, she offered me a full year's salary to cooperate. It was a lot of money for just turning my back, and since neither your grandmother nor your mother wanted the baby . . . well, I did as she asked and made myself scarce, went down to Mary Boston's room and waited while Ormand went in and abducted you.

"Mary knew what was happening. She had picked up a hint or two here and there, and then I told her the rest. She never liked your mother. Not many of the staff cared for her, because she was so spoiled and talked down to them.

"Anyway, Mary and I both felt sorry for Sally Jean Longchamp, who had just lost a child she wanted. We thought it was all a good idea. Nobody would be worse off for it.

"Apparently, Randolph still didn't know what was happening and what had happened, so your grandmother continued the ruse by offering a reward. There were times when we thought the police had located Ormand and Sally. Randolph went off to identify the suspects, but it was never them. The rest I guess you know.

"Except," she said, looking down at her hands in her lap, "it got so I regretted my part. No matter how bad a mother Laura Sue would have been and how much Ormand and Sally Jean wanted another child, it was still wrong. They were made into fugitives; you grew up believing you were their daughter, and poor Randolph appeared to be suffering something terrible thinking his newborn baby had been taken.

"I was tempted a few times to tell him the truth, but every time I set out to do that, I lost my courage. Mary kept saying it was for the best anyway. And my daughter . . . she was scared about what might happen if we crossed old Mrs. Cutler, and she and my son-in-law have had enough trouble just caring for me.

"Not long afterward, though, your mother had Clara, and they put that little tombstone in the cemetery to put your memory to rest forever."

"I know; I've seen it."

"I felt terrible about it. I went to look at it myself, and I knew God was watching me. Before long I began to get sick. I got sicker and sicker until you see me now.

"And now you've come back and I'm glad," she said with a sudden burst of energy and strength. "You're my redemption. I can make my peace with the Lord knowing I've told you the truth. I'm sorry, too. I can't right the wrong, but I can tell you I'm sorry I was any part of it.

"You're too young to know and appreciate what forgiveness means, child, but I sure hope someday you can find it in your heart to forgive ole, sick Lila Dalton," she said, smiling softly, hopefully.

"You're not the one who has to ask for forgiveness, Mrs. Dalton," I replied. "You thought you were doing the right thing at the time, even something that would be better for me.

"But," I added, my eyes burning, "Ormand Longchamp shouldn't be sitting in that jail and taking all the blame."

"No, I suppose not."

"Would you tell the truth now, if you were asked to?" I inquired hopefully. "Or are you still afraid of what might happen?"

"I'm too old and too sick to be afraid of anyone or anything anymore," she said. "I'd do what I had to do to make my peace with God."

"Thank you," I said, standing. "For telling me everything. I'm sorry you're so sick, and I hope it does make you feel better."

"That's sweet of you, child. Funny," she said, taking my hand and looking up at me, "you're the grandchild Mrs. Cutler would want the most, and you're the one she gave away."

16
PRIVATE CONVERSATIONS

I returned to the hotel slowly, my head spinning, my whole life whirling by. Every few moments I would stop the wheel of fortune and read off something that now made sense—Momma's last words in the hospital, asking me not to hate her and Daddy, my grandmother's unhappiness at my return, my real mother's cowardice and nervous condition—all of it began to fall into place to create a picture that I didn't like, but that at least made sense.

Lunch had just ended at the hotel. Guests were meandering about the grounds, sitting on the front porch, enjoying the beautiful day. Younger guests were at the tennis courts, and many had gone to the pool. Across the way at the docks other guests were getting into and out of boats that took them for scenic coastal rides. There were smiles and laughter all around me. I was sure I stood out because of the clouds that hovered over me and cast dark shadows over my face.

But I couldn't help it. The bright sunshine, the warm ocean breezes, the happy peal of laughter coming from children, the excitement and energy of the tourists—all of it only pointed up my own sadness. Cutler's Cove was no place to be depressed, I thought, especially not today.

My grandmother was sitting in the lobby smiling and talking to guests. They laughed at something she said and then listened closely as she went on, their attention glued to her as if she were some celebrity. I saw the way other guests were drawn to her, eager to listen. She didn't see that I had entered, so I was able to look at her without her knowing it.

But suddenly she set eyes on me, and her expression frosted. I didn't turn away first. She did. Her smile returned as she continued to talk to her guests. I proceeded through the lobby. I had something to do before I would speak with her, someone else to speak with first.

Clara Sue was behind the front desk. Some of the teenage guests were standing there and talking to her. They all laughed, and then Clara Sue turned my way, her face full of curiosity and without any remorse.

But I didn't care about her right now. Right now she was insignificant to me. I ignored her and walked across the lobby. She made some snide remark about me, I'm sure, because a moment later she and her friends laughed even louder than they had been laughing. I didn't look back. I went to the old section and hurried through the corridor to the stairway.

There I paused, and then I walked up slowly, my eyes fixed ahead of me, my determination building with each step. All I could hear were Momma's last words to me in the hospital; all I could see was Daddy with his head bowed in defeat when the police had arrived.

What I was about to do I was to do for them.

I paused again at the door of my mother's suite, and then I walked in slowly and found her seated at her vanity table, brushing her golden hair and gazing admiringly at herself in the oval mirror. For a long moment she didn't realize I had entered. She was too entranced in her own image. Finally she realized I was standing there staring at her, and she spun around on her stool.

She was dressed in a light blue negligee, but as usual she had on earrings, a necklace, and bracelets. She had been making up her face and wore lipstick, rouge, and eyeliner.

"Oh, Dawn, you frightened me, sneaking in like that. Why didn't you knock? Even though I'm your mother, you've got to learn to knock," she said reproachfully. "Women my age need their privacy respected, Dawn honey," she added and put on her friendly smile that now looked more like a mask to me.

"Aren't you afraid Grandmother will hear you call me Dawn and not Eugenia?" I demanded. She looked more closely at me and saw the angry gleam in my eyes. It unnerved her quickly, and she put her brush down and turned around to get up to go to her bed.

"I'm not feeling too well this morning," she murmured as she crawled over her silk sheets. "I hope you don't have any new problems."

"Oh, no, Mother. All my problems are old ones," I announced, moving closer. She looked up at me curiously and then pulled her blanket over her body and fell back against her fluffy pillows.

"I'm so tired," she said. "It must be this new medication my doctor has prescribed. I'm going to have to have Randolph call him and tell him it's making me too tired. All I want to do is sleep, sleep, sleep. You'll have to leave and let me close my eyes."

"You weren't always like this, Mother, were you?" I asked sharply. She didn't say anything; she kept her eyes closed and her head on the pillow. "Were you, Mother? Didn't you used to be quite a lively young lady?" I asked, stepping up to the bed. She opened her eyes and blazed a wild look at me.

"What do you want? You're acting so strange. I don't have the strength. Go see your father if you have a problem. Please."

"Where shall I find my father?"

"What?"

"Where do I go to find him, my father?" I asked in a sweet, musical voice. "My *real* father."

She closed her eyes and lay back again.

"In his office, I'm sure. Or in his mother's office. You shouldn't have any problem locating him." She waved a hand dismissively.

"Really? I would have thought it would be very hard to find my father. Wouldn't I have to go running about from hotel to hotel, night-club to nightclub, listening to entertainers?"

"What?" She opened her eyes again. "What are you talking about?"

"I'm talking about my real father . . . finally my *real* father. The one by the pool."

My remark had hit home. I savored the look of unease creeping into her face. For once I wasn't the one who had to answer about the past. I wasn't the one made to feel ashamed. She was.

She stared at me uncomprehendingly and then brought her hands to her bosom.

"You don't mean that Mr. Longchamp? You're not still calling him your father, are you?" I shook my head. "Well, what are you talking about? I can't take this." Her eyelids fluttered. "It's making me feel very faint."

"Don't pass out before you tell me the truth, Mother," I demanded. "I won't leave your side until you do anyway. That I promise."

"What truth? What are you babbling about? What have you been told now? Who have you been speaking to? Where's Randolph?" She gazed at the door as if he were right behind me.

"You don't want him here," I said. "Unless it's time he knew it all.

How could you give me up?" I asked quickly. "How could you let someone take your baby?"

"Let . . . someone?"

I shook my head in disgust.

"Were you always this weak and self-centered? You let her force you to give me up. You made your bargain—"

"Who's been filling you with these lies?" she demanded with a surprising burst of energy.

"No one's been filling me with lies, Mother. I have just come from talking with Mrs. Dalton." Her angry scowl wilted. "Yes, Mrs. Dalton, who was my nurse, whom you said Grandmother blamed. You just wanted to shift the blame to someone else. If Grandmother blamed her, why did she give her a year's salary? And why was she rehired to care for Clara Sue?

"There's no sense trying to think of another lie to cover that one," I added quickly when I saw her start to speak. It was better to keep her on her toes. On the defense before she could gather her wits and retaliate with more lies. "Mrs. Dalton's very sick and wants to make her peace with God. She regrets her part in the scheme, and she is willing to tell the truth to anyone now.

"Why did you do it? How could you let anyone have your own child?"

"What did Mrs. Dalton tell you? She's sick; she must be babbling madness. Why did you even go to speak to that woman? Who sent you there?" my mother demanded.

"She's sick, but she's not babbling madness, and there are others here in the hotel who can support her story. I'm the one who is sick," I snapped. "I'm sick of lies, of living a life of lies.

"You lay here in bed pretending to be weak and tired and nervous just to hide yourself from the truth," I said. "Well, I don't care. Do what you want, but don't lie to me anymore. Don't pretend to love me and to have missed me and to pity me for having been taken away to live a poor, hard life. You sent me into that life. Didn't you? *Didn't you?*" I shouted. She winced and looked as if she would burst into tears. *"I want the truth!"* I screamed and pounded my thighs with my fists.

"Oh, God!" she cried and buried her face in her hands.

"Crying and pretending to be sick won't save you this time, Mother. You did a terrible thing, and I have a right to know the truth."

She shook her head.

"Tell me," I insisted. "I won't leave until you do."

Slowly she brought her hands away from her face. It was a changed face, and not just because tears had streaked her makeup and made her eyeliner run. There was a tired, defeated look in her eyes, and her lips trembled. She nodded slowly and slowly turned to me. She looked even younger, more like a little girl who had been caught doing something naughty.

"You mustn't think badly of me," she said in a tiny child's voice. "I didn't mean to do terrible things. I didn't." She pursed her lips and tilted her head as a five-year-old would.

"Just tell me what really happened, Mother. Please."

She glanced toward the doorway and leaned closer to me, her voice in a whisper.

"Randolph doesn't know," she said. "It would break his heart. He loves me very much, almost as much as he loves his mother, but he can't help that. He can't," she said, shaking her head.

"Then you did give me away?" I asked, a sick feeling in the pit of my stomach. Until this moment . . . this moment of truth . . . a secret part of me hadn't wanted to believe what I'd been told. "You *did* let Ormand and Sally Jean Longchamp have me?"

"I had to," she whispered. "She made me do it." She gazed out of the corners of her eyes at the doorway. She was like a little girl trying to shift the guilt onto another little girl. My anger subsided. There was something very pathetic and sad about her. "You mustn't blame me, Dawn. *Please!*" she begged. "You mustn't. I didn't want to do it, honest, but she told me if I didn't, she would tell Randolph things about me and have me cast out a disgrace. Where would I go? What would I do? People would hate me. Everyone respects and fears her," she added angrily. "They would believe anything she said."

"So you did make love with another man and got pregnant with me?" I asked softly this time.

"Randolph was always so involved in the hotel. He's in love with the hotel," she complained. "You don't have any idea how hard it was for me in those days," she said, her face twisting. Tears filled her eyes. "I was young and beautiful and full of energy and wanted to do things, but Randolph was always so busy or his mother was always asking him to do this and do that, and if I wanted to go somewhere or do something, he always had to check with his mother. She ruled our lives like some queen.

"I wasn't going to just sit around all the time. *He never had time for me! Never!* It wasn't fair!" she shouted indignantly. "He didn't tell me it would be that way when he courted me. I was fooled. Yes," she said, nodding and liking her theory, "I was tricked, deceived. He was one kind of a man outside the hotel and another inside. Inside, he is what his mother wants him to be, no matter what I say or do.

"So I can't be blamed," she concluded. "It's all really his fault . . . her fault." The tears streaked down her face. "Don't you see? I'm not to blame."

"She told you you would have to give me up and you agreed," I concluded, as if I were a lawyer cross-examining a witness in a trial, but I did feel like it was a trial of sorts, with me acting as attorney for Ormand and Sally Jean Longchamp, as well as myself.

"I had to agree. What else could I do?"

"You could have said no. You could have fought for me and told her I was your child. You could have told her no, no, no!" I shouted wildly, but it was like trying to tell a four-year-old how to behave like an adult. My mother smiled through her tears, nodding.

"You're right. You're right. I was bad. So very bad! But everything's all right now. You're back. Everything's all right. Let's not talk about it anymore. Let's talk about good things, happy things. Please."

She patted me on the hand and took a deep breath, her expression changing as if all that we had been discussing was instantly forgotten and not very important anyway.

"I was thinking that you should have something done with your hair, and maybe we could go shopping for some nice new clothes for you. And new shoes and some jewelry. You don't have to wear all of Clara Sue's hand-me-downs. You can have your own things now.

"Would you like that?" she asked.

I shook my head. She really was a child. Perhaps she had always been like this and that was why my grandmother had her way with her easily.

"But I'm so tired right now," she said. "I'm sure it's this new medicine. I just want to close my eyes for a while." She dropped her head back to the pillow. "And rest and rest." She opened her eyes and looked up at me. "If you see your father, please tell him to call the doctor. I have to change my medicine."

I stared down at her. She did have the face of a little girl, a face to be pitied and pampered.

"Thank you, honey," she said and closed her eyes again.

I turned away. There was no point in screaming at her anymore or

making any demands on her. In a way she was an invalid, not as sick as
Mrs. Dalton, but just as shut away from reality. I started for the door.

"Dawn?" she called.

"Yes, Mother."

"I'm sorry," she said and then closed her eyes again.

"So am I, Mother," I replied. "So am I."

All my life, I thought as I descended the stairway, I have been carried
along by events beyond my control. As an infant, as a child, and as a
young girl, I was dependent upon adults and had to do whatever they
wanted me to do or, as I had just learned, go along with whatever they
wanted done with me. Their decisions, their actions, and their sins were
the winds that blew me from one place to the next. Even those who
really loved me could turn and go only to certain places. The same was
true for Jimmy and certainly for Fern. Events that had been begun even
before our births had already determined what and who we would be.

But now all the tragedy of the last few months rushed down over and
around me: Momma's death, Daddy's being arrested, having what I
thought was my family broken up, being spirited off in the night to this
new family, Clara's continuous attempts to hurt me, Philip's raping me,
Jimmy's escape and capture, and my learning the truth. I was like
someone caught in the middle of a tornado and spun about. Now, like a
flag that had suddenly snapped in a violent gust and pulled free of the
hinges that held it, I spun on my heels and soared toward the hotel
lobby, my head high, my eyes fixed ahead of me, not gazing left or right,
not seeing anyone else, not hearing any voices.

My grandmother was still sitting on a settee in the lobby, the small
audience of guests surrounding her and listening attentively to whatever
she had to say. Their faces were filled with smiles of admiration.
Whomever my grandmother singled out for a special word, a touch,
beamed like someone blessed by a clergyman.

Something in my face drew the audience back in a wave, made them
part and step away as I approached. Slowly, with her soft, angelic smile
still firmly settled on her face, my grandmother turned to see what had
stolen their attention from the glow of her eyes and the warmth of her
voice. The instant she saw me, her shoulders stiffened and her smile
retreated, bringing dark shadows to her face, which suddenly seemed
more like a hard shell.

I stopped before her, my arms folded under my breasts. My heart was pounding, but I did not want her to see how nervous and frightened I was.

"I want to talk to you," I declared.

"It's impolite to interrupt people like this," she replied and started to turn back to her guests.

"I don't care what's impolite or polite. I want to talk to you right now," I insisted, filling my voice with as much firmness as I could. I did not shift my eyes from her, so she would see just how determined I was.

Suddenly she smiled.

"Well," she said to her admiring circle of guests, "I see we have a little family matter to tend to. Will everyone please excuse me for a few minutes?"

One of the gentlemen at her side moved quickly to help her get up.

"Thank you, Thomas." She glared at me. "Go to my office," she commanded. I glared back and then headed that way while she continued to make excuses for my behavior.

When I entered her office, I looked up at the portrait of my grandfather. He had such a warm, gentle smile. I wondered what it would have been like to know him. How had he put up with Grandmother Cutler?

The door burst open behind me as my grandmother came in like a storm. Her shoes snapped against the wooden floor as she pounded past me and then whipped herself around, her eyes burning in rage, her lips pencil-line thin.

"How dare you? How dare you behave in that manner while I was speaking with my guests? Not even my poorest workers, people who come from the most depressing and lowly backgrounds, act like that. Is there not even a shred of decency in your insolent body?" she ranted. It was as if I had stepped before a coal stove just when the door was open and confronted the raging fire and all its uncovered red heat. I closed my eyes and retreated a few steps, but then I opened them and spit my words back at her.

"You can't speak to me of decency anymore. You're a hypocrite!"

"How dare you? I'll have you shut up in your room; I'll—"

"You won't do anything, Grandmother, but tell the truth . . . finally," I ordered firmly. Her eyes widened in confusion. With a bit of glee I announced my surprise. "I went to see Mrs. Dalton this morning. She's very sick and was happy to finally lift the burden of guilt from her conscience. She told me what really happened after I was born and before."

"This is ridiculous. I won't stand here and—"

"Then I went to see my mother," I added, "and she confessed as well."

Grandmother stared at me a moment, her rage lowering slowly like the flame on a stove, and then she turned and went to her desk.

"Sit down," she ordered and took her own seat. I moved to the chair in front of her desk. For a long moment she and I simply stared at each other.

"What is it you have learned?" she asked in a far calmer tone of voice.

"What do you think? The truth. I found out about my mother's lover and how you forced her to eventually give me up. How you arranged for Ormand and Sally Jean Longchamp to take me and then pretended they had abducted me. How you paid people and got people to go along with your scheme. How you offered a reward just to cover up your actions," I said, all in one breath.

"Who is going to believe such a story?" she replied with such cold control it sent a chill of fear down my spine. She shook her head. "I know how sick Mrs. Dalton is. Did you know that her son-in-law works for the Cutler's Cove Sanitation Company and that I own the Cutler's Cover Sanitation Company? I could have him fired tomorrow just like that," she said, snapping her fingers.

"And if you and I go upstairs together, right now, and confront Laura Sue with this story, she will simply break down and cry and babble so incoherently no one would understand a word. Most likely with me standing beside you, she would not be able to remember anything she had told you." She gave me a look of triumph.

"But it's all true, isn't it?" I cried. I was losing that firmness, that confidence that had put a steel rod in my spine. She was so strong and so sure of herself, she could stand her ground and turn back a herd of wild horses, I thought.

She turned away from me and was quiet for a long moment. Then she looked back.

"You seem to be someone who thrives on controversy . . . harboring that boy here while the police were after him." She shook her head. "All right, I'll tell you. Yes, it's true. My son is not your real father. I begged Randolph not to marry that little tramp. I knew what she was and what she would become, but like all men, he was hypnotized by surface beauty and by her sweet-sounding, syrupy voice. Even my husband was charmed. I watched how she turned her shoulders and dazzled them with her silly little laugh and desperate helplessness," she

said, twisting the side of her mouth up in disgust. "Men just love helpless women, only she wasn't as helpless as she pretended to be," she
added with a cold smile on her lips. "Especially when it came to satisfy-
ing her desires.

"She always knew what she wanted. I didn't want that kind of a
woman as part of my family, part of this . . . this hotel," she said,
holding her arms out. "But arguing with men who are under a woman's
spell is like trying to hold back a waterfall. If you remain under it too
long, it will drown you.

"So I retreated, warned them, and then retreated." She nodded, the
cold smile returning. "Oh, she pretended to want to be responsible and
respectable, but whenever I gave her anything substantial to do, she
would complain about the work and the effort, and Randolph would
plead for her to be relieved of this or that.

" 'We have enough ornaments to hang on our walls and ceilings,' I
told him. 'We don't need another.' But I might as well have directed all
my words to the walls in this office.

"It wasn't long that she began to show her true nature—flirting with
everything that wore pants. There was no stopping her! It was disgusting! I tried to tell my son, but he was as blind to that as to anything else.
When a man is as dazzled by a woman as he was, it's the same as if he
had looked directly at the sun. After that, he sees nothing.

"So I gave up and sure enough, as you have undoubtedly learned, she
had an affair and got herself into trouble. I could have thrown the little
tramp out then. I should have," she added bitterly, "but . . . I wanted
to protect Randolph and the family and the hotel's reputation.

"What I did I did for the good of everyone and for the hotel and
family, for they are one and the same."

"But Daddy . . . Ormand Longchamp . . ."

"He agreed to the arrangements," she said. "He knew what he was
doing."

"But you told him everyone wanted it that way, didn't you? He
thought he was doing what my mother and Randolph wanted, right?
Isn't that true?" I pursued when she didn't respond.

"Randolph doesn't know what he wants; he never did. I always made
the right decisions for him. Marrying her," she said, leaning over the
desk, "is the only time he has ever gone against my wishes, and look
how it turned out."

"But Ormand believed—"

"Yes, yes, so he thought; but I paid him handsomely and kept the police from finding him. It was his own fault he got caught. He should have stayed farther north and never come to Richmond."

"He doesn't belong in prison," I insisted. "It's not fair."

She turned away again, as though what I had to say was unimportant. But it wasn't!

"I don't care if you can force Mrs. Dalton to recant her story and if you can make my mother look so stupid no one will believe her; they'll believe me or at least it will create enough of a scandal to bring embarrassment. And I'll tell Randolph. Just think how hurt he will be to learn it. You let him go off chasing the hope he would recapture me. You offered that reward."

She studied me a moment. I held my gaze as firmly as I could, but it was like looking directly into the center of a campfire. Finally she softened, seeing my resolution.

"What is it you want? You want to embarrass me, rain down disgrace on the Cutlers?"

"I want you to get Daddy out of jail and stop treating me like dirt. Stop calling my mother a tramp, and stop demanding I be renamed Eugenia," I said determinedly.

I wanted a lot more, but I was afraid to make too many demands. In time I hoped I could get her to do something for Jimmy and for Fern.

She nodded slowly.

"All right." She sighed. "I'll do something about Ormand Longchamp. I'll make some calls to people I know in high places and see about getting him an early parole. I was thinking about doing that anyway. And if you insist on being called Dawn, you can be called Dawn.

"But," she added quickly when I began to smile, "you will have to do something for me."

"What? Do you want me to go back to living with him?"

"Of course not. You're here now and you're a Cutler whether you or I like it or not, but," she purred contentedly, quite pleased with herself, sitting back and contemplating me for a moment, "you don't have to be here all the time. I think it would be much better for all of us . . . Clara Sue, Philip, Randolph, even your . . . your *mother,* if you were away."

"Away? Where would I go?"

She nodded, a curious smile on her face. Obviously, she had thought of something very clever, something that pleased her very much.

"You have a very pretty singing voice. I think you should be permitted to develop your talent."

"What do you mean?" Why was she suddenly so eager to help me?

"I happen to be an honorary member of the board of trustees of a prestigious school for the performing arts in New York City."

"New York City!"

"Yes. I want you to go there instead of returning to Emerson Peabody. I will make the arrangements today, and you can leave shortly. They have summer sessions, too.

"Of course, it goes without saying that all this and all you have learned will remain here in this office. No one need know anything more than I decided you are too talented to waste your time cleaning rooms in a hotel."

I could see she liked the idea that everyone would consider her as being magnanimous. She would look like a wonderful grandmother doing great things for her new granddaughter, and I would have to pretend to be grateful.

But I didn't want to return to Emerson Peabody, and I did want to become a singer. She would get her way and rid herself of me, but I would have an opportunity I could only dream of before. New York City! A school for performing arts!

And Daddy would be helped, too.

"All right," I agreed. "As long as you do everything you promised to do."

"I always live up to my word," she said angrily. "Your reputation, your name, your family's honor, are all important things. You come from a world where all those things were insignificant, but in my world—"

"Honor and honesty were always important to us," I snapped back. "We might have been poor, but we were decent people. And Ormand and Sally Jean Longchamp didn't betray each other and lie to each other," I retorted. My eyes burned with tears of indignation.

She gazed at me for a long moment again, only this time I thought I saw a look of approval in her eyes.

"It will be interesting," she finally said, speaking slowly, "very interesting to see what kind of a woman Laura Sue's liaison spawned. I don't like your manners, but you have shown some independence and some spunk, and those are qualities I do admire."

"I'm not sure, Grandmother," I replied, "if what you admire is ever going to be important to me."

She pulled herself back as if I had splashed her with ice-cold water, her eyes turning distant and hard again instantly.

"If that's all, I think you had better go. Thanks to you and your meddling, I have a lot to do. You'll be informed as to when you will be leaving," she added.

I stood up slowly.

"You think you can determine everyone's lives so easily, don't you?" I said bitterly, shaking my head.

"I do what I have to do. Responsibility for significant things requires me to make hard choices sometimes, but I do what is best for the family and the hotel. Someday, when you have something important to take care of and it requires you to make either unpleasant or unpopular choices, you will remember me and not judge me as harshly," she said, as if it were important to her that I have a better opinion of her.

Then she smiled.

"Believe me, when you need something or you get into trouble for one reason or another, you won't call on your mother or even my son. You'll call on me, and you will be happy that you can," she predicted.

What arrogance, I thought, and yet it was true—even from my short stay here I could see that she was responsible for Cutler's Cove being what it was.

I spun around quickly and walked out, unsure as to whether I had won or lost.

Later that afternoon Randolph came to see me. It had become more and more difficult to think of him as my father now, and this just when I had begun to adjust to the idea. From the look on his face I could see that my grandmother had told him of her decision to send me to a school for performing arts.

"Mother just told me about your decision to go to New York. How wonderful, although I must say, I will be sad to see you go off when you've really only just arrived," he complained. He did look somewhat upset by the idea, and I thought how sad it was that he didn't know the truth, that I as well as my mother and Grandmother Cutler kept him fooled. Was that fair? How fragile the happiness and peace was in this family, I thought. His devotion to my mother would surely dwindle to nothing if he knew she had been so unfaithful. In a sense everything was built on a lie, and I had to keep that lie alive.

"I've always wanted to go to New York and be a singer," I said.

"Of course you should go. I'm just teasing you. I'll miss you, but I'll come visit you often, and you'll be back for all the holidays. How exciting it's going to be for you. I've already told your mother, and she thinks it's a wonderful idea that you get formal training in the arts.

"She wants to take you shopping for new clothes, of course. I've already arranged for the hotel car to be at your disposal tomorrow morning so the two of you can go from shopping center to shopping center."

"She feels up to it?" I asked, hardly hiding my disdain.

"Oh, I've rarely seen her as chipper as she is now. As soon as I told her about the decision you and Mother made, she sat up and smiled and began to talk excitedly about the shopping. There are few things Laura Sue loves to do more than go shopping," he said, laughing. "And she always wants to go to New York. She will probably be up there visiting you every other weekend," he added.

"What about my work in the hotel tomorrow? I don't want it all to fall on Sissy's shoulders."

"That's all over. No more chambermaid work for you. Just enjoy the hotel and the family until you have to leave for school," he said. "And don't worry about Sissy. We'll assign someone else to help her and hire someone new quickly."

He tilted his head and smiled. "You don't look as happy about it all as I expected. Is something wrong? I know the situation with the Longchamp boy was not pleasant, and I understand why you were so upset, but you shouldn't have let him hide out here." He slapped his hands together as if he could bust the unpleasant memory by clapping. "But it's over. Let's not worry about it anymore."

"I can't help worrying about Jimmy," I said quickly. "He was just trying to get away from a horrible foster family. I tried to tell you, but no one would listen."

"Um . . . well, at least we know the little girl is doing fine."

"You found out about Fern?" I sat up quickly.

"Not much. They don't like giving out that information, but a friend of your grandmother's knew someone who knew someone. Anyway, Fern was taken by a young, childless couple. Their whereabouts are a mystery to us, but we're still looking."

"But what if Daddy wants her back?" I cried.

"Daddy? Oh, Ormand Longchamp? Under the circumstances, I don't think he will be able to get her back when he is released from prison. That will be some time yet anyway," he added. Obviously, Grandmother Cutler had not told him her part of our bargain. There was no way she could without revealing why she would do such a thing.

"Anyway," he continued, "I wanted to stop by to tell you how happy I was for you. I've got to get back to my office. See you at dinner." He knelt down to kiss me on the forehead. "You will probably become the most famous Cutler of all," he said and left.

I lay back against my pillow. How fast it was all happening now. Fern was with a new family. Perhaps she had already learned to call the man Daddy and the woman Momma. Perhaps her memories of Jimmy and me were already fading. A new home, fine clothing, plenty to eat, and good care would surely erase her earlier life and make it all seem like some vague dream.

I was sure that in a matter of days, Grandmother Cutler would have me carried off to a new life, a life away from her and Cutler's Cove. My great consolation was that I would be in the world of music, and whenever I entered that world, all hardship and misery, all unhappiness and sadness fell away. I made up my mind I would put all my energy and concentration into one thing—becoming a good singer.

That evening I was permitted to sit with my family in the dining room for dinner. The news about my leaving for a performing arts school spread quickly throughout the hotel. Staff members who had previously resented me wished me luck. Even some guests had heard and had something nice to say. My mother made one of her miraculous recoveries. In fact, I had never seen her look more radiantly beautiful. Her hair had a sheen, her eyes were bright and young; she laughed and spoke with more animation than she had ever before demonstrated. To her everything was delicious, people were delightful; it was the most wonderful summer in ages. She rattled on and on about our upcoming shopping spree.

"I have some friends who live in Manhattan," she said, "and first thing in the morning I'm calling them to find out what is in style these days. We don't want you going off and looking like the farmer's daughter," she said and laughed. Randolph found her laughter contagious and was livelier and more charming than ever, too.

Only Clara Sue sat with a dark, dejected look on her face. She glared at me enviously, her emotions confused. She was getting rid of me, which I knew made her happy because once again she would be the little princess and wouldn't have to share the limelight with me in any way; but I was going off to do something very exciting, and I was being pampered, not her.

"I need some new things, too," she complained when she was able to get a word in.

"But you have so much more time, Clara Sue, honey," Mother said. "We'll go shopping for your things closer to the end of the summer. Eugenia is going to New York in a few days. New York!"

"Dawn," I corrected. My mother glanced at me and then at Grandmother Cutler. She saw there was no reprimand pending. "My name is Dawn," I repeated softly.

Mother laughed.

"Of course, if you like and everyone agrees," she said, eyeing Grandmother Cutler again.

"It's what she's used to," Grandmother Cutler said. "If she wants to change her name some time in the future, she can."

Clara Sue looked surprised and upset at the same time. I smiled at her, and she looked away quickly.

Grandmother Cutler and I exchanged a knowing glance. We exchanged a few that evening. Now that our major confrontation was over, I found her acting different toward me, just as she had promised. When some guests stopped by and asked about my singing, she claimed there was an uncle in our family who used to sing and play a violin.

As I gazed around the table, I realized everyone was happy I was leaving, but for different reasons. Grandmother Cutler never wanted me; my mother found me a threat and an embarrassment now; Randolph was sincerely happy for me and my new opportunity; and Clara Sue was happy she was losing her competition for the family's attention. Only Philip, working his waiter's job, cast confused glances in my direction.

After dinner and after I had sat in the lobby with my mother listening to her chat with guests for a while, I excused myself, claiming I was tired. I wanted to write another letter to Daddy describing all that I had learned. I wanted him to know that I didn't blame him for what had been done and that I understood why he and Momma had done it.

But when I opened the door to my room, I found Philip waiting for me. He was lying on my bed, his hands behind his head, looking up at the ceiling. He sat up quickly.

"What are you doing in here?" I demanded. "Get out. *Now!*"

"I wanted to speak to you. Don't worry, I just want to talk," he said, holding his hands up.

"What is it you want, Philip? Don't expect me to forgive you for what you did," I snapped. "I'll never forget what you did to me."

"You told Grandmother something, didn't you? That's why she arranged for you to go to New York so quickly. I'm right, aren't I?" I simply stared at him, not walking in any farther, finding it impossible to be in the same room alone with him after what he had done to me. "Well, did you?" he asked fearfully.

"No, Philip, I didn't, but I think it's true when people say Grandmother Cutler has eyes and ears all over this hotel." That ought to put a scare in him. "Now leave," I ordered, still standing in the doorway and holding the door open. "The sight of you makes me sick."

"Well, why would she do it? Why would she send you off like this?"

"Haven't you heard? She thinks I'm talented," I said dryly. "I thought you did, too."

"I do, but . . . it all seems so strange . . . right at the beginning of the summer season, just when you've been returned to the family, she sends you off to a special arts school?" He shook his head and narrowed his eyes suspiciously. "There's something going on, something you're not telling me. Does it have to do with Jimmy's being found here, then?"

"Yes," I said quickly, but he didn't look satisfied.

"I don't believe you."

"Too bad. I don't care what you believe or what you think. I'm tired, Philip, and I have a lot to do tomorrow. Please, leave." He didn't move. "Haven't you done enough to me?" I cried. "Just leave me alone."

"Dawn, you must understand what came over me before—sometimes a boy my age loses control. It happens especially when a girl leads him along and then pulls back," he said. I thought his attempt at a justification was pathetic.

"I never led you on, Philip, and I would have expected you to understand why I pulled back." I glared hatefully at him. "Don't you dare place the blame on me. You, and only you, are responsible for your actions."

"You're really mad at me, aren't you?" he asked, the smile on his face turning coy. "You're real pretty when you're angry," he said.

I stared at him in disbelief and recalled the excitement I had felt when we had first met at Emerson Peabody. How different things were then. It was like we were two completely different people. In a real way I suppose we were, I thought. We could never go back to the way things had once been . . . when I had believed in fairy tales and happy endings.

"You mustn't hate me," he said, pretending to plead for understanding. "You *mustn't!*" he insisted.

"I don't hate you, Philip." He smiled. "But I feel sorry for you," I added quickly, wiping the smile off his face. "You can never change what happened between us, and you can never change the way I feel about you. Whatever feelings I had for you died the night you raped me."

"I wasn't lying to you," he protested. "Dawn, I love you. With all my heart and soul. I can't help the way I feel about you."

"Well, you'll just have to! You've got to help it, Philip. I'm your sister. Do you understand? Your *sister!* You've got to get over it. *You* can't love me! I'm sure you won't have trouble finding a new girlfriend."

"I suppose not," he said arrogantly, "but that doesn't mean I won't be thinking about you. I don't want a new girlfriend, Dawn. I want *you.* Only you. Why don't we spend one last night together . . . just talking," he suggested and lay back on my pillow. "For old time's sake."

I couldn't believe him! How could he make such a suggestion? After everything I had just said, Philip still wanted to . . . The thought sickened me. *Philip* sickened me. I could no longer stand to look at him. Just as Clara Sue and I would never have a sibling relationship, neither would Philip and I. I had to get him out of my sight. Before I said something I regretted. Before I did something I regretted. I pretended to hear something in the hallway.

"Someone's coming, Philip. It might be Grandmother. She said she wanted to speak with me later."

"Huh?" He sat up quickly and listened. "I don't hear anyone."

"Philip," I said, looking worried. He got up quickly and came to the door.

"I don't hear anybody," he said. I pushed past him and shoved him out, closing the door and locking it quickly.

"Hey!" he cried. "That's sneaky."

"Sneakiness runs in this family," I said. "Now go away."

"Dawn, come on. I want to make it all up to you, show you I can be warm and loving without attacking you. Dawn? I'll stay here all night. I'll sleep at your door," he threatened.

I ignored him, and after a while he got disgusted and left. I was finally alone with my own thoughts. I pulled the chair up to the little table, took out a pen and paper, and began.

Dear Daddy,

No matter what has happened, I realize I will always call you Daddy. I realize I am writing to you before you even had a chance to respond to my first letter, but I wanted you to know I have learned the truth. I have spoken with the woman who had been my nurse, Mrs. Dalton, and after that I confronted my mother and she confessed.

I then demanded a meeting with Grandmother Cutler and learned it all firsthand. I want you to know that I don't blame you or Momma for anything, and I know that once Jimmy learns the facts, he will feel the same way I do.

They are sending me off to a school for performing arts in New York City. Grandmother Cutler mostly wants to get rid of me, but it's what I always wanted to do, and I think it's best I get away from here anyway.

We still don't know where Fern is, but I hope that someday she will be back with you . . . her real father. I don't know what has become of Jimmy yet, but he ran away from one bad family and was found here and taken back. Perhaps you and he will be to-gether again very soon. Grandmother Cutler has promised to do what she can to get you an early parole.

You always said that I brought you sunshine and happiness. I hope this letter brings some to you during what must be your darkest days. I want you to know that whenever I do sing, I will be thinking of you and your smile and all the love you and Momma gave me.

Love,
Dawn

I sealed the letter with a kiss and put it in an envelope. In the morn-ing I would have it mailed.

I really was very, very tired. Moments after my head touched the pillow and my eyes were closed, I began to drift toward a much wel-comed sleep. The sounds of the hotel died away quickly. My short but dramatic life here was coming to an end.

I'm still being whisked away, I thought. I'm not in Daddy's car, and I'm not leaving in the middle of the night, but I'm on the road again, searching, always searching, for a place to call home.

EPILOGUE

Whether it was out of a sense of guilt or merely the excitement of buying clothes, my mother took me off in the hotel limousine and dragged me from store to store. Price was never an object. She bought me more clothing than I had seen in a lifetime: skirts, blouses, jackets, a leather coat and leather gloves, a fur hat, shoes, lingerie, and velvet slippers. We went to a department store to buy makeup, and there she bought me an assortment of powders, lipsticks, blush, rouge, and eye-liner. It took two bellhops four trips to bring all our purchases into the hotel.

Clara Sue's eyes nearly popped out of her head when she saw it all. She cried and moaned and demanded Mother go on a similar shopping spree with her.

The day before I was to leave for New York, one of the bellhops came down to my room to fetch me.

"There's a phone call for you at the main desk," he said. "They said to hurry; it's long distance."

I thanked him and rushed out. I was lucky it was early in the morning and Clara Sue was not on duty, I thought. She would have never permitted the call to go through, because it was Jimmy.

"Where are you?" I cried.

"I'm with a new foster family, the Allans, and I'm back in Richmond, but it's all right. I'm going to go to a regular public school," Jimmy added quickly.

"Oh, Jimmy, I have so much to tell you I don't know where to begin."

He laughed.

"Just start at the beginning," he said, and I told him all that I had learned, described my meeting with Grandmother Cutler, and explained what had resulted.

"So you see, Jimmy, you shouldn't blame Daddy. He thought he was doing the right thing," I said.

"Yeah," he said, "I suppose, but it was still dumb," he added, only not sounding as hard as he could.

"Will you talk to him when he contacts you, Jimmy?" I asked, my voice full of hope.

"Let's see if he ever will," he replied. "I'm glad Fern was adopted by a young couple. They'll give her lots of love, but I can't wait till we find her again," he said. "And I'm glad about your going to a school for performing arts, even though it means I probably won't see you for a long time. But I'll try."

"I'll try to see you, too, Jimmy."

"I miss you," he said.

"I miss you, too," I said, my voice cracking.

"Well, I'd better hang up. They were nice enough to let me make this call. Good luck, Dawn."

"Jimmy!" I cried, realizing he was about to hang up.

"What?"

"I know I can think of you differently," I blurted. He understood.

"I'm glad, Dawn. It's the same with me."

"Bye," I said. I didn't realize I was crying until a tear dropped from my cheek.

On the morning of my departure the chambermaid staff presented me with a going-away present. Sissy gave it to me in the lobby by the front door as the bellhops were loading my suitcases into the hotel limousine.

"Some people are sorry for the cold way you were treated," she said and handed me a tiny package. I unwrapped it and discovered a solid gold mop-and-pail pin.

"We didn't want'cha to forget us," Sissy said. I laughed and hugged her.

Grandmother Cutler stood off to the side during all this, watching with her eagle eyes. I could see that she was impressed with the affection the hotel staff had for me.

Clara Sue stood sullenly in the doorway, Philip at her side, a slight smirk on his face.

I hurried down the steps without a farewell glance to either of them. My mother and Randolph were waiting at the limousine. Mother looked fresh and rested. She hugged me and kissed my forehead. I was surprised at how affectionate she was. Was it just for the audience of guests and staff, or had she come to feel something for me?

I looked into her soft eyes, but I couldn't be sure. It was all too confusing.

"Okay, Dawn," Randolph said. "We'll be up to see you as soon as we can get away from the hotel." He kissed me on the cheek. "If you need anything, just call."

"Thank you," I said. The limousine driver opened the door for me and I got in. I sat back and thought how different this was from my arrival in the night in a police patrol car.

We began to pull away from the hotel. I looked back and waved at everyone and saw Grandmother Cutler step out to gaze after me. She looked different, thoughtful. What a strange woman, I thought, and wondered if I would ever get to know her.

Then I turned to look out at the ocean as we came down the driveway. The sun had turned the water into a bright aqua. The little sailboats looked painted against the blue horizon. It was beautiful here, picture perfect, I thought. My heart was full. I was off to do something I had always dreamt of doing, Jimmy sounded happier, and Daddy would soon be freed from prison.

The hotel limousine turned, and we were off toward the airport.

I couldn't help but remember the games Daddy and I used to play when I was very little and we were in the car and off to a new home.

"Come on, Dawn," he would say. "Let's pretend. Where do you want to be this time? Alaska? The desert? On a ship? In an airplane?"

"Oh, let her sleep, Ormand. It's late," Momma would say.

"You tired, Dawn?"

"No, Daddy," I would say, even though I could barely keep my eyes open.

Jimmy was asleep on his side of the car.

"So? Where shall it be this time?" Daddy asked again.

"I think . . . an airplane," I said. "Soaring above the clouds."

"And so it will be. Feel the lift-off," he said and laughed.

A short while later I really was soaring above the clouds.

Sometimes, when we dream hard enough, those dreams come true, I thought.

And I looked ahead toward the long stretch of blue sky and dreamt of thousands of people in an audience listening to me sing.